PENGUIN CLASSICS

CHILDHOOD, BOYHOOD, YOUTH

LEO TOLSTOY was born in 1828 at Yasnaya Polyana, his family estate near the city of Tula, 125 miles south of Moscow. He was educated there and in Moscow by private tutors before entering the University of Kazan in 1844, first in the Department of Arabo-Turkic Languages in preparation for a diplomatic career, and then in the Department of Jurisprudence. He withdrew from the university in his third year to return to his estate, intending to devote himself to its management and to independent study. Soon losing interest in those projects, he gave himself up to dissipation and gambling in Tula and then in Moscow and St Petersburg, before joining his oldest brother in the Caucasus in 1851 to seek a career in the army. He also began to write at that time, publishing his first work of fiction, *Childhood* (1852), and quickly following it with *Boyhood* (1854) and his *Sevastopol Sketches* (1855–6), the latter based on his experience as a front-line artillery officer in the Crimean War. Resigning his commission in 1856, he returned to Yasnaya Polyana to concentrate on the management of the estate and his writing, publishing *Youth* in 1857. In 1862 he married the much younger Sofya Behrs. They would have thirteen children, as Tolstoy continued to attend to his estate, the innovative school for peasant children he established there and his writing, producing, among many other important works, *The Cossacks* (1863), *War and Peace* (1865–9), *Anna Karenina* (1875–8), *A Confession* (1884), *The Death of Ivan Ilyich* (1886), *The Kreutzer Sonata* (1889) and *Resurrection* (1899). *A Confession* marked a spiritual crisis in his life, leading to a repudiation of church and state, an indictment of the weakness of the flesh and a denunciation of private property. His teachings brought him many followers at home and abroad, but also official disfavour and harassment, and in 1901 he was excommunicated by the Russian Orthodox Church. He died in 1910 at the small railway station of Astapovo during a dramatic flight from home, having become not only one of the world's greatest writers but also one of its most famous men.

JUDSON ROSENGRANT has translated and edited a wide variety of Russian literature and historiography, including works by Yury Olesha, Andrei Platonov, Lydia Ginzburg, Fazil Iskander, Edward Limonov and Edvard Radzinsky. He received his PhD in Slavic Languages and Literature from Stanford University with a dissertation on Vladimir Nabokov, and has taught Russian language, literature and culture at the University of Southern California, Indiana University and Reed College in the United States, and translation theory and practice at St Petersburg State University in Russia. He lives in Portland, Oregon, USA.

LEO TOLSTOY

Childhood, Boyhood, Youth

Translated and with an Introduction and Notes by
JUDSON ROSENGRANT

PENGUIN BOOKS

PENGUIN CLASSICS

Published by the Penguin Group
Penguin Books Ltd, 80 Strand, London WC2R ORL, England
Penguin Group (USA) Inc., 375 Hudson Street, New York, New York 10014, USA
Penguin Group (Canada), 90 Eglinton Avenue East, Suite 700, Toronto, Ontario, Canada M4P 2Y3
(a division of Pearson Penguin Canada Inc.)
Penguin Ireland, 25 St Stephen's Green, Dublin 2, Ireland (a division of Penguin Books Ltd)
Penguin Group (Australia), 250 Camberwell Road, Camberwell, Victoria 3124, Australia
(a division of Pearson Australia Group Pty Ltd)
Penguin Books India Pvt Ltd, 11 Community Centre, Panchsheel Park, New Delhi – 110 017, India
Penguin Group (NZ), 67 Apollo Drive, Rosedale, Auckland 0632, New Zealand
(a division of Pearson New Zealand Ltd)
Penguin Books (South Africa) (Pty) Ltd, Block D, Rosebank Office Park, 181 Jan Smuts Avenue, Parktown
North, Gauteng 2193, South Africa

Penguin Books Ltd, Registered Offices: 80 Strand, London WC2R ORL, England

www.penguin.com

First published in Russian from 1852 to 1857
This edition first published in Penguin Classics 2012

009

Translation, introduction and notes copyright © Judson Rosengrant, 2012
All rights reserved

The moral right of the translator and author of the introduction and notes has been asserted

Set in 10.25/12.25pt Postscript Adobe Sabon
Typeset by Palimpsest Book Production Limited, Falkirk, Stirlingshire
Printed and bound in Great Britain by Clays Ltd, Elcograf S.p.A.

Except in the United States of America, this book is sold subject
to the condition that it shall not, by way of trade or otherwise, be lent,
re-sold, hired out, or otherwise circulated without the publisher's
prior consent in any form of binding or cover other than that in
which it is published and without a similar condition including this
condition being imposed on the subsequent purchaser

ISBN: 978-0-140-44992-1

www.greenpenguin.co.uk

MIX
Paper from
responsible sources
FSC® C018179

Penguin Books is committed to a sustainable
future for our business, our readers and our planet.
This book is made from Forest Stewardship
Council™ certified paper.

Contents

Childhood

Boyhood

Youth

Chronology

1828 9 September (28 August, Old Style). Birth of Count Leo (Lev) Tolstoy, the fourth son of Count Nikolay Tolstoy and Princess Marya Volkonskaya, at Yasnaya Polyana (Clear Glade), their estate 125 miles south of Moscow near the city of Tula.

1830 Death of mother a few months after the birth of her daughter, Marya.

1837 Death of father not long after the five children move from Yasnaya Polyana to continue their education in Moscow in the home of their paternal grandmother.

1838 Death of grandmother. The two oldest children, Nikolay and Sergey, move to the home of their father's older sister, Alexandra Osten-Sacken, to continue their Moscow studies, while Dmitry, Leo and Marya return to Yasnaya Polyana and the care of Leo's beloved 'Auntie' Tatyana Yergolskaya, their father's second cousin and the person who Leo would later say had the greatest and most beneficial influence on him.

1841 Death of Aunt Alexandra. All five children move to the Volga city of Kazan and the home of their father's younger sister, Pelageya Yushkova.

1844 Already a fine linguist with an excellent knowledge of French and German and a good command of English, thanks to his home education and gifts, he enters the University of Kazan in the Department of Arabo-Turkic Languages, the country's best, to study Turkish and Tatar in preparation for a diplomatic career. The year, however, is squandered in drinking, gambling and regular visits to brothels.

1845 After failing his year-end examinations in the Department of Arabo-Turkic Languages, he enrols in the Department of Jurisprudence, where he works with the brilliant young professor of civil law Dmitry Meier. Meier encourages him to make a close study of Montesquieu (*De l'esprit des lois*) in relation to the *Instruction* (*Nakaz*) of Catherine II.

1847 Inherits Yasnaya Polyana in the final distribution of his father's property. Recovering from gonorrhoea, leaves the university for Yasnaya Polyana on the grounds of 'ill-health and domestic circumstances' to pursue his own programme of enlightened estate management, self-improvement and reading, including the complete works of Rousseau.

1848 Leaves Yasnaya Polyana for Moscow, where he engages in dissipation and gambling, incurring large debts.

1849 Goes to St Petersburg, where he decides to take the examinations at the university in the Department of Jurisprudence with the goal of entering government service. Passes the examinations in criminal and civil law, but again lapses into dissipation and gambling, acquiring further debts.

1850 Returns to Yasnaya Polyana, where, determined to put his life in order, he undertakes a serious study of music and once again devotes himself to the management of his estate.

1851 Begins his first literary effort, the soon abandoned 'Story of Yesterday'. Travels to the Caucasus with oldest brother Nikolay, an officer in an artillery brigade. While billeted in a Cossack village on the border of Chechnya and resolving to earn his own commission as a cadet-volunteer or *yunker* involved in actions against the Chechen tribesmen, works on an unfinished translation of Laurence Sterne's *Sentimental Journey* and on *Childhood*, his first completed work of fiction.

1852 *Childhood* published by the poet Nikolay Nekrasov in his influential literary monthly *The Contemporary*. It is very warmly received by the leading writers of the day, including Ivan Turgenev and the influential critic Pavel Annenkov.

1853 'The Raid', an account based on his own Caucasian military experience, is published in *The Contemporary*.

1854 Receives his commission and after the start of the Crimean

War is transferred at his own request to Sevastopol, where he commands a front-line artillery battery in the unsuccessful defence of the port city. *Boyhood* is published in *The Contemporary* and is received even more warmly than *Childhood*.

1855 Gains further celebrity with the publication in *The Contemporary* of the first two of the three *Sevastopol Sketches*, his powerful, brutally realistic treatments of the war. Travels to St Petersburg on army business, where he meets Nekrasov and the staff of *The Contemporary* and makes the acquaintance of the writers in its orbit, including Turgenev, Ivan Goncharov, Alexander Druzhinin, Alexander Ostrovsky, Fyodor Tyutchev, Afanasy Fet and Nikolay Chernyshevsky.

1856 The third of the *Sevastopol Sketches* is published in *The Contemporary*, as are the stories 'The Snowstorm' and 'Two Hussars'. Later that year the long story 'A Landowner's Morning' appears in *Patriotic Annals*. Resigns his commission and returns to Yasnaya Polyana. Tries unsuccessfully to free the peasants of his estate from serfdom. Death of his brother Dmitry from tuberculosis.

1857 Makes his first trip abroad, a six-month visit to Switzerland, France, Germany and Italy. Sees Turgenev in Paris. *Youth*, the last and longest of his three accounts of pychological and social development, is published in *The Contemporary*, as is his story 'Lucerne', written in Switzerland.

1858 Back at Yasnaya Polyana, devotes himself to his literary work and the estate.

1859 The story 'Three Deaths' is published in *The Library for Reading* and the short novel *Family Happiness* in *The Russian Herald*. Starts an innovative school for peasant children at Yasnaya Polyana, an endeavour that would occupy him for the rest of his life.

1860 Takes an even longer second trip abroad, visiting Germany, Switzerland, France and Italy, mainly to study educational practices and methods. Death from tuberculosis of his favourite brother Nikolay in southern France, where he had taken him in the hope that its warm climate would halt the disease.

1861 Visits England and Belgium, meeting the exiled Russian revolutionary and publisher Alexander Herzen and perhaps

Matthew Arnold in London, and the French socialist Proudhon in Brussels. After his return to Russia, serves as an arbitrator dealing with land settlements on behalf of the local peasantry after the emancipation of the serfs by Alexander II earlier that year. Incurs the resentment of his fellow landowners and is relieved of his appointment.

1862 Starts a soon abandoned pedagogical magazine at Yasnaya Polyana. Police carry out a search of the estate, having been falsely informed that Tolstoy is involved in a radical cabal and in possession of an illegal printing press. Marries Sofya Behrs (*b.* 1844), the daughter of a prominent physician and neighbouring landowner.

1863 Publishes *The Cossacks*, a novel based on his time in the Caucasus. Birth of his first child, Sergey. Tolstoy and his wife would have thirteen children – nine boys and four girls – five of them dying in childhood. Starts work on *The Decembrists*, a novel that would eventually become *War and Peace*.

1865–6 Serial publication of the first two parts of *War and Peace* as *1805* in *The Russian Herald*.

1867–9 Book publication of *War and Peace* in its entirety.

1870 Works on unfinished novel about the times of Peter I. Reads the plays of Shakespeare, Molière, Goethe, Pushkin and Gogol. Undertakes a study of Greek, beginning with Xenophon and proceeding to Homer and Plato.

1871 While recovering from an alarming bronchial illness in a Bashkirian village in the steppe, east of the Volga town of Samara, continues his study of Greek, reading Herodotus with the help of a local tutor.

1872 Publishes the first version of his *Abecedary* or *Primer*.

1873 Begins *Anna Karenina*. Works on behalf of famine relief in the Samara province where he has bought an estate, describing the conditions there in an open letter to the *Moscow News*, raising nearly two million roubles on behalf of the afflicted peasants and securing emergency grain allocations.

1874 Much occupied with educational theory. Publishes his *New Abecedary* and the first part of a companion series, *Russian Books for Reading*, of more than a hundred brief, simple stories with a clear message.

1875–7 Serial publication of *Anna Karenina* in *The Russian Herald*. Appearance of a French translation of his story 'Two Hussars' with an introduction by Turgenev in which he declares that with the publication of *War and Peace* Tolstoy 'has assumed first place in the affections of the [Russian reading] public'.

1877 Separate book publication of the eighth and last part of *Anna Karenina*, when Mikhail Katkov, the publisher of *The Russian Herald*, refuses to print its 'unpatriotic' characterization of Russian volunteers in the Russo-Turkish war (1877–8).

1878 Separate publication of *Anna Karenina* in its entirety. Begins work on an unfinished novel about the era of Nicholas I and the Decembrists, as well as on his long autobiographical essay *A Confession*.

1880 Works on *An Examination of Dogmatic Theology* and *A Confession*.

1881 Writes to Alexander III, exhorting him not to punish the revolutionaries who assassinated Alexander II. Moves with his family from Yasnaya Polyana to their new house in the Weavers' district of central Moscow.

1882 Works on a new translation of the Gospels from the original Greek. Starts his short novel *The Death of Ivan Ilyich* and his long autobiographical essay *What Then Shall We Do?*. His passion for languages undiminished, begins a study of biblical Hebrew, taking lessons with a Moscow rabbi.

1883 Finishes his treatise *What I Believe*. Makes the acquaintance of Vladimir Chertkov, who will play a significant role as his disciple and chief confidant, eventually joining his household.

1884 Family relations become strained. *What I Believe* is banned by the Russian censors. *A Confession* is published in Geneva after it, too, is rejected by the censors. Establishes a publishing house (the Intermediary) with Chertkov to produce cheap, edifying literature for the common people.

1885 Writes a number of works for the new publishing venture, including 'Where Love Is, So God Is Too' and 'Strider' ('Kholstomer').

1886 Publishes *The Death of Ivan Ilyich*. Finishes his play *The Power of Darkness* and begins his comedy *The Fruits of Enlightenment*.

1887 Starts work on *The Kreutzer Sonata*. *The Power of Darkness* is published, but permission to stage it is refused by the powerful Procurator of the Holy Synod, who objects to its heterodox religious and social views.

1888 Growing friction between his wife and Chertkov. *The Power of Darkness* is performed in Paris with the help of Émile Zola. Renounces meat, alcohol and tobacco.

1889 Finishes *The Kreutzer Sonata*. Begins work on the novel *Resurrection*.

1890 *The Kreutzer Sonata* is banned from periodical publication by the censor, but is included the next year in the author's *Collected Works*. Begins 'Father Sergius'.

1891 Convinced that personal profits from writing are immoral, renounces the rights to all his works written after 1881. Devotes himself to famine relief in Ryazan province and the surrounding region following widespread crop failures. Helps to bring the neglected situation to public attention and to raise money and organize free food kitchens for the afflicted.

1892 *The Fruits of Enlightenment* is produced at the Maly Theatre, Moscow.

1893 Finishes *The Kingdom of God Is within You*, the summation of his religious and social ideas.

1894 Writes preface to collection of Maupassant stories. *The Kingdom of God Is within You* is published in Germany after its rejection by the Russian censors.

1895 *The Power of Darkness* is produced at the Maly Theatre, Moscow. Writes 'Master and Man' for publication that year by the Intermediary publishing house.

1896 Begins the short historical novel *Hadji Murad*, a work that would occupy him intermittently until 1904.

1897–8 *What Is Art?* is published in the magazine *Questions of Art and Psychology*. Successfully appeals to authorities to allow the emigration to Canada of the Dukhobors, a pacifist religious sect.

1898 Works for famine relief in the Tula province. Resolves to publish 'Father Sergius' and *Resurrection* to provide financial support for the Dukhobors' emigration to Canada.

1899 Finishes *Resurrection*. It is published in instalments in the popular magazine *The Grainfield*, with illustrations by the distinguished artist Leonid Pasternak, Boris Pasternak's father.

1900 After seeing a production of Anton Chekhov's *Uncle Vanya* at the Moscow Art Theatre, begins work on the play *The Living Corpse*.

1901 Excommunicated by the Russian Orthodox church for 'disseminating among the people teachings opposed to Christ and the Church'. Although not a strict excommunication in canonical terms, the decision nonetheless provokes widespread public outrage. Seriously ill with malaria, leaves Yasnaya Polyana for the southern shore of the Crimea, where his many visitors include Chekhov and Maxim Gorky.

1902 Returns to Yasnaya Polyana. Writes to Tsar Nicholas II about the evils of autocracy and the ownership of property.

1903 Begins his unfinished *Memoirs* at the request of his first biographer, Pavel Biryukov. Protests against Jewish pogrom in Kishinyov. Writes the story 'After the Ball'.

1904 *Bethink Yourselves!*, his pamphlet opposing the Russo-Japanese war, is published in a translation by Chertkov in England. Death of his brother Sergey.

1905 Writes an afterword to Chekhov's story 'The Darling'. Produces a variety of public responses to the abortive 1905 Russian revolution, as well as the story 'Alyoshka the Pot' and the long tale 'Posthumous Notes of the Elder Fyodor Kuzmich'.

1906 His article 'Shakespeare and the Drama' is published in the newspaper *The Russian Word* and appears as a separate publication the following year.

1908 'I Cannot Be Silent!', an article denouncing capital punishment, is published illegally in Russia and then in translation in hundreds of newspapers abroad.

1909 Increased hostility between his wife and Chertkov and himself. Corresponds with Gandhi about the doctrine of non-violent resistance to evil.

1910 His wife threatens suicide. Final break in their relationship.

On 10 November (28 October, Old Style), he departs Yasnaya
Polyana. On 20 November (7 November, Old Style) he dies
of pneumonia at the railway station in the town of Astapovo.
At his request, he is buried in an unmarked grave at Yasnaya
Polyana.

1911–12 The stories and tales 'After the Ball', 'The Devil', 'The
False Coupon' and 'Father Sergius', and the short novel *Hadji
Murad* are published posthumously by Chertkov.

Introduction

Count Leo Tolstoy was twenty-three and a cadet-volunteer serving with his oldest brother in an artillery brigade on Russia's
turbulent Caucasian frontier when in July 1852 he sent *Childhood*, his first completed work, to the leading St Petersburg
literary monthly, *The Contemporary*.[1] As he put it in a straightforward letter to the magazine's distinguished editor, the poet
Nikolay Nekrasov, 'Look over the manuscript and if it is not fit
for publication, return it to me. Otherwise, evaluate it, send me
whatever you think it is worth, and publish it in your magazine
. . . In essence, [it] is the first part of a novel, *Four Periods of
Growth*, and the appearance of the following parts will depend
on the success of the first.'[2]

Since Tolstoy had signed his letter and the manuscript with
only the initials of his first name and patronymic, and given as
a forwarding address his brother's name and rank and the remote
Cossack village in which their brigade was headquartered,
Nekrasov's reply was perhaps a little wary, although quick and
very favourable. He supposed that the mysterious L. N. 'had
talent', said that the work possessed 'so much interest' he would
publish it and praised its 'outlook' and the 'simplicity and reality
of its content'.[3] *Childhood* came out six weeks later in the
monthly's September issue, although, to Tolstoy's dismay, in a
heavily edited, even mutilated form, as he saw it, with 'countless' alterations and cuts and even a change in the title to *The
Story of My Childhood*.[4]

Many of the alterations may have simply reflected the
personal taste of Nekrasov and his staff, or at least their
discomfort with the unknown author's innovative style, while

others were evidently the result of the state censor's concern
about sensitive religious and social matters, as in the substitution
in the first paragraph of Chapter One of a portrait of the narrator's mother for the fly-swatter-grazed icon, or the deletion of
most of the first paragraph of Chapter Thirteen with its description of the youthful infatuation and cruel punishment of the serf
Natalya Savishna, a passage that Tolstoy considered essential to
an understanding of her character and condition and therefore
to the story itself: it 'portrayed to a certain extent the old way
of life ... and imparted humanity' to her, as he wrote to Nekrasov
upon seeing the September issue.[5]

Why the title was changed is less clear, however, although
the nature of the change is suggestive. Perhaps in view of the
growing popularity of autobiography and memoir, Nekrasov
and his colleagues felt that their version lent greater familiarity
and personal authority than Tolstoy's own more abstract
choice, or perhaps the sheer vitality of the narrative, its remarkable conviction and vivid, natural detail (for there had been
nothing like it in Russian literature before) led them to conclude,
as many have since, that it must be autobiographical, that a
first-person account of such extraordinary particularity and
rich interiority could only have come from direct personal
recollection, especially considering that the author not only
had no literary standing but, apparently, no literary experience
at all.

However, as Tolstoy firmly objected in his post-publication
letter, the change of title 'contradicts the idea' of the work, for
'who cares about the story of *my* childhood?' (his emphasis).
The objection may not seem especially remarkable against the
vast background of his writings as we regard them today, but
for the young author seeking to defend the method of his first
professional effort, it went to the very heart of the form and
substance not only of *Childhood* but also, as it would turn out,
of *Boyhood* and *Youth* – the next two parts in the series or trilogy, as it has come to be known, since the planned fourth part
was never written.[6] The objection stressed that *Childhood* was
not, nor ever meant to be, a depiction of his own experience, as
interesting as that might have been or as much as it was certainly

utilized and adapted by him, but was offered instead as a work of deliberate art and invention. Indeed, it was a novel, as he said in his first letter to Nekrasov, and moreover one with an 'idea', an overarching conception, that entailed investigation not of a unique personality or sensibility – as Tolstoy's youthful favourite Jean-Jacques Rousseau (1712–78) had famously claimed to undertake in his *Confessions* (1765–70), for example – but of the features and dynamics of a representative or even, in its trajectory and momentum, a universal human experience. *Childhood* was intended, that is, to examine in some broader, more significant way than the merely idiosyncratic the nature of a period or stage in the growth of the self; although, as Tolstoy would render it with his characteristic duality and empiricism, a growth regarded both subjectively from within the perceiving, recollecting, judging mind of the narrator, Nikolenka Irtenyev, and objectively in relation to a fully developed and absolutely authentic social and material world, whose parts and levels stand before us in all their immediacy, thanks to the intensity of Tolstoy's grasp of them and to his phenomenal powers of observation and precisely nuanced expression.

Despite what might have been expected from a first work, especially one with such an elaborate sense of time and place and of the psyche's relation to them, *Childhood* is never tentative or unsure of itself in any of its descriptive, analytic or formal procedures, but creates at once, creates in its very first sentences and paragraphs, a convincing community of complex, rounded characters (even the minor ones have their own irreducible individuality and implied depth and paradox), whose inner life we have no trouble imagining, and whose world is represented, as I have already intimated, with an exactitude and clarity that are as fresh and compelling today as they were for the story's initial readers more than a century and a half ago.

Although Nekrasov obviously could not have realized it at the time, he had been sent the first sustained work of a writer of enormous narrative gifts, ambition and formal and stylistic originality, and, no less importantly, of exceptional social and psychological insight, wit, imaginative sympathy and fierce moral seriousness – the first effort of someone who was

destined to become one of the most potent creative forces not
only of Russian but of world literature, and who, with his
monumental *War and Peace* (1865–9) and *Anna Karenina*
(1875–8), would produce two of the greatest works of fiction
ever written.

The originality and unknown provenance of *Childhood* may
have caught Nekrasov off guard, but if they did, it did not take
him long to recover and recognize the brilliance of the author,
whoever that might be.[7] His admiration for the story measur-
ably increased after he had reread it in proof and could, as he
said, see it free of the clutter of the handwritten copy.[8] His high
opinion was quickly matched by that of the monthly's readership
of educated, thinking Russians and by the literary and intellectual vanguard of the day – the writers and critics who responded
in letters and reviews. Their warm reception acknowledging the
arrival of a new voice of immense promise was followed by an
even warmer response to the trilogy's second part, *Boyhood*,
which was published in *The Contemporary* in September 1854,
although again with changes and cuts by the censor; such as the
omission of Chapter Six, concerning the adolescent Nikolenka's
first sexual stirrings, and Chapter Eighteen, depicting, in vernacular dialogue, the thwarted romance of the domestic serfs Masha
and Vasily.[9] As Nekrasov wrote to the elated young Tolstoy, 'If
I say that I cannot find expressions sufficient to praise your latest
work, then I think it will be the truest that I can say . . . The
talent of the author of *Boyhood* is unique and appealing to the
highest degree, and things like the description of the summer
highway and the thunderstorm or the confinement in the cell,
and much, much more, will give this story a long life in our
literature.'[10]

The publication of *Youth*, the trilogy's last part, in *The
Contemporary* a little more than two years later in January 1857
(once again with cuts by the censor, most notably the treatment
at the end of Chapter Forty-four of the cynical army enlistment
of Nikolenka's talented university classmate Semyonov) was
also met with praise; even if this time it was tempered with
reservations reflecting both the changing ideological climate of
the second half of the 1850s and the expectations (Tolstoy's

identity now having become widely known) created in his readers by the form and stance of his previous works, perhaps especially the powerful *Sevastopol Sketches* of 1855–6, with their unflinching depiction of the brutality and corruption of the Crimean War, which Tolstoy had witnessed as a front-line artillery officer (he received his commission in early 1854 and joined the defence of Sevastopol at his own request). Some readers objected to the relative diffuseness of *Youth*, which is almost as long as the first two parts of the trilogy combined and lacks – as does the period or stage it describes – their more dramatic or at any rate more clearly marked psychological shifts and transitions: the passing in *Childhood* from the rural estate's bright Eden of intimate family life and closeness to nature to the darker, more ambiguous world of Moscow and, ultimately, the death of a parent; or the movement in *Boyhood*, at once amusing and touching, from the confusion and disorder of early adolescence to the partly redeeming social and moral transformation that, through the agency of a new friendship, eventually takes their place.

Other readers were disappointed by the story's aloofness from the urgent social issues and ideological controversies that were assuming an ever more prominent place in Russian literature and intellectual life – the crippling blight of serfdom, for example, or the true nature of Russian culture and the proper direction (native or Western) of its future development.[11] Still other readers were discontented with what they saw as the story's compositional and stylistic defects, its unabashed mixing of reflection, analysis and narrative, or its apparent indifference to lexical and syntactical decorum, as Tolstoy pushed against conventional form and language in his unrelenting search for cognitive accuracy and truth.[12]

Yet despite those reservations (or simply misunderstandings) in its readership, *Youth*'s subtle evocations of character (the psychological complication and pathos of the image of the stepmother, Dunya, in Chapter Forty-two, for example), its lighter moments of satire, parodic pastiche and comedy (Tolstoy's humour is greatly underappreciated), its glancing yet always experientially grounded consideration of such philosophical matters as the varieties of filial love (Chapter Twenty-four) or the nature and discipline of art (Chapter Thirty), and its scrupulously detailed – nothing is ever vague, everything is firmly, uniquely itself – yet surpassingly lyrical descriptions of nature (the progress in Chapter Thirty-two, for example, from deliberate immersion in the lush physicality of the natural world to – in both the implicit structure of its imagery and its explicit theology – a kind of Platonic contemplation of the divinity residing within and beyond it) – all those elements, and many more besides, helped to secure Tolstoy's place in the front rank of Russian prose, and gave further impetus to its movement along the high Realist path that would in the next two decades lead to its golden age.

Of course, with our knowledge of Tolstoy's life, we do not really have to rely on his letters to his first editor, Nekrasov, nor indeed on any of his other correspondence or the many remarks in his notebooks and diaries that might also be cited, to draw confident conclusions about the trilogy's genre – about its mode of literary cognition. We have only to compare the facts and events of Tolstoy's own biography with the relationships and circumstances he assigned to his narrator.

Tolstoy's mother died when he was two and he had no direct memory of her. Nikolenka's mother dies when he is eleven and his sense of her is both intensely physical and a fulcrum of the formal and thematic structure of *Childhood*, if not of the rest of the trilogy. Tolstoy's father died (or was killed) when he was nine, leaving him and his siblings in the care first of their paternal grandmother in Moscow, and then, after her death, of paternal aunts in Moscow and the provincial capital city of Kazan on the upper Volga. Nikolenka's father is a changing, somewhat ambiguous, yet important presence throughout the trilogy, ensuring, however precariously, the financial security of the family and standing, for better or worse, as a main source of its social, psychological and ethical inheritance and character.

Tolstoy was a count (*graf*) with distinguished ancestors on both sides. Nikolenka comes from a somewhat more modest background, although he, too, is a member of the urban nobility and not only blessed with the superb educational and material advantages provided by that milieu, but also, as he grows older, burdened with its characteristic pretensions and moral confusion, as epitomized in the trilogy, but especially in *Youth*, by the notion of *comme il faut* or 'respectability'. Tolstoy had three older brothers and a younger sister with whom he remained close. Nikolenka has a brother and a sister whom he loves and admires (or, as the youngest, sometimes envies and resents), but there is a certain distance in his relations with them, even though they figure prominently in his evolving sense of himself and his place in the world.

Tolstoy attended the University of Kazan, first in the Department of Arabo-Turkic Languages (he was a gifted linguist, with excellent command as a youth of French and German and a good knowledge of English) and then of Jurisprudence, before abandoning his studies to devote himself, until he joined his brother's brigade in the Caucasus, to the enlightened management of Yasnaya Polyana, the estate 125 miles south of Moscow that he had inherited with its numerous serfs. Nikolenka is admitted to Moscow University in the Department of Mathematics, although, like Tolstoy's own first year in Kazan, his Moscow studies end in failure, and, of course, his story, too, moves back and forth between the city and the country (a perennial Tolstoyan motif), with the idyllic world of the latter – of Petrovskoye in the trilogy – playing a central, even transcendental role for him, just as nature did for Tolstoy and many others in the post-romantic Russia and West of his day.

One could continue with such contrasts and oblique similarities in regard to Tolstoy and the members of his large family, including its various retainers and servants, but the point is clear enough. The story of Nikolenka Irtenyev told in the trilogy is a brilliantly sustained imaginative construct, a social and psychological mediation derived, to be sure, from biographical experience as perhaps most works of fiction ultimately are, but not to be confused with that experience or with its merely private meaning. Indeed, to make such a confusion, as some biographers and critics have done, is to overlook or diminish the artistic skill with which the trilogy has been made and to blur the outlines of Tolstoy's own life and its historical reality.[13]

If the trilogy is indeed a novel, just as Tolstoy said it was, and not a veiled account of his own private experience with embellishments, then what kind of novel is it? The broad answer is that it is a *Bildungsroman*, a subgenre that includes such classic antecedents as Rousseau's *Émile* (1762) and Charles Dickens's *David Copperfield* (1849–50), and whose subject, by definition, is the growth and formation of the hero, although in the trilogy the emphasis falls on the turbid, lurching process of that formation, the tangle of feeling, insight and striving self-awareness and realization that inform and impel it.[14]

Among the many who responded to the long and short works produced by Tolstoy during this initial stage of his career, it was the so-called radical critic and novelist Nikolay Chernyshevsky (1828–89) who was the first to describe that special Tolstoyan emphasis systematically, and to explain what set it apart from the methods of older contemporaries like Ivan Turgenev (1818–83) or revered predecessors like Alexander Pushkin (1799–1837) and Mikhail Lermontov (1814–41) and made it important in the then still brief history of modern Russian literature. In an enthusiastic and startlingly prescient 1856 omnibus review of Tolstoy's writings thus far (including the above-mentioned *Sevastopol Sketches* and the publication of *Childhood* and *Boyhood* together in book form with the cuts restored, thanks to a relaxation of censorship after the death of Nicholas I in 1855), Chernyshevsky identified as 'distinctive features' of Tolstoy's 'talent' his 'extraordinary capacity for observation, subtle analysis of mental impulses, precision and poetry in the pictures of nature and elegant simplicity', and then added in a more fundamental summarizing characterization:

> Count Tolstoy is concerned above all with how feelings and thoughts develop from other feelings and thoughts. He is interested in seeing how a feeling spontaneously emerging from a given situation or impression, and yielding to the influence of memories and the power of associations produced by the imagination, is turned into other feelings, goes back to its original starting point,

and then wanders off again and again, changing along a whole
series of memories; how a thought produced by an initial sensation leads to other thoughts and is carried away further and
further, combining daydreams with real sensations and dreams
of the future with reflections about the present. Psychological
analysis may tend in various directions: one poet will be interested
above all in the delineation of character; another, in the influence
on character of social relations and everyday encounters; a third,
in the link between feelings and actions. Count Tolstoy is interested above all in the psychic process itself, in its forms and laws,
in the dialectic of the mind . . .'[15]

This definition of what is offered as the essence of Tolstoy's
method is, with its frequently repeated Hegelian tag, a found-
ing text of the critical line that sees Tolstoy primarily as a
master psychologist, a pioneer literary investigator of conscious
and unconscious states and their behavioural correlates. And
it is undeniably true that the trilogy and Tolstoy's other works
of the 1850s are, like the great masterpieces that would follow,
profoundly attentive to the multilayered interplay of feelings
and thoughts under the pressure of external circumstances and
internal conditions. The depiction of the trilogy's numerous
characters, but especially of the evolving inner life of the narrator, Nikolenka, is indeed remarkable for the subtlety and depth
of its psychological and moral insight.

Reading the novel's three parts with their ever-expanding
scope, their constantly widening circle of interaction and experience, as Nikolenka moves from the safe embrace of country
family life at the beginning of *Childhood* to the large questions
of social and moral identity with which he struggles on the thresh-
old of adulthood at the end of *Youth*, one always has the sense
of encountering not so much conventional fictional projections,
however striking or memorable, of concepts of human personality and situation (the sense that one may have reading Dickens,
for example), as actual human beings whose complexity is never
compromised for a thematic argument or rhetorical manoeuvre,
who are never reduced to mere types, but remain fully, intract-
ably, elusively themselves, whatever their angle of presentation,

be it critical or comical or admiring or, as usually happens, some dynamic blend of all three. Why the trilogy's characters have such human vitality, why readers have returned to the book with such interest and pleasure for so many generations, may, of course, be deemed a mystery, the mystery of any enduring work of art. But for all the attraction of that easy formula, it must be said that there really are sound explanations for that interest and pleasure, and that a principal one lies with Chernyshevsky's insight about the illuminating sensitivity and reach of Tolstoyan psychologism, about Tolstoy's uncanny mastery, even at this early stage of his career, of the complex, shifting mechanisms of personality – of the 'dialectic of the mind' as we know and feel its movement within ourselves, whoever and wherever we may be.

Yet for all the explanatory value of Chernyshevsky's insight into the innovation of Tolstoyan psychologism, there is another, no less important aspect of Tolstoy's art that Chernyshevsky's approach fails to engage: its profoundly empirical apprehension of the objective world; its awareness of the manifold parts and relations of that world, and of the various ways they impinge on human activity, and circumscribe or enable or enrich it. Tolstoy was, it would not be too much to say, a kind of Russian Adam, a first namer of things, a writer who vastly enlarged the purview of the literature of his day, and whose powers of observation were no less wide-ranging than deeply penetrating. He is a writer who is seemingly interested in everything, whether the shape and structure and arrangements of the spaces – the rooms and buildings – his characters inhabit; or the diverse details of the personal dress of boys and girls and men and women of different social conditions and circumstances; or the kinds of conveyances they use, along with descriptions of vehicular technology and function; or agricultural practices; or the customs and procedures of hunting; or the different kinds of dog and horse and their peculiar behaviours, both individual and generic (indeed, dogs in the trilogy may, in the vividness of their portrayal, even emerge as characters: the Borzois Milka and Zhiran in *Childhood*, for example, or Lyubov Sergeyevna's little Bolognese in *Youth*); or the diversity of plant and insect species and, again, their behaviour (Tolstoy's sense of the *intentionality* of plant life is almost palpable: for example, the extraordinary description of the raspberry thicket, of the interaction of the corporeal self with the world of nature already mentioned in regard to Chapter Thirty-two of *Youth*); or the precisely registered modulations and transformations, the behaviour, of meteorological phenomena (the long rhythmic arc of the description of the thunderstorm in Chapter Two of *Boyhood* that Nekrasov mentioned in his letter, or the various other descriptions of clouds, rain and snow, of sunlight and moonlight); and so on. Everything that touches on the characters, or that occurs in and around them, or that is capable of being observed by them, is fully identified, is brought out of the perceptual penumbra into the bright light of consciousness and shown to have a place, a function, a meaning.

That irrepressible cognitive impulse and powerful sense of the intricate interdependence of things pervades the trilogy, and it is this force that ultimately drives the narrative, whatever its immediate subject, whether internal and psychological or external and circumstantial. Tolstoy was not only a supremely rationalistic investigator of feelings and ideas about the world, and the ways they interact and change and manifest themselves in personalities, he was also a gifted poet of material fact, and he shows that fact to us in unprecedented detail with all its colours and sounds and textures and smells vibrantly intact. As Nikolenka puts it on what we may take to be Tolstoy's own behalf in the coda to a splendidly picturesque description of agrarian nature in Chapter Seven of *Childhood*:

> The voices of people, the clattering of horses and carts, the merry chirping of quail, the hum of insects hovering in motionless swarms, the smell of wormwood, straw and horse sweat, the myriad colours and shadows the scorching sun cast upon the light-yellow stubble, the distant blue wood and pale-lilac clouds, and the white gossamer carried through the air or lying across the stubble – all that I saw, heard and felt.

This poignant concluding declaration pertains, as is always the case in Tolstoy, to a very specific, very concrete moment of experience and memory, but it may also stand as a kind of summary of the stance of the trilogy as a whole: its eager receptivity to the phenomenal world and its scrupulous representation of that world's extraordinary multiplicity, complexity and beauty.

There is, of course, much more to say about the trilogy – about its forms, structure, evolving technique and themes – than may even be alluded to, let alone addressed, in a brief introduction. For although the trilogy lacks the scale and integrative power of Tolstoy's masterpieces, it is nonetheless a work of genuine subtlety and art in its own right, a small classic of durable psychological and social insight and compelling charm. Tolstoy had by the end of his long and extraordinarily productive life (he died at the age of eighty-two in 1910) become an internationally famous literary artist and inspiring moral thinker, whose collected works would, in their standard Russian edition, reach an astonishing one hundred volumes and include many permanent additions to the canons of world literature and philosophy. He was a complicated but always fascinating figure, whose 2010 centenary inspired popular films and other expressions of public esteem, and whose writings have, in the numerous languages into which they have been translated, reached far more readers than he enjoyed in his own lifetime or could ever have foreseen.

Yet even writers and thinkers of such enormous power and lasting achievement must have their more modest beginnings, must take their first steps in search of their distinctive voices and styles and subjects and their roles within the human cultures that give them being and nourish and sustain them. Tolstoy was no exception to that rule, and the work in which he took those first steps, the one in which he laid the groundwork for the great edifice that would follow, was, of course, the trilogy. Although there are many other reasons for its continued presence in our reading life, the last is perhaps sufficient in itself. The trilogy allows us to see Tolstoy's preoccupations as an artist and thinker in their initial form; it shows us, as perhaps no other work of his can, how those preoccupations developed, how his ideas about human nature and the world first engaged the world and then were changed and modified by his growing experience of it – by his intellectually powerful and morally serious examination of its myriad parts and relations and the ways they ineluctably shape us and then are shaped by us in turn.

NOTES

1. In the Russian army until 1864, a cadet-volunteer (*yunker* or *volontër*) was an irregular non-commissioned officer from the nobility promotable to regular status and a commission after a short term of active service (two years or less) and the passing of a set of examinations.

2. L. N. Tolstoy, *Perepiska s russkimi pisateliami* (Correspondence with Russian Writers), ed. S. A. Rozanova, 2nd ed., 2 vols (Moscow, 1978), 1: 49–50. This and all subsequent translations are my own and may differ in detail from the available English versions mentioned in the Further Reading section, below.

3. *Perepiska*, 1: 50–51. The term rendered here and in the translation as 'outlook' (*napravlenie*), in the sense of 'a mental attitude or point of view' (*Shorter Oxford English Dictionary*), had for liberals like Nekrasov the further meaning of 'progressive orientation' or even 'commitment', as Sir Isaiah Berlin has rendered it in his *Sense of Reality* (New York, 1997), 208–9. Nekrasov was thus acknowledging what he took to be the story's social engagement, just as Tolstoy had chosen *The Contemporary* not only for its literary pedigree (it had been founded by Pushkin in 1836 and published the very best writers of the day) but also for its enlightened social views, which, as they grew more strident, would eventually lead to the closing of the magazine and the brief arrest of its staff.

4. '*Istoriia moego detstva*', *Sovremennik* (*The Contemporary*) 9 (1852). *Perepiska*, 1: 55.

5. *Perepiska*, 1: 57.

6. Perhaps feeling that he had taken the subject and its somewhat restrictive first-person method as far as he could, Tolstoy never returned to the series, although he did publish what might be taken as a kind of variation on the projected fourth part, the 1856 long story, 'A Landowner's Morning'.

7. Despite Nekrasov's increasingly insistent pleas (he was required by Russian law to know who his contributors were), Tolstoy, perhaps still unsure that the quality of his effort had matched the scale of his ambition, stubbornly refused for a time to identify himself,

leaving the exasperated editor to publish not only *Childhood* but several other pieces virtually anonymously with the private conjecture that they had been written by Tolstoy's brother.

8. *Perepiska*, 1: 51.
9. *Sovremennik* 9 (1854). The Russian title, *Otrochestvo*, has, in a tradition going back to the first translation by Isabel Hapgood in the late nineteenth century, always been rendered in English as *Boyhood*, but it could as easily and, given the developmental stage depicted in the story, perhaps even more accurately be rendered as *Adolescence*.
10. *Perepiska*, 1: 61–2. The allusions are to Chapters 1, 2 and 15–16, respectively.
11. The public debate about Russia's true character and appropriate future famously coalesced into the two camps of the so-called Slavophiles and Westernizers and entailed a variety of ancillary issues, many of them addressed, in very different ways to be sure, in the great topical fiction of Turgenev and Dostoevsky, as well as in numerous other minor works. Tolstoy, however, was, at least at this early stage in his career, opposed in principle to that kind of direct engagement with public intellectual life, as he eloquently argued in 1859 in a speech to the Society of the Lovers of Russian Literature after his induction along with Turgenev: '. . . however great the significance of a political literature reflecting the temporary interests of a society, however necessary it may be for a nation's development, there is another literature reflecting eternal, broadly human interests and the most precious, intimate feelings of a people, a literature accessible to any person of any nation and time, and one without which no nation of strength and vitality has ever developed' (L. N. Tolstoi, *Sobranie sochinenii* [Collected Works], ed. M. B. Khrapchenko et al., 20 vols [Moscow, 1983], 15: 8).
12. See, for example, the blend of discriminating insight and blank incomprehension in the long, frank letter of the editor and minor novelist Alexander Druzhinin, a close friend to whom Tolstoy had sent *Youth* in manuscript (*Perepiska*, 1: 266–9). Druzhinin's remarks on Tolstoy's style are especially interesting: 'Every one of your defects has its part of strength and beauty, and nearly every one of your merits contains within it the kernel of your defects. Your style fits that conclusion perfectly. You're dreadfully illiterate, sometimes with the illiteracy of the innovator and strong poet who's remaking the language in his own way and forever, and sometimes with that of an army officer scribbling to a comrade while squatting in some *blindage*' (1: 267).

13. As, for example, Ernest J. Simmons did in his very well documented scholarly account by blithely interpolating into his own
narrative long unmarked sections of the trilogy as if they were
autobiography or historical fact. Another approach to the issue
is that of the brilliant critic and literary historian Lydia Ginzburg,
who characterized the trilogy as 'autopsychological' rather than
'autobiographical'. Her approach does not really resolve the issue,
however, since all psychological analysis in all fiction, and indeed
all human experience, is at base 'autopsychological' – is derived
or extrapolated from self-perception: we know others in large
part through our knowledge of ourselves. If, however, Ginzburg
meant that Tolstoy had changed the external facts yet retained
the internal mechanisms and processes of his own particular
psyche, then that too will tend to discount the achievement of
empathic imagination that is the hallmark of the trilogy, as it is
indeed of all of Tolstoy's fiction; that is, it will discount both the
power of his insight and the degree of his conscious, calculated
artistry.

14. Although one should not ignore the importance of *Émile* for
Tolstoy, the example of *David Copperfield* (1849–50) is perhaps
especially pertinent here. According to his diary, Tolstoy was reading Dickens's novel in 1852 as he worked on *Childhood*, most
likely in the loose translation of Irinarkh Vvedensky published in
Patriotic Annals (*Otechestvennye zapiski*) in 1851, since in
November 1853, evidently wishing to reread the book in English,
he asked his brother Sergey to obtain a copy for him and send it
to the Caucasus along with an English-French dictionary. Be that
as it may, we know that Tolstoy held *David Copperfield* in high
regard throughout his life and reread it often in English as a special
favourite, and that, as he indicated in a letter of 1891, it made an
'enormous' impression on him the first time he read it. Nonetheless, given the very great, indeed fundamental, differences between
Dickens's treatment of childhood, boyhood and youth and
Tolstoy's, not to mention their very different ways of representing
character (Dickens tends to operate from schemata, while Tolstoy
proceeds as it were inductively), it would be much more accurate
to say that *David Copperfield* was a kind of sanction or inspira-
tion in the use of first-person narration rather than a direct
influence on the trilogy's structure and stance.

15. *Sovremennik* 12 (1856). Perhaps from a confusion about the full
semantic range of the Russian term, which has both a spiritual and
a more strictly mental meaning, the concluding phrase (*dialektika*

dushy) is sometimes translated as 'dialectic of the soul', even though the doctrinaire materialist Chernyshevsky is speaking of mental, rather than of spiritual processes, of definite psychic events and mechanisms rather than of a transcendental religious or metaphysical category whose existence he would probably have denied anyway.

Further Reading

TRANSLATIONS

The following two editions are very well translated and annotated, with detailed indexes and excellent contextual commentary, and are highly recommended for their great literary interest and biographical value.

Christian, R. F. (ed. and trans.), *Tolstoy's Letters*, 2 vols (New York: Charles Scribner's Sons, 1978).
— (ed. and trans.), *Tolstoy's Diaries*, 2 vols (New York: Charles Scribner's Sons, 1985).

BIOGRAPHIES

Despite his literary and cultural importance and enduring place in the English-speaking world, and the vast literature in English devoted to his art and thought and to various aspects of his life and career, there is unfortunately no recent biography of Tolstoy in English of genuine scholarly authority and reach, let alone literary merit. The Russian Formalist scholar Boris Eikhenbaum's superb *Lev Tolstoy* (Leningrad, 1928–31) remains, eighty years on, the most thorough examination of Tolstoy's early and mid-career in the context of the evolving literary culture of his day, but only the second part is available in English: *Tolstoi in the Sixties*, trans. Duffield White (Ann Arbor: Ardis, 1982), and it is, in any case, largely indifferent to details of private history.

The works cited below, however, are good sources of information about that private history, especially the Maude and Simmons contributions, while the other two books, although confidently written and often entertaining, are unfortunately marred by trite, melodramatic conjecture and careless factual errors, and should be used with care.

Maude, Aylmer, *The Life of Tolstoy*, 2 vols, revised edition (Oxford: Oxford University Press, 1930). First published in 1908–10.

Simmons, Ernest J., *Leo Tolstoy*, 2 vols (New York: Vintage Books, 1960). First published in 1946.

Troyat, Henri, *Tolstoy*, trans. Nancy Amphoux (New York: Grove Press, 2001). First published in 1967.

Wilson, A. N., *Tolstoy* (London: Hamish Hamilton, and New York: W. W. Norton, 1988).

CRITICISM

Although the critical literature devoted to Tolstoy in English or English translation is very large, as I have indicated, it has tended to neglect his early writings. Nonetheless, the following studies are of particular relevance to the trilogy, either for their direct discussion of it or their examination of larger issues of genre, style and form, and (in the case of Sir Isaiah Berlin *par excellence*) of Tolstoy's thought and its provenance.

Bayley, John, *Tolstoy and the Novel* (London: Chatto & Windus, 1966).

Berlin, Isaiah, 'The Hedgehog and the Fox' and 'Tolstoy and Enlightenment', in his classic *Russian Thinkers*, ed. Henry Hardy and Aileen Kelly (New York: The Viking Press, 1978).

Christian, R. F., *Tolstoy: A Critical Introduction* (Cambridge: Cambridge University Press, 1969).

Eikhenbaum, Boris, *The Young Tolstoy*, ed. Gary Kern (Ann Arbor: Ardis, 1972). Original first published in 1922.

Ginzburg, Lydia, *On Psychological Prose*, ed. and trans. Judson

Rosengrant (Princeton: Princeton University Press, 1991).

Gustafson, Richard F., *Resident and Stranger: A Study in Fiction and Theology* (Princeton: Princeton University Press, 1986).

Knowles, A. V., *Tolstoy: The Critical Heritage* (Boston: Routledge and Kegan Paul, 1978).

Orwin, Donna Tussing, *Tolstoy's Art and Thought, 1847–1882* (Princeton: Princeton University Press, 1993).

— (ed.), *The Cambridge Companion to Tolstoy* (Cambridge: Cambridge University Press, 2002).

—, *Consequence of Consciousness: Turgenev, Dostoevsky, Tolstoy* (Stanford: Stanford University Press, 2007).

Wachtel, Andrew Baruch, *The Battle for Childhood: Creation of a Russian Myth* (Stanford: Stanford University Press, 1990).

Williams, Gareth, *Tolstoy's 'Childhood'* (Bristol: Bristol Classical Press, 1995).

Zweers, A. F., *Grown-up Narrator and Childlike Hero* (Paris and The Hague: Mouton, 1971)

Note on the Text and Translation

The translation is completely new and is based on a study of the young Tolstoy's language in relation both to its social and historical context and to its use within the trilogy as a self-contained work of art – in relation, that is, to how the language may reflect a particular time and place (Russia in the 1840s and 1850s), yet acquire distinctive internal meaning and resonance as its elements are arranged according to Tolstoy's own cognitive and aesthetic purposes.

The source text of the translation is that in the most recent and authoritative Russian academic edition of Tolstoy's *Complete Collected Works*.[1] That text was compared with earlier versions, including those published in *The Contemporary*, as well as with material abandoned or cut by Tolstoy, a relentless reviser.[2]

In view of the distance between our own time and that of the trilogy, and the extraordinary specificity of Tolstoy's depiction of his world, the translation has been furnished with endnotes. They are meant to provide background information of the sort that Tolstoy's first readers would have brought to the work and that he clearly assumed them to have. For English-speaking readers, that information includes translations of the German and French phrases used in the text, identification of its geographical, cultural, historical and literary references, and clarification of its social and material world, including the technologies current in Tolstoy's day, since he is, as I have indicated, interested in everything that touches his characters, describing it with unprecedented exactitude, and bringing to bear for that purpose the full lexical range of the Russian language. That language, it should be observed, is less the received literary instrument of Tolstoy's time (roughly the middle style established by Pushkin) than it is the vernacular usage of his own highly educated, polyglot milieu, augmented with terminologies from a wide variety of subjects and spheres. The sheer extent of that uniquely Tolstoyan variety is, for many, a source of the great pleasure of the trilogy, of the satisfying sense that his representations have a firm empirical grounding and a rigorous conceptual order – that he is, in fact, showing us exactly how things are, exactly how they look and work and feel and act upon or exist in greater or lesser proximity to the particular human experience he is portraying.

Some items of Tolstoy's vocabulary are, as has been indicated above, historically specific, and they have been glossed in the notes accordingly, while others are bound to individual characters, to their speech habits or physical attributes or gestures, or mark thematic motifs (in which case the verbal link has been scrupulously repeated in the translation), or denote with almost ethnographic or scientific zeal particular features of social behaviour or aspects of the natural and material world. Whether because the Russian language has changed in subtle ways since Tolstoy's time and blurred or obscured distinctions that were important for him, or because of what might be called a rashly assimilative translation philosophy, or simply because of haste, there has been a tendency in English versions of the trilogy (and not only of the trilogy) to substitute broad generic terms for Tolstoy's much more specific notations. There are numerous examples of this tendency, but a simple and telling one is the translation in *Youth* of the unusual Russian word *bolonka*. It has been variously rendered as 'small dog', 'lapdog' and even 'spaniel', whereas it in fact means a Bolognese, a small breed of the Bichon type still popular today. As such, the word has a distinct function in the text. It conveys (or in its denotation metonymically projects) something of the identity and personality of the pet's owner, the peculiar Lyubov Sergeyevna, and it imparts a far more vivid, even oddly familiar sense of her world and its possibilities than does 'small dog'. Tolstoy used the word *bolonka*, that is, because he wanted the concrete, particular meaning it brought, and not some colourless verbal marker lacking nuance or depth. I have dwelt on this seemingly minor point because I think it is an important one that concerns not so much the accurate translation of a single term as it does the preservation of a fundamental Tolstoyan principle. The trilogy's lexical variety and precision are not merely a feature of its style in some inadvertent or formal sense, but rather, and much more importantly, a reflection of its cognitive orientation and method, of its semantics and perhaps even of its phenomenology.

I have mentioned the vernacular or colloquial nature of many of Tolstoy's usages. This is a very complex matter best illustrated by the translation itself, but suffice it to say that I have striven to replicate the trilogy's movement not only among numerous terminological domains but also among highly diverse registers (from formal to informal, from bookish, scientific or technical to macaronic), while at the same time seeking to avoid disruptive lexical anachronism by using no words not active in English before 1850 (as documented by the *Oxford English Dictionary*). That last criterion might, in the colloquial usages at least, seem to entail the equal risk of archaism or quaintness, but, in fact, the colloquial stock of English is quite old, with many words we might suppose to be contemporary often dating from at least the eighteenth century. The historical complexity and richness of contemporary English have thus made it possible, at least theoretically, for the translation to be not only true to Tolstoy's own time and place, but also fresh and vivid – have made it possible, that is, to respect the trilogy's reflection of an apparently remote period, on the one hand, and its extraordinary vitality and remarkable modernity of conception, attitude and voice, on the other.

Another feature of Tolstoy's language and style is his syntax. In fact, there are several varieties of it in the trilogy. They range from the naturalistic ellipsis and disjunction of the dialogue and other reported speech (Tolstoy had a fine ear for such things); to elegant eighteenth-century discourse with formulaic antitheses and strict parallelism (the portraits of Papa and Prince Ivan Ivanych in *Childhood*, or of Katenka and Lyubochka in *Boyhood*); to lyrical or dramatic nature descriptions (the hunt in *Childhood* or the thunderstorm in *Boyhood*), with their strong rhythms, alliteration, onomatopoeia and other aural and syntactic combinations, including morphemic repetition and a fondness for triads; to the already mentioned romantic pastiche with its naïvely earnest or self-indulgent emotionalism; to the broken or pidgin language of the non-Russian Karl Ivanych (his list of reimbursable expenses in *Childhood*, or his unconsciously parodic autobiographical picaresque in *Boyhood*). There are also Tolstoy's more or less neutral descriptions of character, scene and situation, with their famously intricate, compressed and sometimes even convoluted syntax. That 'convolution' is yet another dimension of Tolstoy's stylistic innovation and not a matter of carelessness or a rejection of grammatical elegance on his part, but an expression of his sense of reality as a multiplicity of simultaneously interactive principles and conditions. It is, therefore, for him, an indispensable stylistic tool, and as such it has been preserved in the translation.

Tolstoy famously remarked in one of his *Sevastopol Sketches* that his hero was truth. The remark may also stand as a guide for anyone undertaking to translate him: to tell the truth about his text in its own terms, and to do so by recognizing that the truth lies pre-eminently in the wonderful particularity of the text's representation of the world. If the translator is alert to that particularity and at the same time responsive to the constantly shifting angles of its presentation, then the rest may, if he is lucky, follow of its own accord.

NOTES

1. L. N. Tolstoy, *Polnoe sobranie sochinenii*, ed. L. D. Gromova-Opul'skaia et al., 100 vols (Moscow: Nauka, 2000), 1: 11–276.
2. As Tolstoy put the issue in an aphoristic notebook entry of 16 October 1853: 'The art of writing well . . . consists not in knowing what to write but in knowing what doesn't need to be written; no additions, however brilliant, can improve a work so much as deletions will.'

Note on Names, Languages and Transliteration

As in most works of nineteenth-century Russian prose, the trilogy's system of personal naming is complex. It conveys not only identity but also gradations of intimacy, social position and even linguistic and cultural orientation (Western European versus Russian), thereby instantly establishing for the reader familiar with the system both the characters' attitudes towards and their status in relation to each other. Thus, the narrator, usually called by his diminutive *Nikolenka* (with the stress on the second syllable), may also, depending on the context and speaker, be addressed more formally by his given name and patronymic, *Nikolay Petrovich*; officially by his last name only, *Irtenyev*; more intimately by his secondary diminutives, *Koko* or *Nikolasha*; or more or less neutrally by the French equivalent of his given name, *Nicolas*. His older brother, usually called by his own diminutive, *Volodya*, may also be addressed by his given name and patronymic, *Vladimir Petrovich*; by a second, more affectionate diminutive, *Volodenka*; or by a German equivalent of his given name, *Woldemar*; while their sister, formally *Lyubov Petrovna Irtenyeva* (with her last name in the obligatory feminine form), is usually referred to by one of two diminutives, *Lyuba* or, more affectionately, *Lyubochka*.

As a rule, for both nineteenth-century and modern Russian speakers, diminutives tend to be used by social equals on familiar terms, by superiors addressing inferiors, or by adults speaking to children; whereas the combination of given name and patronymic is used by social inferiors addressing superiors, by younger people as a sign of respect when speaking to or of older people, regardless of social rank, and by adult equals who are not on familiar terms. The use of a given first name without an accompanying patronymic – as in regard to the serf and servant *Nikolay* in the trilogy – may express a degree of respect for an older social inferior, but without the acknowledgement of standing and authority that the addition of his patronymic would imply – as it does, for example, with the German tutor *Karl Ivanych* (a colloquial contraction of *Ivanovich*), or the former serf and nurse *Natalya Savishna* (her patronymic deriving from the old Russian name *Savva*). Similarly, the use at different times of the Russianized first name and patronymic *Marya Ivanovna* ('*Marie*, daughter of *Jean*') and the French diminutive *Mimi* (instead of its Russian cognate *Masha*) in regard to the Irtenyev French governess reflects, in the first instance, her status as a respected (by virtue of her age and authority) retainer and, in the second, her place as a family intimate and confidante of the children's mother.

In sum, the naming system serves both to identify individuals per se and to limn the social arrangements and dynamics of the world they inhabit and help to sustain. It is thus not only a matter of received onomastic convention, but also, in the hands of a virtuoso like Tolstoy, a subtle instrument of narrative structure and theme. As such it has naturally been retained in the translation without adaptation or simplification, other than the provision, below, of a list of the main characters and the different names associated with them.

The milieu from which Tolstoy himself derived and that he describes with such unremitting care was highly cosmopolitan and comfortably multilingual, and its members, especially the older ones, were often more proficient in their 'foreign' languages than they were in their 'native' Russian. As mentioned above, Tolstoy as a young man was fluent in French and German, and had a good knowledge of English, but he was also acquainted with Italian and Tatar; and later in life he would undertake the study of Greek and biblical Hebrew, as well as refine his English to a very impressive level of skill. He was, to be sure, exceptional in the extent and depth of his knowledge of other languages, but not at all exceptional in his command of German and French,

which were both commonly used in his milieu as still vital leg-
acies of the programmatic Europeanization of Russian culture
undertaken first by Peter I, the Great (reigned 1682–1725), whose
sympathies were Dutch and German, and then by Catherine II,
the Great (reigned 1762–96), whose orientation was Franco-
phone and Francophile, despite her Pomeranian birth. It follows
that Tolstoy has therefore included German and French in the
trilogy because those languages were living idioms of the world
he wanted to describe and analyse in the full complexity of its
historical, social and linguistic life. Indeed, he is as scrupulous in
his representation of the diverse non-Russian usages as he is in
conveying the distinctive Russian speech of different individuals
and groups, even groups as small as an immediate family or a
circle of acquaintances – for example, the 'sociolinguistic' discussion of family idioms in Chapter Twenty-nine of *Youth* and of
the distinctive speech habits of Nikolenka's fellow students in
Chapter Forty-three of the same section, or the systematic representation of verbal tics, like Papa's fondness for the word
'splendid' (*slavny* and its derivations) or the steward Yakov's
characteristic repetition of the nonce phrase 'once again' (*opyat-
taki*), or the already mentioned comic deformities of Karl
Ivanych's insecure, German-inflected Russian.

It would be incorrect to say that Tolstoy would have agreed
with his near-contemporary Wilhelm von Humboldt (1767–1835)
that language may determine thought, but it is certainly true that
he not only accepted but applied in a fairly elaborate way in the
trilogy the idea that language embodies and instils a powerful,
multilayered cultural orientation and impetus, and even, to some
degree, an ideology; as in his milieu's link through French to the
Enlightenment, a connection that was no less strong than its other
link through Russian to the ancient East Slavic culture of Orthodox Christianity and the peasantry or common people. Indeed, it
was arguably the blending of – and productive tension between
– those two historical, social and linguistic principles that
ultimately produced the extraordinarily vital hybrid culture from
which Tolstoy and his contemporaries emerged; the culture that
gave the world the great achievements of nineteenth-century
Russian literature, and that, as I have already indicated in various

ways, is one of the subjects of the trilogy's own intricate investigations and elaborations. In view of those facts and their vital importance, I have retained the German and French without alteration as integral components of the text, although, as mentioned above, English translations have been provided in the endnotes.

The problem of transliterating names and words from the Cyrillic alphabet of Russian to the Latin alphabet of English is a notoriously difficult one. There seems to be no satisfactory solution, other than a provisional compromise that tries, in the best instances, to render the rough phonetic shape (the pronunciation) of the Russian words and names without burdening the English-speaking reader with superfluous, distracting or meaningless orthographic detail, while yet providing, where necessary, reasonably reliable information for any readers with Russian who may want to consult the original sources. The compromise of this edition has been to use the popular Penguin system for the translation itself, but a simplified Library of Congress system in the Notes and other explanatory materials for the convenience of scholars and students.

List of Characters

Dubkov: an army officer and friend of the Irtenyev brothers
Frost: the Ivin German tutor
Grandmother: the narrator's maternal grandmother
Grap, Ilenka: an Irtenyev childhood friend
Irtenyev, Nikolay Petrovich; Nikolenka, Nikolasha, Koko: the narrator
Irtenyev, Pyotr Aleksandrovich (or **Aleksandrych**); **Pierre**: the narrator's father
Irtenyev, Vladimir Petrovich; Volodya, Volodenka, Woldemar: the narrator's brother
Irtenyeva, Lyubov Petrovna; Lyuba, Lyubochka: the narrator's sister
Irtenyeva, Natalya Nikolayevna; Natasha: the narrator's mother
Ivin brothers: distant Irtenyev relations and childhood friends
Ivin, Sergey; Seryozha: the middle Ivin brother
Katya, Katenka, Catherine: the French governess's daughter
Kornakov, Prince Stepan Mikhailovich; Étienne: Princess Kornakova's son
Kornakova, Princess Varvara Ilinishna: first cousin of the narrator's mother
Lyubov Sergeyevna: a Nekhlyudov family friend and member of their household
Marya Ivanovna; Mimi: the Irtenyev French governess
Mauer, Karl Ivanych: the Irtenyev German tutor
Mikhailov, Yakov Kharlampych: the Petrovskoye estate steward and a serf
Natalya Savishna; Natashka, Nasha: the Petrovskoye housekeeper and a freed serf

Nekhlyudov, Prince Dmitry; Mitya: the narrator's best friend
Nekhlyudova, Princess Marya Ivanovna: Dmitry's mother
Nekhlyudova, Princess Varvara; Varenka: Dmitry's sister
Nikolay (or **Nikolay Dmitrich**): an Irtenyev servant and serf
Prince Ivan Ivanych: Grandmother's cousin
St-Jérôme, Auguste: the Irtenyev French tutor
Sofya Ivanovna: Dmitry's aunt and a member of the Nekhlyudov
    household
Valakhina (or **Madame Valakhina**): an Irtenyev relation
Valakhina, Sofya; Sonyechka: Mme Valakhina's daughter
Yepifanov, Pyotr Vasilyevich; Petrushka: Avdotya Vasilyevna's
    brother
Yepifanova, Anna Dmitriyevna: Avdotya Vasilyevna's mother
Yepifanova, Avdotya Vasilyevna; Dunyechka, La belle Flamande:
    the narrator's stepmother

CHILDHOOD, BOYHOOD, YOUTH

Childhood

ONE

Our Teacher, Karl Ivanych

On the 12th of August 18**, exactly three days after my tenth birthday when I received such wonderful presents, Karl Ivanych woke me at seven in the morning by hitting a fly right over my head with a swatter made of sugar-bag paper on a stick. He did it so clumsily that he grazed the little icon of my patron saint hanging on the oak headboard of my bed, and the fly fell on my head. I poked my nose out from under the blanket, steadied the swaying icon with my hand, flicked the dead fly onto the floor and glanced over at Karl Ivanych with sleepy, angry eyes. But he, in a multicoloured quilted dressing gown wrapped with a belt of the same material, a knitted red skullcap with a tassel, and soft kidskin boots, continued to patrol the walls, aiming and swatting.

'Perhaps I am little,' I thought, 'but why is he bothering me? Why isn't he killing the flies by Volodya's bed? There are so many over there! No, Volodya's older than I am. I'm the youngest; that's why he's tormenting me. All he's thought about his whole life is doing nasty things to me,' I murmured. 'He saw very well that he woke and startled me, but he acts as if he didn't. What a horrible man he is! And his dressing gown and cap and tassel are horrible too!'

As I was thus mentally expressing my vexation with Karl Ivanych, he went over to his bed, looked at the watch suspended above it in a beaded slipper, hung the swatter on a nail and then turned to us, clearly in the best of moods.

'*Auf, Kinder, auf! 'S ist Zeit. Die Mutter ist schon im Saal!*'[1] he boomed in his kind German voice, and then he came over to me, sat down at the foot of my bed and removed his snuffbox from his pocket. I pretended to be asleep. Karl Ivanych took some snuff, wiped his nose, flicked his fingers and only then got after me. With a chuckle, he started to tickle my heels. '*Nu, nun, Faulenzer!*' he said.[2]

Ticklish as I was, I didn't jump out of bed or answer, but only stuck my head deeper under the pillows and kicked with all my might, trying as hard as I could not to laugh.

'What a kind person he is and how fond of us, and yet I could think such bad things about him!'

I was vexed both with myself and with Karl Ivanych, and felt like laughing and crying – my nerves were all in a jumble.

'*Ach, lassen Sie,*[3] Karl Ivanych!' I yelled with tears in my eyes as I pulled my head out from under the pillows.

Karl Ivanych was taken aback, and leaving my soles alone he anxiously started to ask what the matter was. Had I had a bad dream? His kind German face and the concern with which he tried to guess the reason for my tears made them flow even faster. I was ashamed and didn't understand how only a moment before I could have disliked Karl Ivanych and found his gown and cap and tassel so horrible, for now on the contrary they all seemed extraordinarily nice to me, and even the tassel struck me as clear proof of his goodness. I told him that it *was* a bad dream that had made me cry, that *maman* had died and was being taken for burial. I made it all up, since I had absolutely no idea what I had dreamed that night, but when Karl Ivanych, touched by my story, began to comfort and console me, it seemed to me that I really had dreamed that frightening dream, and I started to cry again for a different reason.

After Karl Ivanych left me and I sat up in bed and began to pull my stockings on my little feet, my tears started to recede, although dark thoughts about the made-up dream remained. Then our servant Nikolay came in, a tidy little man, always serious, correct and respectful, and a great friend of Karl Ivanych's. He had our clothes and footwear with him – boots for Volodya and insufferable pumps with bows for me. I would have been ashamed to cry in front of Nikolay, and anyway the morning sun was gaily shining through the windows and Volodya, mimicking Marya Ivanovna (our sister's French governess), was laughing so loudly and merrily at the washstand that even the serious Nikolay, a towel over his shoulder and soap in one hand and a ewer in the other, said with a grin, 'That will do, Vladimir Petrovich, now please get on with your washing.'

I was completely cheered up.

'*Sind Sie bald fertig*?'[4] Karl Ivanych's voice came from the classroom.

The voice was stern without the gentle expression that had earlier brought me to tears. Karl Ivanych was an entirely different person in the classroom: he was a schoolmaster. I quickly got dressed, washed and still brushing my wet hair responded to his call.

Karl Ivanych, with spectacles on his nose and a book in his hand, was sitting in his usual place between the door and the window. To the left of the door were two small shelves, one ours – the children's – and the other Karl Ivanych's *own*. Ours contained books of every kind, school and non-school, some upright and others lying flat. Only two large volumes in red bindings of the *Histoire des voyages*[5] stood primly against the wall, and then came tall books, thick books, big books and small books, books without covers and covers without books, all crammed in the same space, as happened whenever you were ordered before breaks to straighten up the library, as Karl Ivanych grandly called our little shelf. The collection of books on his *own* shelf, although not so numerous as ours, was even more varied. I remember three: a German pamphlet, without a cover, on manuring cabbage gardens; a volume of a history of the Seven Years War[6] in parchment with a burnt corner; and a complete course on hydrostatics. Karl Ivanych spent the better part of his spare time reading and had even hurt his eyesight doing so, although he read nothing but the books on his shelf and the *Northern Bee*.[7]

Among the things on Karl Ivanych's shelf was one that recalls him to me more than any other. It was a cardboard disc on a wooden support, up and down which the disc could be moved on pegs. Glued to the disc were caricatures of a lady and a hairdresser. Karl Ivanych was good at gluing things and had devised the disc himself to protect his weak eyes from bright sunlight.

As if it were today, I see before me a tall figure in a quilted dressing gown and a red cap with thin grey hair sticking out from under. He's sitting next to a small table on which the cardboard disc with the hairdresser stands, casting a shadow over his face. He's holding a book in one hand, while the other is resting on the arm of his chair. Beside him on the table are a watch with a hunter painted on the dial, a checked handkerchief, a round black snuffbox, a green spectacle case and a pair of candle snuffers on a little tray. It all sits so neatly, so tidily in place, that you might conclude from the order alone that Karl Ivanych's conscience is clear and his soul at peace.

After running around the salon downstairs to your heart's content, you would creep up to the classroom on tiptoe to take a look. Karl Ivanych would be sitting alone in his armchair reading one of his favourite books with an expression of calm majesty. Sometimes I would catch him when he wasn't reading, his spectacles resting on the tip of his long aquiline nose, his blue, half-closed eyes gazing with a special sort of expression, and a wistful smile on his lips. The room would be silent, except for his regular breathing and the chiming of the watch with the hunter.

He wouldn't notice me, and I would stand in the doorway and think, 'Poor, poor old man! There are many of us, we play and have fun, but he's completely by himself with no one to be affectionate to him. He's right when he says that he's an orphan. And the story of his life is such an awful one! I remember his telling Nikolay about it – it would be terrible to be in his position!' And you would become so sad that you would go over and take his hand and say, '*Lieber* Karl Ivanych!'[8] He liked it when I talked to him that way and always petted me and was clearly moved.

On the middle wall hung the geography maps, most of them badly tattered but skilfully glued from behind by Karl Ivanych. On one side of the third wall with the doorway downstairs in the middle hung two rulers, one nicked and ours, and the other quite new and his *own* and used more for urging us on than for drawing lines. On the other side of the same wall was a blackboard on which our major transgressions were marked with circles and our minor ones with crosses. To the left of the blackboard was the corner in which we were made to kneel.

What memories I have of that corner! I remember the stove vent and the noise it made whenever you opened it. You would kneel in the corner until your knees and back started to ache and think, 'Karl Ivanych has forgotten all about me. He's probably calmly sitting in his soft armchair reading his hydrostatics, but what about me?' And to remind him, you would quietly start to open and close the vent or peel the plaster from the wall. But if too large a piece suddenly fell to the floor with a thud, the fright alone really would be worse than any punishment. You would glance back at Karl Ivanych, but he would be sitting there with a book in his hand as if he hadn't noticed anything.

In the middle of the room stood a table covered with a worn black oilcloth through which the table's edge, picked by penknives, stuck out in several places. Around the table were some stools, unpainted but polished from long use. The room's fourth wall was taken up by three windows. This was the view from them: directly below was the driveway, in which every hollow, every stone, every rut had long been familiar and dear to me; across the driveway was a mown avenue of lindens, behind which parts of a wattle fence could be seen; and beyond the fence was a meadow with a threshing barn on one side and a wood on the other with the watchman's hut in the distance. Partly visible in the window on the right was the terrace where the grown-ups usually gathered before dinner.[9] While Karl Ivanych corrected the pages of dictation, you would gaze in that direction and see Mama's dark head and someone else's back and hear muffled talk and laughter, and it would vex you that you couldn't be there, too, and you would think, 'When shall I at last be grown up and done with lessons and not always sitting over dialogues, but be with the ones I love?' Your vexation would turn to sadness and, goodness knows why or about what, you would fall into such a reverie that you wouldn't even hear Karl Ivanych fuming over your mistakes . . .

Then Karl Ivanych took off his dressing gown, put on a blue tailcoat with pads and gathers at the shoulders, adjusted his cravat in the mirror and led us downstairs to greet Mama.

TWO

Maman

Mama was sitting in the drawing room pouring tea. In one hand she held the teapot, and in the other the tap of the samovar, from which the water ran over the lip of the teapot onto the tray. But even though she was staring at it, she noticed neither that nor our coming into the room.

So many memories of the past rise up when you try to resurrect in your imagination the features of a beloved being, that peering through those memories you see the features dimly, as if through tears – the tears of imagination. When I try to recall Mama as she was then, I see only her brown eyes that always expressed the same gentleness and love, the mole on her neck just below where the little hairs curl, her embroidered white collar and her thin, tender hand that caressed me so often and that I kissed so much. But her general expression eludes me.

To the left of the sofa was an old English grand piano. Sitting at it was my dark-haired sister Lyubochka, playing études by Clementi[10] with obvious effort, her pink little fingers having just been rinsed in cold water. She was eleven. She was dressed in a short muslin shift and white pantalettes with lace ruffles and could only do octaves in arpeggios. Marya Ivanovna, wearing a blue padded jacket and a mobcap with pink ribbons, was seated alongside, but turned towards her with an angry red face that assumed an even sterner expression the moment Karl Ivanych came in. She glared at him and, ignoring his bow, continued to tap her foot while counting, '*Un, deux, trois! Un, deux, trois!*' even louder and more insistently than before.

Karl Ivanych paid exactly no attention to any of that, but went over to Mama with a German greeting, just as he always did. She came to with a start, shook her head, as if hoping by that movement to dispel sad thoughts, and offered her hand to Karl Ivanych, who kissed it while she kissed his wrinkled temple.

'*Ich danke,*[11] *lieber* Karl Ivanych,' and continuing in German, she asked, 'Did the children sleep well?'

Karl Ivanych was deaf in one ear and now, because of the noise of the piano, he couldn't hear anything. He bent closer to the sofa, leaned with his hand on the table while standing on one foot, raised his cap with a smile that at the time seemed to me the height of refinement, and said, 'Will you forgive me, Natalya Nikolayevna?'

So as not to catch cold from his bare head, Karl Ivanych never took off his red cap, although whenever he came into the drawing room he would ask permission to leave it on.

'Keep it on, Karl Ivanych. I was asking, did the children sleep well?' *maman* repeated quite loudly, moving closer to him.

But again hearing nothing, he covered his bald spot with the red cap and smiled even more sweetly.

'Stop for a moment, Mimi,' *maman* said to Marya Ivanovna with a smile. 'We can't hear anything.'

When Mama smiled, as fine as her face was, it was made incomparably better, and everything around seemed more cheerful. If in the difficult moments of my life I could have had just a glimpse of that smile, I would never have known the meaning of sorrow. It seems to me that what is called beauty in a face lies entirely in the smile: if it adds charm to the face, the face is beautiful; if it leaves the face unchanged, the face is plain; and if it spoils the face, the face is ugly.

After greeting me, *maman* took my head in her hands, tilted it back, looked intently at me, and asked, 'Have you been crying?'

I didn't answer. She kissed my eyelids and asked in German, 'What were you crying about?'

Whenever she talked to us in an intimate way, she always spoke that language, which she knew perfectly.

'I was crying in my sleep, *maman*,' I said, recalling my made-up dream in all its detail and involuntarily shuddering at the thought.

Karl Ivanych confirmed my words, but said nothing about the dream itself. After a few remarks about the weather – a conversation in which Mimi also took part – *maman* put six lumps of sugar on the tray for a few appreciated servants, got up and went over to her embroidery frame, which stood by the window.

'Well, children, run along to Papa now, and tell him to be sure to come to me before he goes out to the barn.'

The music, counting and glaring resumed, and we went to see Papa. After passing through the room that since my grandfather's day has been called the 'waiters' room', we entered the study.

THREE

Papa

Papa was standing by his desk and pointing at some envelopes, papers and a pile of money, while heatedly explaining something to the steward Yakov Mikhailov, who stood in his usual place between the door and the barometer, his hands clasped behind his back and his fingers rapidly moving in various directions.

The more exercised Papa became, the more rapidly the fingers moved, and conversely, whenever Papa fell silent, the fingers would stop moving too; but whenever Yakov started to talk, the fingers would become extremely agitated and desperately begin to leap in every direction. It seemed to me that you could tell Yakov's innermost thoughts from those movements, even though his face was invariably calm, conveying awareness of his own merit but also of his dependence – that is, 'I'm right, but it will be as you wish.'

On seeing us, Papa merely said, 'Wait, I'll be with you in a moment.'

And with a movement of his head he indicated the door for one of us to close it.

'Good Lord, Yakov! What *is* the matter with you today?' he continued to the steward, shrugging a shoulder, a habit of his. 'This envelope with the eight hundred roubles . . .'

Yakov moved the abacus, cast off eight hundred, and gazed into the distance, waiting for what would come next.

'. . . is for expenses while I'm away. Understood? You should get a thousand roubles from the mill . . . Is that right or not? You should get eight thousand from the trustee bank[12] on the mortgages. For the hay, of which, by your own calculations, you can sell a hundred and twenty-five tons, you should get three thousand – I'm reckoning at twenty-four roubles a ton. What will be your total then? Twelve thousand? Is that right or not?'

'Quite right, sir,' Yakov said.

But from the rapid movement of his fingers, I could tell that he wanted to object. Papa interrupted him.

'Well, of that money you'll send ten thousand to the Council for Petrovskoye. Now the money in the office,' Papa continued (Yakov returned the previous twelve and cast off twenty-one thousand), 'you'll bring to me and show as an expenditure as of today.' Yakov removed the sum and tipped the abacus, very likely indicating thereby that the twenty-one thousand would also disappear. 'But the money in this envelope you'll convey from me to the person indicated thereon.'

I was standing next to the desk and glanced at the inscription. It said, 'For Karl Ivanovich Mauer'.

Very likely noticing I had read something that didn't concern me, Papa put his hand on my shoulder and with light pressure indicated movement away from the desk. I didn't know if it was an affectionate gesture or a reproof so, just in case, I kissed the large, veiny hand resting on my shoulder.

'It will be done, sir,' Yakov said. 'What are your instructions with respect to the Khabarovka money?'

Khabarovka was *maman*'s village.

'To leave it in the office and not to use it for any purpose without my orders.'

Yakov was silent for a few seconds, and then his fingers started to wriggle with increasing speed and, replacing the expression of stolid obedience with which he had listened to his master's instructions with his more usual one of crafty intelligence, he moved the abacus closer and began to speak.

'Allow me to inform you, Pyotr Aleksandrych, that it will be as you wish, but we won't be able to pay the Council on time. You were pleased to say,' he continued after a pause, 'that there will be money from the mortgages, mill and hay . . .' Entering each of those items, he cast them off on the abacus. 'But I'm afraid that our calculations may be mistaken,' he added, after falling silent for a moment and looking at Papa with a gravely thoughtful expression.

'How so?'

'Well, if you'll allow me, with respect to the mill, the miller has been to see me twice already to ask for a delay and swears by God and Christ that he has no money, and is here now. Would you like to speak to him yourself?'

'What's he saying?' Papa asked, indicating with a shake of his head that he had no wish to talk to the miller.

'The usual thing – that there hasn't been any grain to mill, that there was a little money, but he put it all into the dam. So if we leave him out, *sire*, how, once again, will we come up with the total? You were pleased to speak of the mortgages, but I think I've already reported to you that our money's sitting there and won't be released soon. The other day I sent a shipment of flour to Ivan Afanasevich in town with a note about the matter. So he replies, once again, that he would be glad to do something for you, but that the matter isn't in his hands and that it's clear from everything that you're unlikely to get your payment, even in two months. With respect to the hay, if you'll permit me, once again, let's assume that we do sell it for three thousand . . .'

He cast off three thousand on the abacus and was silent for a moment as he looked back and forth between it and Papa with an expression that said, 'Well, you yourself see how little it is!'

'But even if we do sell it for that, we'll lose money on it again, as you yourself know, if I may say so . . .'

It was obvious that he had a large store of other arguments, which is probably why Papa cut him off.

'I won't change my orders,' he said, 'but if there really is going to be a delay in getting the money, then the only thing you can do is take whatever you need from the Khabarovka account.'

'Very well, sir.'

It was clear from the expression on his face and from his fingers that the last instruction gave Yakov great satisfaction.

Yakov was a serf and an extremely zealous and devoted man. And like all good stewards he was stinting to a fault on his master's behalf, although with the strangest notions about his master's interests. He constantly worried about increasing the property of his master at the expense of that of his mistress, endeavouring to show that it was necessary to use all the income from her estate for Petrovskoye (the village in which we lived). He was now triumphant, since he had fully accomplished his goal.

After greeting us, Papa said that we had been twiddling our thumbs in the country long enough, that we were no longer little boys, and that it was time for us to begin serious study.

'You already know, I think, that I'm going to Moscow tonight and taking you with me,' he said. 'You'll live at Grandmother's, and *maman* will remain behind with the girls. And be aware that the only thing that will be a comfort to her will be to know that your studies are going well and that people are satisfied with you.'

Even though we had anticipated something unusual from the preparations that had been evident for the last few days, the news had a terrible effect on us. Volodya turned red and passed on Mama's message in a trembling voice.

'So that's what my dream portended!' I thought. 'Heaven forbid that anything worse should happen.'

I felt very, very sorry for Mama, but at the same time the idea that we were now big made me glad.

'If we're leaving today, then there probably won't be any more lessons, which is splendid!' I thought. 'Although I do feel sorry for Karl Ivanych. They're probably letting him go, or else they wouldn't have prepared an envelope for him . . . It would be so much better if we could just go on studying here for ever and not part with Mama or hurt poor Karl Ivanych's feelings. He's so unhappy as it is!'

Such were the thoughts that flitted through my mind, but I continued to stand where I was and stare at the black bows of my pumps.

After exchanging a few words with Karl Ivanych about the falling barometer, and ordering Yakov not to feed the dogs so he could go out after dinner for a farewell sounding of the young hounds, Papa sent us, against my expectation, off to our lessons again, consoling us, however, with the promise to take us hunting with him.

On the way upstairs I ran out to the terrace. Lying by the

door in the sunshine with her eyes closed was my father's favourite Borzoi, Milka.

'Dear Milka,' I said, petting her and kissing her on the muzzle. 'We're leaving today. Goodbye! We'll never see each other again!'

I was overwhelmed and started to cry.

FOUR

Lessons

Karl Ivanych was extremely put out. It was apparent from his scowl and the way he threw his tailcoat into a drawer of his chest and angrily tied the belt of his dressing gown and made a deep mark in the dialogue book with his fingernail to show how far we were to memorize. Volodya studied well enough, but I was so upset that I could do absolutely nothing. I stared blankly at the book of dialogues, but couldn't read it because of the tears welling in my eyes at the thought of our imminent departure. When it was time to recite the dialogues to Karl Ivanych, who listened to them with narrowed eyes (a bad sign), I couldn't hold back my tears any longer, and at the point where one of the people asks, '*Wo kommen sie her?*' and the other replies, '*Ich komme vom Kaffeehaus,*' I started sobbing and couldn't say the words, '*Haben Sie die Zeitung nicht gelesen?*'[13] When it was time for penmanship, I made so many smudges from the tears falling on the paper that it was as if I had been writing with water on wrapping paper.

Karl Ivanych lost his temper, ordered me to kneel, kept repeating that it was obstinacy and a puppet show (a favourite expression of his), threatened me with his ruler, and insisted that I apologize, although from sobbing I couldn't utter a word. No doubt realizing in the end how unfair he was being, he went into Nikolay's room and slammed the door behind him.

Their conversation could be heard from the classroom.

'Did you know that the children were going to Moscow, Nikolay?' Karl Ivanych asked as he entered the room.

'Well, of course I did, sir.'

Nikolay must have meant to get up, because Karl Ivanych

said, 'Sit, Nikolay,' and shut the door all the way. I went over to it from my corner to listen.

'However much good you do for people and however devoted you are, it seems that gratitude isn't to be expected, Nikolay,' Karl Ivanych said with feeling.

Sitting next to the window, repairing a boot, Nikolay nodded affirmatively.[14]

'I've lived in this house for twelve years, Nikolay, and I can say before God,' Karl Ivanych went on, raising his eyes and snuffbox to the ceiling, 'that I've loved them and looked after them better than if they had been my own children. You remember, Nikolay, when Volodenka had a fever and I sat by his bedside for nine days without shutting my eyes. Then it was "dear, kind Karl Ivanych", then I was needed, but now,' he added with a derisive grin, 'now the "children are grown and it's time for serious study". As if they haven't been studying here, Nikolay?'

'Well, certainly they have, I think,' Nikolay replied, inserting the awl and pulling the waxed twine through with both hands.

'Yes, but now I'm no longer needed, now it's time to send me away, and where are the promises? Where's the gratitude? I respect and love Natalya Nikolayevna,' he said, placing his hand over his heart, 'but what can she do? Nobody in this house cares what she wants,' he added, hurling a piece of leather onto the floor for emphasis. 'I know who's behind it and why I'm no longer needed; it's because I don't flatter and make allowances for everything, the way *some people* do. It's always been my way to speak the truth to everyone,' he said proudly. 'So be it, then! They won't get rich from my going, and with God's help I'll find a crust of bread somewhere. Isn't that right, Nikolay?'

Nikolay looked up and gazed at Karl Ivanych, as if wishing to reassure himself that the teacher would indeed be able to find a crust of bread, but said nothing.

Karl Ivanych went on for quite a while in the same spirit: he talked about how there had been more appreciation for his services at a certain general's where he had lived before (it hurt me very much to hear that), and he talked about Saxony and his parents and his friend the tailor Schönheit, and so on and so forth.

I sympathized with his bitterness, and it distressed me, too, that Father and Karl Ivanych, whom I loved almost equally, didn't understand each other. I returned to the corner, sat back down on my heels and thought about how to restore the accord between them.

Returning to the classroom, Karl Ivanych ordered me to stand up and prepare my exercise book for dictation. When we were ready, he fell majestically back into his armchair and in a voice that seemed to come deep from within began to dictate the following: '*Von al-len Lei-den-schaf-ten die grau-samste ist . . . Haben Sie geschrieben?*' He stopped there, slowly took some snuff and then resumed with greater emphasis, '*Die grausamste ist die Un-dank-bar-keit . . . Ein grosses U.*'[15] After writing the last word, I looked up, expecting him to go on.

'*Punctum*,'[16] he said with a barely visible little smile, and then gestured for us to turn in our exercise books.

Several times with various intonations and a look of immense gratification, he repeated that expression which had put his heartfelt thought into words. Then he assigned a history lesson and sat down by the window. His face was no longer grim; rather, it expressed the satisfaction of someone who had properly avenged a wrong.

It was a quarter to one, but Karl Ivanych apparently still had no idea of letting us go and kept assigning new lessons. The tedium and hunger increased in equal measure. With great impatience I followed all the signs of dinner's approach. A maidservant with a handful of bast went out to wash some plates. The noise of banging dishes could be heard in the pantry, as could the sound of the table being extended and the chairs being placed around it. Mimi and Lyubochka and Katenka (Katenka was Mimi's twelve-year-old daughter) had returned from the garden, but Foka was still nowhere to be seen – the butler Foka, who always came to announce that dinner was ready. Only then could we abandon our books and, paying no attention to Karl Ivanych, run downstairs.

Then footsteps were heard on the stairs, only it wasn't Foka! I had learned his tread and could always recognize the squeak of his boots. And then the door opened, revealing a figure completely unfamiliar to me.

FIVE
The Holy Fool

Into the room came a man of about fifty with a long, pale, pock-marked face, stringy grey hair and a wispy red beard. He was so tall that to enter the doorway he had not only to lower his head but bend his whole body. He was dressed in a ragged garment that resembled both a peasant caftan and a cassock. In his hand he held an enormous staff. Once inside the room, he banged the staff on the floor with all his might and then, scowling and opening his mouth extraordinarily wide, he guffawed in a most terrifying and unnatural way. He was blind in one eye, and its white pupil constantly leapt about, imparting to his already ugly face an even more repellent expression.

'Aha! Caught!' he yelled and, running with little steps over to Volodya, he seized his head and carefully examined its crown, and then with a completely serious expression he moved away from him to the table and started blowing under the oilcloth and making the sign of the cross over it. 'Oh-oh, what a pity! Oh-oh, how sad! The dears will fly away,' he began in a sobbing voice, while gazing at Volodya with feeling and then wiping with his sleeve the tears that really were falling from his eyes.

His voice was gruff and hoarse, his movements hurried and jerky, and his speech nonsensical and disjointed (he almost never used pronouns), but his intonation was so moving, and his ugly yellow face sometimes had such a sincerely mournful expression, that listening to him it was impossible not to feel a mixture of pity, fear and sadness.

It was the holy fool[17] and wanderer, Grisha.

Where was he from? Who were his parents? What had prompted him to choose the itinerant life he led? No one could

say. I know only that he had from the age of fifteen become well
known as a holy fool who went barefoot winter and summer,
visited monasteries, gave little icons to those he liked and spoke
cryptic words that some people regarded as prophetic; that no
one had ever seen him in any other guise; that from time to time
he had visited Grandmother's; and that some claimed he was
the unhappy son of rich parents and a pure soul, while others
said he was just a peasant layabout.

The long-desired but punctual Foka at last appeared and we
went downstairs. Sobbing and continuing to talk nonsense of
one kind or another, Grisha followed behind, banging his staff
on each step of the stairs. Papa and *maman* were walking around
the drawing room, arm in arm, and quietly talking about something. Marya Ivanovna was primly sitting in one of the armchairs
placed symmetrically at right angles to the sofa and in a severe
but restrained tone admonishing the girls, who were on the sofa
next to her. As soon as Karl Ivanych came into the room, she
glanced at him, then instantly looked away and assumed an
expression that conveyed something like 'You're beneath notice,
Karl Ivanych.' It was clear from the way the girls were looking
at us that they wanted to share some very important news as
soon as possible, but jumping up from their places and coming
over to us would have been against Mimi's rules. We first had
to go over to her and say, '*Bonjour*, Mimi!' with a click of our
heels, after which conversation might begin. What an intolerable
person that Mimi was! Around her you couldn't talk about
anything; she found it all improper. Moreover, she would
constantly pester you with '*Parlez donc français*,'[18] and, as if
from spite, always just when you felt like chattering away in
Russian. Or at dinner when you were just starting to enjoy
something and didn't want to be distracted, she would invariably say, '*Mangez donc avec du pain*,' or '*Comment est-ce que
vous tenez votre fourchette*?'[19] 'What business of hers are we?'
you would think. 'Let her teach the girls! We have Karl Ivanych
for that.' I fully shared his loathing for *some people*.

'Ask your mama for them to take us hunting, too,' Katenka
whispered, stopping me by holding onto my jacket after the
grown-ups had gone ahead into the dining room.

'All right, we'll try.'

Grisha ate in the dining room, but at a special little table. He kept his eyes on his plate, sighing from time to time and making dreadful faces and saying, as if to himself, 'What a pity! Flown away . . . The dove will fly away to heaven . . . Oh, there's a stone on the grave . . . ,' and so forth.

Maman had been upset since morning, and Grisha's presence, words and actions noticeably aggravated that state.

'Oh yes, there's something I meant to ask you,' she said, handing Father a bowl of soup.

'What is it?'

'Tell them, please, to lock up their awful dogs. They almost bit poor Grisha as he was crossing the yard. They could go after the children, too.'

Hearing that the talk was about him, Grisha turned towards the table and started showing the torn skirts of his garment, and repeating as he chewed, 'Wanted them to bite . . . God wouldn't let. A sin to set dogs! A great sin! Don't beat, boss,[20] why beat? God forgives . . . Times are different.'

'What's he talking about?' Papa asked, giving him a hard, searching look. 'I don't understand a word of it.'

'Well, I do,' *maman* answered. 'He told me a hunter had set the dogs on him on purpose, so he's saying, "He wanted them to bite me, but God wouldn't allow it," and he's asking you not to punish the man for it.'

'Hah! So that's it!' Papa said. 'Why does he think I want to punish the man? You know I'm not very fond of these fellows,' he continued in French, 'but I especially don't like this one, and he must be –'

'Oh, don't say that, my dear,' *maman* stopped him, as if frightened of something. 'How do you know?'

'I think I've had occasion to study the species – enough of them come by here to see you – and they're all of the same cut. It's always the same story . . .'

It was clear that Mama had an entirely different view of the matter, but didn't want to argue.

'Please pass me a pasty,' she said. 'They're good today, aren't they?'

'No, it makes me angry,' Papa went on, picking up a pasty, but holding it too far away for *maman* to reach. 'It makes me angry to see clever, educated people allowing themselves to be duped.'

And he rapped the table with his fork.

'I asked you to pass me a pasty,' she repeated, holding out her hand.

'And it's quite right,' Papa continued, moving his hand away, 'to turn them over to the police. All they're good for is upsetting the already weak nerves of certain persons,' he added, finally handing Mama the pasty with a smile, when he realized that she didn't care for the conversation at all.

'I'll say just one thing to you about that: it's hard to believe that someone who despite being sixty years old goes around barefoot winter and summer, and without ever removing them wears seventy pounds of chains under his clothes, and has more than once refused offers of a quiet life with everything taken care of – it's hard to believe that such a person is doing all that merely from laziness. As for his prophecies,' she added with a sigh, after a brief pause, '*je suis payée pour y croire*.[21] I think I've mentioned how Kiryusha foretold my own late papa's death to the very day and hour.'

'Oh no, what have you done?!' Papa said with a grin, and brought his hand to his face on the side where Mimi was sitting. (Whenever he did that, I always listened with particular attention, expecting something funny.) 'Why did you remind me of his feet? I just looked at them and now I can't eat any more!'

Dinner was nearly over. Lyubochka and Katenka kept winking at us and fidgeting in their chairs and generally showed extreme restlessness. The winking meant, 'Why haven't you asked them to take us hunting?' I nudged Volodya with my elbow. Volodya nudged back and at last made up his mind. First in a hesitant and then in a fairly strong and loud voice he explained that since we had to leave today, we would like the girls to go hunting with us in the wagonette. After a brief consultation among the grown-ups, the question was decided in our favour and, what was even nicer, *maman* said that she would come too.

SIX

Preparations for the Hunt

Yakov was called in during pastries and given orders regarding the wagonette, the dogs and our mounts – all in the greatest detail with every horse called by name. Volodya's own horse was lame and Papa ordered a courser saddled for him. For some reason, the word 'courser' struck *maman* oddly: she decided that it must be some sort of savage beast that would surely bolt and kill Volodya. Despite Papa's and Volodya's reassurances, Volodya remarking with splendid pluck that it was nothing and that he actually liked it when horses bolted, poor *maman* continued to say that it would be a torment to her the whole outing.

Dinner was over, the grown-ups retired to the study for coffee, and we ran out to the garden to scrape our feet along the paths covered with fallen yellow leaves and talk. We talked about Volodya's riding a courser, about what a shame it was that Lyubochka couldn't run as fast as Katenka, about how interesting it would be to see Grisha's chains, and so on, but not a word about parting. Our conversation was interrupted by the clatter of the approaching wagonette with servant boys sitting alongside each spring. Behind the wagonette came the hunters with the dogs, and behind the hunters, on the horse meant for Volodya, rode Ignat the coachman, leading my ancient Klepper by its reins.[22] First we ran over to the fence, where all those interesting things could be seen, and then, with squeals and pounding feet, we raced upstairs to dress, and dress to look as much like hunters as possible. One of the main ways of doing that was to tuck your trousers into your boots. We set about doing this as quickly as possible, hurrying to finish and run out onto the front steps to enjoy the sight of the dogs and the horses and conversation with the hunters.

The day was hot. Whimsically shaped white storm clouds had
been on the horizon all morning. Then a light breeze started to
drive them closer and closer, so that they covered the sun from
time to time. Yet however much the clouds shifted and darkened
it was obvious that they wouldn't, in the end, gather into a storm
and spoil our pleasure. Later in the afternoon they started to
disperse: some turned pale, grew elongated and sped off towards
the horizon, while others right overhead turned into translucent
white scales, with only one large black storm cloud coming to
rest in the east. Karl Ivanych always knew which way storm
clouds would go. He announced that this one would proceed in
the direction of Maslovka, that there would be no rain and that
the weather would be superb.

Despite his advanced years, Foka ran down the steps with
great nimbleness and speed and cried, 'Drive up!' and then with
his feet wide in the stance of someone who didn't need to be
told his duties, he took a position by the entrance, midway
between the steps and the place where the coachman was to
bring the wagonette. The ladies came down and after a brief fuss
about who would sit on which side and who would hold on to
whom (although it didn't seem necessary to me to hold on at
all), they took their seats, opened their parasols and set off. As
the wagonette began to move *maman* pointed at the courser and
asked the coachman in a tremulous voice, 'Is that the one for
Vladimir Petrovich?'

When the coachman confirmed that it was, she waved her
hand and looked away. I was eager to start. Climbing onto my
own little horse, I took aim between its ears and made several
turns about the yard.

'Kindly don't trample the dogs, sir,' one of the hunters said.

'Have no fear, this isn't my first time out,' I proudly replied.

Despite his determined character, Volodya mounted his
courser with some trepidation and, stroking it, asked several
times, 'Is it gentle?'

But he looked very fine on horseback, just like a grown-up.
His tightly clad thighs lay upon the saddle so well that it made
me envious, especially since I was, judging by my own shadow,
far from having such an excellent appearance.

Then Papa's feet were heard on the steps. A whipper-in rounded up the hounds that had wandered off, and the hunters with the Borzois called their dogs over and began to mount up. A groom led a horse up to the front steps. The dogs in Papa's pack, which had been lying nearby in various picturesque poses, rushed over to him. Behind him happily loped Milka in a beaded collar with a short, jingling chain. She always greeted the kennel dogs when she came out, playing with some, sniffing and growling at others and looking for fleas on a few.

Then Papa mounted his horse and we were off.

SEVEN

The Hunt

Wearing a shaggy cap and carrying a knife in his belt and an enormous horn over his shoulder, the master of hounds, nick-named Turka, rode in front of everyone on a blue roan with a bent nose. From his sullen, ferocious look, you might have thought he was going into deadly combat rather than off on a hunt. Around the hind legs of his horse trotted the leashed hounds in an excited, motley throng. It was pitiful to behold the fate of any unfortunate who thought of lagging behind. A great effort was needed to pull his leashmate back, but no sooner had he done so than one of the whippers-in riding behind would unfailingly whack him with his riding crop and say, 'Back to the pack!' Coming out of the gate, Papa ordered the hunters and the rest of us to proceed down the road, while he turned into the rye field.

Harvesting was at its height. The immense, brilliant-yellow field was limited on one side only by a tall bluish wood that at the time seemed to me a most remote and mysterious place, beyond which either the world came to an end or uninhabited regions began. The field was covered with people and ricks of grain. Visible here and there in a harvested strip of the tall, dense rye were the bent back of a reaper, the sweeping movement of the ears as she grasped them between her fingers, a woman leaning over a cradle in the shade, and sheaves strewn about the cornflower-dotted stubble. Standing on carts on the other side and wearing only their shirts, men were stacking the sheaves in ricks and raising the dust on the dry, sun-baked ground. Noticing Papa in the distance, the headman, in tall boots with a heavy coat thrown over his shoulders and tally sticks in his hand, removed his felt hat, wiped his red hair and beard with a towel and shouted at the women. The little sorrel Papa was riding moved with a light, frolicking gait, from time to time dropping her head to her chest, pulling the reins taut, and swishing with her thick tail the flies and botflies that were greedily clinging to her. Two Borzois, lifting their legs high and holding their tails in the air like sickles, followed behind the horse's feet in graceful bounds over the tall stubble. Milka ran in front, her head turned back in anticipation of a treat.[23] The voices of people, the clattering of horses and carts, the merry chirping of quail, the hum of insects hovering in motionless swarms, the smell of wormwood, straw and horse sweat, the myriad colours and shadows the scorching sun cast upon the light-yellow stubble, the distant blue wood and pale-lilac clouds, and the white gossamer carried through the air or lying across the stubble – all that I saw, heard and felt.

When we reached Kalinov's wood, we found the wagonette already there and, beyond all expectation, a one-horse cart with a serving man sitting in the middle. Sticking out from under the straw were a samovar, a tub with an ice-cream mould and various other enticing little boxes and bundles. There was no mistaking it: we were going to have tea outside in the fresh air with ice cream and fruit. Seeing the cart, we noisily expressed our delight, since drinking tea in the wood on the grass and in a place where no one had ever drunk tea before was considered a great treat.

Turka rode up to the grove, stopped, and, after listening intently to Papa's detailed instructions as to where to line up and where to come out (although he never followed the instructions but did everything his own way), unleashed the dogs, leisurely tied the leashes to his saddle, mounted his horse and, with a whistle, disappeared behind the young birches. The unleashed hounds first expressed their pleasure by wagging their tails, then shook themselves, straightened up, and trotted off in various directions, sniffing and wagging.

'Have you got a handkerchief?' Papa asked.

I pulled one out of my pocket and showed him.

'Well, tie it around that grey dog . . .'

'You mean Zhiran?' I asked with an expert look.

'Yes, and then run along the road. Stop when you come to a

little clearing and keep your eyes open. And don't come back to me without a hare!'

I tied my handkerchief around Zhiran's shaggy neck and started running headlong towards the designated place. Papa laughed and called out after me, 'Hurry or you'll be too late!'

Zhiran kept stopping and pricking up his ears in response to the hallooing of the hunters. I wasn't strong enough to pull him from his spot, so I started to yell, 'Tally-ho! Tally-ho!' Then he strained so hard it was all I could do to hold him back, and I fell down more than once before I reached the clearing. Choosing a flat, shady spot at the foot of a large oak, I took my place on the grass, sat Zhiran down beside me and began my vigil. As invariably happens in such situations, my imagination far outstripped reality. When only the first hound was giving tongue in the wood, I imagined that I was already on my third hare. Turka's voice boomed ever more loudly and excitedly through the wood. A hound yelped, its voice was heard more and more frequently, then another base voice joined in, and after that a third and a fourth. Then the voices either fell silent or broke in on one another. Gradually they grew stronger and more continuous, finally merging in a single undulating drone. 'The wood had acquired a voice and the hounds were in full pursuit.'[24]

Hearing it, I froze in place. Directing my gaze to the edge of the wood, I smiled pointlessly and the sweat poured from me in streams, and even though the drops rolling down my chin tickled, I didn't wipe them away. I thought that nothing could be more critical than that moment. But a position of such intensity was too unnatural to hold for very long. The hounds were baying either at the very edge of the wood or gradually moving away. There was no hare to be seen. I started to look along the sides. It was the same with Zhiran: first he strained and whimpered, then lay down beside me with his muzzle in my lap and was silent.

On the grey, dry ground next to the exposed roots of the oak under which I was sitting, ants were swarming among the dry oak leaves, acorns, desiccated moss-covered twigs, yellow-green moss and occasional thin blades of grass poking through. One after another the ants proceeded along the smooth paths they had worn: some with loads, others carrying nothing. I picked up a twig and blocked their path. It had to be seen how one ant, despising the danger, crawled under the twig, while others, especially those with loads, were completely at a loss and didn't know what to do. They stopped, looked for a way around, turned back, or moved along the twig to my hand, apparently meaning to go up the sleeve of my jacket. I was diverted from those interesting observations by an exceptionally attractive butterfly with yellow wings hovering in front of me. As soon as I turned my attention to it, it flew a couple of paces away, came to a stop over an almost completely wilted floweret of white clover, and then settled on it. I don't know if it was sunning itself or drawing nectar from the clover; all that was clear was that it was happy. It moved its wings from time to time, pressing itself against the floweret, and then became completely still. I rested my head on my arms and watched it with pleasure.

Suddenly Zhiran began to whine and strain with such force that I almost fell over. I looked around. At the edge of the wood hopped a hare with one of its ears erect and the other flat. The blood rushed to my head and in an instant I forgot everything. I shouted something in a frenzied voice, released the dog and rushed after him. But no sooner had I done so than I regretted it: the hare leaned back on its haunches, sprang into the air and disappeared from sight.

But what was my shame when right after the hounds, whose baying had led him to the edge of the wood, Turka appeared from behind a bush! He had seen my blunder (which consisted of not *waiting*) and, looking at me with scorn, he merely said, 'Oh, master!' Only it's necessary to know how he said it! It would have been easier for me if he had tossed me over his saddle like a hare.

I stood rooted in the same spot for a long time in deep despair, without calling the dog back, but repeating over and over, while pounding my thighs, 'My goodness, what have I done!'

I heard the hounds in pursuit farther on, the tally-hoes of the men on the other side of the grove, the retrieving of a hare and then Turka calling in the dogs with his enormous horn – but I still didn't move from my spot.

EIGHT

Games

The hunt was over. A rug had been spread out in the shade of the young birches and the whole company was sitting around it. The serving man Gavrilo, who had trampled down the juicy green grass next to himself, was wiping the plates and taking leaf-wrapped plums and peaches out of a box. The sun shone through the green branches of the young birches and cast round shimmering shafts of light on the designs of the rug, my legs, and even the bald, perspiring head of Gavrilo. The light breeze blowing through the leaves of the trees and my hair and over my perspiring face was extraordinarily refreshing.

After we had all been presented with ice cream and fruit, there was nothing left to do on the rug, and despite the oblique, scorching rays of the sun, we got up and went off to play.

'All right, what will it be?' Lyubochka asked, squinting in the sunlight and hopping about on the grass. 'Let's play Robinson.'

'No, it's boring,' Volodya said, lazily collapsing on the grass and chewing some leaves. 'It's always Robinson! But if you all really want to, then let's build an arbour.'

Volodya was plainly putting on airs. Probably he was proud of having ridden there on a courser and was pretending to be worn out. Or maybe it was because he had too much common sense and too little power of imagination to enjoy the game of Robinson completely. It consisted of acting out scenes from *Robinson Suisse*,[25] which we had just been reading.

'Oh, please ... Why won't you give us the pleasure?' the girls pleaded with him. 'You can be Charles or Ernest or the father, or anyone you like,' Katenka said, trying to pull him up by the sleeve of his jacket.

'The truth is I just don't feel like it. It's boring!' Volodya said with a complacent smile, stretching out where he lay.

'It would have been better to stay at home if nobody wants to play,' Lyubochka stammered through her tears.

She was a terrible crybaby.

'Well, all right then. Only please don't cry. I can't stand it!'

Volodya's patronizing attitude gave us very little pleasure; quite the contrary, his bored, indolent look took all the fun out of the game. When we sat on the ground and pretended we were going fishing in a boat and started to row with all our might, Volodya sat with his arms crossed in a posture that had nothing whatever to do with that of a fisherman. I observed as much to him, but he answered that whether we moved our arms more or moved them less wouldn't gain or lose anything or get us very far. I was forced to agree. When I set off for the wood with a stick over my shoulder, pretending I was going hunting, Volodya lay down on his back, put his hands behind his head, and said that it was as if he were going with me, too. Such words and actions, cooling our ardour for the game, were quite unpleasant, all the more so since you couldn't help but agree in your heart that his behaviour made sense.

I myself knew that the stick not only wouldn't kill birds, but wouldn't even shoot. It was a game. If you were going to look at it like that, then you couldn't ride chairs either, and I think Volodya himself remembered how on the long winter evenings we covered an armchair with shawls and made a barouche out of it, with one of us the driver and the other a footman, and the girls in the middle, and three chairs a troika of horses as we set off down the road. And what adventures we had along the way! How happily and quickly we passed those winter evenings! If you're going to judge by what's real, there can be no play at all. And if there's no play, what's left?

NINE

Something Like First Love

Pretending to pick some American fruit from a tree, Lyubochka tore off a leaf with an enormous worm on it and threw it in horror on the ground, raised her arms and jumped back, as if afraid the worm might squirt something. The game came to a halt and we got down on the ground with our heads together to examine the curiosity.

I watched over Katenka's shoulder as she tried to lift up the worm on a leaf by placing it in its path.

I've noticed that many girls have a habit of hitching their shoulders in an attempt thereby to return to its proper place an open-neck dress that has slipped down. I also remember that Mimi would always get angry about it and say, '*C'est un geste de femme de chambre.*'[26] Bent over the worm, Katenka made that movement at the same time that the breeze lifted her kerchief from her white cheek. During the movement her little shoulder was two fingers from my lips. I wasn't looking at the worm any more but at Katenka's shoulder, which I kept staring at and then kissed as hard as I could. She didn't turn around, although I could see that her cheek and ear had turned red. Without looking up, Volodya said with disdain, 'Why the tenderness?'

But there were tears in my eyes.

I couldn't stop looking at Katenka. I had long been used to her fresh, fair little face and had always been fond of it. But now I began to look at it more closely and to like it even more. When we returned to the grown-ups, Papa announced to our great delight that at Mama's request our departure had been postponed until morning.

We rode back with the wagonette. Wishing to outdo each

other in bravado and riding skill, Volodya and I pranced along-side. My shadow was longer than before, and judging by it, I supposed that I now had the look of a rather handsome rider. But that self-satisfied feeling was soon spoiled by the following circumstance. Meaning to captivate completely those seated in the wagonette, I first lagged slightly behind and then urged on my little horse with my crop and heels, and assumed a carelessly graceful posture, meaning to rush past in a whirl on the side where Katenka was sitting. Only I didn't know which would be better: to gallop past silently or with a yell. But when my little horse drew abreast of the horses pulling the wagonette, the insuf-ferable beast came to a stop so abruptly, despite all my efforts, that I was thrown from the saddle onto its neck and nearly went flying.

TEN

What Kind of Man Was My Father?

He was a man of the last century and shared with the youth of that time an elusive character combining chivalry, enterprise, self-assurance, courtesy and profligacy. He regarded people of the present century with scorn; a view derived as much from innate pride as from hidden disappointment that he could have neither the influence nor the success in our century that he had enjoyed in his own. His two chief passions in life were cards and women. He had won several million roubles in his lifetime and had had affairs with countless women of every caste.[27]

Tall and imposing with a peculiar shuffling gait, a habit of shrugging his shoulder, constantly smiling little eyes, a large aquiline nose, irregular lips that were somewhat awkwardly yet pleasantly shaped, a defect in pronunciation (a slight lisp) and a large, completely bald head – such was my father's appearance from my earliest memory of him, an appearance with which he knew not only how to pass for and be a man *à bonnes fortunes*,[28] but also how to be liked by everyone without exception – by people of every caste and circumstance, but especially by those he wanted to like him.

He also knew how to take the upper hand in his dealings with everyone. Never a man of 'very high society' himself, he nevertheless always associated with people of that circle, and in such a way that he was respected. He knew the utmost degree of pride and self-assurance that would, without offending others, elevate him in the eyes of the world. He was eccentric, but not always so, and sometimes used his eccentricity as a substitute for breeding and wealth. Nothing in the world could surprise him, and however brilliant the situation in which he found himself, it seemed that he was born to it. He was so adept at hiding from others and avoiding himself the dark side of life, with its petty vexations and disappointments familiar to everyone, that you couldn't help envying him. He was an expert in all things that bring comfort and pleasure and knew how to use them. His hobby-horse was his brilliant connections, which he enjoyed partly through my mother's relatives and partly through the companions of his youth, whom he secretly resented for having risen so high in rank, while he remained forever a retired Guards lieutenant. Like all former officers, he didn't know how to dress fashionably, but on the other hand he did dress with originality and elegance, always in very loose and light clothes with superb linen and large, turned-out collars and cuffs . . . All of it, however, went with his tall stature, strong build, bald head and calm, self-confident movements. He was sensitive and even given to tears. Often when he came to a passage of heightened feeling when reading out loud, his voice would start to break, his eyes would well up, and he would put the book down in vexation. He was fond of music and, while accompanying himself on the piano, would sing the romances of his friend A., Gypsy songs and several opera airs. But he didn't care for serious music and, disregarding the common view, frankly admitted that Beethoven's sonatas put him to sleep and that he knew of nothing better than 'Do Not Wake Me, a Bride', sung by Semyonova, and 'Not Alone',[29] sung by the Gypsy girl Tanyusha. His was one of those natures that require an audience for their good deeds. And the only things he considered good were those that the audience called good. Heaven knows if he had any moral convictions. His life was always so full of enthusiasms of every kind that he never had time to form convictions of his own, and he was, in any case, so fortunate in life that he never saw any need to.

As he got older he acquired a permanent view of things and unchanging rules, but only in a practical sense: he regarded as good the actions and mode of life that brought him happiness or pleasure, and thought that everyone else should act the same way. He talked very engagingly, and I think that ability increased the elasticity of his rules: he could speak of one and the same action as the sweetest mischief or low villainy.

ELEVEN

Activities in the Study and Drawing Room

It was already dusk when we got home. *Maman* sat down at the piano and we children brought paper, pencils and paints and arranged ourselves around the table to make pictures. I had only blue paint, but neverthless decided to represent a hunt. After vigorously depicting blue dogs and a blue boy mounted on a blue horse, I was unsure whether you could paint a blue hare and ran to the study to consult Papa about it. He was reading something, and to my question 'Are there blue hares?' he replied, without looking up, 'Indeed there are, my friend, indeed there are.' Returning to the table, I painted a blue hare, but then found it necessary to redo it as a blue shrub. I didn't care for the shrub either and turned it into a tree, the tree into a haystack, and the haystack into a cloud, in the end so smearing the whole sheet of paper with blue paint that I tore it up in vexation and went to nap in the Voltaire armchair.

Maman was playing the second concerto of her teacher, John Field.[30] I dozed off, and light, luminous, limpid memories rose up in my imagination. Then she started to play Beethoven's Pathétique Sonata, and I recollected something sad, heavy and gloomy. *Maman* played those two pieces often, and I remember very well the feeling they evoked in me. It was like a recollection, but a recollection of what? You seemed to be recalling something that had never existed.

Across from me was the door to the study, and I saw Yakov go in with some other bearded men wearing peasant caftans. The door immediately closed behind them. 'Well, business has begun!' I thought. It seemed to me that nothing in the world could be of greater importance than the business transacted in the study. That thought was confirmed in me by the fact that everyone approached the door in whispers and on tiptoe. From it, on the other hand, came Papa's loud voice and the fragrance of his cigar, which – I don't know why – was always very attractive to me. I was startled from my half-awake state by a familiar squeaking of boots in the waiters' room. Karl Ivanych, on tiptoes but with a sombre, determined face and a note of some kind in his hand, went up to the door and knocked lightly on it. He was admitted and the door banged shut again.

'I hope nothing terrible happens,' I thought. 'Karl Ivanych is angry and liable to say anything.'

I dozed off again.

But nothing terrible did happen. An hour later I was woken by the same squeaking. Using his handkerchief to wipe the tears I could see on his face, Karl Ivanych came out of the study and went upstairs, mumbling something to himself. Papa came out immediately after him and went into the drawing room.

'You know what I've just decided?' he said in a cheerful voice, putting his hand on *maman*'s shoulder.

'What, my dear?'

'I'm taking Karl Ivanych along with the children. There's room in the britzka.[31] They're used to him, and he seems to be quite attached to them. The seven hundred roubles a year won't make any difference, *et puis au fond c'est un très bon diable.*'[32]

I couldn't at all understand why Papa was cursing Karl Ivanych.

'I'm very happy for the children and for him,' *maman* said. 'He's a dear old man.'

'If you could have seen how touched he was when I told him that he could keep the five hundred roubles as a gift ... But the most amusing part is the bill he brought me. It's worth a look,' he added with a smile, handing her a note written in Karl Ivanych's hand. 'It's charming!'

Here are the note's contents:

'Two fishingpoles for childs – 70 kopeeks.

'Colour paper, gold border, paste and mould for box, as gifts – 6 r., 55 k.

'Book and archery bow, gifts for childs – 8 r., 16 k.

'Trouser for Nikolay – 4 roubles.

'Promised of Pyotr Aleksandrovish in Moscow in 18 –, gold watch for 140 roubles.

'Total due to Karl Mauer, beside hees salary – 159 roubles, 79 kopeeks.'

Anyone reading that note in which Karl Ivanych asked for repayment of all the money he had spent on gifts, and even the money for a gift that had been promised to him, would think that he was nothing more than an insensitive, greedy egotist – and that person would be wrong.

Entering the study with the note in his hand and a prepared speech in his mind, Karl Ivanych had meant to lay out eloquently before Papa all the injustices that he had endured in our home. But when he started to speak with the same touching voice and sensitive intonations that he had used when dictating to us, his eloquence acted most powerfully of all on himself, so that on coming to the place where he said, 'As sad as it will be for me to part with the children,' he completely lost his way, his voice started to quaver and he had to take his checkered handkerchief out of his pocket.

'Yes, Pyotr Aleksandrovich,' he said through his tears in a part that hadn't been in his prepared speech at all, 'I'm so used to the children that I don't know what I'll do without them. It would be better to serve you without pay,' he added, wiping his tears with one hand, while handing Papa the bill with the other.

That Karl Ivanych was speaking sincerely at that moment I can confirm, since I know his kind heart, yet in what way that bill was in agreement with his words remains a mystery to me.

'If it makes you sad, then it would make me even sadder to part with you,' Papa said, patting him on the shoulder. 'I've changed my mind now.'

Just before supper, Grisha came into the room. From the moment he entered our home he hadn't stopped sighing and weeping, which, in the view of those who believed in his ability to foretell the future, augured some calamity for us. He began his farewells and said that he would be leaving the next morning. I winked at Volodya and went out of the room.

'What is it?'

'If you want to have a look at Grisha's chains, let's all go up to the men's quarters, since he's sleeping in the second room. We can sit very nicely in the storage closet and see everything.'

'Excellent! Wait here. I'll get the girls.'

The girls ran out and we went upstairs. After arguing over who would enter the dark closet first, we took our places and waited.

TWELVE

Grisha

We were all afraid of the dark and pressed close together without speaking. Grisha came in with quiet steps almost immediately after us. He held his staff in one hand and in the other a tallow candle in a copper candlestick. We held our breath.

'Lord Jesus Christ! Most Holy Mother of God! Father and Son and Holy Spirit!' he recited, taking large breaths and using the various intonations and elisions that are typical of those who repeat the words often.

He placed his staff in a corner with a prayer and examined the bed, and then began to undress. After unwinding his old black sash, he slowly took off his torn nankeen coat, carefully folded it, and draped it over the back of the chair. His face no longer expressed its usual haste and obtuseness; on the contrary, he was serene, thoughtful, and even majestic. His movements were slow and deliberate.

Dressed only in his underwear, he quietly lowered himself onto the bed, made the sign of the cross over it in every direction, and with evident effort – since he winced – rearranged the chains under his shirt. After sitting for a while and carefully examining his underwear, which was torn in several places, he got to his feet, lifted the candle to the level of the icon case in which several icons stood, crossed himself before them, and turned the candle upside down. It went out with a crackle.

A nearly full moon shone brightly through the windows, which faced the wood.

The tall white figure of the holy fool was illumined on one side by pale, silvery moonbeams, and hidden on the other in a dark shadow that, along with those of the window frames, fell on the floor and on the opposite wall up to the ceiling. Outside, the night watchman banged on his cast-iron bar.

Folding his enormous hands over his chest, bowing his head and breathing heavily, Grisha stood silently in front of the icons, then lowered himself with effort onto his knees and started to pray.

First he quietly recited familiar prayers, stressing only a few words, and then repeated them, but louder with more animation. Then he began to speak his own words, trying with evident effort to express himself in Church Slavonic.[33] His own words were awkward but moving. He prayed for all his benefactors (as he called those who took him in), including Mama and us, and he prayed for himself, asking God to forgive him his grievous sins, and repeated, 'God, forgive my enemies!' Then he raised himself up with a groan and, while repeating the same words over and over, prostrated himself, and then raised himself up again, despite the weight of the chains, which produced a harsh, dry sound as they struck the floor.

Volodya pinched my leg very painfully, but I didn't even turn around. I merely rubbed the place with my hand and continued to follow all of Grisha's movements and words with a feeling of astonishment, pity and awe.

Instead of the fun and laughter I was expecting when I entered the storage closet, I felt trembling and a sinking heart.

Grisha remained in that condition of religious ecstasy a long time, improvising prayers. Either he repeated 'God, have mercy' several times in succession, each time with new strength and expression, or he would say, 'Forgive me, Lord, and teach me what to do! Teach me what to do, Lord!' but as if he were expecting an immediate reply to his words; or else only mournful sobbing would be heard. Then he got onto his knees again, crossed his hands on his chest and fell silent.

I quietly stuck my head out of the door and held my breath. Grisha didn't move. Heavy sighs tore from his breast and a tear welled in the clouded pupil of his blind eye, illumined by the moon.

'Thy will be done!' he suddenly cried with incomparable expression, and then fell with his forehead to the floor and began to sob like a child.

Much water has flowed by since then, many memories of the past have lost their meaning for me or have become confused dreams, and even the wanderer Grisha has long since finished his last pilgrimage, but the impression he made on me and the feeling he aroused will remain in my memory forever.

O great Christian, Grisha! Your faith was so strong that you felt the nearness of God. Your love was so great that the words flowed of their own accord from your lips – you did not test them with your reason. And what lofty praise you gave to His majesty when, not finding words, you fell to the floor in tears!

The tender feeling with which I listened to Grisha couldn't last, first because my curiosity had been satisfied, and second because my legs were numb from sitting in one place, and I wanted to join in the whispering and rustling I heard behind me in the dark. Someone took hold of my arm and murmured, 'Whose arm is this?' The closet was completely dark, but I knew at once that it was Katenka by her touch and by the voice whispering by my ear.

Completely unconsciously, I took hold of her arm in its short little sleeve ending at her elbow and raised it to my lips. Katenka was evidently surprised by that action and jerked her arm away, bumping as she did a broken chair standing in the closet. Grisha raised his head, quietly looked around, and, while reciting a prayer, made the sign of the cross at all four corners. We tumbled out of the closet with noisy whispering.

THIRTEEN

Natalya Savishna

In the second half of the last century a merry, plump, rosy-cheeked girl named Natashka ran about the yards of the village of Khabarovka in bare feet and a coarse cotton frock. At the request of her father, the clarinet player Savva, and in recognition of his services, my grandfather 'took her up' into the household as a lady's maid for my grandmother. As a chambermaid, Natashka was distinguished by her diligence and mild temperament. When Mama was born and a nurse was needed, the responsibility was given to Natashka. And in that new duty, too, she earned praise and rewards for her industry, fidelity and devotion to her young mistress. But the powdered head and gartered stockings of the lively young waiter Foka, who in his work came into frequent contact with Natalya, captured her rough-hewn but loving heart. She even decided to go to Grandfather herself to ask for permission to marry him. Grandfather took her wish for ingratitude, became enraged, and in punishment exiled the poor Natalya to a village cattle yard in the steppe. Six months later, however, she was called back to the household to her previous duties, since no one had been able to replace her. Returning from exile in her coarse frock, she presented herself to Grandfather, fell down at his feet, and begged him to restore his kindness and favour and to forget the foolishness that had overcome her and that, she swore, would never happen again. And she was true to her word.

From that day forth Natashka became Natalya Savishna, put on a mobcap, and gave to her young lady all the love that was in her.

When a governess took her place by Mama's side, Natalya

Savishna was given the keys to the storeroom and care of the linen and provisions. She carried out her new duties with the same diligence and love. She lived entirely for her masters' property and saw waste, spoilage and pilfering in everything, and took every measure to resist them.

Wishing after her own marriage to repay Natalya Savishna in some way for her twenty years of labour and devotion, *maman* sent for her and, expressing in the most affectionate terms all her appreciation and love, presented her with a stamped piece of paper granting her her freedom, and told her that whether or not she continued to serve in our home, she would always receive an annual pension of three hundred roubles. Natalya Savishna listened to it all without a word and then took the document in her hands, angrily looked at it, muttered something between her teeth, and ran out of the room, slamming the door behind her. Not understanding the reason for that strange reaction, *maman* went to Natalya Savishna's room a little later. Natalya Savishna, her eyes red from weeping, was sitting on a trunk and turning her handkerchief over and over in her hands, while staring at the letter of manumission lying in fragments on the floor in front of her.

'What's wrong, darling Natalya Savishna?' *maman* asked, taking her hand.

'Nothing, ma'am,' she replied. 'It must be that I've offended you in some way, since you're driving me out of the house. So, I'll leave.'

She pulled her hand away and, barely holding back her tears, tried to run out of the room. *Maman* restrained her, embraced her, and they both started to cry.

For as long as I can remember, I remember Natalya Savishna and her love and affection, but it's only now that I'm able to appreciate them. It never occurred to me then what a rare, marvellous creature that old woman was. She not only never talked but also, I think, never even thought about herself. Her whole life was one of love and self-sacrifice. I was so used to her selfless, tender love for us that I never imagined it could be otherwise, and I was therefore in no way grateful to her, nor did I ever ask myself the questions, 'Is she happy?' 'Is she satisfied?'

Sometimes it would happen, on the pretext of an urgent need, that you would run from the lesson to her room, seat yourself and start to muse out loud, not in the least embarrassed by her presence. She was always occupied with something, whether knitting a stocking or rummaging in the trunks that filled the room or making a list of the linen, and as she listened to me chatter away about when 'I become a general, I'll marry a remarkable beauty, buy a bay horse, build a glass house and send to Saxony for Karl Ivanych's relatives' and the like, she would say, 'Yes, little master, yes.' When I got up to leave, she would usually open a blue trunk with, as I remember it now, the tinted image of some hussar, a picture from a pomade jar, and one of Volodya's drawings pasted on the lid, and take out a pastille, light it and say, while waving it around, 'This is still the Ochakov incense, little master. When your late grandfather – may he rest in the kingdom of heaven – marched against the Turks,[34] his lordship brought it back with him. There are only a few pieces left,' she would add with a sigh.

The trunks filling her room contained absolutely everything. Whatever might be needed, the servants would say, 'Go ask Natalya Savishna,' and, in fact, after going through the trunks, she would find the item and say, 'It's a good thing I put it aside.' There were a thousand such things in those trunks that no one in the house but she either knew or cared about.

Once I lost my temper with her. This is how it happened. While pouring some kvass at dinner I dropped the pitcher and soaked the tablecloth.

'Well, go call Natalya Savishna, so she can enjoy her darling's work,' *maman* said.

Natalya Savishna came in and, on seeing the mess I had made, shook her head. Then *maman* whispered something to her and Natalya Savishna, after a threatening gesture at me, went out.

After dinner, as I was skipping in the direction of the salon in the merriest of moods, Natalya Savishna suddenly sprang from behind a door with the tablecloth in her hand, grabbed hold of me and, even though I desperately resisted, began to rub my face with the wet part, saying, 'Don't soil the tablecloths! Don't soil the tablecloths!' I was so offended that I started to howl with rage.

'What!' I said to myself as I paced back and forth in the salon, choking on my tears. 'Natalya Savishna – or just "Natalya" – uses the intimate "thou" with *me* and hits *me* in the face with a wet tablecloth like some servant boy? No, it's an outrage!'

When Natalya Savishna saw me sobbing, she immediately ran off, and I continued to walk up and down, thinking how to repay the insolent 'Natalya' for the insult I had suffered.

A few minutes later Natalya Savishna returned, meekly came over to me, and started to plead.

'Enough, little master, don't cry . . . Forgive me for being so stupid. I was wrong. Please forgive me, my darling. Here's something for you.'

She took from under her shawl a cornet made of red paper with two caramels and a dried fig in it, and handed it to me with a trembling hand. I didn't have the strength to look that kind old woman in the face. Turning away, I accepted her gift and my tears flowed all the more abundantly, although no longer from rage but from love and shame.

FOURTEEN

Parting

Around noon the day after the events I've described, the barouche and britzka were standing by the front steps. Nikolay was dressed for the road; that is, his trousers were tucked into his boots, and his old frock coat was tightly bound with a sash. He stood in the britzka, stowing overcoats and pillows under the seat. When the seat seemed too high, he sat on the pillows and bounced up and down to flatten them.

'Take pity, Nikolay Dmitrich, and see if you can't put the master's travelling *cheest* in with you,' said Papa's valet, sticking his head out of the barouche and breathing hard. 'It isn't big.'

'You should have said something before, Mikhey Ivanych,' Nikolay shot back in vexation, hurling a bundle to the floor of the britzka with all his strength. 'As God is my witness, my head's already spinning, without you and your *cheests*,' he added, pushing his cap back and wiping large beads of sweat from his sunburnt forehead.

Standing around the front steps and chatting among themselves were bareheaded servants in frock coats or in peasant caftans and shirts, women in coarse cotton frocks and striped kerchiefs with babies in their arms, and barefoot little children. One of the drivers, a humpbacked old man wearing a winter cap and heavy coat, held the shaft of the barouche in one hand, tapped it with the other, and gravely examined its play. The other driver – a portly young fellow in a white shirt with red calico gussets and a black felt hat with a fez-shaped crown that he knocked from ear to ear as he scratched his blond curls – put his own coat up on the coach box, tossed the reins up there, too, and lashed out with his plaited whip from time to time, while looking first at his boots and then at the coachmen lubricating the britzka. While one strained to lift the britzka, the other leaned over a wheel and carefully smeared the axle and sleeve and even all around underneath, so that none of the leftover birch tar would go unused. Jaded post horses of various colours stood by the iron fence swishing the flies away with their tails. Splaying their shaggy, swollen legs, a few rolled their eyes up and dozed, while others nuzzled each other from boredom or nibbled at the tough leaves and stems of the dark-green ferns growing near the steps. Several Borzois lay panting in the sun or moved about in the shade under the barouche and britzka to lick the tallow from their axles. The air was filled with a kind of dusty haze, and the horizon was a lilac-grey, but there wasn't a cloud in the sky. A strong westerly wind raised columns of dust on the road and fields, bent the crowns of the tall lindens and birches in the garden, and carried their falling yellow leaves a good distance away. I sat by the window and waited impatiently for all the preparations to end.

Even when everyone had gathered by the round table in the drawing room to spend a last few minutes together,[35] I still had no idea how sad it would be. Thoughts of the most idle kind wandered through my mind. I wondered which driver would go in the britzka and which in the barouche, and who would ride with Papa and who with Karl Ivanych, and why they would certainly want to wrap me up in a scarf and a long quilted coat.

'Am I really so delicate? I'm not likely to freeze. If they would just hurry up and finish so we can get going.'

'Whom shall I give the children's linen list to?' Natalya Savishna asked *maman*, entering the room with a tear-stained face and the list in her hand.

'Give it to Nikolay,' *maman* said, 'and then come and say goodbye to the children.'

The old woman was going to say something else, but suddenly stopped, covered her face with her handkerchief and left the room with a wave of her hand. It made my heart ache a little to see that gesture, but my eagerness to get going overpowered that feeling, and instead I listened with complete indifference to Father's conversation with Mama. They were talking about things that were obviously of no interest to either of them: what needed to be purchased for the house, what to tell Princess Sophie or Mme Julie, and whether the road would be good.

Then Foka came to the doorway, and in exactly the same voice with which he announced 'Dinner is ready,' he said, 'The horses are ready.' I noticed *maman* shudder and turn pale at the news, as if it had caught her by surprise.

Foka was told to close all the doors in the room. That amused me – 'as if we're all hiding from someone'.

After everyone was seated, Foka, too, sat down on the edge of a chair, but no sooner had he done so than a door creaked and Natalya Savishna hurried in and, without lifting her eyes, found refuge by the door on the same chair with Foka. As if it were today I see Foka's bald head and impassive, wrinkled face, and the kindly, bent figure of Natalya Savishna in a mobcap that doesn't quite cover her grey hair. They're pressed together on the chair and it's awkward for both of them.

I continued to be carefree and impatient. The ten seconds we sat there with the doors closed seemed like an hour to me. Finally we got up, crossed ourselves, and began to say our farewells. Papa embraced *maman* and kissed her several times.

'That's enough, my dear,' Papa said. 'After all, we're not parting forever.'

'All the same, it's sad!' *maman* said, her voice breaking.

When I heard that voice and saw her trembling lips and eyes filled with tears, I forgot about everything else and became so sad and distressed and afraid that I felt it would be better to run away than to say goodbye to her. I realized at that moment that in embracing Father she was already saying farewell to us.

She kissed Volodya and made the sign of the cross over him so many times that I pushed forward, assuming that she would now turn to me, but she kept blessing him and pressing him to her breast. Finally, I embraced her and, clinging to her, cried and cried, aware only of my grief.

When we went to get in the carriages, the entryway was filled with a tedious throng of servants waiting to say goodbye. Their 'I beg your hand, sir' and noisy kisses on the shoulder[36] and the smell of lard in their hair aroused in me the feeling nearest to regret in touchy people. Under the sway of that feeling, I kissed Natalya Savishna on her mobcap with unusual coldness as she said goodbye to me, completely in tears.

It's strange that I see the faces of the servants as if it were today and could draw them all in the minutest detail, yet *maman*'s face and stance have completely vanished from my imagination, perhaps because I couldn't bring myself to look at her the whole time. It seemed to me that if I did look, her distress and mine would reach intolerable extremes.

I threw myself into the barouche before anyone else and took a place on the back seat. I couldn't see anything on the other side of the raised hood, but all the same some instinct told me *maman* was there.

'Shall I take a look at her again or not? Well, one last time!' I said to myself and leaned out of the barouche towards the front steps. At the same time, *maman* came up to the barouche on the other side with the same idea and called my name. Hearing her voice behind me, I turned around, but so quickly that we bumped heads. She smiled sadly and kissed me one last time as hard as she could.

After we had gone a few yards, I decided to look again. The wind lifted the light-blue kerchief tied around her chin as she slowly went up the front steps with her head bowed and her hands covering her face. Foka was holding her by the arm.

Papa was sitting next to me and said nothing, while I choked on my tears and something else that pressed so hard in my throat I was afraid I might suffocate. Coming out onto the main road, we saw someone waving a white handkerchief from the balcony. I started to wave my own and the gesture calmed me a little. I continued to cry, but the thought that the tears were evidence of my sensitivity gave me pleasure and comfort.

After a mile or so I settled down and turned my unwavering attention to the thing right before my eyes, the rear of the piebald trace horse running on my side of the barouche. I watched the horse flick its tail and strike one foot against the other, and then the lash of the driver's plaited whip to make the feet jump together. I watched the movement of the harness breechband and the breechband ring, and kept watching until the breechband was covered with lather near the horse's tail. I started to look around: at the billowing fields of ripe rye; at the dark haze in which a plough, a peasant or a horse with a foal would turn up from time to time; at the mileposts; and even at the box to see which driver was with us. My face still wasn't completely dry of tears, but my thoughts were already far from the mother with whom I had parted, perhaps forever. Yet every recollection brought me back to thoughts of her. I recalled the mushroom I had found the day before in the birch avenue, and how Lyubochka and Katenka had argued over who should pick it. And I recalled their tears as they said goodbye to us.

I felt sorry for them! And I felt sorry for Natalya Savishna and for the birches and for Foka! And for the bad-tempered Mimi – even for her. I felt sorry for everyone and everything. But poor *maman*? The tears welled up again, but not for long.

FIFTEEN

Childhood

The happy, happy unrecoverable days of childhood! How could I not love, not cherish its memories? They have lifted up and refreshed my soul and served as the source of its finest pleasures.

After running around to my heart's content, I would be sitting at the tea table in my own tall chair. It would already be late and I would have long since drunk my cup of warm milk with sugar. Sleep would weigh on my eyelids, but I would still sit and listen. And how could I not? *Maman* would be talking to someone, and the sound of her voice would be so sweet and amiable. That sound alone spoke so much to my heart! I would look at her with eyes clouded with sleepiness and she would suddenly become very, very small, her face no bigger than a button, although it would still be just as clearly visible: I could see her gazing back at me and smiling. I liked to see her so tiny. I would squint even harder and she would become no bigger than a speck in my eye, but then I would shift a little, and the spell would be broken. I would narrow my eyes, move about and try in every other way to recover it, but to no avail.

Then I would get up, climb into an armchair and cosily settle in it.

'You'll fall asleep again, Nikolenka,' *maman* would say. 'Why don't you go upstairs?'

'I don't want to sleep, Mama,' I would answer, and sweet, vague reveries would fill my imagination, the healthy sleep of childhood would close my eyes, and a moment later I would be fast asleep and remain so until I was wakened. Then I would become aware through my sleep of the touch of someone's tender hand. I would recognize it from the touch alone, and still not fully awake would involuntarily take hold of it and press it hard to my lips.

Everyone had gone to bed and a single candle burned in the drawing room. *Maman* had said that she would wake me herself, and it was she who had sat down on the edge of the chair where I was sleeping and run her wonderfully tender hand through my hair, and it was her dear familiar voice that had whispered in my ear, 'Get up, my darling. It's time to go to bed.'

No indifferent gazes inhibited her. She wasn't afraid to pour out on me all her tenderness and love. Without moving, I would kiss her hand even harder.

'Come, my angel, get up.'

She would take hold of my neck with her other hand and rapidly wiggle her fingers and tickle me. It would be quiet in the room and half-dark. My nerves would be stimulated by the tickling and awakening. Mama would be sitting right next to me and touching me, and I would smell her fragrance and hear her voice. All of which would make me jump up, wrap my arms around her neck, press my head against her breast and say breathlessly, 'Oh, dear, dear Mama, how I love you!'

She would smile her sad, bewitching smile, take my head in both her hands, kiss me on the forehead and set me on her knees.

'So you love me very much?' Then she would fall silent for a moment before adding, 'See that you always love me and never forget me. If your mama were no more, you wouldn't forget her, would you? You wouldn't forget her, Nikolenka?'

And she would kiss me even more tenderly.

'Oh, don't say that, my dove, my darling!' I would shriek, kissing her knees with tears running from my eyes, tears of love and rapture.

After I had gone upstairs and was standing before the icons in my room in my quilted dressing gown, what a marvellous feeling it was to say the words, 'Lord, protect dear Papa and Mama.' As I repeated the prayers that I had first murmured as a small child after my beloved mother, my love for her and for God somehow became strangely fused in a single feeling.

After saying my prayers, I would wrap myself up in my little blanket. My soul would be clear, comforted and at ease. One dream would quickly replace another, but what were they about? They were elusive, but full of pure love and a hope for radiant happiness. I would remember Karl Ivanych and his bitter lot (he was the only unhappy person I knew), and become so sorry for him and so fond of him that the tears would flow from my eyes and I would think, 'God grant him happiness, and me the opportunity to help him and ease his sorrow. I'm ready to sacrifice everything for him.' And then I would stick my favourite porcelain toy – a little hare or dog – into a corner of the down pillow and admire how well, warm and comfortably it lay there. I would pray again for God to grant happiness to all, for everyone to be content, and for good weather for the next day's outing, and then I would turn over on my other side, my thoughts and dreams would grow muddled and confused, and I would quietly and calmly fall asleep, my face still wet from my tears.

Will the freshness, unconcern, need for love and strength of faith you possess as a child ever return? What time could have been better than when the two finest virtues – innocent gaiety and a limitless need for love – were life's only impulses?

Where are those ardent prayers? Where is the best gift – those pure tears of tenderness? A comforting angel would fly down to dry those tears with a smile and waft sweet reveries into the uncorrupted imagination of childhood.

Has life really left such a heavy mark on my heart that those tears and raptures are gone forever? Are the memories really all that remain?

SIXTEEN

Verses

Almost a month after our move to Moscow I was sitting upstairs at a large table in my grandmother's house and writing. Across from me sat our drawing teacher, putting the finishing touches on a pencil sketch of the head of a Turk in a turban. Volodya stood behind the teacher and, craning his neck, watched over his shoulder. The head was Volodya's first work in pencil and was to be presented to Grandmother that very day, her name-day.

'Shouldn't there be more shading there?' Volodya asked the teacher, standing on tiptoe and pointing at the Turk's neck.

'No, there's no need,' the teacher said, putting his pencils and stub holder away in a little box with a sliding lid. 'It's excellent as it is. Don't touch it any more. Well, what about you, Nikolenka?' he added, getting up and continuing to look at the Turk from the side. 'Tell us your secret at last. What are you going to give your grandmother? It really ought to be a head, too. Goodbye, gentlemen,' he said, and picking up his hat and coupon,[37] he left.

I, too, was thinking at that moment that a head would have been better than what I was struggling with. When we were told that it would soon be Grandmother's name-day and that we should prepare gifts, I thought I would write her a poem for the occasion and immediately found a suitable rhyming couplet, hoping that the rest of it would come just as quickly. I've absolutely no recollection of where that idea, a very odd one for a child, came from, but I do remember that it pleased me very much, and that my response to every question on the subject was that I would certainly give Grandmother a present, but that I couldn't say what it was.

My expectation notwithstanding, it turned out that except for the couplet that had come to me in the heat of the moment, I couldn't compose anything else, however hard I tried. I started reading the poems in our books, but neither Dmitriev nor Derzhavin[38] were of any help; on the contrary, they convinced me even more of my own inability. Knowing that Karl Ivanych liked to copy out doggerel, I started to go through his papers, where, among some German poems, I found one in Russian that must have been from his own pen.

> *To Mademoiselle L. Petrovskaya. 1828. 3 June.*
> Remember near,
> Remember far,
> Remember of me
> From today forth and until forever,
> Remember even unto my grave,
> How faithful I have knowed how to love.
> *Karl Mauer*

The poem was written in a beautiful, round hand on fine postal tissue, and I liked it for the touching feeling with which it was imbued. I memorized it at once and decided to use it as a model. Everything got much easier after that. My name-day congratulation in twelve lines was finished and I was sitting at the table in our classroom and copying it out on vellum paper.

I had already ruined two sheets. Not because I thought of altering anything in the poem – it seemed superb to me – but because after the third line the ends started to curl up more and more, so that even from a distance you could see that it had been written crookedly and wasn't any good.

The third sheet was just as crooked as the other two, but I decided not to recopy any more. In my poem I congratulated Grandmother, wished her many years of health, and concluded this way:

> To comfort you we'll never fear,
> And love you like our mother dear.

That would have been quite fine, I think, had not the last line strangely grated.

'And love you like our mother dear,' I repeated to myself. 'What other rhyme is there besides "mother dear"? "Mother near"? "Mother here"? Oh, it's all right, and better than Karl Ivanych's stuff at any rate!'

I copied out the last line. Then I read my entire composition out loud in the bedroom with feeling and gestures. There were lines that didn't scan at all, but I didn't dwell on them, since the last line struck me even more forcefully and unpleasantly. I sat down on the bed and started to brood.

'Why did I write "like our mother dear"? She isn't here, so it wasn't necessary to mention her at all. Certainly, I love Grandmother and respect her, but even so it's not the same. Why did I write that? Why did I lie? Even if it's only a poem, it still wasn't necessary.'

At that moment the tailor came in with our new short jackets.

'Well, so be it!' I said in exasperation, sticking the poem under a pillow in vexation and running off to try on the Moscow clothes.

They turned out to be superb: the short brown jackets with bronze buttons were made to fit snugly, unlike in the country where they had been cut with room for growing, and the black trousers were also tight – it was wonderful how well they outlined your muscles and lay on your boots.

'I finally have trousers with foot straps – real ones!' I mused, beside myself with joy as I examined my legs from every side. Even though I felt awkward and confined in the new clothes, I kept it from everyone and said that, on the contrary, they were very comfortable, and that if there was any defect, it was that they were a trifle loose. After that I combed my heavily pomaded hair in front of the mirror a long time. But however hard I tried, I couldn't smooth down the cowlicks on top. As soon as I stopped pressing on them with the brush to test their obedience, they popped back up and stuck out in various directions, imparting a ridiculous expression to my face.

Karl Ivanych was getting dressed in the other room, and a blue tailcoat and some white articles had already been brought

for him through the classroom. I heard the voice of one of Grandmother's chambermaids in the doorway leading downstairs. I
went to see what she wanted. She was holding a stiffly starched
shirtfront and said that she had brought it for Karl Ivanych and
hadn't slept all night in order to get it washed and ready in time.
I told her that I would give it to him and asked if Grandmother
was up yet.

'Well, of course she is, sir! My lady has already had her coffee
and the archpriest has come. Don't you look smart!' she added
with a smile, inspecting my new clothes.

That remark made me blush, but I twirled on one foot,
snapped my fingers, and hopped, intending by that to give her
a sense of just how smart I really was.

When I brought Karl Ivanych the shirtfront, he no longer
needed it. He had put on another and was leaning over the little
mirror on his desk and holding the magnificent bow of his cravat
in both hands to see if his cleanly shaven chin moved freely above
and around it. After straightening our clothes and asking Nikolay
to do the same for him, he took us down to see Grandmother.
It makes me laugh to recall how much the three of us reeked of
pomade as we made our way downstairs.

Karl Ivanych was holding a little box of his own manufacture,
Volodya had his drawing and I had my poem, and each of us
carried on the tip of his tongue the greeting with which he would
present his gift. Karl Ivanych opened the door to the salon just
as the clergyman was putting on his vestments and intoning the
first words of the office.[39]

Grandmother was already in the salon, bent over the back of
a chair by the wall and devoutly praying, with Papa standing
beside her. Noticing our hurried concealment behind our backs
of the gifts we had brought and our effort to remain incon-
spicuously by the door, he turned towards us and smiled. The
whole effect of surprise that we had been counting on was lost.

As we were about to go over to the cross, I was suddenly
gripped by an overwhelming, stupefying shyness, and realizing
that I would never have the courage to present my gift, I hid
behind Karl Ivanych, who greeted Grandmother in the choicest
language, transferred the box from his right hand to his left,

held it out to her, and then withdrew a few steps to let Volodya take his turn. Grandmother seemed to be delighted with the box, on which golden edging had been glued, and she expressed her gratitude with a most affectionate smile. It was obvious, however, that she didn't know what to do with it, and probably for that reason suggested to Papa that he look at the marvellous skill with which it had been made.

After satisfying his curiosity, Papa handed the box to the archpriest, who appeared to be quite taken with it. He shook his head, while gazing first at the box and then at the craftsman who had been able to make such a beautiful thing. Volodya presented his Turk and also received the most flattering praise from every side. Then came my turn, and Grandmother gazed at me with an encouraging smile.

Anyone who has experienced shyness knows that the feeling increases in direct proportion to its duration, and that resolve decreases in the same proportion; that is, the longer the condition lasts, the more insurmountable it becomes and the weaker the resolve that remains.

My shyness reached its uttermost limit and my last courage and resolve left me just as Karl Ivanych and Volodya were presenting their gifts: I felt the blood rush from my heart to my head, my face change from one colour to another, and large beads of sweat appear on my forehead and nose. My ears burned, my whole body trembled and perspired, and I rocked from one foot to the other, while continuing to stand where I was.

'Well, show us what you have, Nikolenka. Is it a box or a drawing?' Papa said. There was nothing to be done, so with a trembling hand I held out the fateful, now crumpled scroll, but in silence, since my voice, too, had completely refused to serve me. I was overwhelmed by the thought that instead of the expected drawing, my worthless verses would now be read in everyone's hearing, along with the words 'like our mother dear', which would clearly prove that I had never loved her and had forgotten her. How can I convey my sufferings when Grandmother began to read my poem out loud and, unable to make sense of a line, paused in the middle to glance at Papa with a smile that seemed mocking to me; or when she articulated differently than I meant; or when, from weak eyesight, she handed the paper to Papa without finishing and asked him to read the poem to her again from the start? I thought she did that because she was tired of reading such poor and crookedly written verses and wanted Papa to read the last line himself, with its glaring proof of my insensitivity. I expected that he would rap me on the nose with the poem and say, 'Don't forget your mother, you wretched boy. Take that!' although nothing like that happened. On the contrary, after the poem had been read, Grandmother said, '*Charmant!*' and kissed me on the forehead.

The box, the drawing and the poem were placed beside two batiste handkerchiefs and a snuffbox with a portrait of *maman* that were already lying on the little extension table of the Voltaire armchair Grandmother always sat in.

'Princess Varvara Ilinishna,' announced one of the two enormous footmen who rode behind Grandmother in her coach.

Grandmother was absorbed in looking at the portrait set into the tortoiseshell snuffbox and didn't answer.

'May I show her in, your highness?' the footman repeated.

SEVENTEEN

Princess Kornakova

'Yes, do,' Grandmother replied, settling into her armchair.

The princess was a woman of about forty-five, small, frail, thin and bilious, with unpleasant little grey-green eyes, whose expression was conspicuously at odds with the unnaturally ingratiating shape of her little mouth. Light-red hair was visible under her velvet hat with its ostrich plume, and her eyebrows and eyelashes seemed even lighter and redder against the unhealthy pallor of her face. Despite that, and thanks to her relaxed movements, tiny hands and the spareness of all her features, her general appearance still had something noble and energetic about it.

The princess talked a lot and belonged in her volubility to the category of people who always speak as if they've been contradicted, even if no one has said anything. She would first raise her voice, gradually lower it, and then suddenly speak out again with renewed energy, while gazing at those not taking part in the conversation, as if trying in that way to enlist their support.

Although the princess kissed Grandmother's hand and continually called her *ma bonne tante*,[40] I could tell that Grandmother was displeased with her. She raised her eyebrows particularly high as she listened to the princess's story about why Prince Mikhailo was simply unable to come to congratulate Grandmother himself, despite his very great wish to do so, and then replying to the princess's French in Russian, she said, drawing out her words, 'I'm very grateful to you, my dear, for being so attentive, and that Prince Mikhailo hasn't come, well, what is there to say about it? He always has such a lot of things to do, and, if the truth be told, what pleasure is there for him in the company of an old woman?'

And without giving the princess a chance to object, she continued, 'And how are your children, my dear?'

'Well, thank goodness, *ma tante*, they're growing and studying and up to their usual tricks, especially Étienne, the oldest, who's becoming such a scamp that there's no peace with him. On the other hand, he's capable, *un garçon qui promet*.[41] Can you imagine, *mon cousin*?' she went on, addressing Papa, since Grandmother, not at all interested in the princess's children but wishing to boast of her own grandsons, had carefully taken my poem out from under the box and begun to unroll it, 'can you imagine what he did a few days ago?'

And the princess, leaning towards Papa, started to tell him something with great animation. Finishing her story, which I didn't hear, she immediately laughed and then said with an enquiring look at Papa, 'What sort of boy is that, *mon cousin*? He deserved a thrashing, but it was such a clever and amusing prank that I forgave him, *mon cousin*.'

And the princess, directing her gaze back at Grandmother, continued to smile without saying anything more.

'Do you actually *beat* your children, my dear?' Grandmother asked, significantly raising her eyebrows and giving particular emphasis to the word 'beat'.

'Ah, *ma bonne tante*,' the princess answered in a sweet little voice with a quick glance at Papa, 'I know your opinion on the matter, but allow me in this one thing to disagree with you. However much I've thought about it, however much I've read and consulted with others on the subject, my experience still convinces me of the need for fear in influencing children. To make anything out of a child, you need fear . . . Isn't that right, *mon cousin*? And what, *je vous demande un peu*,[42] do children fear more than the rod?'

As she said that, she looked enquiringly at us, too, and I'll admit it made me quite uncomfortable.

'Whatever you say, a boy of twelve or even fourteen is still a child. Girls are a different story.'

'It's a good thing I'm not her son,' I thought.

'Yes, that's very fine, my dear,' Grandmother said, rolling up my poem and putting it back under the box, as if, after that last remark, considering the princess unworthy of hearing such a work, 'that's all very fine, but tell me, please, how, after that, you can expect refined feelings from your children.'

And regarding that argument as irrefutable, Grandmother added, in order to end the conversation, 'But, of course, we all have our own views on the subject.'

The princess didn't answer, but merely smiled indulgently, expressing thereby her tolerance of those strange prejudices in someone for whom she had such respect.

'Oh, but do introduce me to your young people,' she said, looking at us with an amiable smile.

We stood up and, after gazing into the princess's face, had no idea what else we should do to acknowledge the introduction.

'Well, kiss the princess's hand,' Papa said.

'I hope you will love your old aunt,' she said, kissing Volodya on the head. 'Although I'm a distant relation, I go more by connections of friendship than degrees of kinship,' she added, mainly to Grandmother, although Grandmother continued to be displeased with her and replied, 'Does kinship really mean anything these days, my dear?'

'This one of mine will be a young man of the world,' Papa said, indicating Volodya, 'and this one's a poet,' he added just as I was kissing the princess's thin little hand and imagining with exceptional vividness a birch rod in it, and beneath the rod a bench, and so on and so forth.

'Which one?' the princess asked, holding on to my hand.

'This little one with the cowlicks,' Papa said with a merry smile.

'What have my cowlicks done to him? Is there really nothing else to talk about?' I thought and withdrew to a corner.

I had the strangest notions about beauty and even considered Karl Ivanvych the handsomest man in the world. But I knew quite well that I wasn't good-looking myself, and wasn't at all mistaken about it, and therefore every hint about my appearance was a painful affront.

I remember very well how once at dinner – I was six at the time – they were talking about my looks and *maman* was trying to find something good in my face, and said that I had clever eyes and a pleasant smile, but yielding in the end to my father's arguments and her own eyesight, she was forced to admit I was homely. Afterwards, as I was thanking her for dinner, she stroked my cheek and said, 'Remember, Nikolenka, no one will love you for your face, so you must try to be a good and clever boy.'

Those words convinced me not only that I was no beauty, but also that I would certainly be a good and clever boy.

Despite that, there were often moments when I was overwhelmed with despair. I imagined that there could be no happiness on earth for someone with the broad nose, thick lips and tiny grey eyes I had. I asked God to perform a miracle and turn me into a handsome man, and I would have exchanged all that I had then and all that I might have in the future for a handsome face.

EIGHTEEN

Prince Ivan Ivanych

After the princess had listened to my poem and showered its author with praise, Grandmother relented, started to speak French to her, stopped using the formal pronoun and the phrase 'my dear' and invited her to come back that evening with her children, which the princess agreed to do, and then, after sitting a little while longer, she left.

So many guests arrived with greetings that morning that there was never a moment when several carriages weren't parked at once in the yard by the entrance.

'*Bonjour, chère cousine,*' said one of the guests, upon entering the room and kissing Grandmother's hand.

He was a tall man of about seventy in a military tunic with large epaulettes and a big white cross visible from under its collar, and a calm, forthright expression on his face. I was struck by the freedom and simplicity of his movements. Although his only remaining hair was a sparse crescent at the back of his head, and the position of his upper lip clearly indicated a scarcity of teeth, his face was still remarkably handsome.

Prince Ivan Ivanych had at a very young age made a brilliant career at the end of the last century, thanks to his noble character, handsome appearance, remarkable valour, distinguished and powerful family, but especially good luck. He remained in the service, and his ambition was very quickly satisfied to such a degree that there was nothing left for him to desire in that regard. From early youth he had conducted himself as if he were preparing to assume the brilliant place in society to which fate eventually assigned him. Thus, although he had, like everyone, encountered setbacks, disappointments and distress in his brilliant and rather vainglorious life, he never once changed either his always calm character or his mode of thought or his basic rules of religion and morality, and he enjoyed universal respect not so much for his brilliant position as for his firmness and consistency. He wasn't a man of great intelligence, but thanks to his position, which permitted him to regard the petty aggravations of life from above, his mode of thought was a lofty one. He was kind and sensitive, yet cold and even aloof in his manner of address. That came from the need to protect himself from the constant importunity and flattery of those who merely wanted to take advantage of his influence, since from his high position he could be useful to many. His coldness, however, was softened by the gracious courtesy of a man of 'very high society'. He was well educated and well read, but his education ended with what he had acquired in his youth – at the end of the last century, that is. He had read everything remarkable written in France in the eighteenth century in the areas of philosophy and rhetoric, and had a sound knowledge of all the best works of French literature, so that he could and often did cite passages from Racine, Corneille, Boileau, Molière and Fénelon.[43] He had a brilliant knowledge of mythology and had with profit studied in French translation the ancient monuments of epic poetry, and he had an adequate knowledge of history, gleaned from Ségur,[44] but no understanding at all of mathematics beyond arithmetic, nor of physics, nor of contemporary literature. He could in conversation maintain a dignified silence or offer a few general remarks on Goethe, Schiller and Byron,[45] but he had never read them. Despite that French classical education, of which so few exemplars survive today, his conversation was simple, the simplicity both concealing his ignorance of certain things and displaying toleration and a pleasant tone. He was a great foe of eccentricity of every kind, calling it a ruse of the vulgar. Society was essential to him wherever he resided, and whether in Moscow or abroad he always lived in the same accessible way and on certain days was at home to the whole city. His standing was such that an invitation from him could serve as an entrée to any drawing room, and such, too, that many a young and pretty lady readily offered the prince her rosy cheek, which he kissed as if with paternal feeling, while other, seemingly quite important and respectable people experienced indescribable joy on being admitted to the prince's company.

Few people like my grandmother remained for the prince – people of the same circle and upbringing with the same views about things and of the same age. He therefore especially valued his long friendship with her and always treated her with great respect.

I couldn't stop staring at the prince. The deference that every-one showed him, his large epaulettes, the particular joy that Grandmother expressed on seeing him, and the fact that he was apparently the only person who wasn't afraid of her and was free and easy in his dealings with her, even daring to call her *'ma cousine'*, inspired in me a respect that was equal to if not greater than the one I felt for Grandmother herself. When my poem was shown to him, he called me over and said, 'Who knows, *ma cousine*, perhaps he'll be another Derzhavin.'

Saying that, he pinched my cheek so hard that if I didn't cry out, it was only because I realized I should take it as affection.

The other guests had departed, Papa and Volodya had gone out and the prince, Grandmother and I were left alone in the drawing room.

'Why didn't our dear Natalya Nikolayevna come too?' the prince suddenly asked Grandmother after a brief silence.

'Ah, *mon cher*,' Grandmother replied, lowering her voice and resting her hand on the prince's sleeve, 'she probably would have, if she had been free to do as she wished. She wrote to me to say that *Pierre* had suggested it, but that she herself had refused, since they apparently have had no income at all this year, and as she wrote, "Moreover, there's no reason this year for me to bring the whole household to Moscow. Lyubochka's still too young, and as for the boys, I'm more comfortable with them there with you than I would have been with them here." That's all very fine!' Grandmother continued in a tone that clearly meant that she viewed it as nothing of the sort. 'Sending the boys here so they could learn something and get used to society was long overdue – what kind of education could they receive in the country? Why, the older one will soon be thirteen, and the other's eleven. You've noticed, *mon cousin*, that they're like absolute savages here. They don't even know how to enter a room.'

'But I don't understand,' the prince answered. 'What's the reason for the continual complaining about their disordered circumstances? *He* has a very good living, and Natasha's Khabarovka, in whose theatre you and I used to play in our day – I know it like the back of my hand – is a splendid estate and should always produce an excellent income.'

'I'll tell you as a true friend,' Grandmother stopped him with a rueful expression. 'I think it's all a subterfuge for *him* to live here by himself, and loaf about his clubs and dinners and goodness knows what else, while she doesn't suspect a thing. You know her angelic goodness – she trusts *him* in everything. He persuaded her that the boys needed to be taken to Moscow and that she needed to remain behind in the country with that stupid governess, and she believed him. Let him tell her that the children should be beaten the way Princess Varvara Ilinishna beats hers, and she would, I think, agree to it at once,' Grandmother said, turning around in her armchair with a look of utter contempt. 'Yes, my friend,' Grandmother continued, after a moment of silence while she picked up one of the new handkerchiefs to wipe away a welling tear, 'I often think that *he* can neither appreciate her nor understand her, and that despite all her goodness and her love for him and all her efforts to hide her sorrow – as I know very well – she cannot be happy with him and, mark my words, if he doesn't . . .'

Grandmother covered her face with her handkerchief.

'Ah, *ma bonne amie*,'[46] the prince said reprovingly, 'I see that you still haven't got any more sensible and continue as ever to grieve and weep over imaginary woes. Aren't you ashamed of yourself? I've known *him* a long time, and I know him to be an attentive, kind and excellent husband, and, the main thing, to be the noblest of people, *un parfait honnête homme*.'[47]

Having overheard a conversation that I shouldn't have, I tiptoed out of the room in great agitation.

NINETEEN

The Ivins

'Volodya! Volodya! The Ivins!' I started to yell on seeing out of the window three boys in fitted blue overcoats with beaver collars crossing over to our house from the other side of the street behind their foppish tutor.

The Ivins were relatives of ours and nearly the same age. We had made their acquaintance and become friends shortly after our arrival in Moscow.

The second Ivin, Seryozha, was a swarthy, curly-haired, snub-nosed boy with beautiful dark-blue eyes, very fresh red lips that rarely covered his slightly protruding upper row of white teeth and an exceptionally lively expression on his face. He never smiled but either gazed with complete seriousness or heartily laughed his sharp, ringing, extraordinarily appealing laugh. His unique beauty struck me at once. I felt an irresistible attraction to him. Seeing him was enough to make me happy, and all the powers of my soul were for a time concentrated on that desire: whenever I happened to pass three or four days without seeing him, I started to miss him and grew sad to the point of tears. All my dreams, asleep and awake, were of him; going to bed, I wanted to dream of him; closing my eyes, I saw him before me and cherished that apparition as the finest of pleasures. There was no one in the world in whom I would have confided that feeling, so much did I treasure it. But either because he was getting tired of my restless eyes staring at him all the time, or because he simply had no real liking for me, he clearly enjoyed playing and talking with Volodya more. But I was content, even so, and wished for and required nothing and was ready to sacrifice everything for him. Besides the passionate attraction he inspired, his presence awoke in me another, equally strong feeling – the fear of upsetting him or offending or displeasing him in some way, perhaps because his face had a haughty expression, or because in my contempt for my own looks I had too high a regard for the advantages of beauty in others, or, most likely, because my feeling for him contained as much fear in it as it did adoration – a sure sign of love. The first time Seryozha spoke to me, I was so abashed by the sheer unexpected happiness of it that I turned pale and then red and couldn't answer anything. He had the bad habit when absorbed in thought of focusing his gaze on a single point and blinking and twitching his nose and eyebrows. Everyone was of the opinion that the habit spoiled his looks, but I found it so appealing that I involuntarily started to do the same thing myself, and a few days after I had made his acquaintance, Grandmother asked me if my eyes didn't hurt, since I was blinking like an eagle owl. No words of affection ever passed between us, but he sensed his power over me and made unconscious but tyrannical use of it in our relations, while I, however much I wanted to tell him everything that was in my heart, was too afraid of him for such candour. I pretended not to care and submitted uncomplainingly. Sometimes his influence was an intolerable burden for me, but freeing myself of it was beyond my power.

It's sad for me to recall that fresh, beautiful feeling of unselfish and boundless love that died without ever expressing itself or finding a sympathetic response.

Strange how as a child I tried to be like a grown-up, but that ever since I stopped being a child, I've often wanted to be childlike. How many times did the desire not to be like a little boy in my relations with Seryozha check the feeling that was ready to express itself and make me dissemble instead? Not only did I dare not kiss him, a thing that I sometimes very much wanted to do while taking his hand in mine and telling him how happy I was to see him, but I didn't even dare to use his diminutive 'Seryozha', invariably calling him 'Sergey' instead, as we were all accustomed to doing. Every expression of sensitivity was taken as proof of childishness and of the fact that whoever allowed it in himself was still a 'little boy'. Not yet experienced through the bitter trials that lead adults to caution and reserve in their relationships, we deprived ourselves of the pure pleasures of tender childhood attachment, merely from the strange desire to be like 'grown-ups'.

I went down to meet the Ivins while they were still in the footmen's room, greeted them, and then ran headlong to Grandmother to tell her they had come, as if the news would be sure to fill her with joy. And then, never taking my eyes off Seryozha, I followed him into the drawing room, watching all his movements. When Grandmother said that he had grown a lot and fixed her penetrating gaze on him, I experienced the same mixture of hope and fear that an artist must feel waiting for a respected judge's verdict on his work.

With Grandmother's consent, the Ivins' young tutor, Herr Frost, led us down to the front garden, where he took his seat on a green bench, picturesquely crossed his legs after placing his stick with its bronze knob between them, and lit a cigar with the look of someone quite content with his actions.

Herr Frost was a German, but a German of a completely different cut than our kind Karl Ivanych. First, he spoke Russian correctly and French with a bad accent, and generally enjoyed the reputation, especially among the ladies, of being very learned; second, he had a red moustache and wore lustrous light-blue trousers with foot straps and a large ruby pin in a black satin scarf whose ends had been tucked under his braces; and third, he was young and had a handsome, self-satisfied air and exceptionally muscular legs. It was clear that he especially prized the last advantage, regarding its effect on persons of the female sex as irresistible, and probably for that reason would try to put his legs in the most conspicuous position, and whether standing or sitting always flexed his calves. He was the type of young Russian-German who wants to be a rake and a gallant.

The front garden was great fun. Our game of robbers had never gone better, although one incident did come close to spoiling it all. Seryozha was the robber, and as he was running after the travellers, he stumbled and struck his knee against a tree so hard that I thought he had certainly smashed it. Although I was the gendarme and supposed to arrest him, I went over and asked with concern if he was all right. That made him angry, and he clenched his fists and stamped his foot, and in a voice that clearly showed that he had hurt himself very painfully, he started to yell,'Well, what's this, then? If you're going to do that, there can't be any game! Well, why don't you arrest me?' he repeated several times with sidelong glances at Volodya and the eldest Ivin, who, representing travellers, were galloping along the path, and then with a yelp and a loud laugh he ran after them.

I can't convey how stunned and captivated I was by that heroic action. Despite the terrific pain, he not only didn't cry out, but didn't even show he was hurt or forget the game for a moment.

Soon after we had been joined by Ilenka Grap and gone upstairs before dinner, Seryozha had a chance to astonish and captivate me even more with his remarkable fortitude and firmness of character.

Ilenka Grap was the son of an impoverished foreigner, who at one time had lived in my grandfather's house and somehow been in his debt, and who now considered it his binding duty to send his son to us for regular visits. If he supposed that acquaintance with us would bring honour or pleasure to his son, he was badly mistaken, for we were not merely unfriendly to Ilenka, but paid attention to him only when we wanted to laugh at him. Ilenka Grap was a boy of about thirteen, tall, thin and pale with a bird-like little face and a diffident, good-natured expression. He was very badly dressed, but on the other hand he was always so abundantly pomaded that we swore that on a sunny day the pomade would melt on his head and run down inside his jacket collar. When I recall him now I realize that he was a very obliging, quiet and kind boy. At the time, however, he seemed to me to be the sort of contemptible creature who deserved neither pity nor even thought.

After the game of robbers was over and we had gone upstairs, we started to 'romp' and show off various gymnastic tricks to each other. Ilenka watched us with a smile of timid amazement, and when it was suggested that he try them too, he declined, saying he wasn't strong enough. Seryozha was remarkably fine. He took off his jacket and with a glowing face and gleaming eyes and constant guffaws kept coming up with new antics: he leapt over three chairs placed end to end, executed a cartwheel the length of the room and stood on his head on Tatishchev's lexicons,[48] stacked in the middle of it like a pedestal, all the while doing such hilarious things with his legs that it was impossible not to laugh. After that last trick, he fell to thinking, blinked his eyes, and then suddenly went over to Ilenka with a completely serious face. 'Try it, it's not so hard.' Grap, realizing that everyone was looking at him, blushed and then in a barely audible voice assured us there was no way he would be able to do it.

'Really, now, why doesn't he want to show us anything? What a little girl he is. He definitely must stand on his head!'

And Seryozha took him by the arm.

'Definitely, definitely on his head!' we all started to yell, and surrounding Ilenka, who had turned white and was clearly frightened, we grabbed him by his arms and dragged him over to the lexicons.

'Let me go, I'll do it myself! You'll tear my jacket!' the unfortunate victim cried. But those cries of despair only egged us on, and when his green jacket came apart at the seams, we all burst into laughter.

Volodya and the oldest Ivin bent Ilenka's head down and positioned it on the lexicons, while Seryozha and I grabbed the poor boy by his skinny legs, which he had been kicking in various directions, rolled his trousers up to his knees, and then with a loud laugh jerked his legs up. The youngest Ivin kept his torso balanced.

It happened after our noisy laughter that we all suddenly fell silent, and it became so still in the room that the only sound was the unfortunate Grap's laboured breathing. I wasn't entirely convinced at that moment that it was all so merry and amusing.

'Well, you're a brave fellow now,' Seryozha said, slapping him on the back.

Ilenka said nothing and, trying to break free, struck out with his feet in different directions, striking Seryozha in the eye so hard with his heel in one of those desperate movements that Seryozha immediately let go of his leg, grabbed his eye, which was watering, and pushed Ilenka with all his might. No longer held by us, Ilenka fell to the floor like some lifeless thing, and because of his tears could only say, 'Why are you tormenting me?'

The pitiful figure of poor Ilenka with his tear-stained face and tousled hair and his rolled-up trousers exposing his unpolished boot tops took us aback. We said nothing and tried to smile.

Seryozha was the first to recover.

'What a sniveller! What a ninny!' he said, prodding him with his foot. 'Can't take a joke? Enough of that, get up.'

'I said you were a worthless brat,' Ilenka angrily retorted, turning away, and starting to sob.

'A-ha! He kicks people with his heels and then calls them names!' Seryozha shouted, picking up one of the lexicons and brandishing it at the unfortunate Ilenka, who didn't even try to defend himself, but merely covered his head with his hands.

'Take that! And that! Leave him be, if he doesn't understand jokes. Let's go downstairs,' Seryozha said, laughing unnaturally.

I gazed in sympathy at poor Ilenka, who was lying on the floor and sobbing so hard with his face in the lexicons that it seemed just a little more, and he would perish from the convulsions racking his body.

'Sergey!' I said to him. 'Why did you do that?'

'That's a good one! I didn't start crying, I hope, when I smashed my knee today almost to the bone.'

'Yes, that's true,' I thought. 'Ilenka's nothing but a crybaby, whereas Seryozha's a brave fellow, a really brave fellow!'

It didn't occur to me then that poor Ilenka was probably crying not so much from physical pain as from the thought that five boys, whom he perhaps liked, had all agreed for no reason at all to hate and torment him.

I'm simply unable to explain to myself the cruelty of my own actions. Why didn't I go over and defend and comfort him? Where had the compassion gone that had once made me sob violently at the sight of a jackdaw chick thrown from its nest, or an unwanted puppy about to be tossed over the fence, or a chicken being carried off by the kitchen boy for soup?

Had that fine feeling really been stifled in me by my affection for Seryozha and my desire to seem to him to be the same sort of brave fellow he was? How unenviable then were that affection and the desire to seem brave! They produced the only dark spots on the pages of my childhood memories.

TWENTY

Company Arrives

Judging by the particular bustle in the pantry, by the bright illumination imparting a kind of festive new look to the already long-familiar things of the drawing room and salon, and especially by the fact that Prince Ivan Ivanych had certainly not sent his musicians for nothing, a great deal of company was expected that evening.

I ran over to the window at the sound of every passing carriage, cupped my hands by my temples against the glass, and looked out at the street with impatient curiosity. Emerging little by little from the darkness that at first covered everything were the long-familiar shop and lantern across the street, the big house next to it with its two downstairs windows lit, and, on the street, a hack with two passengers or else an empty barouche returning home at an amble. But then a coach drove up to our front steps and, certain it was the Ivins, who had promised to come early, I ran downstairs to greet them in the entry room. But instead of the Ivins, two persons of the female sex appeared from behind the liveried arm holding the door: one big and wearing a blue pelerine with a sable collar, the other small and completely wrapped in a green shawl from under which only her little feet in fur boots could be seen. Paying no attention at all to my presence in the entry room, even though I had considered it my duty at the appearance of the two to bow to them, the small one silently went over to the big one and stood in front of her. The big one unwound the kerchief that completely covered the small one's head, unbuttoned her pelerine, and then when the liveried footman had taken those things into his care and removed her fur boots, from the wrapped-up person emerged a wonderful twelve-year-old girl in a short open-neck muslin dress, white pantalettes and tiny black slippers. She wore a black satin ribbon around her little white neck and her head was completely covered with dark-chestnut curls that went so well with her beautiful little face in front and her bare little shoulders behind, that no one, not even Karl Ivanych himself, could have convinced me that they looked that way because they had been set with a hot curling iron and wrapped since morning with strips of the *Moscow News*. It seemed to me that she had been born with that head of curls.

The most striking feature of her face was the exceptional size of her prominent, hooded eyes, which made an odd but pleasing contrast to her small mouth. Her lips were shaped in such a way, and the look in her eyes was so grave, that her general expression was the kind from which you wouldn't have expected a smile, so that when one did come it was all the more enchanting.

Hoping not to be noticed, I slipped through the doorway into the salon, where I regarded it necessary to pace back and forth, pretending to be immersed in thought and quite unaware that company had arrived. When the guests were halfway through the salon I, as if coming to, bowed with a scrape of my foot and informed them that Grandmother was in the drawing room. Mme Valakhina, whose face I liked very much, especially since I saw in it a great resemblance to that of her daughter, Sonyechka, graciously nodded.

Grandmother seemed to be very glad to see Sonyechka. She called her closer, set right a curl that had fallen onto her forehead and, looking carefully at her face, said, '*Quelle charmante enfant!*'[49] Sonyechka smiled, blushed and became so sweet that watching her made me blush too.

'I hope that you won't be bored in my home, my little friend,' Grandmother said, lifting Sonyechka's little face by the chin. 'Please enjoy yourself and dance as much as you like. Now we have one lady and two cavaliers,' she added, addressing Mme Valakhina and stretching out her hand to me.

That intimate association gave me so much pleasure that I blushed again.

Sensing that my shyness was increasing, and hearing the

clatter of another carriage, I considered it best to withdraw. In the entry room I found Princess Kornakova with her son and an improbable quantity of daughters. The daughters all looked alike: they resembled the princess and were homely, and therefore not one of them caught your eye. As they took off their pelerines and foxtails, they all started to talk at once in high-pitched little voices and to bustle about and laugh at something – no doubt at the fact that there were so many of them. Étienne was a boy of about fifteen, tall, stout, with a haggard face, sunken eyes with dark-blue circles under them and, for someone his age, enormous hands and feet. He was awkward and had a rough, unpleasant voice, but seemed very pleased with himself and was, according to my notions, precisely the sort of boy someone thrashed with a birch rod should be.

We stood facing and examining each other without a word for quite some time. Then, after moving closer, presumably to kiss, we for some reason changed our minds upon looking each other again in the eye. After the dresses of his sisters had all rustled past, I asked him, in order to make conversation, if it hadn't been crowded in the coach.

'I have no idea,' he carelessly replied. 'You see, I never ride in the coach, because as soon as I get in I start to feel sick, and Mama knows that. Whenever we go out in the evening, I always sit on the box. It's a lot more fun. You can see everything. Filipp lets me drive, and sometimes I take the whip. And sometimes, you know, I go like that! at those passing by,' he added with an expressive gesture. 'It's excellent!'

'Your highness,' said a footman, coming into the entry room, 'Filipp wants to know where you were kind enough to put the whip.'

'What do you mean, where did I put it? I gave it to him.'

'He says that you didn't.'

'Well, then I hung it on the lantern.'

'Filipp says that it isn't on the lantern either, and that it would be better for you to say that you took it and lost it, or else Filipp will have to pay for your prank out of his own pocket,' the irritated footman said, becoming increasingly exercised.

The footman, who seemed to be a dour, respectable man, was

warmly taking Filipp's side and meant to get to the bottom of
it, whatever the cost. From an involuntary sense of tact, I moved
off to the side as if I hadn't noticed anything, but the other footmen who were present reacted quite differently: they moved
closer, looking at the old servant with approval.

'Well, if I lost it, then I lost it,' Étienne said, avoiding further
explanation. 'Whatever the whip costs I'll pay. It's hilarious!' he
added, coming over to me and pulling me into the drawing room.

'No, permit me, master, but with what will you pay? I know
how you pay. You've been saying for eight months that you'll
pay back Marya Vasilyevna two kopeks, and in my own case
it's been well over a year, and Petrushka –'

'Silence, you!' the young prince shouted, livid with rage. 'See
if I don't tell everything!'

'I'll tell everything! I'll tell everything!' the footman muttered.
'It's not good, your highness!' he added with particular emphasis as we were entering the salon, and then he left to put the
pelerines away in the bin.

'Quite right!' an approving voice was heard behind us in the
entry room.

Grandmother had a special knack for using the second-person
singular and plural pronouns with a certain tone of voice in
certain situations to express her view of people. Her use of 'thou'
and 'you' inverted the generally accepted practice, with their
nuances acquiring a completely different meaning on her lips.
When the young prince came over to her, she said several words
to him, addressed him as 'you', and gazed at him with such
disdain that had I been in his place, I would have been utterly
crushed. But Étienne was clearly not a boy of that 'make-up'.
He ignored not only Grandmother's reception of him, but even
her entire person and bowed instead to the whole company, if
not gracefully then with complete nonchalance. It was Sonyechka,
however, who occupied my full attention. I remember that when
Volodya, Étienne and I were talking in the salon in a place where
Sonyechka could be seen and could see and hear us, I talked
with pleasure, and whenever I produced what to my mind was
an amusing or spirited *mot*, I said it louder and glanced around
at the door to the drawing room. But when we went off to a

different part where we could be neither seen nor heard from the drawing room, I was silent and took no more pleasure in the conversation.

The drawing room and salon gradually filled up with guests. Among them, as always at children's parties, were several older children, who didn't want to miss out on the opportunity to dance and enjoy themselves, but were taking part as if the only reason they were doing so was to please the hostess.

When the Ivins arrived, instead of the pleasure I usually experienced on seeing Seryozha, I felt a kind of strange vexation at the fact that he would see Sonyechka and that she would see him.

TWENTY-ONE

Before the Mazurka

'Well, it looks like you're going to have dancing,' Seryozha said, coming out of the drawing room and taking a new pair of kid gloves out of his pocket. 'I'll have to put my gloves on.'

'How can it be that we have no gloves?' I thought. 'I had better go upstairs and find some.'

Yet even though I dug around in all the chests, I found only our green travelling mittens in one, and in another a single kid glove that didn't suit me at all, first because it was extraordinarily old and filthy, second because it was too big, but mainly because it had no middle finger, which had probably been cut off long before by Karl Ivanych for an injured hand. Nevertheless, I put on that relic of a glove and stared at the place on my finger that was always stained with ink.

'If Natalya Savishna were here, she would surely have found some gloves among her things. I can't go downstairs looking like this, for if someone should ask me why I'm not dancing, what would I say? And I can't stay here either, since I'll certainly be missed. What shall I do?' I said to myself, throwing my hands up.

'What are you doing up here?' asked Volodya, running in. 'Go engage a partner. It's about to start.'

'Volodya,' I said in a voice verging on despair as I showed him my hand with two fingers sticking out of the filthy glove. 'Volodya, you didn't think of it either!'

'Think of what?' he asked impatiently. 'Oh! Gloves,' he added with complete indifference as he looked at my hand. 'No, I certainly didn't. We'll have to see what Grandmother says.' And without giving it another thought, he ran downstairs.

The calmness of his response to a situation that had seemed

so important to me put my mind at ease, and I hurried off to the drawing room, completely forgetting the misshapen glove on my left hand.

Cautiously approaching Grandmother's chair and lightly touching her mantle, I said to her in a whisper, 'Grandmother! What are we to do? We have no gloves!'

'What, my friend?'

'We have no gloves,' I repeated, moving closer and putting both hands on the arm of her chair.

'What's this?' she said, suddenly grabbing my left wrist. '*Voyez, ma chère,*' she continued, addressing Mme Valakhina. '*Voyez comme ce jeune homme s'est fait élégant pour danser avec votre fille.*'[50]

Grandmother held on tightly to my wrist and looked with a serious but enquiring expression at everyone present, until the curiosity of all the guests was satisfied and the laughter was general.

I would have been mortified if Seryozha had seen me then, cringing in embarrassment as I attempted in vain to pull my hand free, but I wasn't at all embarrassed in front of Sonyechka, who was laughing so hard that her curls bounced up and down beside her flushed little face and there were tears in her eyes. I realized that her laughter was too loud and natural to be mocking. On the contrary, laughing together while looking at each other seemed to draw us closer. The episode with the glove, although it could have ended badly, had the benefit of putting me at ease in the circle that had always seemed the most intimidating – that of the drawing room – and I no longer felt the least shy in the salon.

The suffering of the shy comes from uncertainty about the opinion others have of them, but once that opinion has been clearly expressed – whatever it may be – their suffering ends.

How sweet Sonyechka Valakhina was as she danced the French quadrille across from me with the awkward young prince! How sweetly she smiled as she offered me her hand *en chaîne*! How sweetly her chestnut curls bounced in time, and how naïvely she did a *jeté-assemblé* with her tiny feet! In the fifth figure, when my partner ran over to the other side, and I, waiting for the beat, got ready for my solo, Sonyechka compressed her lips in a grave expression and looked away. But there was nothing to fear. I boldly performed the *chassé en arrière* and *glissade*, and when I came even with her, I playfully showed her the glove with my two fingers sticking out. She burst out laughing and minced even more sweetly across the parquet. I remember, too, how, when we were making a circle and had all taken each other by the hand, she dipped her head and, without removing her hand from mine, rubbed her little nose against her glove. I see everything right before my eyes as if it were now, and I hear the quadrille from the *Danube Maiden*,[51] to the strains of which it all took place.

Then came the second quadrille, which I had engaged to dance with Sonyechka. Taking my place beside her, I felt an extraordinary awkwardness and had absolutely no idea what to say to her. When my silence had gone on too long, I began to fear that she might take me for a dunce and resolved, whatever the cost, to set her straight on that account. '*Vous êtes une habitante de Moscou?*' I asked her, and after her affirmative reply I continued, '*Et moi, je n'ai encore jamais fréquenté la capitale,*' relying in particular on the effect of the verb *fréquenter*.[52] I sensed, however, that although my beginning was quite splendid and completely demonstrated my lofty knowledge of the French language, continuing the conversation in that vein was beyond my ability. Our turn to dance wasn't to come for a good while yet, and the silence returned. I looked at her in dismay, wanting to know what sort of impression I had made and hoping for help from her. 'Where did you find such a hilarious glove?' she asked all of a sudden, and that question gave me great pleasure and relief. I explained that the glove belonged to Karl Ivanych, even enlarging a little ironically on the person of Karl Ivanych himself, and how ridiculous he looked when he took off his red cap, and how he once fell off a horse into a puddle while wearing a green fur-trimmed overcoat and so on. The quadrille proceeded without our noticing it. It was all very fine, but why had I made fun of Karl Ivanych? Would I really have lost Sonyechka's good opinion if I had described him with all the love and respect I actually felt?

After the quadrille ended, Sonyechka said '*Merci*' with such

a sweet expression that it was as if I really had earned her gratitude. I was delighted and beside myself with happiness and no
longer recognized myself: where had all that boldness, assurance
and even audacity come from? 'There isn't anything that could
frighten me now!' I thought, as I walked unconcernedly about
the salon. 'I'm ready for anything!'

Seryozha suggested that we be *vis-à-vis*.[53] 'All right,' I said. 'I
don't have a partner, but I'll find one.' A quick, resolute glance
around the salon established that all the ladies were taken, except
for one grown-up girl standing by the drawing-room door. A tall
young man was walking towards her with the aim, I surmised, of
asking her. He was two paces from her, while I was at the other
end of the salon. Gracefully gliding across the parquet, I flew the
entire distance separating her from me in the twinkling of an eye,
and with a scrape of my foot asked her in a firm voice for the
contredanse. The grown-up girl extended her hand to me with a
patronizing smile, and the young man was left without a partner.

I was so full of my own strength that I didn't notice the young
man's chagrin, although I did learn afterwards that he had asked
who that tousled boy was who had skipped past him and
snatched a partner right from under his nose.

TWENTY-TWO

The Mazurka

The young man from whom I had stolen a partner for the *contredanse* was dancing the mazurka in the first couple. He leapt from his place, holding his partner by the hand and, instead of doing *pas de Basques*, as Mimi had taught us, he simply ran forward. Reaching the corner, he paused, spread his legs, stamped his heel, pivoted, and then with a skipping movement made another run.

Since I had no partner for the mazurka, I sat behind Grandmother's tall armchair and watched.

'Why is he doing that?' I wondered to myself. 'That's not at all what Mimi taught us. She assured us that everyone dances the mazurka on tiptoe, moving the feet in a smooth semicircle, but it turns out it isn't danced that way at all! The Ivins and Étienne and the others are all dancing without doing *pas de Basques*, and our Volodya has adopted the new way too. It's not bad! And isn't Sonyechka a darling?! There she goes.' I was having an extraordinarily good time.

The mazurka was nearing its end. Several older men and ladies had come over to Grandmother to say goodnight before leaving. Carefully avoiding the dancers, the footmen were taking supper things to the rooms at the back. Grandmother was noticeably tired and spoke as if reluctantly, drawling her speech. The musicians were listlessly starting the same tune for the thirtieth time. The grown-up girl with whom I had danced caught sight of me as she was executing a figure, and with an arch smile – no doubt meant to please Grandmother – she led Sonyechka and one of the innumerable young princesses over to me. '*Rose ou hortie?*'[54] she asked.

'Ah, there you are!' Grandmother said, turning around in her armchair. 'Go on, my little friend, go on.'

Although at that moment I felt more like hiding my head under Grandmother's armchair than coming out from behind it, how could I refuse? I stood up and said 'rose' and glanced timidly at Sonyechka. Almost before I realized what was happening, I felt a white-gloved hand in mine, and the young princess set off ahead with a most pleasant smile, not at all suspecting that I had absolutely no idea what to do with my feet.

I now knew that *pas de Basques* were inappropriate and out of place and could even put me completely to shame, but as the mazurka's familiar strains acted on my hearing, they imparted a certain impetus to my auditory nerves, which in their turn transmitted movement to my feet. And the latter, quite involuntarily and to the astonishment of all who were watching, began to execute the fatal smooth semicircular *pas* on tiptoe. As long as we proceeded in a straight line, that was all right, but at the turn I realized that if I didn't do something, I would certainly pull ahead. In my attempt to avoid that dilemma, I paused, meaning to execute the same 'caper' the young man in the first couple had done so beautifully. But just as I was separating my legs and about to skip, the young princess, who was hurriedly circling me, looked down at my feet with an expression of dull curiosity and surprise. That look was the end of me. I was so flustered that instead of dancing, I stamped my feet in place in the strangest way, neither with the beat nor with anything else that made sense, finally coming to a complete stop. Everyone was staring at me, some with astonishment, some with curiosity, some with derision, some with compassion. Only Grandmother was completely indifferent.

'*Il ne fallait pas danser, si vous ne savez pas!*'[55] Papa's angry voice said above my ear, and, lightly pushing me away, he took the hand of my partner, performed the *tour* with her in the old-fashioned way to the loud approval of the spectators, and returned her to her place. And with that the mazurka ended.

'O Lord, why dost Thou punish me so horribly!'

———

'Everyone despises me and always will. The road to everything is closed for me: friendship, love, honours. They're all gone! Why did Volodya make signs to me that everyone could see and that didn't help? Why did the horrible young princess look at my feet that way? Why did Sonyechka . . . She's a darling, but why did she smile at that moment? Why did Papa turn red and grab me by the arm? Oh, it was awful! If only Mama were here. She wouldn't have blushed for her Nikolenka.' And her sweet likeness carried my imagination far away. I recalled the meadow in front of the house, the tall lindens in the garden, the clear pond with swallows swirling above it, a blue sky in which translucent white clouds had come to a rest, and fragrant ricks of fresh hay, among many other bright, serene memories that wafted through my distraught imagination.

TWENTY-THREE

After the Mazurka

The young man who had danced in the first couple sat down at the children's table with us during supper and was especially attentive to me, which would have greatly flattered my self-esteem, had I been able to feel anything after my disaster. But the young man wanted, I think, to cheer me up in whatever way he could. He started to joke with me, called me a brave fellow, and as soon as the grown-ups weren't looking, poured me a small glass of wine from one of the various bottles and made me drink it. Towards the end of the meal, after the butler had poured me a quarter goblet of champagne from a bottle wrapped in a napkin and the young man had insisted that he pour a full glass and had made me drink that, too, I felt a pleasant warmth throughout my body, along with a particular fondness for my merry patron, and burst out laughing at something.

Suddenly we heard the strains of the *Grossvater*[56] and everyone started to get up. With that, my friendship with the young man ended: he went off to join the grown-ups, and since I didn't dare follow him, I went from curiosity over to listen to what Mme Valakhina and her daughter were saying to each other.

'Just another half-hour,' Sonyechka said in a wheedling tone.

'Really, my angel, we can't.'

'Please, just for me,' she pleaded in an affectionate little voice.

'Well, will it really be much fun for you if I'm sick tomorrow?' Mme Valakhina said, rashly smiling.

'Then it's all right? We'll stay?' Sonyechka said, hopping with joy.

'What am I to do with you? Go and dance, then. Here's a partner for you,' she said, pointing at me.

Sonyechka offered me her hand and we ran off to the salon.

The wine I had drunk and Sonyechka's merry presence put the disastrous mazurka adventure completely out of mind. I made the most amusing moves with my feet, either imitating a horse with a little prance, or proudly lifting them high, or stamping them in place like a ram provoked by a dog, and laughing with all my heart and not worrying about the impression I might be making on anyone watching. Sonyechka didn't stop laughing either. She laughed at the fact that we were twirling in a circle, holding each other's hands; she guffawed while watching some old nobleman slowly raise his feet while stepping over a handkerchief as if it were a very hard thing to do; and she shrieked with laughter when I jumped almost to the ceiling to show how agile I was.

Passing through Grandmother's study, I glanced at myself in the mirror. My face was wet with sweat, my hair was tousled, my cowlicks stuck out even more, but my general expression was so gay and kind and healthy that I liked myself.

'If I could always be the way I am now,' I thought, 'someone might still like me.'

But when I gazed again at the beautiful little face of my partner, there was, besides that expression of mirth, health and unconcern that I had liked in my own, so much elegant, tender beauty that I grew quite vexed with myself. I realized how silly it was for *me* to hope for the attention of such a wonderful creature.

I couldn't hope for mutual feeling, so I didn't think about it. My heart was overflowing with happiness even without it. I didn't understand that besides the feeling of love that filled my heart with joy, it was possible to ask for even greater happiness and hope for more than that the feeling would never end. It was fine as it was. My heart beat like a dove, my blood flowed ceaselessly into it, and I felt like crying.

As we were walking down the hallway past the dark storage closet under the staircase, I glanced at it and thought, 'How happy I would be if I could spend a hundred years with her in that dark closet with no one knowing we were living there.'

'It really has been a lot of fun today, hasn't it?' I said in a soft, trembling voice, and quickened my step, frightened not so much by what I had said as by what I meant to say.

'Yes . . . lots!' she answered, turning her little head in my direction with such an unaffectedly warm expression that I was no longer afraid.

'Especially after supper . . . But if you only knew how sorry I am' – I wanted to say 'sad' but didn't dare – 'that you'll be leaving shortly and we won't see each other again.'

'But why not?' she said, staring at the toes of her slippers and running her little finger along the edge of the latticed screen we were walking past. 'Mama and I drive to Tverskoy Boulevard every Tuesday and Friday. Don't you go for walks?'

'We'll certainly ask to on Tuesday, and if they won't let me, then I'll run off by myself without my hat. I know the way.'

'You know what?' Sonyechka said all of a sudden. 'I always say "thou" with some of the boys who come to see us. Dost thou want to?' she added, giving her little head a shake and looking me in the eyes.

We were entering the salon just as another, livelier part of the *Grossvater* was beginning.

'If . . . you like,' I said when the music was loud enough to drown out my words.

'Don't say *you*, say *thou*,' Sonyechka corrected me with a laugh.

The *Grossvater* ended, but I still hadn't managed to utter a single sentence containing 'thou', although I thought of many in which the intimate pronoun could have been repeated several times. I just didn't have the courage to. 'Dost *thou* want to?' and 'Say *thou*' echoed in my ears and produced a kind of intoxication: I saw nothing and no one except Sonyechka. I saw her curls gathered up and tucked behind her ears, revealing parts of her forehead and temples I hadn't seen before. I saw her wrapped so snugly in her green shawl that only the tip of her nose was visible. I noticed that if she hadn't made a small opening by her mouth with her pink little fingers, she would surely have suffocated. And then as she was descending the stairs with her mother, I saw her suddenly look back and nod her little head to us before disappearing through the door.

Volodya, the Ivins, the young prince and I were all in love with Sonyechka and followed her with our eyes as we stood on the stairs. Exactly to whom she had nodded, I don't know, although at that moment I was firmly convinced it was me.

As we said goodbye to the Ivins I spoke to Seryozha in a rather free and easy and even distant way, before shaking his hand. If he realized he had that day lost all the love I felt for him, and along with it his power over me, he probably regretted it, although he tried to seem completely indifferent.

I had for the first time in my life been unfaithful in love, and for the first time had experienced the sweetness of it. I was happy to exchange a worn-out feeling of habitual devotion for a fresh one of love filled with mystery and the unknown. Besides, to fall out of love and into it at the same time is to fall in love twice as much as before.

TWENTY-FOUR

In Bed

'How could I have loved Seryozha so passionately for so long?'
I wondered as I lay in bed. 'No, he never understood or knew
how to appreciate my love and didn't deserve it. But Sonyechka!
How charming! "Dost *thou* wish?" "It's for *thee* to begin."'

Vividly picturing her little face, I hopped up onto my hands
and knees, pulled the quilt over my head, tucked it under all
around, and when there was no opening left, lay down and
luxuriated in the pleasant sensation of warmth, while immersing
myself in sweet daydreams and memories. Staring fixedly at the
lining of the quilt, I saw her as clearly as I had seen her an hour
before. I conversed with her in my mind, and that conversation,
even though it made no sense at all, gave me indescribable pleasure, inasmuch as 'thou', 'thy', 'thee' and 'thine' constantly figured
in it.

Those daydreams were so vivid that I couldn't fall asleep from
the excitement and delight, and I wanted to share that excess of
happiness with someone.

'Darling Sonyechka!' I almost said out loud, suddenly turning
over. 'Volodya, are you awake?'

'Yes,' he answered in a sleepy voice. 'What is it?'

'I'm in love, Volodya! Completely in love with Sonyechka!'

'Well, what of it?' he replied, stretching.

'Oh, Volodya! You can't imagine what's happening to me.
I've been lying here wrapped in my quilt and I saw her and talked
to her so clearly that it's just amazing. And do you know what
else? When I lie here thinking about her, it makes me terribly
sad, goodness knows why, and I feel like crying.'

Volodya shifted his body.

'The only thing I want,' I went on, 'is to be with her always, to see her always, and nothing more. Are you in love too? Admit the truth, Volodya.'

It's strange that I wanted everyone to be in love with Sonyechka and to talk about it.

'What has that got to do with you?' Volodya said, turning his face towards me. 'Maybe.'

'You don't want to sleep, you're only pretending,' I cried, noticing from his gleaming eyes that he wasn't thinking of sleep at all and had thrown off his quilt. 'Let's talk about her instead. She's a charmer, isn't she? So charming that if she said to me, "Nikolasha, jump out of the window or throw yourself in a fire!" I swear I would do it,' I said. 'I would do it at once and gladly. Oh, what charm!' I added, vividly imagining her in front of me, and in order to enjoy that image more fully, I suddenly turned back over and stuck my head under the pillow. 'I feel like crying so much, Volodya!'

'What a ninny!' he said with a grin, and, after a brief pause, 'I'm not like you at all. I think if it were possible, I would first want to sit down beside her and talk.'

'Ah, so you're also in love?' I interrupted.

'Then,' Volodya continued with a tender smile, 'then I would kiss her little fingers and eyes and lips and nose and feet. I would kiss her all over.'

'How silly!' I yelled from under the pillow.

'You don't understand anything,' Volodya scornfully replied.

'No, I do, but you don't and are saying silly things,' I said through my tears.

'Only there's nothing to cry about. What a little girl you are!'

TWENTY-FIVE

A Letter

On 16 April, almost six months after the day I've just described,
Father came upstairs during lessons and announced that we
would be going with him that night to the country. Something
about that news made my heart skip a beat, and my thoughts
turned at once to Mama.

The reason for the unexpected trip was the following letter.

Petrovskoye. 12 April.

*Only now, at ten in the evening, have I received your good
letter of 3 April, and in keeping with my usual habit, I'm answering at once. Fyodor brought it from town yesterday, but since it
was late, he gave it to Mimi this morning. And Mimi, on the
pretext that I wasn't well and was upset, kept it all day. I did in
fact have a small fever, and to tell you the truth, it's been four
days that I've been sick and in bed.*

*Please don't let that alarm you, my dear: I'm feeling quite well,
and if Ivan Vasilyevich allows it, I think I'll get up tomorrow.*

*Last Friday I went for a ride with the children, but near the
exit to the main road by the little bridge that has always scared
me, the horses got stuck in the mud. It was a beautiful day, so I
thought I would walk out to the main road while they pulled the
barouche out. When I got to the chapel I was feeling very tired
and sat down to rest, but since it took a half hour or so to round
up people to pull the carriage out, I got cold, especially my feet,
since I was wearing boots with thin soles and they were soaked.
After dinner I had chills and a fever but continued to walk around
as I usually do, and after tea I sat down with Lyubochka to play
a piece for four hands. (You won't recognize her; she's made such*

progress!) But imagine my astonishment when I noticed that I couldn't hold the measure. I tried several times, but everything in my mind was completely muddled, and there was a strange hum in my ears. I counted one, two, three, and then all of a sudden eight, fifteen, but the main thing was that I saw I was talking nonsense but still couldn't help it. Mimi finally came to my rescue and put me to bed almost by force. So there's a detailed account for you, my dear, of how I got sick and how it was my own fault. The next day I had a fairly high fever and our kind old Ivan Vasilyevich came and is still here and promises to let me back out into God's world soon. What a splendid old man he is! While I had a fever and was delirious, he stayed awake by my bedside the whole night, and now, since he knows that I'm writing, he's in the sitting room with the girls, and I can hear him from the bedroom telling them German folk tales while they die of laughter listening to him.

La belle Flamande,[57] as you call her, has been staying here with me over a week now, since her mother's off visiting somewhere, and she has shown the most sincere attachment in her care of me. She's been confiding all the secrets of her heart to me. With her beautiful face, kind heart and youthful freshness, a fine young woman in every respect might come from her if she were in good hands. But judging by her stories, she'll be completely ruined in her present society. It occurred to me that if I didn't have so many children of my own, I would be doing a good deed to take her in.

Lyubochka wanted to write to you herself, but she's already torn up her third sheet of paper and says, 'I know what a mocker Papa is: if you make even one tiny little mistake, he'll show it to everybody.' Katenka is just as darling as before, and Mimi is just as kind and tedious.

Let's talk about something serious now. You wrote that your affairs have been going badly this winter and that you'll have to use the Khabarovka money. It's even strange to me that you've asked for my consent. Doesn't everything that belongs to me also belong as much to you?

You're so kind-hearted, my dear, that from fear of upsetting me you hide the true state of your affairs, but I can guess: you've probably lost a great deal, and I'm not, cross my heart, at all upset about it. Therefore, if it can all be set right, please don't fret too much about it and don't torment yourself unnecessarily. I've grown used in regard to the children not only not to rely on your winnings but, forgive me, not even on any of your living. Your winnings give me no more pleasure than your losses cause me pain. The only thing that distresses me is your unfortunate passion for gambling, which deprives me of a part of your tender attachment and forces me to speak such bitter truths to you as I'm doing now – and God knows how painful that is for me! I won't cease praying to Him to spare us one thing . . . not poverty (what does it matter?) but the awful situation wherein the interests of the children, which I'll have to defend, come into conflict with our own. So far the Lord has heard my prayers: you haven't crossed the line beyond which we would either have to sacrifice our living, which no longer belongs to us but to the children, or . . . It's frightening to think about, but that terrible calamity has always threatened us. Yes, it's a heavy cross the Lord has sent us both!

You also wrote about the children and have returned to our old quarrel to ask my consent to send them away to school. You know my prejudice against that kind of education . . .

I don't know if you'll agree with me, my dear, but I implore you in any event to give me your promise, out of love for me, that as long as I live and even after my death, should it please God to part us, that you'll never let that happen.

You wrote that you'll have to go to Petersburg in connection with our affairs. Christ be with you, my dearest, go and come back soon. We all miss you so! The spring has been miraculously fine: the balcony door has already been removed, the path to the greenhouse has been completely dry for four days now, the peach trees are in bloom, there are only a few patches of snow here and there, the swallows have returned, and Lyubochka has brought me the first spring flowers. The doctor says that in three days or so I'll be completely well and able to breathe fresh air, and warm myself in the April sunshine. Farewell, my dear, and don't worry, please, either about my health or your losses. Finish up your business and come back to us with the children for the whole summer. I'm making wonderful plans for how we'll spend it, and the only thing needed to realize them is you.

The next part of the letter was written in French in an uneven, barely legible scribble on another piece of paper. I translate it word for word.

Don't believe what I wrote about my illness. No one suspects how serious it is. I know only that I'll never leave my bed. Don't wait another moment but come at once and bring the children. Perhaps I'll succeed in embracing you once more and in blessing them: that's my one last wish. I know what a terrible blow I'm inflicting on you, but all the same, sooner or later, from me or from others, you would have received it. But let us try with firmness and hope for God's mercy to endure this calamity. Let us submit to His will.

Don't think that what I'm writing is the delirium of a distraught imagination. On the contrary, my thoughts are exceptionally clear at this moment and I'm utterly serene. Don't console yourself with the empty hope that they're the vague, deluded forebodings of a fearful soul. No, I feel and I know, and I know because God has seen fit to reveal it to me, that I have not long to live.

Will my love for you and the children end with my life? I've realized that that is impossible. I feel too strongly at this moment to think that the feeling without which I cannot comprehend existence could ever be destroyed. My soul can't exist without my love for all of you, and I know that it will last forever, if only because a feeling like my love could not have come into being if sometime it had to end.

I won't be with you, but I'm certain that my love will remain with you always, and that thought gives such comfort to my soul that I calmly await my approaching death without fear.

I'm serene and God knows that I've always looked and even now look upon death as a transition to a better life, but why then do tears choke me? Why deprive the children of a beloved mother? Why inflict such a heavy, unexpected blow on you? Why should I die when your and the children's love has made life infinitely happy for me?

His holy will be done.

I cannot write any more from my tears. Perhaps I won't see you. But I thank you, my precious one, for all the happiness with

which you've surrounded me in this life, and I'll ask God to
reward you. Farewell, my dear. Remember that I'll be gone, but
my love will remain with you forever. Farewell, Volodya, farewell,
my angel, farewell, Nikolenka, my Benjamin.[58]
  Can it be that they'll forget me someday?!

Enclosed with the letter was the following note in French
from Mimi.

The doleful forebodings of which she speaks have been only
too well confirmed by the doctor's words. Last night she ordered
that this letter be sent at once for posting. Thinking that she had
said it in a delirium, I waited until this morning and then decided
to open it. As soon as I had done so Natalya Nikolayevna asked
me what had happened to the letter and ordered me to burn it,
if it hadn't been sent. She keeps talking about it and is sure that
it will be the death of you. Don't put off your trip if you want to
see that angel before she has left us. Excuse my scrawl. I haven't
slept for three nights. You know how much I love her!

Natalya Savishna, who spent the whole night of 11 April in
Mama's bedroom, told me that after writing the first part of the
letter, *maman* put it beside her on the bedtable and fell asleep.

'I'll admit,' Natalya Savishna said, 'that I dozed off myself in
the armchair and the stocking I was knitting fell out of my hands.
It was only in my sleep – it was sometime before one – that I
seemed to hear her talking to someone. I opened my eyes to
look: my darling was sitting on the covers with her arms crossed
like this with tears running in three streams down her face. "So,
it is over?" was all she said, and then she covered her face with
her hands. I jumped up and started to ask, "What's the matter?"'

'"Oh, Natalya Savishna, if only you knew whom I have just
seen."

'However many times I asked, she wouldn't say anything
more, but only told me to hand her the bedtable, wrote something else, and told me to seal the letter in her presence and send
it at once. After that, everything got worse and worse.'

TWENTY-SIX

What Awaited Us in the Country

The travelling barouche arrived at the front steps of the Petrovskoye house on 18 April. Driving out of Moscow, Papa was preoccupied and, when Volodya asked him if *maman* was ill, he looked at him sadly and silently nodded. During the trip he was noticeably calmer, but as we got closer to home, his expression grew increasingly sombre, and when, on getting out of the barouche, he asked the breathless Foka, who had run from the house, 'Where's Natalya Nikolayevna?' his voice was unsteady and there were tears in his eyes. With a quick glance at us, the kind old Foka lowered his eyes, turned aside to open the door to the entryway, and answered, 'It's the sixth day now that my lady has been confined to her bedroom.'

Milka, who I later learned had whined pitifully from the very first day that *maman* got sick, joyfully rushed to Papa and licked his hands, but he pushed her aside and passed on to the drawing room, and then to the sitting room with its door leading directly to the bedroom. The closer he got to that room, the more his movements betrayed his anxiety. On entering the sitting room, he proceeded on tiptoe, barely breathing, and crossed himself before taking hold of the latch of the closed door. At that moment the tear-stained, uncombed Mimi ran in from the hallway. 'Oh, Pyotr Aleksandrovich!' she said in a whisper with an expression of genuine despair, and then, noticing that Papa was turning the handle of the latch, she added almost inaudibly, 'You can't go in that way; you'll have to enter through the maids' room.'

Oh, how cruelly that affected my young imagination, already disposed to grief by a terrible foreboding!

We went to the maids' room. In the hallway we ran into the

halfwit Akim, who had always amused us with his faces, but this time not only did he not seem funny to me, but nothing struck me so painfully as the sight of his mindlessly indifferent gaze. In the maids' room two young women who were sitting over some work got to their feet to bow to us, but with such sorrowful expressions that it terrified me. After passing through Mimi's room, Papa opened the door to the bedroom and we went in. The two windows to the right of the door were covered with shawls. Natalya Savishna was sitting next to one of them with spectacles on her nose, knitting a stocking. She didn't kiss us as she usually did, but merely got to her feet and gazed at us through her spectacles with tears streaming down her face. I didn't like it that, although they had been perfectly calm before, they all started to cry as soon as they saw us.

To the left of the door stood a screen and behind the screen the bed, a little table, a small chest filled with medicines, and a large armchair in which the doctor was dozing. Beside the bed stood a young, very fair, remarkably beautiful young woman in a white morning gown with the sleeves pushed slightly back, who was applying ice to *maman*'s forehead, but I still couldn't see *maman* herself.

The young woman was *La belle Flamande*, about whom *maman* had written and who would later play such an important role in the life of our family. As soon as we entered, she removed her hand from *maman*'s head and rearranged the folds of her own gown over her breast and then said in a whisper, 'She's unconscious.'

I was overwhelmed with grief at that moment, but involuntarily took in all the details. It was almost dark in the room and hot, and it smelled of a mixture of mint, eau de cologne, camomile and Hoffmann's anodyne. The odour made such an impression on me that not only when I smell it now but even when I simply remember it, my imagination instantly transports me to that dismal, stuffy room and reproduces the smallest details of that terrible moment.

Maman's eyes were open, but she saw nothing. I'll never forget that frightening gaze! So much suffering was expressed in it!

We were led out.

When I asked Natalya Savishna later about Mama's last moments, this is what she said: 'After you were led out, my darling continued to toss and turn a long time, as if something was crushing her right here. Then her head slipped off the pillows and she dozed so quietly and calmly that she was like a heavenly angel. I had just gone out to see why something hadn't been brought for her to drink, and when I came back she, the poor dear, was throwing off the bed clothes and beckoning to your papa to come to her. He bent over her, but it was clear that she didn't have the strength to say what she wanted to; she only parted her lips and moaned, "O God! O Lord! The children! The children!" I wanted to run and get you, but Ivan Vasilyevich stopped me and said, "You had better not; it will only upset her more." After that she just raised her arm and let it drop. What she meant by that God alone knows. I think she was blessing you unseen, since the Lord had not, right before her final end, allowed her to see her little ones. Then my darling propped herself up, put her hands like this, and started saying in such a voice that I can't bear to remember it, "Holy Mother, don't abandon them!" Then the pain reached her heart and you could see in her eyes that the poor thing was suffering terribly. She fell back on the pillows and bit down on the sheet, while the tears, little master, poured down her cheeks.'

'Well, and what happened then?' I asked.

Natalya Savishna couldn't say any more, and turned away and bitterly wept.

Maman died in dreadful agony.

TWENTY-SEVEN
Grief

The next day, late in the evening, I wanted to look at her again and, overcoming an involuntary feeling of fear, I quietly opened the door and tiptoed into the salon.

The coffin stood in the middle of the room on a table with sooty candles in tall silver candlesticks around it. In a far corner sat a lector reading from the Psalter in a low monotone.

I paused at the door and looked around, but my eyes were so swollen from crying and my nerves were in such a jumble that I couldn't make out anything at all. It was somehow all strangely blended: the candlelight, the brocade, the velvet, the tall candlesticks, the pink lace-trimmed pillow, the funeral band,[59] the beribboned bonnet, and something translucent with a waxy colour. I got up onto a chair to examine her face, but instead found that same pale-yellow translucent thing. I couldn't believe that it was her face. I stared harder at it, and little by little I began to make out her dear, familiar features. I shuddered in horror upon assuring myself that it was *maman*, but why were her closed eyes so sunken? And what was the reason for that awful pallor and the dark smudge under the translucent skin of one cheek? What made her whole face so severe and cold? Why were her lips so pale and their placement so beautiful and majestic, expressing such unearthly serenity that a cold shiver ran over my scalp and down my spine as I gazed at them?

As I looked, I sensed that some mysterious, irresistible power was drawing my eyes to her lifeless face. I continued to look at it, but my imagination limned pictures teeming with life and happiness. I forgot that the dead body lying in front of me, and at which I was senselessly staring, as if at an object that had nothing in common with my memories, was *maman*. I imagined her one way and then another – as lively, gay, smiling – until I was suddenly struck by some feature of her pallid face as my gaze dwelt on it, and I remembered the horrible reality with a shudder, even as I continued to gaze. And then dreams again replaced the reality, and again awareness of the reality dispersed the dreams. In the end my imagination grew weary and stopped deceiving me, and awareness of the reality vanished, too, and I became completely oblivious. I don't know how long I remained in that state, or what it consisted of; I know only that for a time I ceased to be aware of my own existence and experienced a kind of lofty, inexplicably pleasing, yet sad bliss.

Perhaps as it was flying away to a better world, her beautiful soul looked back with sadness on the one in which it had left us, saw my sorrow, took pity, and on the wings of love and with a heavenly smile of compassion returned to earth to comfort and bless me.

The door creaked and another lector entered the room to relieve the first. The sound roused me, and the first thought that came to me was that since I wasn't crying and was standing on a chair in a posture that had nothing touching about it, the reader might take me for an unfeeling boy who had climbed on to the chair from mischief or curiosity, and I crossed myself, bowed and started to cry.

Remembering my impressions now, I find that my only real grief was that moment of oblivion. I didn't stop crying before the funeral or after it, and was overwhelmed with sadness, although I'm ashamed to recall it now, since there was always an admixture of pride in it: either a desire to show that I was more unhappy than everyone else, or a concern about the impression that I was making on others, or an idle curiosity that led to observations about Mimi's mobcap and the faces of the rest of those present. I despised myself for not experiencing only grief, and tried to conceal the other feelings, and that made my sorrow insincere and unnatural. Moreover, I took a kind of pleasure in knowing that I was unfortunate and tried to heighten that awareness, and, more than anything else, that egotistical feeling stifled the genuine sorrow in me.

After sleeping soundly and peacefully through the night, as always happens after a great sadness, I awoke with dried tears and calmed nerves. At ten we were called for the memorial service that came before the procession. The room was full of weeping servants and peasants who had come to bid farewell to their mistress. During the service I wept befittingly, crossed myself and bowed to the ground, but I didn't pray from my heart and was rather unfeeling. I worried about whether the new jacket they had put on me was too tight in the armpits, I thought about how to keep the knees of my trousers from getting too soiled, and I engaged in furtive scrutiny of everyone present. Father stood at the head of the coffin, was as white as his handkerchief, and was holding back his tears with conspicuous effort. His tall figure in its black tailcoat, his pale expressive face, and his ever graceful, confident movements as he crossed himself, bowed and brushed the ground with his hand, took a candle from the priest or stepped over to the coffin, produced a remarkable impression. But, I don't know why, I didn't care for it in him that he could, in fact, seem so impressive at such a moment. Mimi leaned against the wall and seemed barely able to stand. Her dress was wrinkled and flecked with down, her mobcap was pushed over to the side, her eyes were swollen and red, her head shook, and she sobbed unceasingly in a harrowing voice and kept covering her face with her handkerchief and hands. To me it seemed that she was doing it all to hide her face from view and gain a brief respite from her feigned sobbing. I remembered her saying to Father the day before that *maman*'s death was such a terrible blow that she had no hope of ever recovering from it, for it had deprived her of everything, and that the angel, as she called *maman*, had not forgotten her at the brink of death, and had indicated a desire to provide for her and Katenka's future forever. She wept bitter tears as she reported that, and perhaps her grief was genuine, but it wasn't purely or entirely so. Lyubochka, wet with tears and wearing a short black dress trimmed with weepers, bowed her head and rarely looked at the coffin, her face expressing only childish terror. Katenka stood beside her mother and was as rosy as ever, despite her solemn face. Volodya's forthright nature was just as forthright in grief: he either stood preoccupied, directing an unwavering gaze at some object, or his mouth would suddenly start to twist and he would hurriedly cross himself and bow. All the other people at the funeral were unbearable to me. The comforting phrases they spoke to Father – that she was in a better place, that she wasn't made for this world – provoked in me a kind of vexation.

What right did they have to speak about and weep for her? Some of them referred to us as 'orphans'. As if we didn't know without them that that's what children are called who have no mother! It pleased them, apparently, to be the first to use that name, much as people hurry to call a just married young woman 'madame' for the first time.

In a far corner of the salon, nearly hidden behind the open door of the pantry, knelt a grey, bent old woman. Clasping her hands and looking up towards heaven, she didn't weep but prayed. Her soul strained towards God, she entreated Him to reunite her with the one she had loved more than anything in the world, and she fervently hoped that it would come soon.

'That's who truly loved her!' I thought, and felt ashamed of myself.

The service ended. The face of the deceased was still uncovered, and one after another all those present, except us, started to file past the coffin to pay their respects.

Among the last to bid farewell to the deceased was a peasant woman carrying a pretty five-year-old girl whom, goodness knows why, she had brought with her. I had accidentally dropped my damp handkerchief and was going to pick it up, but no sooner had I bent over than I was startled by a terrible, piercing cry full of such horror that if I should live to be a hundred I'll never forget it, and whenever I do remember it, a cold shiver always passes through my body. I looked up – standing on the stool beside the coffin was the same peasant woman, struggling to hold the little girl, who had thrown her own frightened little face back and was staring goggled-eyed at the face of the deceased and screaming in a frenzied, terrifying voice and flailing her arms. I cried out in another voice that was, I think, even more terrible than the one that had frightened me, and ran out of the room.

It was only then that I understood the source of the strong, oppressive smell that had filled the room together with the odour of frankincense, and the thought that the face of the one whom I loved more than anything in the world, a face that had just a few days before been suffused with such beauty and tenderness, could nonetheless evoke so much horror, revealed to me as if for the first time the bitter truth and filled my soul with despair.

TWENTY-EIGHT
Last Sad Memories

Maman was gone, but our life continued the same round as before: we went to bed and got up at the same time and in the same rooms; morning and evening tea and the other meals were served at their regular times; and the tables and chairs remained in their usual places. Nothing in the house or in our way of life had changed, except that she was gone.

I thought that after such a calamity everything would have to change. Our usual way of life seemed an affront to her memory and reminded me all too vividly of her absence.

The day before the burial, I was feeling sleepy after dinner and went to Natalya Savishna's room, intending to get in her soft feather bed under her warm quilt. Natalya Savishna was lying down, probably asleep, when I came in. Hearing my footsteps, she sat up, threw off the wool shawl that had covered her head to keep off the flies, and put her legs over the edge of the bed, while adjusting her mobcap.

Since I had gone to her room many times before to nap after dinner, she guessed what had brought me this time, and getting up from the bed she said to me, 'Come for a rest then, darling? Go ahead and lie down.'

'What do you mean, Natalya Savishna?' I said, taking her hand. 'That isn't the reason I came at all. I just came . . . And you're tired yourself. Why don't you lie down instead?'

'No, little master, I've slept enough,' she said, even though I knew that she hadn't slept for three days. 'Anyway, I don't feel like it now,' she added with a deep sigh.

I wanted to talk to Natalya Savishna about our calamity. I

knew how sincere and loving she was, and having a cry with her would be a comfort to me.

'Natalya Savishna,' I said after a brief silence as I sat down on the bed, 'did you expect it?'

The old woman looked at me in bewilderment, probably not understanding why I was asking her that.

'Could anyone have expected it?' I repeated.

'Oh, little master,' she said, looking at me with an expression of tender compassion, 'not only didn't I expect it, I don't believe it even now. It's high time for an old woman like me to lay her old bones to rest, but I've outlived them all: the old master, your grandfather Prince Nikolay Mikhailovich, eternal memory to him, and my two brothers and my sister Annushka, and all of them younger than I am, little master; and now, clearly for my sins, I've come to outlive her, too. His holy will be done! He took her because she was worthy and He needs good people there, too.'

That simple thought impressed and comforted me, and I moved closer to Natalya Savishna. She folded her hands over her breast and looked up. Her moist, sunken eyes expressed a great but tranquil sadness. It was her firm hope that God had not separated her for long from the one on whom all the power of her love had been concentrated for so many years.

'Yes, little master, it doesn't seem so very long ago that I took care of her and swaddled her and she called me "Nasha".[60] She would run to me, take hold of me with her little hands, and start to kiss me and say, "My Nashik, my handsome one, my little turkey hen." And I would say in fun, "That isn't so, missy, you don't love me. Why, when you grow up to be a big girl and get married, you'll forget all about your Nasha." Then she would start thinking. "No," she would say, "it would be better not to get married if I can't take Nasha with me. I'll never leave Nasha." But she didn't wait, and now she's left me. And she did love me, but now she's gone! But whom didn't she love, to tell the truth of it? No, little master, you must never forget your mama; she wasn't a human being but an angel from above. When her soul goes to the kingdom of heaven, she'll love you there, too, and rejoice in you.'

'But Natalya Savishna, why do you say *when* her soul goes to the kingdom of heaven?' I asked. 'It's already there now, I think.'

'No, little master,' Natalya Savishna said, lowering her voice and moving closer to me on the bed. 'Her soul's still here.'

And she gestured upward. She spoke almost in a whisper, and with such feeling and conviction that I involuntarily looked up at the cornices, expecting to see something there.

'Before the soul of a righteous person goes to heaven, it passes through forty ordeals, little master, for forty days, and may still be in its home.'

She talked that way for a long time, and did so with such simplicity and conviction it was as if she were talking about quite ordinary things that she herself had seen and no one would even think of doubting. I held my breath as I listened, and although I didn't understand most of what she said, I believed her completely.

'Yes, little master, she's here, watching us now and perhaps listening to what we're saying,' Natalya Savishna concluded.

And looking down, she fell silent. She needed a handkerchief to dry her tears. She got up, looked directly at me and said in a voice shaking in agitation, 'The Lord has moved me many steps closer to Him with this. What's left for me here? For whom shall I live? Whom shall I love?'

'But don't you love us?' I said reproachfully, barely holding back my tears.

'God knows how much I love you, my darlings, but I've never loved and cannot love anyone the way I loved her.'

She couldn't say any more, and turned away from me and broke into loud sobs.

I was no longer thinking about sleep. We silently sat across from each other and wept.

Just then Foka came into the room. Noticing our state and probably not wishing to disturb us, he remained by the door and watched in silence.

'What have you come for, Fokasha?' Natalya Savishna asked, drying her tears with her handkerchief.

'A pound and a half of raisins, four pounds of sugar and three pounds of rice for the *kutya*,[61] ma'am.'

'In a moment, in a moment, my dear,' Natalya Savishna said, hurriedly taking some snuff and quickly stepping over to a trunk. The last traces of the sorrow produced by our conversation disappeared as she set about her duties, which she regarded as very important.

'Why four pounds?' she asked querulously, as she got out the sugar and weighed it on her scale. 'Three and a half will be plenty.'

And she removed several pieces from the scale.

'And what do they mean by asking for more rice when I gave them eight pounds only yesterday? You may do as you like, Foka Demidych, but I won't give them the rice. That Vanka's glad there's a to-do in the house now: he thinks no one will notice. No, I'm not going to be a party to pilfering the masters' property. Whoever heard of such a thing? Eight pounds!'

'But what can I do, ma'am? He says it's all gone.'

'Well, here, take it, then! Take it! Let him have it!'

I was struck at the time by the shift from the tender feeling of her conversation with me to peevishness and petty calculation. Reflecting on it afterwards, I realized that, regardless of what was in her heart, she still had enough presence of mind to do her work, and force of habit pulled her back to her usual activities. Grief affected her so powerfully that she found it unnecessary to hide her ability to deal with other things. She wouldn't even have understood where such an idea could have come from.

Vanity is the feeling most incompatible with genuine grief, but it's so tightly intertwined in human nature that it's quite rare for even the strongest grief to drive it out. Vanity in grief is expressed in the desire to seem grief-stricken or miserable or strong, and those base desires, which we don't admit but which almost never leave us, even in the greatest sorrow, deprive our sorrow of its force and dignity and sincerity. But Natalya Savishna was so profoundly affected by her unhappiness that not a single desire remained in her heart, and she lived by habit alone.

After handing over the requested provisions to Foka, and reminding him of the pie that would have to be baked as a treat for the parish priests, she let him go, picked up the stocking she was knitting and sat back down beside me.

We started to talk about the same thing again, and wept again, and dried our tears again.

Those talks with Natalya Savishna were repeated every day. Her quiet tears and calm, devout words provided comfort and relief.

But we were soon parted. Three days after the funeral, the entire household moved to Moscow and I was destined never to see her again.

It was only with our arrival that Grandmother received the terrible news, and her grief was extraordinary. We weren't allowed in to see her, since she was delirious the whole week and the doctors were concerned for her life, all the more since she not only refused to take any medication but wouldn't talk to anyone, sleep or eat. Sometimes while sitting alone in her room in her armchair, she would suddenly start laughing and then sob convulsively without tears or scream terrible or meaningless words in a frenzied voice. It was the first powerful grief to affect her, and it brought her to despair. She needed to blame someone for her unhappiness, and would say appalling things and make threats with exceptional violence, jump up from her armchair, move around the room with long, rapid strides, and then collapse in a swoon.

One time I went into her room. She was sitting in her armchair as usual and seemed calm enough, although I was struck by her gaze. Her eyes were open very wide, but with an unfocused, absent look. She was staring straight at me, but probably didn't see me. Her lips slowly started to smile and she began to speak in a tender, touching voice: 'Come here, my friend, come here, my angel.' I thought she was speaking to me and moved closer, but she wasn't looking at me at all. 'Ah, if you only knew, dear heart, how much I've suffered and how happy I am that you've come.' I realized she was imagining that she saw *maman* and I stopped. 'And they told me you were gone,' she continued with a frown. 'What nonsense! Could you really die before me?' And she started to laugh in terrifying, hysterical guffaws.

Only those capable of strong love can experience strong grief, but the very need to love serves as a counterweight to their grief and heals them. For that reason, a person's mental nature is even more resilient than his physical one. Grief never kills.

A week later Grandmother was finally able to cry and she got better. Her first thought, when she was herself again, was of us, and her love for us increased. We didn't leave her armchair. She wept quietly, and talked about *maman* and tenderly petted us.

It would never have occurred to anyone observing Grandmother's sorrow that she exaggerated it, and the expression of that sorrow was powerful and moving, but, I don't know why, I had greater sympathy for Natalya Savishna, and I remain convinced to this day that no one loved *maman* more sincerely and purely, or felt greater sorrow at her passing, than that simple-hearted and loving creature.

With my mother's death, the happy period of childhood ended and a new one began, that of boyhood. But since my memories of Natalya Savishna belong to that first period, and she had such a strong and beneficial influence on my outlook and the development of my sensibility, even though I never saw her again, I'll say a few more words about her and her passing.

As those who had remained behind in the country told me later, she got very bored with the lack of anything to do after we had gone. Although the trunks remained in her care and she hadn't stopped rummaging in them or moving things around or weighing and distributing them, she missed the noise and bustle of the country house occupied by masters she had known since childhood. Grief, the change in her way of life, and the lack of responsibilities aggravated the infirmities of age to which she was already prone. A year after Mama passed away, she developed dropsy and took to her bed.

It was hard, I think, for Natalya Savishna to live alone, and harder still for her to die that way in the large, empty Petrovskoye house without either family or friends. Everyone in the house liked and respected her, but she wasn't on intimate terms with any of them and took pride in that. She felt that in her position as housekeeper, as someone who enjoyed the confidence of her masters and was responsible for so many trunks of every kind of property, friendship with anyone would surely have led to partiality and tolerance of wrongdoing. For that reason, or perhaps merely because she had nothing in common with the other servants, she remained aloof from them all and said that she had neither kith nor kin in the house, and would allow no pilfering of the masters' property.

Confiding her feelings to God in heartfelt prayer, she sought and found solace, but sometimes in those moments of weakness to which all are subject, when the best comfort is the sympathy and tears of another living creature, she would lift up onto her bed her favourite pug (which would lick her hands and fix its yellow eyes on her) and talk to it and quietly weep as she petted it. Whenever the pug would start to whimper, she would soothe it and say, 'That's enough. I know even without you that I'll die soon.'

A month before she died she took out of her own trunk some white calico, white muslin and pink ribbons and, with the help of the young woman who looked after her, made a white dress and bonnet for herself and gave instructions down to the smallest detail about everything else required for her funeral. She also went through all the household trunks and with the utmost care, by inventory list, transferred their contents to the steward's wife. Then she got out two silk dresses and an old shawl that had been given to her by my grandmother, along with my grandfather's gold-braided army uniform, also given to her to use in whatever way she wanted. Thanks to her care, the braiding was like new, and the cloth was untouched by moths.

Just before she died, she expressed the wish that one dress – the pink one – should be given to Volodya to make a dressing gown or quilted jacket, that the other – the puce one with checks – should go to me for the same purpose, while the shawl should be left to Lyubochka. The uniform she bequeathed to whichever of us should become an officer first. All the rest of her possessions and money, except for forty roubles she set aside for her burial and for prayers on her behalf, she left to her brother, who had long since been freed and was living in some distant province where he led a most dissolute life, as a result of which she had no dealings with him at all.

When the brother turned up to claim his inheritance, and the entire property of the deceased turned out to be no more than

twenty-five paper roubles, he couldn't believe it, and
an old woman who had spent sixty years in a rich
been in charge of everything, and had lived her whole li..
and worried about every little scrap, couldn't possibly have left
so little behind. But it really was so.

Natalya Savishna suffered for two months from her illness
and endured her suffering with true Christian forbearance: she
didn't grumble or complain but only prayed continually to God,
as had always been her custom. An hour before she died she
made her confession with quiet joy and received Communion
and unction.

She asked all the servants to forgive her if she had done them
any offence, and she asked her confessor, Father Vasily, to convey
to all of us that she didn't know how to express her gratitude
for our kindness, and begged us to forgive her if from foolishness
she had offended any of us, 'Although I was never a thief and
can say that I never took a single thread at the masters' expense.'
That was the one quality she valued in herself.

After putting on the gown and bonnet she had prepared, and
propping herself up on her pillows, she remembered that she
had left nothing for the poor. She got out ten roubles and asked
the priest to distribute them in the parish, and then continued
to talk with him until the very end. And then she crossed herself,
lay down, and breathed her last, saying the name of God with
a joyful smile.

She departed life without regret, not fearing death but accept-
ing it as a blessing. That is often said, but how rarely it happens!
Natalya Savishna could meet death without fear, because she
was dying with a steadfast faith after fulfilling the law of the
Gospels. Her whole life had been one of pure, unselfish love and
sacrifice.

What if her beliefs could have been loftier or her life directed
towards a higher goal – was that pure soul any the less deserving of love and wonder because of that?

She accomplished the best and greatest thing in this life: she
died without regret or fear.

At her request, she was buried near the chapel that stands over
Mama's grave. The mound under which she lies is overgrown

with nettles and burdocks and surrounded by a black railing, and I never forget to go from the chapel to that railing to prostrate myself.

Sometimes I linger in silence between the chapel and the railing. Painful memories are awakened in my soul. The thought comes to me: could Providence really have bound me to those two beings only to make me regret their loss forever?

Boyhood

ONE

A Trip in Stages

Two carriages are again waiting by the front steps of the Petrov-skoye house, one a coach in which Mimi, Katenka and Lyubochka have taken their places, with the chambermaid Masha and the steward Yakov *himself* up on the box, and the other a britzka in which Volodya and I are to ride with the footman Vasily, recently added to our household.

Papa, who's supposed to join us in Moscow in a few days, stands hatless on the steps, making the sign of the cross at the britzka and the coach's window.

'Well, Christ be with you! Get going!' Yakov and the coachmen (we're using our own horses) doff their caps and cross themselves. 'Gee-up! Gee-up! God speed us!' The coach and britzka start to bounce along the uneven road, and the birches of the wide avenue slip past, one after another. I'm not sad at all: my mental gaze is directed not at what I'm leaving behind, but at what lies ahead. The farther I am from the things linked to the painful memories that have filled my imagination, the less power those memories have, and the more rapidly they're replaced by a joyful sense of life full of strength, vitality and hope.

Rarely have I spent as many days, I won't say merrily, since I was still somehow ashamed to yield to merriment, but pleasantly and well as during the four days of our trip. Gone from sight were the closed door of Mama's room that I had been unable to walk by without a shudder; the piano that we not only didn't go near, but couldn't even look at without a kind of dread; our mourning clothes (we were dressed in simple travel attire); and all the other things that, by vividly bringing to mind our irreparable loss, made me wary of any expression of life, lest I somehow insult the memory of *her*. But now picturesque new places and things continually capture my attention and interest, and springtime nature fills my heart with joyful feelings of contentment with the present and bright hope for the future.

Very early the next morning the pitiless and, as always happens with people in new employment, overly zealous Vasily yanks off my blanket and announces that everything's ready and that it's time to go. Scrunch down, pretend, or show anger as you may to prolong your sweet morning slumber, if only another quarter-hour, it's obvious from Vasily's determined face that he's implacable and prepared to yank the blanket off another twenty times, so you jump out of bed and run out to the yard to wash.

The samovar, into which Mitka the postilion is blowing, red as a lobster, is already boiling in the entryway. Outside it's damp and misty, as if steam were rising from pungent dung. With a bright, merry light, sunshine illuminates the eastern part of the sky, along with the thatched roofs, lustrous with dew, of the spacious open sheds that surround the yard. Tethered in the sheds beside rough-hewn feeding troughs are our horses, their regular chewing quite audible. A shaggy black dog, curled up until dawn on a dry dung-hill, lazily stretches and then sets off at a trot across the yard, wagging his tail. The innkeeper's bustling wife opens the creaking gate, drives her bemused cows out onto the street, along which the rest of the herd is already clattering, mooing and bellowing, and exchanges a word with her sleepy neighbour. Filipp, his shirtsleeves rolled back, cranks up a bucket from the deep well, and then with a splash pours the glistening water into an oak trough, next to which just awakened ducks are bathing in a puddle. I gaze with pleasure at Filipp's impressive face with its broad beard, and at the thick veins and muscles that stand out on his powerful forearms whenever he exerts himself.

Movement is heard where Mimi and the girls have been sleeping behind the partition over which we had talked the night before. Masha, holding various articles that she tries to hide from our curious eyes with her dress, runs by more and more often, until at last the door opens and we're called in for tea.

Vasily, in a paroxysm of excess zeal, keeps running into the room to carry out one thing or another, wink at us, and plead in every way with Marya Ivanovna to make an early start of it. The horses have been harnessed and from time to time express their impatience by shaking their bells. The travelling bags, trunks and large and small boxes have all been packed, and we take our places again. But instead of seats, we find a pile of things in the britzka and simply cannot understand how they were stowed away the day before and how we'll sit today. A walnut tea caddy with a triangular lid that's been transferred to us in the britzka and put under me provokes my fiercest indignation. But Vasily says that it will all press down, and I have no choice but to believe him.

The sun has just risen above the dense white cloud covering the east, and the entire area shines with a serenely joyous light. Everything around me is so beautiful, and there's such calm and ease in my soul . . . The road ahead twists like a broad, unruly ribbon through fields of dry stubble and green glistening with dew. Here and there beside the road a gloomy crack willow or a young birch with small sticky leaves casts a long, motionless shadow over the road's dry ruts and shoots of verdant grass. The monotonous sound of our wheels and bells fails to drown out the singing of the larks that swirl beside the road. The odour of dust, moth-eaten cloth and something sour peculiar to the britzka is overwhelmed by the fragrance of morning, and I feel a joyful restlessness in my soul, and an urge to do something – a sure sign of pleasure.

I didn't have time to say my prayers at the inn, and since I've noticed more than once that some misfortune befalls me whenever I forget that ritual, whatever the reason, I try to correct my mistake: I remove my cap, face a corner of the britzka, say my prayers and cross myself under my jacket so no one will see. But a myriad of different things distracts my attention, and I absently repeat the same words of the prayer over and over.

Then on the path winding alongside the road, slow-moving female figures appear – pilgrims. Their heads are tied with dirty kerchiefs, they have birch-bark knapsacks on their backs, and their feet are bound with dirty, ragged footcloths and shod with clumsy bast shoes. Rhythmically swinging their staffs with barely a look at us, they move along one after another at a slow, deliberate pace, and I wonder where they're going and why, and if their journey will last long, and whether the elongated shadows they cast on the road will soon join the shadow of the crack willow they'll have to pass. Then a barouche and four using post horses hurtles towards us. Two seconds, and the friendly, curious faces looking at us five feet away have already flashed by, and it seems strange in a way that those faces have nothing in common with me and that I may never see them again.

And then cantering along the side of the road come two shaggy, lathered horses in collars with the traces lashed to their breech-bands, and immediately behind them on a third horse a young coachman singing a drawn-out song with his felt hat cocked to one side and his long legs in their tall boots dangling over the flanks of his horse, above whose withers hangs a shaftbow on which a barely audible bell jingles from time to time. His face and posture express so much lazy, carefree contentment that to be a coachman riding home while singing sad songs seems to me the pinnacle of happiness. Far beyond a ravine, the green roof of a village church stands out against the light-blue sky, and behind it the village itself with its green orchard and red manor-house roof. Who lives in that house? Are there children, a father, a mother and a teacher? Why shouldn't we drive over there and make their acquaintance? Then a long train of enormous carts approaches, each drawn by a troika of sturdy, well-nourished horses that we have to skirt to get past. 'What are you carrying?' Vasily asks the first carter, who, with huge feet hanging over the footboard and a little whip in his hand, follows us with a blank stare and replies only when it's no longer possible to hear him. 'What goods are you carrying?' Vasily says to the next cart, in the enclosed front of which another carter lies under new bast matting. A head with light-brown hair, a ruddy face and a ginger beard peeks out from under the bast for a moment, glances with indifferent contempt at our britzka, then disappears again; and the thought occurs to me that those carters have no idea who we are or where we've come from or where we're going.

Absorbed for an hour and a half in diverse observations, I've paid no attention to the crooked numbers on the mileposts. But now the sun is starting to bake my head and back, the road has got dustier, the triangular lid of the tea caddy has begun to bother me a lot, and I shift my position several times: I'm hot, uncomfortable and bored. My attention turns to the mileposts and the numbers inscribed on them, and I make various arithmetical calculations regarding the time of our arrival at the next inn. 'Eight miles is one third of twenty-four, and it's twenty-seven to Liptsy, which means that we've covered one third and how much?' and so on.

'Vasily,' I say, when I notice that he's begun to nod off on the box, 'be a good fellow and let me up there.' He agrees. We trade places, and he immediately starts to snore and to sprawl in such a way that there's hardly any room in the britzka for anyone else, whereas from the high place I occupy a most pleasant view opens up: our four horses, Neruchinskaya, Sexton, Left Shaft and Apothecary, the qualities of each given careful scrutiny by me down to the smallest detail and nuance.

'Why is Sexton the right trace horse today and not the left, Filipp?' I ask a bit timidly.

'Sexton?'

'And Neruchinskaya isn't pulling at all,' I say.

'Sexton can't be harnessed on the left,' Filipp says, ignoring my last remark. 'He's not the kind of horse to be harnessed on the left. On the left you need the kind of horse that, in a word, is a horse, and he isn't a horse of that kind.'

And with those words, Filipp leans to the right, jerking the reins as hard as he can, and starts to whip poor Sexton on the back and the legs in a special way from below, even though Sexton is trying with all his strength and turning the whole britzka. Filipp abandons that manoeuvre only when he feels a need to rest and for some reason to push his hat to the side, even though it had sat very firmly and well on his head before. I take advantage of that lucky moment to ask Filipp to let me 'drive for a while'. He gives me first one rein and then another, until all six and the whip are in my hands and I'm supremely happy. I try to imitate Filipp in every way and ask him how I'm doing, even though it usually ends with his remaining dissatisfied: he says that this one is pulling too much or that one isn't pulling at all, and then he sticks his elbow in front of me and takes back the reins. The heat grows more intense, the fleecy clouds begin to expand like soap bubbles, higher and higher, until they start to merge and take on dark-grey shadows. A hand holding a bottle and a small packet reaches out of one of the coach's windows.

Up on the box again, Vasily jumps from the moving britzka with astonishing agility and brings back some cheese tarts and kvass.

On steep slopes we get out of the carriages and sometimes race each other down to the bridge, while Vasily and Yakov, after putting a slight drag on the wheels, support the coach on either side with their hands, as if they could keep it from tipping over. Then with Mimi's permission, Volodya gets in the coach, or I do, while Lyubochka or Katenka comes over to the britzka. Those changes of place are a source of delight for the girls, since they rightly find that it's a lot more fun in the britzka. Sometimes when passing through a grove during the heat, we let the coach go on ahead and tear off green branches to make a bower in the britzka. The moving bower then chases after the coach at full speed, and Lyubochka screams in her most piercing voice, something she never fails to do on any occasion that gives her great pleasure.

And then comes the village where we'll have dinner and a rest. We've already smelled it – the smoke, birch tar and bread-rings – and heard the sound of voices, hoof beats and wheels. Our harness bells make a different sound than they do in the open fields, and appearing on either side of the road are thatched peasant huts with carved wooden porches and little windows with red and green shutters from which, here and there, the face of a curious peasant woman peers out. Then we see peasant boys and girls in nothing but their smocks. Their eyes open wide and their arms spread apart, they either remain standing where they are, or else – their bare little feet taking short, rapid steps in the dust – they run after the carriages and, ignoring Filipp's threatening movements, try to climb up onto the travelling bags strapped on behind. And then red-haired innkeepers hurry out to the carriages from both sides and with enticing words and gestures try one after another to tempt us in as we pass. 'Whoa!' A gate swings open with a screak, the swingletrees scrape against it, and we enter a yard. Four hours of rest and freedom!

TWO

A Thunderstorm

The sun was declining towards the west, and its slanting, unbearably hot rays burned my cheeks and neck, and so scorched the edges of the britzka that you couldn't touch them. Thick dust rose along the road and filled the air, since there wasn't even a mild breeze to carry it off. Ahead of us, always at the same distance, gently swayed the tall, dusty body of the coach with our trunks on top, and, visible beyond them, the coachman's whip, whenever he flourished it, and his felt hat and Yakov's cap. I didn't know what to do with myself: neither Volodya's dust-blackened face as he dozed beside me, nor the movement of Filipp's back, nor the long shadow of the britzka running after us at an oblique angle offered any diversion. All my attention was on the mileposts, which I would notice while they were still far away, and on the clouds that had earlier been scattered about the sky near the horizon but were now, after acquiring ominous black shadows, gathering in a single large, dark storm cloud. From time to time the crackle of distant thunder could be heard. That circumstance more than any other increased my impatience to get to the next inn quickly. Thunderstorms produced in me an indescribably oppressive feeling of anguish and fear.

It was less than seven miles to the nearest village, but a large dark-purple storm cloud, which had without the slightest breeze come from goodness knows where, was rapidly moving towards us. Not yet hidden by the cloud, the sun brightly illuminates its gloomy shape and the grey strips that reach from it all the way to the horizon. From time to time lightning flashes in the distance and a weak rumbling is heard, which gradually grows stronger, comes closer, and then changes into discontinuous thunderclaps that embrace the whole sky. Vasily gets up from the box and raises the britzka's hood. The coachmen put on their heavy coats and at every clap of thunder remove their hats and cross themselves. The horses prick up their ears and flare their nostrils, as if sniffing the fresh air of the approaching storm cloud, and the britzka rolls faster along the dusty road. I'm terrified and feel the blood moving more quickly through my veins. Then the cloud's leading edge begins to cover the sun, which has looked out for the last time, illuminating half of the frighteningly dark horizon before disappearing. The whole region abruptly changes and takes on a sullen character. A grove of aspens begins to tremble, its leaves rustling and turning a dingy white that stands out vividly against the purple cloud. The crowns of the tall birches begin to heave, and tufts of dry grass blow across the road. Swifts and white-breasted swallows, as if intending to stop us, hover around the britzka and fly right in front of the horses' chests. Jackdaws with ruffled wings somehow fly sideways in the wind. The edges of the leather apron under which we're buttoned begin to lift, letting in gusts of damp air, and then start to flap against the britzka's body. Lightning flashes blindingly, as if inside the britzka itself, for an instant illuminating its grey cloth and braiding and the figure of Volodya pressed into a corner. A second later there's a majestic rumbling right over our heads that seems to rise higher and higher and wider and wider in an enormous spiral, gradually increasing in intensity until it breaks in a deafening crack that makes you tremble and catch your breath. The wrath of God! How much poetry there is in that simple folk idea!

The wheels turn faster and faster. I can tell from the backs of Vasily and Filipp, who is impatiently shaking the reins, that they too are frightened. The britzka rolls swiftly downhill and rattles across the planks of a bridge. I'm afraid to move and expect our destruction at any moment.

'Whoa!' A swingletree has come loose, and despite the constant, deafening thunderclaps, we're forced to stop on the bridge.

Leaning my head against the side of the britzka and gasping

in terror, I grimly follow the movements of Filipp's thick swarthy fingers as he slowly reattaches the loop and adjusts the traces, pushing the trace horse with his hand and the whip handle.

My anguish and fear had grown with the intensity of the storm, and when the majestic moment of silence came that usually precedes a downpour, those feelings had reached such a degree that had they lasted another quarter-hour, I'm sure I would have died of fright. At that moment from under the bridge there suddenly appeared a human being in a filthy, tattered shirt, with a swollen, demented face, wobbling, hatless head, twisted, emaciated legs and, instead of a hand a shiny red stump, which he thrust into the britzka.

'Fa-a-tha! For a cripple, in Christ's name!' the beggar cried in a feeble voice, crossing himself and making a deep bow with each word.

I cannot express the feeling of cold horror that gripped my soul in that instant. My scalp crawled as I stared at the beggar in vacant terror . . .

Vasily, who's responsible for distributing alms on the road, is giving Filipp instructions about securing the swingletree, and only when everything's ready, and Filipp has gathered up the reins again and is climbing back up on the box, does Vasily start to take something out of his pocket. But just as we are beginning to move again a blinding flash of lightning instantly fills the gully with a lurid glow, bringing the horses to a halt, and then, without the least interval, it's followed by a crack of thunder so deafening that it seems the whole sky is collapsing on us. The wind increases even more, and the horses' manes and tails, Vasily's greatcoat and the edges of the apron all start to blow desperately in one direction and flutter with the violent gusts. A large drop of rain falls heavily on the britzka's leather hood, then another, then a third and a fourth, and suddenly it is as if someone were beating a drum right over our heads, and then from all around comes the sound of steadily falling rain. From the movement of his elbows it's clear that Vasily is untying his coin purse, and the beggar, continuing to cross himself and bow, runs beside the wheels, which could crush him in an instant. 'Give in Christ's name!' At last a copper coin flies past, and the pitiful creature, his soaked shirt sticking to his wasted limbs as he staggers in the wind, stops in confusion in the middle of the road, and then disappears from sight.

Driven by the strong wind, the slanting rain falls in buckets, and streams of water run down the back of Vasily's frieze coat into the murky pool that has formed on the apron. Beaten into pellets by the rain, the dust turns first into liquid mud churned by our wheels, and then, as the pelting subsides, into turbid rivulets that flow along our loamy tracks. The lightning becomes broader and paler, and the thunderclaps are less startling against the steady sound of the rain.

And then the raindrops become finer and the storm cloud starts to break up into smaller billows and grow lighter where the sun should be, with bright-blue slivers just showing through along its greyish-white edges. A moment later a tentative sunbeam is already shining in the puddles on the road, on the fine rain falling straight down as if through a sieve and on the road's washed, brilliant green grass. Another black storm cloud is spread just as menacingly across the other end of the sky, but it no longer frightens me. I experience an inexpressibly joyful feeling of hope in life that quickly replaces the oppressive feeling of fear. My soul smiles the same way that refreshed, cheered-up nature does. Vasily turns down the collar of his coat and takes off his cap and shakes it. Volodya throws back the apron. I stick my head out of the britzka and greedily breathe in the now fresh, fragrant air. The shiny, washed body of the coach with its trunks and travelling bags sways ahead of us, and the horses' wet backs, the breech-bands, the reins and the wheel rims all gleam in the sunlight, as if coated with lacquer. On one side of the road an immense field of winter grain, cross-cut here and there by shallow ravines and shining with damp earth, extends like a shadowy carpet all the way to the horizon. On the other side, an aspen grove with an undergrowth of hazelnut and bird cherry stands without moving, as if transfixed with happiness, while glistening raindrops slowly fall from its washed branches onto last year's dead leaves. Crested larks twist and turn and dip on every side with merry songs, the busy movement of little birds is heard in the wet bushes, and from the centre of the grove comes the clear call of a cuckoo. So ravishing is the wonderful fragrance of the woods after the spring thunderstorm – the smell of birches, violets, rotten leaves, morels and bird cherry – that I'm unable to sit still in the britzka and leap from its footboard, run over to the bushes and, despite being showered with raindrops, tear off wet sprays of blossoming bird cherry and lash my face with them, delighting in their marvellous fragrance. Paying no attention to my soaked stockings or to the great clumps of mud sticking to my boots, I run splashing through the mud to the coach's window.

'Lyubochka! Katenka!' I cry, holding out several sprays of bird cherry to them. 'See how fine it is!'

The girls gasp and squeal, and Mimi shouts at me to get away, lest I surely be crushed.

'Just smell how fragrant it is!' I cry.

THREE

A New View

Katenka was sitting beside me in the britzka, her pretty little head inclined in thought as she watched the dusty road running away from under our wheels. I gazed at her silently, surprised by the expression of grown-up sadness that I was seeing on her rosy face for the first time.

'We'll soon be in Moscow,' I said to her. 'What do you suppose it's like?'

'I have no idea,' she answered reluctantly.

'Well, even so, what do you think? Is it bigger than Serpukhov, or not?'[1]

'What?'

'Oh, nothing.'

But by the instinctive feeling that allows one person to divine the thoughts of another, and that serves as the guiding thread of conversation, Katenka realized that her indifference was painful to me. She raised her head and asked, 'Did Papa say that we'll be living at your grandmother's?'

'He did say that. Grandmother wants us to move in with her.'

'Will we all live there?'

'That goes without saying. We'll live upstairs in one half, you'll occupy the other, Papa will be in the guest house, and we'll all dine downstairs together with Grandmother.'

'*Maman* says that your grandmother's very proud. Is she grumpy?'

'No-o! She only seems that way at first. She's proud, but she isn't grumpy at all; on the contrary, she's very kind and jolly. If you had only seen what a ball there was on her name-day!'

'All the same, she scares me, and anyway, goodness knows whether we'll . . .'

Katenka broke off and lapsed into thought again.

'Wha-at?' I asked uneasily.

'Nothing, I was just thinking.'

'No, you said something: "Goodness knows . . ."'

'You were saying what a ball there was at your grandmother's.'

'What a pity you all weren't there! There was a tremendous number of guests, about a thousand people, and music and generals, and I danced . . . Katenka,' I suddenly asked, stopping in the middle of my description, 'are you listening?'

'No, I heard you. You said you danced.'

'Why are you in such a dull mood?'

'One can't always be gay.'

'No, you've changed a lot since we came back from Moscow. Tell me the truth,' I added with a determined look, turning towards her, 'why have you been so strange?'

'Have I really been so strange?' Katenka answered with animation, indicating that my comment had piqued her interest. 'I'm not strange at all.'

'No, you're different than you were,' I went on. 'Before, it was clear that you were with us in everything, that you saw us as your family and loved us the same way we love you, but now you've become so serious and have been avoiding us.'

'That's not true at all –'

'No, let me finish,' I interrupted, already beginning to feel the slight tingling in my nose that always preceded the tears that would start to well in my eyes whenever I expressed some heartfelt thought long held in check. 'You've been avoiding us and talking only to Mimi, as if you didn't want to have anything to do with us.'

'Well, we can't be the same forever, can we? Sometimes you have to change,' Katenka replied. It was her habit to explain everything as a necessity of fate whenever she didn't know what to say.

I remember once when Lyubochka called her a 'stupid girl' in an argument and she replied that not everyone could be clever, that some had to be stupid. But I wasn't satisfied with the reply that sometimes you have to change and continued to question her.

'But why do you have to?'

'Well, we won't always live together,' Katenka replied, blushing slightly and staring intently at Filipp's back. 'Mama could stay in the home of your late mama, who was her friend, but goodness knows if she'll ever be friends with the countess, who's supposed to be so grumpy. Besides, we'll still have to part someday: you're rich – you have Petrovskoye – whereas we're poor – Mama has nothing.'

'You're rich and we're poor': those words and the ideas connected with them seemed quite strange to me. According to my notion at the time, only beggars and peasants could be poor, and there was no way my imagination could combine that idea of poverty with the graceful, pretty Katenka. It seemed to me that if Mimi and Katenka had always lived with us, then they always would, sharing equally in everything. It couldn't be otherwise. But now a myriad of vague new thoughts concerning their lonely position poured into my mind, and I became so ashamed that we were rich while they were poor that I turned red and couldn't bring myself to look at Katenka.

'What if we are rich and they're poor?' I thought. 'How does having to part follow from that? Why can't we share half of what we have?' But I understood that it wouldn't do to talk to Katenka about that, and a sort of practical instinct opposed to those logical reflections was already telling me that she was right, and that it wouldn't be appropriate to share my thought with her.

'Are you really going to leave us?' I said. 'How will we live apart?'

'What else can we do? It hurts me, too. Only if it does happen, I know what I'll do . . .'

'Become an actress . . . How silly!' I took up her thought, knowing that being an actress had always been her favourite dream.

'No, that's what I said when I was little . . .'

'What will you do, then?'

'I'll enter a convent and live there. I'll go around in a little black robe and a velvet cap.'

Katenka started to cry.

Has it ever happened to you, reader, suddenly to realize at a certain time in your life that your view of things was undergoing a complete change, as if everything you had known before had suddenly turned a different, unknown side towards you? That kind of mental change took place in me for the first time during our trip, which I also consider the beginning of my boyhood.

I clearly realized for the first time that we – that is, our family – weren't the only ones in the world, that not all interests revolved around us, that another life existed of people who had nothing in common with us, who didn't care about us and who had no idea we even existed. Certainly, I had known all that previously, but I didn't know it the way I came to know it then: I wasn't conscious of it and I didn't feel it.

A thought becomes a conviction only by following a certain path, one that is often completely unexpected and that may be different from the paths other minds take to reach the same conviction. My conversation with Katenka, which touched me deeply and forced me to think about her future position, was such a path for me. When I looked at the villages and towns we drove through, in each home of which there lived at least one family like ours, and at the women and children who gazed with momentary curiosity at our carriage and then passed from view forever, and at the shopkeepers and peasants, who not only didn't bow as I was used to at Petrovskoye, but didn't even look at us, for the first time the question occurred to me: just what was it that occupied them if they didn't care anything about us? And from that question arose others: how and by what did they live, how did they raise their children, did they teach them, did they let them play, how did they punish them? and so on.

FOUR

In Moscow

The change in my view of people and things and in my attitude towards them was even more palpable after our arrival in Moscow.

When on our first meeting with her I saw Grandmother's thin, wrinkled face and dull eyes, the feeling of servile respect and fear I had felt before was replaced by compassion; and when she pressed her face against Lyubochka's head and began to sob, as if the corpse of her own beloved daughter were standing before her, that compassion was even replaced by a feeling of love. It was awkward for me to see her sorrow when we were with her. I realized that we ourselves were nothing in her eyes, that we were dear to her only as a memory. I sensed that in every one of the kisses with which she covered my cheeks a single thought was expressed: 'She's gone, she's dead and I won't see her any more!'

Papa, who had virtually nothing to do with us in Moscow, only joining us for dinner in a black frock coat or tailcoat with a constantly worried expression on his face, lost a great deal in my eyes, as did his large turned-out collars, dressing gowns, village elders, stewards, strolls to the barn and hunting. Karl Ivanych, whom Grandmother referred to as our 'tutor' and who, goodness knows why, had suddenly taken a notion to substitute for his venerable bald head a light-brown wig with a stitched parting almost in the centre, seemed so strange and ridiculous to me that I was amazed I hadn't noticed it before.

A sort of invisible barrier also emerged between us and the girls. They had their secrets, and we had ours; they took pride in their skirts, which were longer, and we in our trousers with foot straps. And Mimi appeared for our first Sunday dinner in such a gorgeous dress and with such ribbons in her hair that it was clear we weren't in the country any more and everything would now be different.

FIVE

My Older Brother

I was only a year and a few months younger than Volodya, and we had grown up and always studied and played together, making no distinction in age. But then around the time of which I'm speaking I began to realize that he wasn't my comrade in years, inclinations or abilities. It even seemed to me that he was aware of his primacy and proud of it. As wrong as that belief may have been, it inspired in me a pride of my own that chafed at every encounter with him. He was ahead of me in everything – in amusements, in studies, in quarrels, in knowing how to behave – and that created a barrier between us and produced mental sufferings I didn't understand. I'm sure that if the first time fine linen shirts with pleats were made for him, I had immediately said that I resented not having them made for me, too, it would have been easier for me and not have seemed that whenever he adjusted his collar he was only doing it to offend me.

What tormented me most was that it sometimes seemed to me that Volodya understood how I felt, but was trying to hide it.

Who hasn't noticed the secret, wordless relations that reveal themselves in the imperceptible smiles, movements or glances that pass between people who are constantly together – between brothers, friends, a husband and wife, a master and servant – especially when they aren't open with each other about everything. How many unspoken desires, thoughts and fears – of being understood – are expressed in one casual look when your eyes make timid, hesitant contact!

But perhaps I was deceived in that by my inordinate impressionability and penchant for analysis. Perhaps Volodya wasn't feeling the same thing I was at all. He was passionate and outspoken in his enthusiasms, but changeable. Drawn to a great variety of things, he would devote himself to each with all his heart.

Once he was suddenly seized with a passion for pictures: he started to draw, spent all his money on paintings and wheedled them from the drawing teacher, Papa and Grandmother. Or there was his passion for decorating his desk with knick-knacks, which he gathered from all over the house; or for novels, which he quietly obtained and read day and night . . . I was involuntarily drawn to his passions, but too proud to follow after him, and too young and lacking in independence to choose a new path for myself. But there was nothing I envied so much as Volodya's happy, nobly forthright character, which expressed itself with particular clarity in our quarrels. I sensed that he was behaving well, but I was unable to do the same.

Once, at the height of his passion for knick-knacks, I accidentally broke an empty little multicoloured bottle on his desk.

'Who asked you to touch my things?' Volodya said on coming into the room and noticing the disorder I had introduced into the symmetry of the knick-knacks on his desk. 'And where's the bottle? You've definitely –'

'I accidentally dropped it and it broke. Is that really a disaster?'

'Kindly never *dare* touch my things again,' he said, fitting the pieces of the broken bottle together and staring at them in dismay.

'Kindly don't *order me*,' I replied. 'I broke it. What else is there to say?'

And I smiled, even though I didn't feel like smiling at all.

'Yes, it's nothing to you, but it *is* something to me,' Volodya continued with the shrug of his shoulder he had inherited from Papa. 'He broke it and now he thinks it's funny. You're such an insufferable little *brat*!'

'I'm a little brat, but you're a big one, and stupid, too.'

'I have no intention of engaging in name-calling with you,' Volodya said, lightly pushing me away. 'Get out.'

'Don't push me!'

'Out!'

'I said, don't push me!'

Volodya grabbed my arm, intending to pull me away from the desk, but I was at that point as irritated as I could be. I caught the desk with my foot and tipped it over. 'How do *you* like it!' – and all the porcelain and crystal ornaments were thrown to the floor with a crash.

'You disgusting little brat!' Volodya yelled, trying to catch the things as they fell.

'Well, it's all over between us,' I thought as I left the room. 'We've quarrelled for good.'

We didn't speak to each other until evening. I felt guilty and was afraid to look at him, and couldn't work on anything all day. Volodya, however, studied hard and laughed and chatted with the girls after dinner, just as he always did.

As soon as our teacher ended the afternoon lesson, I went out of the room: I was afraid of being left alone with my brother and felt awkward and ashamed. After the evening lesson in history, I picked up my copybook and headed for the door. Walking past Volodya, I puffed myself up and tried to put on an angry face, even though I wanted to go to him and make peace. Volodya lifted his head and looked boldly at me with a barely perceptible, gently mocking little smile. Our eyes met, and I understood that he understood me and knew that I understood that he had, but a feeling I couldn't overcome made me look away.

'Nikolenka!' he said to me in the simplest, most moderate way, 'enough anger. Forgive me if I offended you.'

And he offered me his hand.

It was as if, after rising higher and higher, something had suddenly begun to push against my chest and affect my breathing, if only for a moment, and then tears welled in my eyes and everything got easier.

'Forgi . . . ve . . . me, Volo . . . dya!' I said, taking his hand.

Volodya looked at me, but as if he didn't understand at all why there were tears in my eyes . . .

SIX
Masha

None of the changes that took place in my view of things was more striking, however, than the one that resulted in my seeing in one of our chambermaids no longer merely a servant of the female sex, but a *woman* on whom, to a certain extent, my own peace and happiness might depend.

From as early as I remember myself, I remember Masha in our home, but not until the event that completely altered my view of her, and about which I'm about to speak, did I ever pay the slightest attention to her. Masha was about twenty-five when I was fourteen. She was very pretty, although I'm afraid to describe her, lest my imagination fail to reproduce the enchanting and beguiling image formed in it at the time of my infatuation. To avoid any mistake, I'll say only that she was exceptionally fair, voluptuously developed, and a woman, whereas I was fourteen.

At one of those moments when you're going around the room with a lesson book in your hand and trying to step only along the cracks between the floorboards, or singing some inane tune, or smearing ink along the edge of the desk, or mindlessly repeating some expression or other – in short, at one of those moments when your mind refuses to work and your imagination takes the upper hand and starts to look for impressions, I stepped out of the classroom and idly wandered down to the landing.

Someone in clogs was coming up around another bend in the stairway.

Obviously, I wanted to know who it was, but then the footsteps suddenly came to a stop and I heard Masha say, 'So, you're up to your tricks again, but what if Marya Ivanovna comes along? How will that look?'

'She won't,' Volodya's voice replied in a whisper, and then there was a rustling sound, as if he were trying to restrain her.

'Where are you putting your hands? You are shameless!' And then Masha ran past me, her kerchief pulled to the side, revealing her plump white neck.

I can't convey how much that discovery astonished me, although the feeling of astonishment quickly gave way to sympathy for Volodya's action, so that it was no longer the action itself that astonished me, but how Volodya had grasped that it would be pleasurable to act that way. And involuntarily I wanted to do the same.

Sometimes I would spend whole hours on the landing without any thought, listening intently for the slightest movement upstairs, even though I could never bring myself to imitate Volodya, despite wanting to more than anything in the world. Sometimes, while hiding behind the door, I would listen with a painful feeling of envy and jealousy to the bustle in the maids' room, and I would think, 'What sort of position would I be in if I went upstairs and tried to kiss Masha like Volodya? How would I – with my broad nose and cowlicks – respond if she should ask me what I wanted?' Sometimes I would hear Masha say to Volodya, 'What a nuisance! Why do you keep pestering me? Get out of here, you naughty boy. Why is it that Nikolay Petrovich never comes fooling around?' She had no idea that 'Nikolay Petrovich' was at that very moment sitting on the stairs below and ready to give anything in the world to be in the naughty Volodya's place.

I was bashful by nature, and my bashfulness was increased by my conviction that I was ugly. And I was also convinced that nothing has a more pronounced effect on a person's outlook than his appearance, or if not his appearance itself, then at least his belief that it is or isn't attractive.

I had too much pride to get used to my situation, and so, like the fox, I assured myself that the grapes were sour; that is, I tried to despise all the pleasures that are obtainable with an agreeable appearance, the ones that I had seen Volodya enjoying and that I envied with all my heart, but instead harnessed all the powers of my mind and imagination to find my enjoyments in proud solitude.

SEVEN
Shot

'Good Heavens, gunpowder!' Mimi exclaimed, gasping in alarm. 'What are you doing? Do you want to burn the house down and kill us all?'

And with an indescribably resolute expression she ordered everyone to move out of the way, went with long, determined strides over to the scattered shot and, despising the danger of a sudden explosion, began to stamp on it. When in her view the danger had passed, she called Mikhey and ordered him to throw the 'gunpowder' as far away as possible or, best of all, into water, and then with an imperious shake of her mobcap she went out to the drawing room.

'They're certainly being well looked after!' she growled.

When Papa came in from the guest house and we joined him in Grandmother's room, Mimi was already sitting by the window and looking menacingly past the doorway with a sort of cryptically official expression. In her hand was something wrapped in several pieces of paper. I guessed that it was the shot and that Grandmother knew all about it.

Present in Grandmother's room along with Mimi were the chambermaid Gasha, who from the look of her flushed, wrathful face was extremely upset, and Doctor Blumenthal, a small pockmarked man, who was trying in vain to calm Gasha down by making covert conciliatory gestures with his eyes and head.

Grandmother herself was sitting a bit off to the side and laying out a hand of the solitaire game 'Traveller', which always meant a particularly inauspicious mood.

'How are you feeling today, *maman*? Did you sleep well?' Papa asked as he respectfully kissed her hand.

'Excellent, my dear. You know, it would appear that I'm always completely healthy,' Grandmother answered, her tone implying that Papa's question had been of the most impertinent and offensive kind. 'Well, are you going to give me a clean handkerchief or not?' she continued, speaking to Gasha.

'I just did,' Gasha replied, indicating the snow-white batiste handkerchief that lay on the arm of Grandmother's chair.

'Take this filthy rag away and give me a clean one, my dear.'

Gasha went over to the chiffonier, opened a drawer, and then slammed it shut so violently that the windows rattled. Grandmother glanced menacingly over at us and continued to watch all the chambermaid's movements closely. When Gasha gave her what looked to me like the same handkerchief, she said, 'When are you going to grate me some snuff, my dear?'

'When it's time, I will.'

'What did you say?'

'I'll do it today.'

'If you do not wish to serve me, my dear, you should have told me so. I would have released you long ago.'

'Go ahead, no one will weep,' the chambermaid muttered under her breath.

At that point the doctor started to wink at her, but she glared at him with such a fierce, unyielding expression that he immediately looked down and started to play with his watch key.

'You see, my dear, how they talk to me in my own house?' Grandmother said to Papa after the still muttering Gasha had left the room.

'I'll grind the snuff for you myself, *maman*, if you like,' Papa said, obviously disconcerted at being addressed in that unexpected way.

'Oh no, but I thank you. She allows herself to be so rude because she knows that no one else is able to grind it the way I like. Are you aware, my dear,' Grandmother continued after a pause, 'that your children nearly burned down the house today?'

Papa looked at Grandmother with respectful curiosity.

'Here's what they were playing with. Show it to them,' she said to Mimi.

Papa took the shot in his hands and couldn't help smiling.

'This is shot, *maman*. It's completely harmless.'

'I'm very grateful to you, my dear, for your instruction, but I'm too old . . .'

'Her nerves, her nerves!' the doctor whispered.

Papa immediately turned to us: 'Where did you get this? And how dare you fool with such things?'

'Don't ask them, ask their *tutor*,' Grandmother said, pronouncing the word 'tutor' with special contempt. 'Why isn't he keeping an eye on them?'

'*Woldemar* said that Karl Ivanych himself gave them the *gunpowder*,' Mimi chimed in.

'Well, you see what good he is,' Grandmother continued. 'And where is he, this *tutor*, whatever his name is? Send him in.'

'I gave him the day off for a visit,' Papa said.

'That's no reason; he's supposed to be here all the time. The children aren't mine but yours, and I've no right to advise you, since you're cleverer than I am,' Grandmother went on, 'but it would seem that the time has come to hire a real teacher and not some German peasant *tutor*. And a stupid peasant, at that, who's incapable of teaching them anything but bad manners and Tyrolean songs. Is it really so necessary, I ask you, for the children to know how to sing Tyrolean songs? However, there's no one to think about that *now*, and you may do as you like.'

The word 'now' meant 'now that they have no mother' and called forth sad memories in Grandmother's heart. She glanced down at the portrait on her snuffbox and lapsed into thought.

'I've been thinking about it for some time,' Papa hastened to reply, 'and I wanted to consult you about it, *maman*. Shall we ask St-Jérôme, who's been giving them weekly lessons?'

'He would be a fine choice, my friend,' Grandmother said, dropping the displeased tone she had been using. 'St-Jérôme is at least a *gouverneur* who will understand how *des enfants de bonne maison* ought to behave, and not some simple *menin*,[2] a *tutor* who's only good for taking them out for walks.'

'I'll talk to him tomorrow,' Papa said.

And, in fact, two days after that conversation Karl Ivanych yielded his place to the young French dandy.

EIGHT

Karl Ivanych's Story

Late in the evening of the day before he would leave us for good, Karl Ivanych was standing beside his bed in his quilted dressing gown and red cap and carefully packing his things in a travelling bag.

His treatment of us over the last several days had been especially remote: he seemed to be avoiding all contact with us. And that time, too, he gave me a dour look as I came into the room and then continued with what he was doing. I lay down on my bed, but Karl Ivanych, who had strictly forbidden that, said nothing, and the thought that he would no longer scold or stop us, that we would no longer be any concern of his, vividly reminded me of our imminent separation. It made me sad that he didn't love us any more and I wanted him to know it.

'Let me help you, Karl Ivanych,' I said, going over to him.

Karl Ivanych glanced at me and then looked away, but in that quick glance I saw not the indifference to which I had attributed his coldness but a sincere, concentrated sorrow.

'God sees all and knows all, and His holy will be done in everything,' he said, standing up straight with a heavy sigh. 'Yes, Nikolenka,' he continued upon seeing the expression of unaffected sympathy with which I was looking at him, 'it is my fate to be unhappy from my childhood to my gravestone. The good I have done for people has always been repaid with meanness, and my reward is not here but there,' he said, pointing upward. 'If you only knew my story and all that I have been through in this life! I was a cobbler, I was a soldier, I was a *Deserteur*, I worked in a factory, I was a teacher, and now I am nothing! And like the Son of God, I have no place to lay down my head,' he concluded, closing his eyes and lowering himself into his armchair.

Realizing that Karl Ivanych's mood was a sensitive one in which he would express his heartfelt thoughts for himself alone, regardless of the listener, I sat down on the bed without speaking or taking my eyes off his kind face.

'You are not a little child, you are able to understand. I will tell you my story and everything that I have been through in this life. Someday you will remember the old friend who loved you children very much!'

Karl Ivanych leaned his elbow on the little table beside him, took some snuff, and then, with a heavenward roll of his eyes, he began his narrative using the special flat, guttural voice in which it had been his habit to give us dictation.

'I vas onlocky efen on my *Mutter*'s wombe. *Das Unglück verfolgte mich schon im Schosse meiner Mutter!*' he repeated in German with even greater feeling.

Since Karl Ivanych later told me his story more than once in the same order, with the same expressions and the same unvarying intonations, I hope to convey it virtually word for word, although obviously without the mistakes of language that the reader can judge from that first sentence. Whether it really was his story and not a work of invention born of his time alone in our house, or an embellishment of the true events of his life with imaginary facts that he himself had begun to believe after frequent repetition, I've been unable to decide to this day. On the one hand, he told the story with too much of the lively feeling and consistency of method that are the hallmarks of verisimilitude for it not to be believed, while on the other, there were too many poetical beauties in it, and the beauties raised doubts.

'In my veins flows the noble blood of the Counts of Sommerblat! *In meinen Adern fliesst das edel Blut des Grafen von Sommerblat!* I was born six months after the wedding. My mother's husband (I called him "Papa") was a tenant of Count Sommerblat. He was unable to forget my mother's shame and did not love me. I had a little brother, Johann, and two sisters, but I was a stranger in my own family! *Ich war ein Fremder in meiner eigenen Familie!* When Johann did foolish things, Papa would say, "I will not have a moment's peace with that child Karl!" and I would be scolded and punished. When my sisters got angry with each other, Papa would say, "Karl will never learn to obey!" and I would be scolded and punished. Only my dear kind Mama loved and petted me. Often she would say to me, "Karl, come here to my room," and would secretly kiss me. "Poor, poor Karl!" she would say, "No one loves you, but I would not trade you for anyone. Your mama asks but one thing of you," she would say to me, "study hard and always be an honest German, and God will not abandon you! *Trachte nur ein ehrlicher Deutscher zu werden – sagte sie – und der liebe Gott wird dich nicht verlassen!*" And I did my best. When I was fourteen and old enough to take Communion, my mama said to my papa, "Karl is a big boy now, Gustav. What shall we do with him?" And Papa said, "I don't know." Then Mama said, "Let us give him to Mr Schulz in town. Let him be a cobbler." And my papa said, "Good." *Und mein Vater sagte "Gut".* I lived six years and seven months in the town in the home of a master cobbler and my employer liked me. He said, "Karl is a fine worker and soon he will be my *Geselle!*"[3] But . . . man proposes, while God disposes. In 1796 a *Conscription* was ordered, and all who could serve, from eighteen to twenty-one, had to assemble in the town.

'My papa and brother, Johann, came to the town and together we went to draw lots to see who would be a *Soldat* and who would not be. Johann drew a bad lot – he had to be a *Soldat*. I drew a good one – I did not. And Papa said, "I had only one son and now I must part with him! *Ich hatte einen einzigen Sohn und von diesem muss ich mich trennen!*"

'I took his hand and said, "Why do you say that, Papa? Come with me and I'll tell you something." And Papa came. Papa came with me and we sat down at a little table in a tavern. "Give us two *Bierkrüge*," I said, and tankards were brought. We each drank one, and my brother, Johann, drank one too.

'"Papa!" I said, "do not say that you 'had only one son and now you must part with him'. My heart wanted to *jump out* when I heard *that*. Brother Johann will not serve – it is I who will be a *Soldat*! No one needs Karl here and Karl will be a *Soldat*."

'"You are a worthy fellow, Karl Ivanych!" Papa said and kissed me. "*Du bist ein braver Bursche!*" – *sagte mir mein Vater und küsste mich.*

'And I was a *Soldat!*'

NINE

The Preceding Continued

'It was a terrible time then, Nikolenka,' Karl Ivanych continued. 'It was Napoleon then. He wanted to conquer Germany, and we defended our fatherland to the last drops of blood! *Und wir verteidigten unser Vaterland bis auf den letzten Tropfen Blut!*

'I was at Ulm and at Austerlitz! I was at Wagram! *Ich war bei Wagram!*'[4]

'Did you really fight, too?' I asked, looking at him in astonishment. 'Did you really kill people, too?'

Karl Ivanych immediately put me at ease on that account.

'Once a French *Grenadier* lagged behind his own and fell down on the road. I ran up and was about to stab him with my bayonet, *aber der Franzose warf sein Gewehr und rief pardon*[5] and I let him go!

'At Wagram Napoleon drove us onto an island and surrounded us, so that there was no escape. We went three days without provisions, while standing in water up to our knees. And the scoundrel Napoleon would neither capture us nor let us go! *Und der Bösewicht Napoleon wollte uns nicht gefangen nehmen und auch nicht freilassen!*

'On the fourth day, thank goodness, they took us captive and led us away to a castle. I was wearing blue trousers and a tunic of good cloth and had fifteen thalers and a silver watch, a present from my papa. A French *Soldat* took them all away. Fortunately for me, I had three gold pieces my mama had sewn into my undershirt. No one found them!

'I did not want to remain in the castle for long and decided to escape. Once on a big holiday, I told the sergeant who kept watch on us, "Mister sergeant, today is a big holiday. I want to

celebrate. Bring two bottles of Madeira, if you please, and we
will drink them together." And the sergeant said, "Fine." When
the sergeant brought the Madeira and we had each drunk a glass,
I took his hand and said, "Mister sergeant, perhaps you have a
father and mother?" He said, "I do, Mister Mauer." "My father
and mother," I said, "have not seen me in eight years, and do
not know if I am alive or long dead in my grave. Mister sergeant,
I have two gold coins that were in my undershirt. Take them
and let me go. Be my benefactor, and my mama will pray to
Almighty God for you till the end of her days."

'The sergeant drank a glass of Madeira and said, "Mister
Mauer, I like you very much and I am very sorry for you, but
you are a prisoner and I am a *Soldat*!" I shook his hand and
said, "Mister sergeant!" *Ich drückte ihm die Hand und sagte,
"Herr Sergeant!"*

'And the sergeant said, "You are a poor man and I will not
take your money, but I will help you. When I go to bed, buy a
pail of vodka for the soldiers and they will sleep. I will not keep
watch on you."

'He was a good man. I bought a pail of vodka, and when the
soldiers were drunk I put on my boots and old overcoat and
quietly went out of the door. I went along a rampart and was
going to jump, but there was water and I did not want to ruin
my last clothes. I went to the gate.

'The sentry was walking *auf und ab*[6] with his gun and looked
at me. "*Qui vive?*" *sagte er auf einmal*, and I said nothing; "*Qui
vive?*" *sagte er zum zweiten Mal*, and I said nothing; "*Qui vive?*"
sagte er zum dritten Mal,[7] and I ran. I jumped in the water,
climbed to the other side, and took to my heels in a cloud of
dust. *Ich sprang in's Wasser, kletterte auf die andere Seite und
machte mich aus dem Staube.*

'I ran along the road all night, but when daylight came I was
afraid of being seen and hid in the tall rye. I knelt down and
folded my hands and thanked God Almighty for his mercy, and
with a peaceful feeling I fell asleep. *Ich danke dem allmächtigen
Gott für Seine Barmherzigheit und mit beruhigtem Gefühl schlief
ich ein.*

'I awoke the next evening and continued on my way. Soon a

big German cart with two black horses overtook me. In the cart
was a well-dressed man smoking a pipe and watching me. I
walked slowly, so the cart would pass by, but when I did so the
cart slowed down, too, and the man kept looking at me. I walked
faster and the cart went faster, too, and the man kept looking
at me. I sat down on the road, and the man stopped his horses
and looked at me. "Young man," he said, "where are you going
so late?" I said, "I am going to Frankfurt." "Get in my cart, there
is room, and I will take you. Why are you not carrying anything?
Why are you unshaven, and why is there mud on your clothes?"
he asked after I sat down beside him. "I am a poor man," I said.
"I want to find a job in a *Fabrik*, and my clothes are muddy
because I fell down on the road." "You are not telling the truth,
young man," he said, "the road is dry now."

'And I did not say anything.

'"Tell me the whole truth," the kind man said to me. "Who
are you and where have you come from? I like your face, and if
you are an honest man, I will help you."

'And I told him everything. He said, "All right, young man,
come with me to my rope *Fabrik*. I will give you work, clothes,
money, and you will live in my house."

'And I said, "Good."

'We came to the rope factory, and the kind man said to his
wife, "This is a young man who fought for his fatherland and
escaped capture. He has neither home, nor clothes, nor bread.
He will live with us. Give him clean linen and feed him."

'I lived at the rope factory a year and a half, and my employer
became so fond of me that he did not want to let me go. And it
was good for me. I was a handsome man then; I was young and
tall with blue eyes and a Roman nose . . . And *Frau* L. (I cannot
say her name), my employer's wife, was a young, pretty lady.
And she became fond of me.

'When she saw me, she said, "Mister Mauer, what does your
mama call you?" I said, "Karlchen."

'And she said, "Karlchen, sit down here beside me."

'I sat down beside her, and she said, "Karlchen, kiss me."

'I did so and she said, "Karlchen, I like you so much that I
can hardly stand it," and she started to tremble all over.'

Here Karl Ivanych made a lengthy pause and, rolling his kind blue eyes and slowly shaking his head, he started to smile the way people do when they're overcome with pleasant memories.

'Yes,' he began again, straightening up in the armchair and wrapping his dressing gown tighter, 'I have experienced much good and bad in my life, but here is my witness,' he said, indicating the little needlepoint image of the Saviour hanging over his bed, 'that no one can say that Karl Ivanych was a dishonest man! I did not want to repay with low ingratitude the good that *Herr* L. had done for me, and I decided to run away. Late in the evening when everyone was going to bed, I wrote a letter to my patron and put it on the desk in my room, took my clothes and three thalers, and quietly went outside. No one saw me, and I set off down the road.'

TEN

Further

'I had not seen my mama in nine years and did not know if she was alive or long dead in her grave. I set off for my fatherland. When I arrived in the town, I asked where the Gustav Mauer lived who was a tenant of Count Sommerblat. And they said to me, "Count Sommerblat died and Gustav Mauer now lives on the main street where he keeps a *Likör* shop." I put on my new waistcoat and good frock coat, both gifts of the factory owner, carefully combed my hair, and went to my papa's liqueur shop. My sister Mariechen was sitting behind the counter, and she asked me what I would like. I said, "May I have a glass of liqueur?" And she said, "*Vater!* There is a young man here asking for a glass of liqueur." And Papa said, "Give the young man a glass of liqueur." I sat down at a table, drank my glass of liqueur, smoked my pipe, and looked at Papa, Mariechen and Johann, who had also come into the shop. During our conversation, Papa said to me, "You probably know, young man, where our *Armee* is now." I said, "I myself have come from the *Armee* and it is near Vienna." "Our son," Papa said, "was a *Soldat* and it has been nine years since he has written and we do not know if he is dead or alive. My wife cries about him all the time." I smoked my pipe and said, "What was your son's name and where did he serve? Perhaps I know him." "His name was Karl Mauer and he served in the Austrian chasseurs," my papa said. "He is a tall, handsome man, like you," my sister Mariechen said. I said, "I know your Karl!" "*Amalia!*" *sagte auf einmal mein Vater.*[8] "Come in here! There is a young man who knows our Karl." And my darling mama came out of the back. I recognized her at once. "You know our Karl?" she said and looked at me, turning pale and trembling. "Yes, I saw him," I said, not daring to look at her, my heart wanting to *jump*. "My Karl is alive!" Mama said. "Thank God! Where is he, my dear Karl? I would die peacefully if I could see him once more, see my beloved son, but it is not God's will," and she began to cry. I could not stand it. "Mama!" I said. "I am your son, I am your Karl!" and she fell into my arms.'

Karl Ivanych closed his eyes and his lips started to tremble.

'"*Mutter!*" *sagte ich.* "*Ich bin Ihr Sohn, ich bin Ihr Karl!*" *und sie stürzte mir in die Arme,*' he repeated a little more calmly, as he wiped the large tears that were running down his cheeks.

'But it did not please God for me to end my days in my native land. Bad luck pursued me everywhere! *Das Unglück verfolgte mich überall!* I remained in my native land only three months. One Sunday I was in a coffee house, where I had bought a *Bier-krug* and was smoking my pipe and talking to my friends about *Politik*, the Emperor Franz,[9] Napoleon, the war, and each of us said his opinion. Sitting next to us was a stranger in a grey *Über-rock*,[10] who drank his coffee and smoked his little pipe and kept quiet. *Er rauchte sein Pfeifchen und schweig still.* When the *Nachtwächter*[11] cried ten o'clock, I got my hat, paid my share, and went home. In the middle of the night someone knocked on the door. I awoke and said, "Who is there?" "*Macht auf!*"[12] I said, "Say who it is and I will open." *Ich sagte, "Sagt, wer ihr seid, und ich werde aufmachen.*" "*Macht auf im Namen des Gesetzes!*"[13] came from the other side of the door. And I opened it. Two armed *Soldaten* remained standing outside the door, but into the room came the stranger in the grey *Überrock* who had been sitting beside us at the coffee house. He was a spy! *Er war ein Spion!* "Come with me!" the spy said. "All right," I said. I put on my boots *und Pantalon* and was pulling on my braces, while walking around the room. My blood was boiling. I said, "He is a scoundrel!" When I got to the wall where my sword was hanging, I suddenly grabbed it and said, "You are a spy, defend yourself!" *Du bist ein Spion, verteidige dich!*" *Ich gab ein Hieb*[14] to the right, *ein Hieb* to the left, and one to his head. The spy fell down! I grabbed my travelling bag and wallet and jumped out of the window. *Ich nahm meinen Mantelsack und*

Beutel und sprang zum Fenster hinaus. I came to Ems. *Ich kam
nach Ems.*[15] There I met General Sazin. He took a liking to me,
got a passport from the envoy, and brought me to Russia to
teach his children. After General Sazin died, your mama asked
me to her home. She said, "Karl Ivanych! I am giving you my
children. Love them and I will never abandon you and will be
a comfort to you in your old age." Now she is gone and everything has been forgotten. For my twenty years of service I must
now, in my old age, seek my stale crust of bread in the street.
God sees this and knows this, and it is His holy will, only I am
sorry, children, for you!' Karl Ivanych ended, pulling me towards
him by my hand and kissing me on the head.

ELEVEN
A Low Mark

By the end of her year of mourning, Grandmother had recovered
at least partly from the grief that had overwhelmed her, and had
begun to receive visitors from time to time, especially children
– boys and girls our own age.

On Lyubochka's birthday, 13 December, Princess Korna-
kova and her daughters arrived before dinner, as did Mme
Valakhina and Sonyechka, Ilenka Grap and the two younger
Ivin brothers.

The sound of talking, laughter and quick footsteps reached
us from downstairs, where all the company had gathered, but
we couldn't join them until we finished our morning lessons.
Indicated on the schedule hanging in the classroom were the
words *Lundi, de 2 à 3, Maître d'Histoire et de Géographie*,[16]
and we therefore had to wait for that same *Maître d'Histoire*,
listen to him, and then see him out before we would be free. It
was already twenty past two and the history teacher was still
nowhere to be seen or heard, not even on the street down which
he would have to come, and out at which I looked with a strong
wish never to see him at all.

'Apparently, Lebedev isn't coming today,' Volodya said, for a
moment putting down the volume of Smaragdov[17] from which
he was preparing the lesson.

'God willing, God willing . . . Since I don't know anything.
Although, I think that's him now,' I added in a dejected voice.

Volodya got up and came over to the window.

'No, that's not him but some gentleman,' he said. 'Let's wait
until two-thirty,' he added, scratching the top of his head and
stretching, as he usually did whenever he took a break from

studying. 'If he still hasn't come by then, we can tell St-Jérôme to collect our exercise books.'

'But why does he have to come at a-a-all?' I said, stretching, too, and shaking Kaydanov's history[18] over my head with both hands.

Since there was nothing else to do, I opened the book at the place assigned for the lesson and started to read. It was long and hard, and I knew none of it and realized there was no way I could learn even part of it, especially since I was in that irritable state in which your thoughts refuse to dwell on any subject, whatever it might be.

After the last history lesson – a subject that was always the most boring and difficult for me – Lebedev had complained to St-Jérôme about me and given me a two,[19] which was considered very poor. St-Jérôme told me then that if I got less than a three the next time, I would be severely punished. Now that next time had come, and I was, I'll admit, in a terrible funk.

I was so engrossed in reading through the unfamiliar lesson that the sound of galoshes being removed in the anteroom caught me by surprise. Barely had I turned around to look than in the doorway appeared the repellently pockmarked face and all too familiar awkward figure of the teacher in a blue tailcoat with academic buttons.

He slowly placed his fur hat on the windowsill and his copybooks on the table, spread the tails of his coat with both hands (as if it were quite necessary to do), and, breathing hard, sat down at his place.

'Well, gentlemen,' he said, rubbing his sweaty palms together, 'let's first go over what was covered in the last lesson, and then I'll try to acquaint you with the subsequent events of the Middle Ages.'

That meant: 'Recite your lessons.'

While Volodya was answering him with the fluency and confidence that are characteristic of those who know a subject well, I wandered out onto the stairs and, since I wasn't allowed to go down, it was natural that without realizing it myself I turned up on the landing. But just as I was thinking of assuming my usual observation post behind the door, Mimi, who was always a source of grief for me, suddenly turned up. 'You're here?' she said, glaring at me and then at the door to the maids' room and then at me again.

I felt completely in the wrong both for not being in the classroom and for being in such a forbidden place, so I said nothing and bowed my head, trying to display in my person a most touchingly contrite demeanour.

'No, this is simply unheard of!' Mimi said. 'What have you been doing here?' I said nothing. 'No, this won't do,' she repeated, rapping the banister with her knuckles. 'I'll tell the countess about it.'

It was already five to three when I returned to the classroom. The teacher, as if noticing neither my absence nor my presence, was going over the next lesson with Volodya. After he had finished his explanation and was starting to put his copybooks away, and Volodya had gone to another room to get the coupon, the happy thought occurred to me that they were done and I had been overlooked.

But then the teacher suddenly turned to me with an ominous half-smile.

'I hope you've memorized your lesson, sir,' he said, rubbing his palms together.

'I have, sir,' I responded.

'Then endeavour to tell me something about the first crusade of St Louis,'[20] he said, rocking in his chair and looking thoughtfully down at his feet. 'First, tell me the reasons that induced the king of France to take up the cross,' he said, raising his eyebrows and pointing at the inkwell, 'then explain to me the general features of the crusade itself,' he added, making a movement with his whole hand, as if he wanted to grab something, 'and, finally, describe the influence of the crusade first on the European states in general,' he said, striking the desk on the left side with his copybook, 'and then on the French realm in particular,' he concluded, striking it on the right side and tipping his head in that direction, as well.

I swallowed my saliva several times, coughed, tipped my own head to the side, and said nothing. Then, picking up a pen on the table, I started to pick at it but remained silent.

'The pen, if you please,' the teacher said, holding out his hand. 'It can still be used. Well, sir?'

'Lou . . . King . . . St Louis was . . . was . . . was . . . a kind and clever tsar.'

'Who, sir?'

'The tsar. He came up with the idea of going to Jerusalem and "gave the reins of government" to his mother.'

'What was her name, sir?'

'B . . . B . . . lanka.'

'How's that, sir? Blanka?'

I produced a sort of wry, awkward grin.

'Well, sir, do you happen to know anything else?' he asked with a smirk.

Having nothing to lose, I coughed and began to spout whatever came into my head. The teacher said nothing, brushed the dust from the table with the pen he had taken from me, stared past my ear, and kept repeating, 'All right, sir, all right.' I sensed that I knew nothing and was expressing myself not at all the way I should have, and it was terribly distressing to me that the teacher made no attempt to stop or correct me.

'But how did he come up with the idea of going to Jerusalem?' he asked, repeating my words.

'In order . . . Because . . . So that . . .'

I was at a complete loss and said no more, sensing that if that scoundrel of a teacher should stare enquiringly at me for a year, I would still be in no condition to utter a single word. He gazed at me for three minutes or so, and then, with an expression of profound regret, suddenly said in a sensitive voice to Volodya, who had just come back into the room, 'Give me the record book, please, and I'll enter your marks.'

Volodya gave him the record book and carefully placed the coupon beside it.

The teacher pressed the record book flat, carefully dipped his pen and, in a beautiful hand, entered fives for Volodya in the columns for achievement and behaviour. Then, holding the pen over the columns where my marks were to be entered, he looked at me, shook off some ink, and pondered.

Suddenly his hand made a barely perceptible movement and

in the first column there appeared a beautifully inscribed one, followed by a full stop, and then, after another movement, a second one with a full stop in the column for behaviour.

After gently closing the record book, the teacher got up and went over to the door, as if unaware of my look expressing despair, pleading and reproach.

'Mikhail Larionych!' I said.

'No,' he answered, understanding what I wanted to say to him. 'That's no way to study. I don't want to take your money for nothing.'

He put on his galoshes and camlet overcoat and meticulously wrapped himself in his scarf. As if it were possible to care about anything else after what had just happened to me. For him it had been a mere movement of his pen, but for me, the greatest of calamities.

'Is the lesson over?' St-Jérôme asked, coming into the room.

'Yes.'

'Was the teacher pleased with you?'

'Yes,' Volodya said.

'What did you receive?'

'A five.'

'And *Nicolas*?'

I didn't say anything.

'A four, I think,' Volodya said.

He realized that I needed to be rescued, if only for the day. Let them punish me, only not today while we had company.

'*Voyons, messieurs!*' (It was St-Jérôme's habit to precede every expression with '*voyons*'.) '*Faites votre toilette et descendons.*'[21]

TWELVE

A Little Key

No sooner had we gone downstairs to greet our guests than we were all called to the table for dinner. Papa was in a jolly mood (he had been winning of late) and gave Lyubochka an expensive silver tea service, and then remembered during dinner that he had left a *bonbonnière* for her in the guest house.

'Why send a man for it? Better you go, Koko,' he said to me. 'The keys are in a shell on the big desk, right? Get them and use the big one to open the second drawer on the right. You'll find a little box of sweets wrapped in tissue. Bring everything here.'

'Shall I bring some cigars, too?' I asked, knowing that he always sent for them after dinner.

'Yes, do, but don't touch anything else!' he called out after me.

I found the keys where he said and was about to unlock the drawer when I was stopped by a desire to know what the little key on the ring was for.

On top of the desk, next to the inkwell among numerous other things, was an embroidered portfolio with a tiny padlock, and I wanted to see if the little key would fit it. The test was crowned with complete success, the portfolio opened, and inside I found a whole stack of papers. My curiosity advised me so convincingly to see what they were that I disobeyed the voice of conscience and began to look through them . . .

———

My childhood feeling of unconditional respect for everyone older, but especially for Papa, was so powerful that my mind unconsciously refused to draw any conclusions whatever from what I saw. I felt that Papa must inhabit a sphere that was completely special, excellent, inaccessible and unfathomable to me, and that to try to penetrate the secrets of his life would be something like a sacrilege on my part.

The discoveries made almost inadvertently by me in Papa's portfolio thus left no clear idea in me at all, other than a vague sense that I had behaved badly. I felt uneasy and ashamed.

Impelled by that feeling, I wanted to close the portfolio as quickly as possible, but it was evidently my fate that unforgettable day to experience every possible calamity. After inserting the little key in the lock, I turned it the wrong way, and thinking that the lock was closed, I removed the key, whereupon – to my horror! – only the top part was left in my hand. I tried in vain to unite it with the part remaining inside the lock and by some magic to extract it. In the end I was forced to accept the terrifying idea that I had committed a new crime that would certainly be discovered that very day as soon as Papa returned to his study.

Mimi's complaint, the poor mark, and the little key! Nothing worse could have happened to me. Grandmother for Mimi's complaint, St-Jérôme for the poor mark, and Papa for the little key – it would all come crashing down on me no later than that evening!

'What will happen to me?! O-o-h, what have I done?!' I said out loud as I paced back and forth on the soft rug in the study. 'Oh well,' I said to myself as I got the sweets and cigars, 'what cannot be avoided must be endured . . .' And I ran back to the house.

That fatalistic maxim, which I learned from Nikolay as a small child, has had a beneficial and temporarily calming effect on me in all the difficult moments of my life. I returned to the salon in a slightly irritated and unnatural but extraordinarily mirthful state of mind.

THIRTEEN

The Deceiver

After dinner came *petits jeux*,[22] in which I took a very active part. While playing cat and mouse, I clumsily ran into the Kornakovs' governess, who had joined the game, and accidentally stepped on her dress and tore it. Noticing that all the girls, but especially Sonyechka, took great pleasure in seeing the governess go off with a distressed look to the maids' room to mend her dress, I decided to give them the pleasure again. In keeping with that gracious purpose, as soon as the governess came back, I galloped around and around her until I found an opportune moment to catch my heel on her skirt and tear it again. Sonyechka and the princesses could barely hold back their laughter, which greatly flattered my pride, but St-Jérôme, no doubt having witnessed my antics, came over to me and said with a scowl (which I couldn't bear) that my high spirits seemed to have led to no good, and that if I didn't calm down he would make me regret it, even if it was a special occasion.

But I was in the irritated state of someone who has lost more than he can afford and is afraid to tally up, and so he keeps on playing one desperate card after another, no longer in hope of recouping his losses but simply to avoid thinking about them. I walked away from St-Jérôme with an insolent smirk.

After cat and mouse, someone started a game that I believe we called *Lange Nase*.[23] It involved placing two rows of chairs across from each other with the ladies and cavaliers divided into two groups, and each group choosing from the other in turn.

The youngest princess chose the younger Ivin every time, Katenka chose either Volodya or Ilenka, while Sonyechka chose Seryozha every time and, to my great astonishment, wasn't in the least embarrassed when he went over and sat down directly across from her. She laughed her sweet ringing laugh and motioned with her head that he had guessed correctly. But no one chose me. To the great mortification of my pride, I understood that I was superfluous, the *one left over* – that each time they would have to say, 'Who's left? Oh, Nikolenka. Well, you take him, then.' Therefore, whenever it was my turn to guess, I would go directly to my sister or to one of the homely young princesses and, unfortunately, I was never wrong. Sonyechka, I think, was so preoccupied with Seryozha Ivin that I didn't exist for her at all. I don't know on what grounds I mentally called her a 'deceiver', since she had never promised to choose me instead of Seryozha, but I was firmly convinced that she had acted in the vilest way towards me.

After the game I noticed that the 'deceiver', whom I despised but couldn't stop looking at, had gone off into a corner with Katenka and Seryozha, where they were talking among themselves. Creeping up behind the piano to find out their secrets, I saw the following: Katenka was holding up two ends of a batiste handkerchief as a screen to hide Seryozha and Sonyechka's heads. 'No, you lost, and now you have to pay up!' Seryozha was saying. Her arms hanging down, Sonyechka stood before him like a guilty person and said with a blush, 'I didn't lose. Isn't that right, *mademoiselle Catherine*?' 'I love the truth,' Katenka answered. 'You did lose the bet, *ma chère*.'

Hardly had Katenka managed to say those words than Seryozha bent down and kissed Sonyechka. He kissed her right on her rosy lips. And Sonyechka laughed as if it was nothing at all, as if it was lots of fun. Awful!!! 'O, treacherous deceiver!'

FOURTEEN
A Temporary Derangement

I suddenly felt scorn for the entire female sex, and especially for Sonyechka. I persuaded myself that those games weren't any fun at all, that they were only good for 'silly girls', and I felt an extraordinary urge to make a row and play a trick so bold that it would astonish everyone. An opportunity wasn't long in coming.

St-Jérôme, after talking to Mimi about something, left the room, and the sound of his footsteps was heard first on the stairs and then overhead in the direction of the classroom. It occurred to me that Mimi had told him where she had seen me during the lesson, and that he had gone to look at the record book. At the time, I attributed to St-Jérôme no other purpose in life than to punish me. I've read somewhere that children from twelve to fourteen, that is, those at the transitional age of boyhood, are particularly susceptible to arson and even murder. Recalling my own boyhood, and especially the state of mind I was in on that unhappy day, I see very clearly how the most terrible crime might be committed not from a desire to cause harm or for any other reason, but 'just so', out of curiosity or an unconscious need for action. There are times when the future presents itself to a person in such a dismal light that he's afraid to let his mental gaze dwell on it, and completely suspends the operation of his mind, convincing himself that there won't be any future and that there hasn't been any past. At such times, when thought no longer weighs every determination of the will in advance, and the only vital impulses are bodily instincts, it's understandable how a child might, from inexperience, be especially vulnerable to such a state, and without the least hesitation or fear, but with a little smile of curiosity, first set and then fan a fire under his own house in which his brothers, father and mother, all of whom he dearly loves, are fast asleep. Under the sway of that same temporary absence of thought – of distraction, almost – a peasant boy of seventeen, while examining the blade of a just sharpened axe next to a bench on which his old father is lying face-down asleep, might all of a sudden swing the axe, and then with dull curiosity watch the blood from the severed neck pool beneath the bench. And under the sway of that same instinctive curiosity and absence of thought, a person might take a kind of pleasure in stopping at the very edge of a cliff and thinking, 'What if I jump?' Or in putting a loaded pistol to his forehead and thinking, 'What if I pull the trigger?' Or in looking at some very important personage before whom a whole society feels servile respect and wondering, 'What if I go over to him, grab him by the nose, and say, "What about this, my dear fellow?"'

It was under the sway of that same inner turmoil and absence of reflection that when St-Jérôme came back downstairs and said that, since I had behaved and studied so badly, I had no business being there that day and would have to go up to my room at once, I stuck out my tongue at him and announced that I wasn't going anywhere.

St-Jérôme was at first speechless with astonishment and fury.

'*C'est bien*,'[24] he said, coming after me. 'I've promised to punish you several times before and it's always been your grandmother's wish to spare you, but now I see that the only thing that will make you obey is a good birching, and you've certainly earned one today.'

He said it so loudly that everyone heard him. The blood rushed into my heart with terrific force: I felt it pound, and the colour drain from my face, and my lips quiver involuntarily. I must have been an awful sight at that moment, for St-Jérôme, avoiding my gaze, quickly came over to me and seized me by the arm. But as soon as I felt his hand, I was so overcome with rage that I tore my arm away and hit him with all my child's strength.

'What's the matter with you?' Volodya said, coming over to me after watching my behaviour in astonishment and horror.

'Leave me alone!' I screamed at him through my tears. 'No one cares anything about me or understands how unhappy I am! You're all vile and disgusting!' I added in a sort of frenzy, addressing the entire company.

But at that instant, St-Jérôme came after me again with a pale, determined face, and before I could defend myself had seized both my arms in a strong, vice-like grip and started to drag me away. I was delirious with rage, and the only thing I remember is desperately lashing out with my head and knees while I still had the strength to do so, banging my nose against someone's thighs several times, getting someone's coat in my mouth, and being aware of the proximity on every side of someone's legs and the smell of dust and the *violette* that St-Jérôme used as a scent.

Five minutes later the storage-closet door closed behind me.

'*Vasile!*' he said in a hideous, exultant voice. 'Bring me a birch rod!'

FIFTEEN
Daydreams

Could I really have thought then that I would survive the disasters that had befallen me, or that a time would come when I could calmly remember them?

As I recalled what I had done, I couldn't imagine what would happen to me, although I did have a vague sense that I was irretrievably lost.

At first, complete silence reigned below and around me, or so it seemed to me in my overwrought state, but then I gradually began to make out different sounds. Vasily came upstairs, and after tossing something like a broom onto the windowsill, stretched out on a bin with a yawn. Down below the loud voice of Avgust Antonych[25] could be heard, no doubt talking about me, and then children's voices, and then laughter and running around, and then, after a few more minutes, the whole house returned to its previous movement, as if no one knew or cared that I was sitting in the dark storage closet.

I didn't cry, although something lay heavily on my heart like a stone. Thoughts and images passed through my distraught imagination with increasing speed, but the memory of what had happened kept interrupting their fantastical train, and I would find myself back in a closed labyrinth of despair, fear, and ignorance about what lay ahead.

Then it occurred to me there must be some unknown reason for the general dislike and even loathing of me. (I was firmly convinced at the time that everyone, from Grandmother to Filipp the coachman, hated me and and took pleasure in my sufferings.) 'It must be that I'm not my mother and father's son, nor Volodya's brother, but a wretched orphan, a foundling taken in for charity's sake,' I said to myself, and that ridiculous idea not only provided a kind of melancholy solace, but even seemed quite plausible. It was comforting to think that I was unhappy not through any fault of my own, but because it had been my fate from birth – that my lot was like that of the unhappy Karl Ivanych.

'But why keep it a secret any more, when I myself have already guessed?' I said to myself. 'Tomorrow I'll go to Papa and say to him, "Papa, there's no reason for you to hide the secret of my birth from me. I know it." He'll say, "What's to be done, my friend? Sooner or later, you were going to find out. You're not my son, but adopted, and if you're worthy of my love, I'll never abandon you." And I'll say to him, "Papa, even though I've no right to call you that, and say it now for the last time, I've always loved you and will love you, and never will I forget that you are my benefactor, but I cannot remain in your home any longer. No one cares about me here, and St-Jérôme has sworn to destroy me. Either he or I must leave your home, for I cannot answer for my actions; my hatred of that man is so great that I could do anything. I'll kill him." That's what I'll say: "Papa, I'll kill him!" Papa will start to plead with me, but I'll wave my hand and say, "No, my friend, my benefactor, we cannot live together, so let me go," and I'll embrace him and say, in French for some reason, "*Oh mon père, oh mon bienfaiteur, donne-moi pour la dernière fois ta bénédiction et que la volonté de dieu soit faite!*"[26] And sitting on a trunk there in the dark storage closet, I sob uncontrollably at the thought. But then I suddenly remember the shameful punishment awaiting me, and reality presents itself in its true light and my daydreams are instantly dispelled.

Then I imagine myself at liberty and outside our home. I've joined the hussars and gone off to war. I'm beset by foes on every side. I swing my sabre and kill one, and then with a second blow, another, and then a third. Finally, faint from my wounds and exhaustion, I fall to the ground and cry, 'Victory!' A general rides up and asks, 'Where is he, our saviour?' They point to me and he embraces me with tears in his eyes and cries, 'Victory!' I recover from my wounds, and with my arm in a black sling I'm walking along Tverskoy Boulevard. I'm a general! And then the *sovereign* drives by and asks who that wounded young man is. They tell him it's the famous hero, Nikolay. The sovereign comes to me and says, 'You have my gratitude. I'll grant whatever you ask of me.' I bow respectfully, and leaning on my sabre I say, 'I'm happy, great sovereign, that I could shed my blood for my fatherland, and I would die for it, but if you will be so kind as to grant a request, then I do have one: permit me to destroy my enemy, the foreigner St-Jérôme. I want to destroy my enemy, St-Jérôme.' I stand menacingly before St-Jérôme and say to him, 'You're the cause of my unhappiness. *À genoux!*'[27] But then it suddenly occurs to me that the real St-Jérôme might at any moment walk in with a birch rod, and I no longer see myself as a general saving his fatherland, but once again as a miserable wretch.

And then I begin to think about God and brazenly ask Him why He's punishing me. 'I have, I think, never forgotten to pray morning and night, so why do I suffer?' I can positively say that the first steps towards the religious doubts that troubled me in boyhood were taken then, not because my unhappiness provoked grumbling and disbelief, but because the idea of the injustice of Providence that came to me in that time of complete mental disorder and day-long isolation quickly began to germinate and put down roots, like a bad seed fallen on soft earth after rain. I imagined then that I would certainly die, and vividly pictured St-Jérôme's surprise on finding a lifeless body in the storage closet instead of me. Recalling Natalya Savishna's stories that the soul of the deceased remains in its home for forty days, I mentally hover as an invisible spirit in all the rooms of Grandmother's house after my death and listen to Lyubochka's sincere tears, Grandmother's sorrow and Papa's conversation with Avgust Antonych. 'He was a fine lad,' Papa will say with tears in his eyes. 'Yes,' St-Jérôme will reply, 'but a tremendous scamp.' 'You ought to respect the dead,' Papa will tell him. 'You were the cause of his death, you filled him with fear and he could not tolerate the humiliation you were preparing for him ... Depart, scoundrel!'

And St-Jérôme will fall on his knees, and weep and beg forgiveness. After forty days my soul then flies to heaven. There

I see something astonishingly beautiful, white, translucent and tall, and sense it is my mother. That white something surrounds and caresses me, but I feel uneasy and barely recognize her. 'If it really is you,' I say, 'show yourself to me more clearly, so I can embrace you.' And her voice replies, 'We're all like this here and I can't embrace you any better. Do you really not like it?' 'No, it's very good, but you can't tickle me and I can't kiss your hands.' 'That isn't necessary; it's beautiful here, even so,' she says, and I sense that it really is beautiful, and together we fly higher and higher. Then I awake and find myself again on a trunk in the dark storage closet, my cheeks wet with tears as I vacantly repeat the words, 'we all fly higher and higher'. For a long time I make a great effort to understand my position, but the only thing that presents itself to my mental gaze is a terrifyingly gloomy, impenetrable expanse. I try to return to the happy, comforting daydreams that had been interrupted by the consciousness of reality, but to my surprise, as soon as I enter the track of my earlier musings, I find that their continuation is impossible and, what is more surprising, that they no longer give me any satisfaction at all.

SIXTEEN

It Will All Work Out in the End

I spent the night in the storage closet, and no one came to see me. The next day, on Sunday, that is, I was taken to the little room next to the classroom and locked in again. I was beginning to hope that my punishment would be limited to confinement, and thanks to a sweet, fortifying sleep, the bright sunshine playing in the hoarfrost on the windows, and the usual daytime noise in the streets, my thoughts were growing calmer. But the isolation was still very hard: I wanted to move around and tell someone about all the things that had accumulated in my heart, but there wasn't any living creature near. The situation was made all the more unpleasant by the fact that, as loathsome to me as it was, I still couldn't help hearing St-Jérôme calmly whistling merry tunes to himself as he walked around his room. I was fully convinced that he didn't really want to whistle, but was only doing it to torment me.

At two o'clock St-Jérôme and Volodya went downstairs and Nikolay brought me dinner, and after I talked to him about what I had done and what might lie in store for me, he said, 'Don't fret, sir, it will all work out in the end.'

Although that saying, which afterwards would bolster my spirits more than once, did comfort me a bit, the fact that I had been sent not bread and water but a whole dinner and even sweet rolls required serious thought. If they hadn't sent sweet rolls, that would have meant that confinement was the punishment, but now it turned out that I still hadn't been punished, that I had only been separated from the others like some dangerous person, and the punishment still lay ahead. While I was engaged in the solution to that problem, a key turned in the lock of my cell and St-Jérôme came into the room with a stern, official expression on his face.

'Let's go and see your grandmother,' he said, without looking at me.

Before leaving the room, I wanted to brush off the sleeves of my jacket, which were covered with chalk dust, but St-Jérôme said that it wasn't necessary, as if I were already in such a pitiful mental state that my appearance wasn't worth troubling over.

As St-Jérôme led me by the arm through the salon, Katenka, Lyubochka and Volodya looked at me exactly the same way that we looked at the convicts led past our windows every Monday. And when I went up to Grandmother's chair with the intention of kissing her hand, she turned away and put it under her mantilla.

'Yes, my dear,' she said after a rather lengthy silence, during which she gazed at me from head to toe with such an expression that I didn't know where to look or what to do with my hands, 'I can say that you have held my love in high regard and been a genuine comfort to me. *Monsieur* St-Jérôme, who undertook your education at my request,' she added, drawing out every word, 'now no longer wishes to remain in my home. Why? Because of you, my dear. I had hoped that you would be grateful,' she continued after a pause and in a tone that showed that her words had been prepared beforehand, 'for his efforts and care, that you would appreciate his services, but you, you sniveller, you little boy, have dared to raise your hand against him. Very well! Excellent!! I, too, am starting to think that you're incapable of understanding nobler treatment, that for you other, baser means are required. Now apologize to him,' she added in a severe, peremptory voice, pointing at St-Jérôme. 'Do you hear?'

I looked in the direction of Grandmother's hand, but on seeing St-Jérôme's frock coat, I turned away and remained standing where I was, again feeling my heart sink.

'What's this? Do you really not hear what I'm saying to you?'

My whole body shuddered, but I didn't move from my place.

'Koko!' Grandmother said, no doubt sensing the anguish I was feeling. 'Koko,' she said in a no longer peremptory but tender voice, 'is this you?'

'Grandmother, I won't apologize to him for anything,' I said and then stopped, realizing that if I said another word, I wouldn't be able to hold back the tears that were welling up within me.

'I'm ordering you. I'm asking you. What is wrong with you?'

'I . . . I . . . don't . . . want to . . . I can't . . . ,' I stammered, and the tears pent up in my breast suddenly broke through the barrier that had been holding them and burst out in a desperate torrent.

'*C'est ainsi que vous obéissez à votre seconde mère, c'est ainsi que vous reconnaissez ses bontés?*'[28] St-Jérôme said in a tragical voice. '*À genoux!*'

'My goodness, if she had seen this!' Grandmother said, turning away from me and wiping the tears that were filling her own eyes, 'if she had seen . . . It's all for the best. She wouldn't have survived this grief, she wouldn't have survived it.'

And Grandmother wept harder and harder. I wept, too, but I still had no thought of apologizing.

'*Tranquillisez-vous au nom du ciel, madame la comtesse,*'[29] St-Jérôme said.

But Grandmother was no longer listening to him. She covered her face with her hands, and her sobbing rapidly passed into gasping and hysteria. Mimi and Gasha ran into the room with frightened faces; there was an odour of spirits of some kind, and the whole house erupted in running about and whispering.

'Admire your deed,' St-Jérôme said as he led me back upstairs.

'My goodness, what have I done? What a terrible criminal I am!'

No sooner had St-Jérôme gone downstairs after telling me to go to my room than, without a thought about what I was doing, I started to run down the main staircase to the front door.

Whether I meant to run away from home for good or drown myself, I don't recall; I know only that after covering my face with my hands to keep from seeing anyone, I ran farther and farther down the stairs.

'Where are you going?' a familiar voice suddenly asked me. 'You're just the one I want, my good fellow.'

I tried to run past him, but Papa grabbed me by the arm and said in a stern voice, 'Come along with me, dear fellow!' And he led me into the small sitting room. 'What possessed you to touch the portfolio in my study?' he added, taking hold of my ear. 'Well? Why don't you answer me? Well?'

'I'm sorry,' I said. 'I don't know what came over me.'

'So you don't know what came over you, you don't know, you don't know, you don't know,' he repeated, pulling my ear each time. 'Will you stick your nose where it doesn't belong in the future? Will you? Will you?'

Despite the excruciating pain in my ear, I didn't cry out, but felt a pleasant mental sensation. As soon as Papa let go of my ear, I grabbed his hand and started to kiss it.

'Hit me again,' I said through my tears, 'harder and more painfully. I'm a vile, worthless, miserable person!'

'What is the matter with you?' he said, lightly pushing me away.

'No, nothing will make me go,' I said, tightly holding on to his frock coat. 'Everyone hates me, I know that, but listen to me for heaven's sake, protect me or send me away. I can't live with him. *He*'s always trying to humiliate me and makes me kneel before him. He wants to flog me. I can't allow it. I'm not a little child. I won't tolerate it. I'll die. I'll kill myself. *He* told Grandmother that I'm worthless, and now she's sick and will die because of me. I . . . with . . . him . . . for heaven's sake, beat me . . . why . . . do . . . they . . . tor . . . ment . . . ?'

I was choking on my tears. I sat down on the sofa, and unable to say anything more, fell with my head on his knees, sobbing so hard I thought I would certainly die that very instant.

'What are you talking about, little fellow?' Papa asked sympathetically, leaning over me.

'*He*'s a tyrant, a torturer . . . I'll die . . . No one loves me!' I said, barely able to pronounce the words and shaking with convulsions.

Papa picked me up in his arms and carried me to my bedroom. I fell asleep.

When I awoke, it was already very late, only one candle was burning beside my bed, and Mimi, Lyubochka and our family doctor were sitting nearby. It was apparent from their faces that they were worried about my health. But I felt so good after my twelve-hour sleep that I would have jumped out of bed at once, had I been willing to disappoint their belief that I was very ill.

SEVENTEEN

Hatred

Yes, it was a genuine feeling of hatred, not the to me unbelievable kind written about only in novels, the one that supposedly enjoys doing harm to another person, but rather the kind that inspires an uncontrollable aversion in you for someone who is nonetheless entitled to your respect, and that makes his hair, his neck, his way of walking, the sound of his voice, and all his parts and movements odious to you, while at the same time some mysterious power draws you to him and compels you to follow his smallest movements with anxious attention. That's how I felt about St-Jérôme.

St-Jérôme had been with us a year and a half. Reflecting dispassionately on him now, I find that he was a good Frenchman, but a Frenchman to the utmost degree. He wasn't stupid – he was, in fact, quite learned, and scrupulously carried out his duties with us – but he possessed the features common to all his countrymen, yet so opposed to the Russian character, of frivolous egoism, vanity, impudence and ignorant self-assurance. And I didn't care for any of that. It goes without saying that Grandmother had explained her views on corporal punishment to him and that he didn't dare beat us, but even so he often threatened us, and especially me, with a birch rod and pronounced the word '*fouetter*'[30] so revoltingly (something like '*fouatter*') and in such a tone of voice that it was as if flogging me would have given him the greatest pleasure.

I wasn't at all afraid of the pain of the punishment, since I had never known it, but the very idea that St-Jérôme could strike me left me in a state of muffled rage and despair.

Karl Ivanych had in moments of irritation used a ruler or his braces to deal with us, but I recall it without the slightest resentment. Even if at the time I'm speaking of (when I was fourteen) Karl Ivanych had given me a thrashing, I would have calmly put up with the blows. I loved Karl Ivanych and remembered him for as long as I remembered myself, and was used to regarding him as a member of our family. St-Jérôme, however, was a smug, conceited person for whom I felt only the involuntary respect that all 'grown-ups' inspired in me. Karl Ivanych was an absurd old man, a 'tutor', whom I loved with all my heart, but still ranked below myself in my childish understanding of social position.

St-Jérôme, on the other hand, was an educated, handsome young dandy who tried to be on equal terms with everyone. Karl Ivanych always scolded and punished us without rancour, so it was clear he considered it an unpleasant but necessary duty. St-Jérôme, however, loved to drape himself in the role of preceptor. It was obvious when he punished us that he was doing it more for his own pleasure than our benefit. He was infatuated with his own splendour. His florid French phrases, which he spoke with a heavy stress on the last syllable with an *accent circonflexe*,[31] were for me unspeakably obnoxious. When Karl Ivanych got angry, he would say in Russian, 'It's a puppet show, you naughty boy, you Spaniard flea.'[32] St-Jérôme would call us '*mauvais sujet*', '*vilain garnement*',[33] and so on, names that injured my pride.

Karl Ivanych made us kneel facing the corner, and the punishment lay in the physical pain produced by that position; St-Jérôme, squaring his chest and making a grandiose gesture with his hand, would cry in a tragical voice, '*À genoux, mauvais sujet!*' and order us to kneel facing him and beg his forgiveness. The punishment lay in the humiliation.

I wasn't punished again, and no one even reminded me of what had happened, but I still couldn't forget any of what I had gone through – the despair, shame, fear and loathing of those two days. Even though St-Jérôme had, as it seemed, from that time washed his hands of me, having virtually nothing to do with me, I still couldn't get used to regarding him with indifference. Every time our eyes met, it seemed to me that the hostility expressed in my own was too conspicuous, and I quickly assumed an expression of unconcern, but then it would seem to me that he had seen through my pretence, and I would blush and turn away.

In short, it was extremely difficult to have any relationship with him at all.

EIGHTEEN
The Maids' Room

I felt more and more alone, and my main pleasures were solitary reflections and observations. I'll speak of the subject of those reflections in the next chapter; the theatre of my observations, however, was primarily the maids' room, where for me a highly interesting and touching romance was underway. Its heroine, needless to say, was Masha. She was in love with Vasily, who had known her even before she was taken into service, and who had promised to marry her then. The fate that separated them five years earlier had brought them back together in Grandmother's house, although it had also placed a barrier between their love for each other in the form of Nikolay, Masha's uncle, who wouldn't even hear of marriage to Vasily, whom he regarded as 'incompatible' and 'unbridled'.

The barrier had resulted in the previously self-possessed and rather negligent Vasily suddenly falling in love with Masha, and doing so as only a pomaded, pink-shirted servant who worked as a tailor could.

Even though the expressions of his love were often bizarre and incongruous (whenever he ran into Masha, for example, he would always try to inflict pain by pinching or hitting her, or hugging her so hard she could barely breathe), the love itself was sincere, as shown by the fact that the first time Nikolay refused him the hand of his niece, Vasily 'took to drink' from grief, and began to hang about taverns and get into brawls – in a word, to behave so badly that he more than once suffered the disgrace of a jail cell. But those actions and their consequences had, it seemed, a merit in Masha's eyes, and made her love him even more. Whenever Vasily was 'detained by the police', she would weep for days, complain of her bitter lot to Gasha (who took an active interest in the unhappy lovers' affairs) and, scorning the abuse and blows of her uncle, secretly run to the station house to visit and calm her friend.

Reader, do not disdain the society into which I am taking you. If the strings of love and sympathy still vibrate in your own heart, then in the maids' room, too, they'll find sounds with which to resonate. Whether you care to follow me or not, I'll go to the stairway landing from which all that happens in the maids' room may be seen. There's the wide shelf of the stove with an iron, a cardboard doll with a battered nose, a basin and a ewer on it; there's the windowsill, where a chunk of black wax, a spool of silk thread, a partly eaten cucumber and a box of sweets are scattered; and there's the large red table on which new sewing waits under a calico-wrapped brick, and at which *she*'s sitting in my favourite pink cotton dress and a blue kerchief that particularly attracts my attention. *She*'s sewing, and as she pauses from time to time to scratch her head with the blunt end of her needle or reposition a candle, I watch her and think, 'Why, with her light-blue eyes, long chestnut braid and firm bosom, wasn't she born a lady? How it would become her to sit in a drawing room in a bonnet with pink ribbons and a crimson silk dressing gown, not the kind that Mimi wears, but the one I saw on Tverskoy Boulevard. She would be working with an embroidery frame, and I would gaze at her in the mirror, and whatever she wanted, I would do; I would help her with her pelerine or serve her dinner myself . . .'

What an appalling figure Vasily makes with his drunkard's face and the narrow frock coat he wears over a filthy, untucked-in pink shirt! In every movement of his body, in every bend of his back, I seem to detect unquestionable signs of the terrible punishment he endures.

'What, again, Vasya?' Masha said, sticking her needle in a pin cushion, but without looking up at him as he entered.

'Well, what of it? Can any good really come from *him*?' Vasily answered. 'Just let him finish it, one way or the other. As it is, I'm going under for nothing, and all on account of *him*.'

'Will you have some tea?' asked Nadezha, another chamber-maid.

'I thank you kindly. Why does he hate me, that thief uncle of yours? Because I've got real clothes of my own, because of my strut, because of the way I walk? One word: it's a shame!' Vasily concluded with a wave of his hand.

'You should be humble,' Masha said, biting off the thread, 'but you always . . .'

'I haven't got the strength for it, that's what!'

At that moment the sound of Grandmother's door was heard, followed by the grumbling voice of Gasha coming up the stairs.

'Just try and please her when she herself doesn't know what she wants. A *cussed* life of hard labour! If there's one thing I wish – forgive my sin, O Lord,' she muttered, waving her hands.

'My respects to you, Agafya Mikhailovna,' Vasily said, getting up to greet her.

'You? Spare me your respects,' she menacingly replied, looking at him. 'What are you doing here? Is the maids' room really a place for men?'

'I wanted to enquire after your health,' Vasily timidly answered.

'I'll pop off soon enough, that's the kind of health!' Agafya Mikhailovna shouted even more angrily.

Vasily started to laugh.

'There's nothing to laugh about, and if I say get going, then march! Why, the rascal wants to get married, too, the scoundrel! Well, march! Get going!'

And stomping her feet, Agafya Mikhailovna went into her room, slamming the door so hard the glass in the windows rattled.

For a long time she could be heard on the other side of the partition abusing everything and everyone and cursing her life, as she tossed her things about and pulled the ears of her favourite cat. Finally, the door opened and with a pitiful meow the cat came flying out, flung by its tail.

'Maybe I'll come for tea another time,' Vasily whispered. 'Till then.'

'It's nothing,' Nadezha said with a wink. 'I'll check on the samovar.'

'Yes, I'll put an end to it myself,' Vasily continued, moving closer to Masha after Nadezha left the room. 'Either I'll go straight to the countess and say, "One way or the other," or else I'll . . . give it all up and run far, far away, I truly will, so help me God. '

'But what about me?'

'You're the only one I feel sorry for, or else this body of mine would have been lo-ong gone, it truly would, so help me God.'

'Why don't you let me wash your shirts for you, Vasya?' Masha asked after a pause. 'Look how dirty this one is,' she added, taking a hold of his collar.

Just then Grandmother's little bell was heard downstairs, and Gasha came back out of her room.

'Well now, what are you trying to get from her, you scoundrel?' she said, pushing Vasily towards the door after he quickly stood up. 'You brought the girl to this and you're still pestering her? It's clear you like to see her cry, you shameless rascal. Out! And don't let me catch you here again. What do you see in him?' she continued to Masha after Vasily had left. 'Hasn't your uncle beaten you enough over him today? No, it's always got to be your way: "I won't marry anyone but Vasily Gruskov." Fool!'

'No, I won't marry anyone else! I don't love anyone else, even if you beat me to death over him!' Masha said, bursting into tears.

I watched Masha a long time as she sat on a trunk, wiping her tears with her kerchief, and I tried in every way I could to change my idea of Vasily, seeking the point of view from which he could be so attractive to her. But although I sincerely sympathized with her sorrow, I still couldn't grasp how a creature as charming as Masha seemed in my own eyes could ever love Vasily.

'When I'm grown up,' I reasoned with myself after I had gone back up to my room, 'Petrovskoye will be mine, and Vasily and Masha will be my serfs. I'll be sitting in my study smoking a pipe, and Masha will pass by with an iron on her way to the kitchen. I'll say, "Send Masha to me." She'll come and no one else will be in the room. Then Vasily will come, too, and on seeing Masha will say, "This body's done for!" and Masha will start to cry. And I'll say, "Vasily! I know that you love her and that she loves you. Here's a thousand roubles. Marry her, and may God grant you happiness," and I'll go out to the sitting room.' Among the countless thoughts and daydreams that pass through your mind and imagination without a trace, there are a few that leave a deep, sensitive furrow behind, so that even after you've forgotten the essence of the thought, you still remember that there was something good in your mind and sense the thought's trace and try to reproduce it. The thought of sacrificing my feelings for the happiness that Masha could only find in marriage to Vasily had left just such a deep furrow in my own mind.

NINETEEN

Boyhood

It will scarcely be believed what my favourite and most constant subjects of reflection were in boyhood, so incompatible were they with my age and position. But a lack of compatibility between a person's position and his mental activity is, in my opinion, the surest sign of truth.

During the year in which I led a solitary mental life concentrated on itself alone, all the abstract questions about human purpose, the future life and immortality of the soul had already presented themselves to me, and my feeble child's intellect tried with all the ardour of inexperience to make sense of those questions, the posing of which is the highest rung the human intellect can reach, even if the answers aren't given to it.

I believe that the development of the intellect in each person follows the same path that it takes over whole generations – that the ideas that have served as the foundations of various philosophical theories are integral parts of the intellect, and that everyone becomes more or less clearly aware of them, even before knowing about the existence of the philosophical theories themselves.

Those ideas presented themselves to my own intellect so clearly and strikingly that I even tried to apply them to life, imagining that I was the *first* to discover such great and useful truths.

Once the idea came to me that happiness depends not on external circumstances but on our attitude towards them – that the person who has learned to tolerate suffering cannot be unhappy, and to inure myself to it, I would hold Tatishchev's lexicons at arm's length for five minutes, despite the terrific pain, or go to the storage closet and lash my bare back with a rope so hard that my eyes would water.

Another time, after suddenly remembering that death could come to me at any hour or minute, I decided, not understanding why people hadn't realized it before, that there's no other way to be happy than to enjoy the present without any thought for the future, and under the influence of that idea I abandoned lessons for three days and did nothing but lie in bed reading some novel and eating spice cakes with Krohn[34] mead that I had bought with the last of my money.

Yet another time as I was standing at the blackboard drawing various shapes with chalk, I was suddenly struck by the thought: why is symmetry pleasant to the eye? What is symmetry? It's an innate feeling, I answered myself. But on what is it based? Is there symmetry in everything in life? On the contrary, here's life, and I drew an oval on the blackboard. After life, the soul enters eternity; here's eternity, and I made a line extending from the oval all the way to the edge of the blackboard. But why isn't there another line on the other side? And, indeed, what sort of eternity could there be on only one side? We probably existed before this life, although we've lost all memory of it.

That argument, which seemed extraordinarily novel and lucid to me, although I can barely make sense of it now, pleased me very much, and getting out a sheet of paper I thought I would put it down in writing. But such a welter of thoughts came to me in the meantime that I had to get up and walk around the room. When I reached the window, my attention was caught by the water horse, which the coachman happened to be harnessing, and all my thoughts were directed at answering a new question: into what animal or person would the soul of the water horse pass when it died? Volodya, who was walking through the room just then, smiled on noticing that I was pondering something, and that smile was enough to make me realize that everything I had been thinking about was the most awful rubbish.

I've recounted this instance, memorable to me for some reason, to give the reader an idea of the nature of my cogitations.

But there was no philosophical outlook that I was more taken with than scepticism, which for a while brought me to a state verging on lunacy. I imagined that except for me, no one and nothing else existed in the whole world, that things weren't things but images that existed only when I directed my attention to them, and that as soon as I stopped thinking about them those images would instantly vanish. In a word, I converged with Schelling[35] in the conviction that it isn't things that exist but my relation to them. There were moments under the influence of that 'fixed idea' when I reached such a degree of extravagance that I would suddenly turn around, hoping to catch nothingness (*néant*) by surprise where I no longer was.

What a pitiful, insignificant mainspring of mental activity the human intellect is!

My own feeble intellect couldn't penetrate the impenetrable, and one after another, in an effort beyond my strength, I lost all the convictions that for the sake of my own happiness I should never have touched.

I derived nothing from all that hard mental labour except a facility of mind that weakened my willpower, and a habit of continual analysis that destroyed freshness of feeling and clarity of reasoning in me.

Abstract ideas are formed as a result of a person's ability to capture with his consciousness the state of his mind at a certain moment and transfer it to memory. My penchant for abstract reflection developed consciousness in me to such an unnatural degree that often, when starting to think about the simplest matter, I would fall into a closed circle of analysis of my own thoughts and think not about the question at hand, but about the fact that I was thinking about it. Asking myself, 'What am I thinking about?' I would answer, 'I'm thinking about what I'm thinking about.' 'What am I thinking about now?' 'I'm thinking about what I'm thinking about what I'm thinking about,' and so on. I was at the end of my tether . . .

Nevertheless, the philosophical discoveries I made were extremely flattering to my self-esteem: I frequently imagined myself a great man disclosing new truths for the benefit of all humanity and looked on other mortals with a proud awareness of my own merit. Yet, oddly enough, whenever I came into contact with those other mortals I was intimidated by them, and the higher my regard for myself, the less I was able with others not only to convey an awareness of my own merit but even to get used to not being ashamed of my simplest words and gestures.

TWENTY
Volodya

Yes, the further I go in describing this period of my life, the more distressing and difficult it is for me. Very, very rarely among the memories of that time do I find moments of the truly warm feeling that so brightly and constantly illumined the start of my life. In spite of myself, I want to hurry through the wilderness of boyhood to reach the happy days when truly tender, noble feelings of friendship again lit up that period with a bright light and marked the beginning of a new one filled with charm and poetry – that of youth.

I won't retrace my recollections hour by hour, but will quickly look at the main ones between the point to which I've already brought my narrative and that of my friendship with an exceptional person who had a decisive and beneficial influence on my character and outlook.

Volodya is to take his entrance examinations for the university in a few days; the teachers have been coming to work separately with him, and I listen with envy and involuntary respect as he briskly taps the blackboard with chalk, while explaining functions, sines, coordinates and the like, all of which seem like expressions of unintelligible intricacy to me. But then one Sunday after dinner, all the teachers and two professors gather in Grandmother's room, and in the presence of Papa and a few guests conduct a rehearsal for the university examinations, and to Grandmother's great delight Volodya demonstrates exceptional knowledge. I, too, am asked questions on a few subjects, although I prove to be quite poor, and it's clear the professors are trying to conceal my ignorance from Grandmother, which only embarrasses me more. Actually, they pay little attention to me at all:

I'm only fifteen, which means I have another year before my own examinations. Volodya only comes down for dinner, spending all day and even all evening upstairs at his studies – not from need but because he wants to. He's extremely proud and means to pass his examinations not with satisfactory but with superior marks.

And now the day of the first examination has arrived. Volodya puts on a blue tailcoat with bronze buttons and a gold watch and patent-leather boots. Papa's phaeton drives up to the front steps, Nikolay throws back the apron, and Volodya and St-Jérôme set off for the university. The girls, but especially Katenka, look out of the window with joyful, delighted faces at the graceful figure of Volodya in the carriage; Papa says, 'God willing, God willing'; and Grandmother, who has come to the window, too, makes the sign of the cross at Volodya with tears in her eyes, and whispers something as the phaeton disappears around the corner of our lane.

Volodya returns. All impatiently ask, 'Well? Good? What mark?' but it's clear from his merry face that all went well. He received a five. The next day he's sent off with the same anxiety and wishes for success and greeted on his return with the same impatience and joy. Thus nine days pass. On the tenth is to be the last and most difficult examination, the one on religion,[36] and everyone's standing by the window and waiting for his return with even greater impatience. It's already two o'clock, but Volodya still isn't back.

'Oh my goodness! Heavenly father! It's them! It's them!' Lyubochka screams, pressed against the glass.

And indeed Volodya is sitting in the phaeton beside St-Jérôme, although no longer in a blue tailcoat and grey cap, but in a student uniform with a light-blue embroidered collar, a cocked hat, and a gilt sword at his side.

'If only *you* were alive!' Grandmother exclaims upon seeing Volodya in his uniform, and then falls back in a swoon.

Volodya runs into the entry room with a beaming face and embraces and kisses me, Lyubochka and Katenka, who blushes to her very ears. Volodya is beside himself with joy. And how handsome he is in his uniform! How well its light-blue collar suits his emerging black moustache! How slim his long waist is and how noble his walk! On that memorable day we all dine in Grandmother's room, happiness shines in every face, and over the pastries the butler, with an expression both properly dignified and merry, brings a bottle of champagne wrapped in a napkin. It's the first time Grandmother has drunk champagne since *maman*'s death and she empties an entire goblet while congratulating Volodya, and weeps again with joy as she gazes at him. Volodya now goes out for drives by himself in his own carriage, receives his *own* friends, smokes, goes to balls, and has even, as I myself saw, consumed two bottles of champagne in his room with his friends, toasting the health of certain mysterious ladies with each goblet and arguing over who would get *le fond de la bouteille*.[37] He usually dines at home, however, and after dinner goes into the sitting room, just as before, where he talks about something with Katenka, always in private. But as far as I can tell without taking part in their conversations, they're only talking about the heroes and heroines of novels they've read, and about jealousy and love, although I don't understand at all why those conversations are so interesting to them, or what makes them smile so slyly and argue so vehemently.

In general, I've noticed that besides their understandable friendship as childhood companions, strange relations of a new kind have developed between Katenka and Volodya that distance them from us and mysteriously connect them to each other.

TWENTY-ONE
Katenka and Lyubochka

Katenka's sixteen and has grown. The angularity of form, shyness and awkward movements characteristic of girls at a transitional age have all yielded to the harmonious freshness and grace of a just opened flower, although she herself hasn't changed: the same light-blue eyes and cheerful gaze, the same little nose making an almost straight line with her forehead, the same flared nostrils and small mouth with its bright smile, the same little dimples in her clear pink cheeks, and the same little white hands; and just as before the epithet 'pure young girl' for some reason fits her extraordinarily well. The only new things about her are the thick chestnut braid that she wears like a grown-up and her young bosom, whose emergence clearly both pleases and embarrasses her.

Although Lyubochka has grown up and been raised with Katenka, she is in every respect a completely different girl.

Lyubochka is short and, as a result of her rickets, she still has bandy legs and a terrible waist. The only good thing about her appearance is her eyes, which really are beautiful: large, dark and with such an indefinably pleasant expression of gravity and naïveté that they cannot fail to catch your attention. Lyubochka is simple and natural in everything; Katenka, however, seems to want to be like someone else. Lyubochka's gaze is always direct, and sometimes when she fixes her enormous dark eyes on someone, she doesn't remove them for such a long time that people rebuke her for it, saying it isn't polite; Katenka, on the contrary, drops her eyelashes, squints and claims to be short-sighted, although I know very well her vision is perfect. Lyubochka doesn't like to play-act with strangers, and when anyone tries to kiss her in front of guests, she makes a wry face and says that she can't stand 'mushy' displays; Katenka, by contrast, is always particularly affectionate with Mimi in front of guests and likes to walk around the salon arm in arm with other girls. Lyubochka is an awful giggler, and sometimes in a fit of laughter she flaps her arms and gallops around the room; Katenka, on the contrary, covers her mouth with her handkerchief or her hands whenever she starts to laugh. Lyubochka always sits straight and walks with her arms hanging down; Katenka carries her head slightly to the side and walks with her arms folded in front. Lyubochka is always extremely happy whenever she manages to converse with a grown-up man and says that she'll certainly marry a hussar; Katenka says that all men are disgusting, that she'll never marry, and changes completely, as if she were afraid of something, whenever a man speaks to her. Lyubochka is endlessly indignant with Mimi for lacing her up in corsets 'until she can't breathe', and she likes to eat; Katenka, by sticking her finger under the scalloping below her bodice, often shows us how loose it is for her, and eats extraordinarily little. Lyubochka likes to draw heads; Katenka, however, draws only flowers and butterflies. Lyubochka plays Field's concertos and several of Beethoven's sonatas with great precision; Katenka plays waltzes and variations, slows down the tempo, bangs the keys, pedals constantly and, before beginning anything, always plays three chords in *arpeggio* with feeling . . .

But according to my opinion at the time, Katenka seems more grown-up and is thus much more to my liking.

TWENTY-TWO

Papa

Papa's been particularly jolly since Volodya entered the university and dines at Grandmother's more often than usual. But the real reason for his jollity, as I learned from Nikolay, is that he's won an extraordinarily large amount of late. It even happens now that before going out to the club in the evening, he drops by to see us, sits down at the piano, gathers us around him, and sings Gypsy songs, while tapping with his soft boots (he can't stand stacked heels and never wears them). And then you would have to see the absurd delight of his favourite, Lyubochka, who for her part simply adores him. Sometimes he comes up to the classroom and listens with a stern face as I recite my lessons, although from the few words he says by way of correction, I can tell he has little knowledge of what I'm being taught. Sometimes he gives us a sly wink and makes signs to us whenever Grandmother starts to grumble and get angry with us for no reason. 'Well, *we* really caught it, didn't we, children?' he says afterwards. In general, he's come down a bit from the unattainable summit on which my childish imagination had placed him. I kiss his large white hand with the same sincere feeling of love and respect, but now permit myself to think about him and judge his actions and, in spite of myself, have thoughts about him that scare me. I'll never forget the event that inspired many of those thoughts and that was the occasion of a good deal of mental distress in me.

Once, dressed in a black tailcoat and white waistcoat, Papa came into the drawing room late in the evening just before going out to a ball with Volodya, who was still getting ready in his room. Grandmother was waiting for Volodya to come and present himself (it was her custom to call him to her before every ball, bless him, look him over, and give him instructions). Mimi and Katenka were walking up and down the salon, which was lit by a single lamp, and Lyubochka was sitting at the piano practising Field's second concerto, *maman*'s favourite.

I've never seen in any other family a resemblance like that between my sister and mama. It wasn't in Lyubochka's face or figure, but in something more elusive: her hands, the way she walked, and especially her voice and some of her expressions. When she got angry and said, 'We haven't been let out for ages,' the phrase 'for ages', which *maman* also had the habit of using, was enunciated in a way that made it sound drawn out: 'for a-a-ges'. But the most extraordinary resemblance was in the way Lyubochka played the piano and all her little manoeuvres when she did so: just like *maman*, she would smooth her dress, turn the pages with her left hand from above and, whenever a difficult passage was slow in coming, pound the keys with her fist in vexation and say 'Good Lord!' Her playing also had the same elusive tenderness and precision, the same lovely Field style that has been so well termed '*jeu perlé*'[38] and whose charm will not be forgotten, despite the hocus-pocus of the newest pianists.

Papa came into the room with quick little steps and went over to Lyubochka, who stopped playing when she saw him.

'No, don't stop, Lyuba, keep on playing,' he said, sitting her back down. 'You know how much I enjoy listening to you ...'

Lyubochka continued to play, and Papa sat across from her a long time, resting on his elbow. Then with a sudden shrug of his shoulder, he got up and started to walk around the room. Each time he came to the piano, he stopped and gazed at Lyubochka. I could see from his movements and the way he walked that he was agitated. After going around the salon several times, he stopped behind Lyubochka's seat, kissed her dark head, then quickly turned and continued to pace. When she finished the piece and went over to him to ask 'Was it all right?' he silently took her head in his hands and began to kiss her forehead and eyes with a tenderness I had never seen in him before.

'Good Lord, you're crying!' Lyubochka suddenly said, letting go of his watch chain and fixing her large, astonished eyes on his face. 'Forgive me, darling Papa, I completely forgot it was *Mama's piece.*'

'No, my friend, play it more often,' he said in a voice trembling with feeling. 'If you only knew how good it is for me to have a cry with you . . .'

He kissed her again and, trying to control his inner turmoil, shrugged his shoulder and went out of the door leading through the hallway to Volodya's room.

'*Woldemar!* Are you just about ready?' he shouted, stopping in the middle of the hallway. At that moment the chambermaid Masha was passing through and, seeing the master, she lowered her eyes and tried to get by him. He stopped her.

'You're getting prettier and prettier,' he said, leaning over her.

Masha blushed and lowered her head even more.

'Please allow me to pass,' she whispered.

'*Woldemar*, how about it, are you quite ready?' Papa repeated, shrugging his shoulder and coughing after Masha had gone past and he saw me.

I love my father, but the human mind lives independently of the heart and often contains thoughts that offend our feeling and seem incomprehensible and cruel to it.

And such thoughts come to me despite my effort to dispel them . . .

TWENTY-THREE
Grandmother

Grandmother has been getting weaker each day. Her little bell, Gasha's grumbling voice, and the sound of slamming doors have been heard more frequently in her room, and she no longer receives us in the study in her Voltaire armchair, but in her bedroom on her high bed with its lace-edged pillows. Greeting her, I notice a shiny, pale-yellowish growth on her hand and the same oppressive odour that I was aware of in Mama's room five years before. The doctor sees her three times a day, and there have been several consultations with specialists. But her character and her proud, imperious treatment of the entire household, and especially of Papa, haven't changed at all. She draws out her words just as before, and raises her eyebrows and says 'my dear'.

And then for several days we aren't allowed in to see her and one morning during lessons St-Jérôme suggests that I go for a ride with Lyubochka and Katenka. Although I notice as I'm getting into the sleigh that the pavement in front of Grandmother's windows is covered with straw and that people in long blue coats are standing by our gate, I don't at all understand why we've been sent for a ride at such an inappropriate hour. That day Lyubochka and I are for some reason in an especially merry mood the whole way, and every little occasion, every word, every movement makes us laugh.

A hawker grabs his tray and scampers across the street and we laugh. A dilapidated hack, flapping the ends of its reins, overtakes our sleigh at a gallop and we guffaw. Filipp gets his whip caught under the sleigh's runners and, turning around, says 'Oh, my!' and we collapse in hilarity. Mimi says with a disapproving look that only 'silly people' laugh for no reason, and Lyubochka, her face red from the effort not to laugh, looks at me from under her brow, our eyes meet, and we let loose such Homeric guffawing that there are tears in our eyes and we're no longer capable of holding back the explosions of laughter that overcome us. No sooner do we calm down a bit than I look over at Lyubochka and say a cryptic little word that has lately been in favour with us and that always produces a laugh, and we're overcome again.

Approaching the house on the way back, I've just opened my mouth to make one more excellent face at Lyubochka when I'm startled to see a black coffin cover leaning against one side of the front door, and my mouth remains fixed in the same distorted position.

'*Votre grande-mère est morte*,'[39] St-Jérôme says with an ashen face as he comes out to meet us.

The whole time Grandmother's body is in the house, I'm oppressed by the fear of death; that is, her dead body vividly and unpleasantly reminds me that some day I too must die – a feeling that for some reason we confuse with sorrow. I'm not sorry about Grandmother, nor is hardly anyone else truly sorry about her either. Although the house is full of visitors in mourning, no one feels sorry about her death, except for one person whose frenzied grief is inexpressibly astonishing to me. That person is the chambermaid Gasha. She goes up to the attic, locks herself in, can't stop crying, curses herself, tears her hair, won't listen to any counsel, and says that death remains the only comfort for her after the loss of her beloved mistress.

I repeat that implausibility in matters of feeling is the surest sign of truth.

Grandmother is no more, but memories and various rumours about her live on in our home. Those rumours mostly pertain to the will she made just before her death, and about which no one but her executor, Prince Ivan Ivanych, knows anything. I observe a certain anxiety among Grandmother's serfs and hear frequent talk about who will go to whom, and, I'll admit, I involuntarily have glad thoughts about our receiving a legacy.

Six weeks later Nikolay, a perpetual source of news in our

home, informs me that Grandmother has left her entire estate to Lyubochka, naming as its trustee until she marries not Papa but Prince Ivan Ivanych.

TWENTY-FOUR
Me

I have only a few months left before my university entrance examinations. I have been studying hard, and not only await the teachers without fear but even take pleasure in my classes.

It's fun for me to recite the memorized lessons clearly and precisely. I'm preparing for the mathematics department and, to tell the truth, the only reason I chose it is that I have an exceptional liking for the words 'sine', 'tangent', 'differential', 'integral', etc.

I'm much shorter than Volodya, but broad-shouldered, muscular and just as ugly as before and just as tormented by it. I try to seem original. One thing comforts me: that Papa once said of me that I have a 'clever mug', and my faith in that is complete.

St-Jérôme is satisfied with me and praises me, and not only do I not hate him, but when he sometimes says that 'with your abilities, with your mind' it would be a shame not to do this or that, I even think I like him.

My surveillance of the maids' room is a thing of the past. I'm ashamed to hide behind the door, and the certainty that Masha was in love with Vasily has, I'll admit, rather cooled my ardour anyway. I was finally cured of that unhappy infatuation by their marriage, for which I myself asked Papa's permission at Vasily's request.

When the young people came to Papa with sweets on a tray to express their thanks, and Masha, in a bonnet with blue ribbons, also thanked us all for something, kissing the shoulder of each, I was aware of the smell of rose pomade in her hair but of no feeling at all in myself.

In general, I'm starting to recover little by little from my
boyhood defects, except, of course, the main one, which is
destined to do a good deal of harm in my life – my penchant for
philosophizing.

TWENTY-FIVE

Volodya's Friends

Even though the role I played in the company of Volodya's friends hurt my pride, I still liked to sit in his room when he had guests and silently observe everything that went on there. The aide-de-camp Dubkov and the student Prince Nekhlyudov visited Volodya more than the others. Dubkov was a small, wiry brunet, no longer in the first bloom of youth, a bit short of leg, but not bad-looking and always jovial. He was one of those limited people who are especially agreeable thanks to their limitations, people who are incapable of looking at things from different sides, but are invariably enthusiastic. Their judgements are one-sided and mistaken, but are always pure of heart and attractive. Even their narrow egoism somehow seems forgivable and nice. Dubkov had in addition to that a double charm for Volodya and me: his martial appearance and – the main thing – his age, which young people for some reason are wont to confuse with the idea of respectability (*comme il faut*),[40] held in very high regard in those years. But Dubkov really was what is called *un homme comme il faut*.[41] The only unpleasant part of it for me was that Volodya sometimes seemed ashamed before Dubkov of my most innocent actions, but most of all of my being so young.

Nekhlyudov wasn't good-looking. His little grey eyes, low, sloping forehead and disproportionately long arms and legs couldn't be called handsome. His only good features were his unusually tall stature, fair complexion and excellent teeth. But such original and energetic character was imparted to his face by his narrow gleaming eyes and the constantly changing expression of his smile, now stern, now childishly vague, that you couldn't help but notice it.

He was, I think, quite shy, since every little thing made him blush to his very ears, but his shyness differed from mine. The more he blushed, the more determined his face became, as if he were angry with himself for his weakness.

Although he seemed to be on very friendly terms with Dubkov and Volodya, it was clear that he and they had only come together by chance. Their outlooks were completely different from his. Volodya and Dubkov seemed to be afraid of anything resembling serious discussion or sensitivity; Nekhlyudov, on the contrary, was enthusiastic to the highest degree about such things, and often, despite their mocking, would launch into a discussion of philosophical questions and feelings. Volodya and Dubkov liked to talk about the objects of their love (and were in love with several ladies at once, and often the same ones); Nekhlyudov, on the contrary, always got extremely angry whenever his love for a certain 'redhead' was mentioned.

Volodya and Dubkov often allowed themselves to joke about their relatives, even though they loved them; Nekhlyudov, on the contrary, could be sent into a fury by any untoward reference to his aunt, whom he regarded with a kind of rapturous adoration. After supper, Volodya and Dubkov would go off somewhere without Nekhlyudov, calling him a 'blushing girl'.

Prince Nekhlyudov impressed me from the start with his conversation as much as with his appearance. Yet even though I found in his outlook much in common with my own, or perhaps simply because I did, the feeling he inspired in me the first time we met was far from amicable.

I disliked his quick glance, hard voice and proud appearance, but most of all his complete indifference to me. Often in conversation I badly wanted to contradict him and, as a punishment for his pride, better him in argument and prove to him that I was clever, even if he didn't want to pay any attention to me.

But my shyness prevented it.

TWENTY-SIX

Discussions

Volodya was lying on his sofa, propped on his elbow with his feet up and reading a French novel, when I made my usual visit to his room after my evening classes. He lifted his head for a second to look at me, before continuing to read, a movement of the simplest and most natural kind, but it made me flush. It seemed to me that expressed in the look was a question about why I had come, and in the quick lowering of his head, a wish to conceal the look's meaning from me. That tendency to attribute significance to the simplest movements was a characteristic of mine at that age. I went over to the desk and picked up a book, too, but before I started to read, it occurred to me that since we hadn't seen each other all day, there was something ridiculous about our not saying anything to each other.

'So, are you going to be at home this evening?'

'I don't know. Why?'

'No reason,' I said, and realizing that the conversation wasn't going anywhere, I took the book and started to read.

It's strange that although Volodya and I could spend whole hours side by side without a word, it was enough for a third person, even a silent one, to be present for the most interesting and varied conversations to start up between us. We sensed that we knew each other too well. And knowing too much or too little about someone may each get in the way of closeness.

'Is Volodya at home?' Dubkov's voice was heard in the entry.

'I am,' Volodya said, dropping his feet to the floor and putting his book on the desk.

Dubkov and Nekhlyudov came into the room in their over-coats and hats.

'Well, what do you say, Volodya, shall we go to the theatre?'

'No, I don't have time to,' Volodya replied, turning red.

'What nonsense! Come with us, please.'

'But I don't have a ticket.'

'You can get as many tickets as you like at the door.'

'Just a moment, I'll be right back,' Volodya answered evasively, and with a shrug of his shoulder went out of the room.

I knew that he very much wanted to go to the theatre with Dubkov, and that the reason he had refused was because he didn't have any money, and therefore had gone to borrow five roubles from the butler until he got his next allowance.

'Hello, Diplomat!' Dubkov said, shaking my hand.

Volodya's friends called me 'Diplomat', because my late Grandmother, while talking once about our futures in their pres-ence after dinner, had said that Volodya would join the army, while she hoped to see me as a diplomat in a black tailcoat with my hair combed *à la coq*,[42] a necessary condition of the diplo-matic calling, in her view.

'Where did Volodya go?' Nekhlyudov asked.

'I've no idea,' I answered, blushing at the thought that they had probably already guessed why he had left.

'He probably hasn't any money! True? Oh, Diplomat!' he added in reply to my smile. 'I don't either! How about you, Dubkov?'

'Let's have a look,' Dubkov said, getting out his coin purse and carefully feeling around inside with his stubby fingers. 'Here's a five-kopek piece, and here's a twenty-kopek piece, but otherwise poof-f-f!' he said, making a comical gesture with his hand.

At that moment Volodya came back.

'Well, are we going, then?'

'No.'

'How ridiculous you are!' Nekhlyudov said. 'Why didn't you say you had no money? Take my ticket, if you like.'

'But what about you?'

'He'll join his cousins in their box,' Dubkov said.

'No, I won't go at all.'

'Why not?'

'Because, you know, I don't like sitting in the box.'

'Why not?'

'I don't like it. I feel awkward about it.'

'The same old stuff! I don't understand how it can be awkward for you where everyone's so glad to see you. It's ridiculous, *mon cher*.'

'What can I do, *si je suis timide*?[43] I'm sure that you've never blushed in your life, but I do it all the time over the smallest things!' he said, blushing then, too.

'*Savez-vous d'où vient votre timidité? D'un excès d'amour propre, mon cher*,'[44] Dubkov said in a patronizing tone.

'Just what *excès d'amour propre* do you mean?' Nekhlyudov replied, stung to the quick. 'On the contrary, I'm shy because I have too little *amour propre*. On the contrary, I always think that I'm unpleasant and boring to be with . . . As a result –'

'Get dressed, Volodya,' Dubkov said, taking him by the shoulders and removing his frock coat. 'Ignat, the gentleman needs to get ready!'

'As a result, it often happens to me that –' Nekhlyudov continued.

But Dubkov was no longer listening to him. 'Tra-la-la, ta-ra-ra-la-la!' he started to sing some tune.

'You won't get off that easily,' Nekhlyudov said. 'I'll prove to you that shyness doesn't come from pride at all.'

'You will if you come with us.'

'I said I'm not going.'

'Well, then stay here and prove it to Diplomat, and he'll tell us about it when we come back.'

'And I will prove it,' Nekhlyudov retorted with childish obstinacy. 'Only come back soon. What do you think, am I proud?' he asked, sitting down next to me.

Even though I had an opinion about it, I was so disconcerted by the unexpectedness of the question that it took me a moment to answer.

'I think you are,' I said, feeling my voice tremble and my face flush from the thought that the time had come to prove to him that I was 'clever'. 'I think everyone is, and that whatever anyone does, it's all done from pride.'

'Then what is pride, in your view?' Nekhlyudov asked with a slightly superior smile, as it seemed to me.

'Pride,' I said, 'is the conviction that I'm better and cleverer than anyone else.'

'But how can everyone be convinced of that?'

'I don't know if it's fair or not, only no one but me admits it. I'm convinced that I'm cleverer than everyone else in the world, and I'm sure that you're convinced of the same thing.'

'No, I would be the first to say that I've met people whom I've acknowledged to be cleverer than I am,' Nekhlyudov said.

'That's impossible,' I replied with conviction.

'Is that really what you think?' Nekhlyudov said, staring intently at me.

'I'm serious,' I answered.

And then an idea suddenly came to me, which I at once put into words.

'I'll prove it to you. Why is it that we love ourselves more than we do other people? Because we regard ourselves as better than others, as more worthy of love. If we found others to be better than ourselves, then we would love them more than we do ourselves, yet that never happens. And even if it did, I'm still right,' I added with a smug little smile.

Nekhlyudov was silent for a moment.

'Well, I never thought that you were so clever!' he said to me with such a nice, good-natured smile that all of a sudden I felt extraordinarily happy.

Praise has such a powerful effect not only on a person's feelings but also on his mind that it seemed under its pleasant influence that I had become much cleverer, and new thoughts entered my mind one after another with unusual speed. From pride we moved indiscernibly to love, and the conversation on that subject seemed inexhaustible. Although our discussions might have sounded like arrant nonsense to anyone listening – so vague and one-sided were they – they still held a lofty meaning for us. Our souls were so well attuned that the slightest brushing of a string by one found an echoing response in the other. And it was in the resonance of those different strings struck in conversation that we found our pleasure. It seemed to us that we had neither words nor time to express to each other all the ideas that wanted to come out.

TWENTY-SEVEN
The Start of a Friendship

From that time rather odd but extraordinarily pleasant relations were established between Dmitry Nekhlyudov and me. Around others, he paid almost no attention at all to me, but as soon as we were alone we would sit down in a comfortable corner and start discussing, forgetting everything and not noticing the time fly.

We talked about our future lives, about the arts, about government service, about marriage, about raising children, and it never occurred to us that everything we were saying was the most awful rubbish. It didn't occur to us because the rubbish was nice, clever rubbish, and when you're young you still value cleverness, you still believe in it. When you're young all the powers of your soul are directed towards the future, and it assumes such varied, vivid and entrancing forms under the sway of an optimism based not on past experience but on an imagined possibility of happiness, that those shared conceptions of future happiness are themselves the true happiness of that time of life. In the metaphysical discussions that were the mainstay of our conversations, I liked the moment when the ideas followed each other ever more rapidly and, growing more and more abstract, ultimately reached such a degree of nebulosity that you saw no way of ever expressing them, and while assuming you were saying what you thought, you said something completely different. I liked the moment when, soaring higher and higher in the realm of thought, you suddenly grasped the boundlessness of it all and became aware of the impossibility of going any further.

It happened the week before Lent,[45] however, that Nekhlyudov was so preoccupied with various pleasures that although he came to see us several times for the day, he and I didn't talk even once, and I was so offended by it that he again seemed like a proud, unpleasant person to me. All I was waiting for was the chance to show that I placed no value at all on his company, and had no particular affection for him.

The first time he showed an interest in conversation with me after that, I told him I needed to prepare some lessons and went upstairs, but a quarter-hour later the classroom door opened and Nekhlyudov came in.

'Am I disturbing you?' he asked.

'No,' I answered, even though I meant to say that I really did have things to do.

'Why did you leave Volodya's room? After all, it's been a long time since we've had a discussion. And I'm so used to them that it's as if something has been missing.'

My vexation evaporated in an instant, and Dmitry again became in my eyes the same kind and dear person he had been before.

'You probably know why I left, don't you?'

'Perhaps I do,' he answered, sitting down next to me, 'but even if I can guess, I still can't say why, whereas you can.'

'Then I will. I left because I was angry with you. Or not angry but vexed. It's just that I've always been afraid that you despise me for being so young.'

'Do you know why you and I became such friends?' he said, responding to my admission with a kind-hearted, clever look, 'or why it is that I like you more than I do people I know better and have more in common with? I've just decided why. You have a remarkable, rare quality: candour.'

'Yes, I always say the very things that I'm embarrassed to admit,' I confirmed, 'but only to people I'm sure of.'

'Yes, but to be sure of someone, you have to be complete friends with him, and you and I still aren't, *Nicolas*. You remember what we said about friendship – that true friends must have confidence in each other?'

'To be confident that whatever I tell you, you won't tell anyone else,' I said, 'for the most important, interesting thoughts are, in fact, the ones we won't tell each other for anything.'

'And such vile thoughts! Such base thoughts that if we knew we had to admit to them, we would never dare to let them into our minds. You know what idea has just occurred to me, *Nicolas*?' he added, getting up from his chair and rubbing his palms together with a smile. 'Let's *do* that, and you'll see how beneficial it will be for both of us. We'll give each other our word to admit everything to each other. We'll know each other and won't be embarrassed. And so we won't be afraid of outsiders, we'll give each other our word *never to say anything to anybody* about each other. Let's do that.'

'All right,' I said.

And we really *did* do that. Of what came of it, I'll speak later.

Karr[46] said that there are two sides in every attachment: one loves and the other lets himself be loved; one kisses and the other offers his cheek. That's absolutely right: in our friendship I kissed and Dmitry offered his cheek, but he was also ready to kiss me. We loved equally, because we knew and appreciated each other mutually, even if that didn't keep him from influencing me, or me from allowing him to.

It goes without saying that under Nekhlyudov's influence I involuntarily adopted his outlook, the essence of which was a rapturous adoration of the idea of virtue, and the conviction that man's purpose lies in continual self-improvement. To reform all humanity and eradicate all human vice and unhappiness seemed plausible enough to us at the time, just as it seemed an easy and uncomplicated matter to reform ourselves, to master all virtues and be happy . . .

God alone knows, however, just how absurd those noble dreams of youth were, or who was to blame that they were never realized . . .

Youth

ONE

What I Consider the Beginning
of Youth

I said that my friendship with Dmitry revealed to me a new view of life and its purpose and relations. The essence of that view was the conviction that it is the goal of each to strive for moral improvement, and that such improvement is easy, possible and lasting. So far, however, the only enjoyment I had obtained was discovering the new ideas that followed from that conviction, and making brilliant plans for an active moral future, since my life continued the same trivial, confused and idle round as before.

The ideas of virtue I examined in conversation with my cherished friend Dmitry – with 'marvellous Mitya' as I sometimes called him in a whisper to myself – had appealed only to my intellect and not to my feelings. But the time came when those ideas entered my mind with such a fresh power of revelation that it scared me to think how much time I had wasted, and I wanted at once, wanted that very second, to apply them to life with the firm intention of never betraying them.

And it's that time that I consider the beginning of *youth*.

I was nearly sixteen. The teachers continued to come, St-Jérôme supervised my studies, and against my will and reluctantly I prepared for the university. Besides studying, my activities consisted of solitary, disconnected daydreaming and reflection, doing gymnastics to make myself the strongest man in the world, wandering with no particular purpose or idea in all the rooms, but especially in the hallway to the maids' room, and looking at myself in the mirror, even if the last activity always left me with a painful feeling of dejection and even disgust. Not only was I ugly, I was convinced, but I couldn't even depend on the usual consolation in such cases. I couldn't say that I had an expressive, clever or noble face. There was nothing expressive about it – the most common, coarse, homely features and tiny grey eyes that were more stupid than clever, especially when I examined myself in the mirror. Of manliness there was even less, for although I was very strong for my age and fairly tall, the features of my face were soft, limp and vague. And there wasn't anything noble either; on the contrary, it was the face of a simple peasant, and I had the same big hands and feet, which seemed quite shameful to me at the time.

TWO

Spring

Bright week came quite late in April the year I was to enter the university, and the entrance examinations were scheduled for Thomas week, with the result that during Passion week I had to fast[1] and finish my studies.

Following the wet snow, which Karl Ivanych used to refer to as 'the son coming for the father',[2] the weather had been calm, warm and clear for three days or so. There wasn't a wisp of snow to be seen on the streets, and the dirty slush had been replaced by glistening wet pavement and rapid rivulets. The last drops on the rooftops were evaporating in the sunshine, buds were swelling on the trees in the front garden, the backyard path leading past a pile of frozen dung to the stable was dry, and the moss between the flagstones by the back steps was turning green. It was the special time in spring that acts most powerfully on the human soul: a brilliant but not hot sun shining down on everything, rivulets and thawed patches, a fresh fragrance in the air, and a delicate blue sky with long, translucent clouds. I don't know why, but it seems that the effect on the soul of that first period of spring's rebirth is felt even more strongly in a big city – you see less, but anticipate more.

I was standing next to a double-frame window, through which the morning sun cast dusty beams on the floor of the insufferable classroom, and working out a long algebra equation on the blackboard. In one hand I held a tattered copy of Francoeur's[3] soft-cover *Algebra*, and in the other a small piece of chalk, which I had got all over my hands and face and the elbows of my jacket. Nikolay, in an apron and with his sleeves rolled up, was using pliers to remove the putty and bend back the nails of the inner frame of the window, which looked out onto the front garden. His activity and the noise it made kept me from concentrating. I was, moreover, in an extremely bad, dissatisfied mood. None of it was working out for me: I had made a mistake at the beginning of the calculation and had to start again; I had dropped the chalk twice and could feel it all over my face and hands; the sponge had disappeared somewhere; and the tapping noise Nikolay was making was getting painfully on my nerves. I was about to get angry and start grumbling, and threw down the chalk and the *Algebra* and started to walk around the room. But then I remembered that I should refrain from doing anything bad, since it was Passion Wednesday, when we had to make our confessions, and my mood changed at once to a sort of special, mild one, and I went over to Nikolay.

'Let me help you, Nikolay,' I said, trying to give my voice the mildest expression, my mood made even milder by the thought that in suppressing my vexation and helping him I was doing good.

The putty had been removed and the nails bent back, but although Nikolay was pulling on the crosspiece with all his might, the frame wouldn't yield.

'If it comes out at once when I pull on it with him,' I thought, 'that will mean that it's a sin to study and I should stop for the day.' The frame gave to the side and slipped out.

'Where shall I take it?' I asked.

'I'll deal with it myself, with your permission,' Nikolay replied, apparently surprised by my zeal and, I think, unhappy with it. 'They mustn't get mixed up, since I keep them in the storage closet by number.'

'I'll take note of that,' I said, picking up the frame.

I think that if the storage closet had been a mile away and the frame twice as heavy, I would have been even more pleased. I wanted to wear myself out doing that service for Nikolay. When I came back, the little bricks and salt pyramids had been moved to the sill, and Nikolay was sweeping the grit and drowsy flies out of the open window with a goose wing.[4] Fresh, fragrant air had already entered the room and begun to fill it. Through the window came the noise of the city and the chirping of sparrows in the front garden.

Everything in the room was brightly lit, cheering it up, and a light breeze rustled the pages of my *Algebra* and the hair on Nikolay's head. I went over to the window, sat down on the sill, leaned out over the garden, and lapsed into thought.

A new, exceptionally strong and pleasurable feeling suddenly filled my soul. The moist earth in which bright-green blades of grass with yellow stems were breaking through here and there, the sunshine gleaming in the rivulets along which swirled tiny fragments of wood and earth, the swelling buds on the reddening branches of lilac swaying just below the window, the fussy chirping of little birds hopping about in the lilac, the fence darkened with melted snow, and especially the fragrant damp air and the joyful sun – all that spoke clearly and distinctly to me of something new and wonderful that I'm unable to convey as it expressed itself to me then, although I'll try to do so as I perceived it. It spoke to me of beauty, happiness and virtue, saying that each was possible and easy for me, that none could exist without the others, and that beauty, happiness and virtue were even the same thing. 'How could I have failed to realize that? How bad I was before, and how good and happy I could have been and might be in the future!' I said to myself. 'I must hurry, hurry, and this very minute become a different person and start to live differently.' Despite that, however, I continued to sit in the window a long time, daydreaming and doing nothing.

Has it ever happened to you in the summer to lie down for a nap in the afternoon in overcast, rainy weather and then, on waking around sunset, to open your eyes and, in the expanding rectangle of a window under the linen blind as it fills with air and bangs against the sill like a branch, to see the violet, shady side of an avenue of lindens wet from the rain, and a damp garden path lit up with bright slanting rays, or suddenly to hear the joyful life of birds in the garden, or glimpse in the opening of the window hovering insects translucent in the sunlight, or smell the air after the rain and think, 'How shameful to sleep away such an evening,' and then to jump up and run out to the garden to rejoice in life? If that has ever happened to you, then you will have a sample of the strong feeling I was experiencing that day.

THREE

Daydreams

'I'll make my confession today and purify myself of all my sins,' I thought, 'and never again will I ...' (and here I recalled all the sins I was most tormented by). 'I'll go to church every Sunday without fail, and afterwards I'll read the Gospel a whole hour, and then from the twenty-five roubles I'll receive every month after I've entered the university, I'll give two roubles fifty (a tithe) to the poor without fail, and in such a way that no one will know, and not to beggars, but I'll find some poor people, an orphan or an old woman, whom no one knows about.

'I'll have my own room (St-Jérôme's, very likely), and I'll take care of it myself and keep it exceptionally clean, and I won't make my servant do anything for me. After all, he's the same as I am. Then I'll walk to the university every day (if they give me a droshky,[5] I'll sell it and put that money aside for the poor), and I'll carry out everything just so.' Exactly what that 'everything' was I certainly couldn't have said at the time, although I did vividly understand and feel that it was all a rational, moral, irreproachable life entailed. 'I'll summarize the lectures and even go over the subjects beforehand, so that I'll be at the top of the first-year class and write a thesis. In the second year I'll already know everything in advance, and they'll able to move me directly to the third year, so that at eighteen I'll finish the year with a first-class baccalaureate and two gold medals, and then I'll do a master's and a doctorate and become the leading scholar in Russia ... Or even in Europe ... Well, and what then?' I asked myself, but then I remembered that such daydreams were pride, a sin I would have to tell my confessor that very evening, and I returned to the beginning of my reflections. 'To prepare for the lectures I'll walk to Sparrow Hills,[6] choose a place under a tree there for myself, and read through the previous lectures, sometimes taking something to snack on: some cheese or a pastry from Pedotti's[7] or something else. I'll have a rest and then I'll start to read some good book or sketch the view or play an instrument (I'll learn to play the flute without fail). Then *she*'ll start taking walks to Sparrow Hills, too, and at some point will come over to me and ask who I am. I'll look at her sadly like this, and say I'm the son of a priest and only happy when I'm there alone, completely by myself. She'll give me her hand, say something and sit down beside me. And we'll both go there every day and become friends and I'll kiss her . . . No, that's no good. On the contrary, from this day forward I won't look at women. I'll never, never go to the maids' room and will try not to walk past it, and in three years I won't be a dependant any more and will get married without fail. I'll make a point of exercising as much as possible and do gymnastics every day, so that when I'm twenty-five I'll be stronger than Rappo.[8] The first day I'll hold twenty pounds at arm's length for five minutes; the next day, twenty-one pounds; the third day, twenty-two; and so on, ending with 160 pounds in each hand and stronger than any of the servants. And if someone should all of a sudden think he can insult me or start referring to *her* disrespectfully, then I'll just take him by the chest like this, and lift him several feet off the ground with one hand, and hold him there long enough for him to feel my strength, and then let him go. Actually, that's no good either. No, it's all right, since I won't be doing him any harm, but only showing that I . . .'

Let me not be reproached that the daydreams of my youth were as puerile as those of my childhood and boyhood. I'm sure that if it should be my lot to live to a venerable old age and my story keeps pace with my years, my daydreams as an old man of seventy will be just as impossibly puerile as they are now. I'll daydream of some charming Maria who'll fall in love with me, a toothless old man, just as she did with Mazeppa,[9] or of how through some extraordinary circumstance my dim-witted son will become a government minister, or of how I'll suddenly have piles of money in the millions. I'm sure there's no human being of any age who lacks that comforting and beneficial ability to daydream, although, except for the common feature of impossibility, of magicalness, the daydreaming of each person and age will have its own distinctive character.

In the period I regard as the end of boyhood and the beginning of youth, four feelings formed the basis of my own daydreaming. The first was love for *her*, for an imagined woman of whom I always dreamed in the same way, and whom I expected to meet at any moment. That *she* had a little of Sonyechka in her, a little of Vasily's wife, Masha, when she was washing our linens in the tub, and a little of the woman with the pearls on her white neck, whom I had seen long ago in a box next to ours at the theatre. The second feeling was love of love. I wanted everyone to know and love me. When I spoke my name, Nikolay Irtenyev, I wanted everyone to be impressed by the news and to gather around me and be grateful to me for something. The third feeling was a vain hope for some extraordinary good fortune, a hope so strong and firm that it verged on insanity. So sure was I that some magical event would suddenly make me the richest and most famous man in the world that I was in constant, eager expectation of it. I kept thinking that it was about to *begin*, and that I would now attain all that anyone could wish for, and I hurried everywhere, supposing that it had already *begun* wherever I wasn't. The fourth and main feeling was one of disgust with myself and remorse, but a remorse so fused with hope for happiness that there wasn't anything sad about it. It seemed so easy and natural to me to break free of everything in the past, make a fresh start, forget all that had gone before, and begin my life and all its relations anew, that the past didn't oppress or bind me. I even took pleasure in my disgust and tried to see the past as gloomier than it was. The blacker the circle of memories from the past, the more purely and radiantly did the bright point of the present stand apart from it and the rainbow colours of the future unfurl. That voice of remorse and of a passionate desire for improvement was in fact the chief new mental sensation of that period of my development, and it laid the foundation for a new view of myself, of others, and of the world. How often in melancholy times, when my soul was quietly submitting to life's falsehood and depravity, has that virtuous, consoling voice suddenly and boldly risen up against every untruth, fiercely unmasking the past, indicating the clear point of the present, making me love it, and promising goodness and happiness in the future? Can it really be, O virtuous, consoling voice, that one day you will be heard no more?

FOUR

Our Family Circle

Papa was rarely home that spring. But on the other hand, when he was at home he was exceptionally gay, tapping out his favourite ditties on the piano, gazing at us with sweet little eyes, and making up little jokes about us and Mimi, such as that the Georgian heir apparent had seen Mimi out driving, and was so in love with her that he had petitioned the Synod[10] for a divorce, or that I had been made an aide to the envoy to Vienna, all of it said with a straight face. He teased Katenka with spiders, which she was afraid of, and was quite genial with our friends Dubkov and Nekhlyudov, regaling them and us with his plans for the coming year. Although the plans changed almost daily and contradicted each other, they were so fascinating that we were spellbound, and Lyubochka stared without blinking at Papa's mouth, in order not to miss a single word. The plans involved leaving us behind in Moscow, while he and Lyubochka went to Italy for two years, or buying an estate on the southern shore of the Crimea and going there every summer, or moving the entire family to Petersburg, and so forth. But besides that particular gaiety another change had lately taken place in Papa that greatly surprised me. He had ordered fashionable clothes for himself: an olive tailcoat, stylish trousers with foot straps and a long fur-trimmed overcoat that suited him very well, and he often smelled of fine scent when he went out, especially if it was to call on a certain lady of whom Mimi never spoke without a sigh and a face that said, 'Poor orphans! A regrettable passion! It's a good thing *she* isn't here!' and so on. I learned from Nikolay, since Papa told us nothing about his gambling, that he had been especially lucky over the winter, winning terrific sums, and had put the money in a savings bank, intending not to gamble any more that spring. Probably afraid that he couldn't resist otherwise, he wanted to depart for the country as soon as possible and had even decided not to wait for my examinations but to set out for Petrovskoye with the girls right after Easter, leaving Volodya and me to join them later.

Volodya had been inseparable from Dubkov that whole winter, even as he and Dmitry had started to drift apart. Volodya and Dubkov's main pleasures, as far as I could tell from the conversations I heard, were constant champagne drinking, sleigh rides under the windows of a young lady with whom they were both apparently in love, and dancing opposite each other at real balls instead of the children's variety. Even though we loved each other, that last circumstance did much to distance Volodya and me. We felt too great a difference – between a boy who was still visited by teachers and someone who danced at great balls – to share our thoughts with each other. Katenka was already quite grown up and reading a great many novels, and the thought that she might get married soon no longer seemed a joke to me. But even though Volodya was grown up, too, he and Katenka were not only not friends, but even seemed to despise each other. Generally, whenever she was at home alone she did nothing but read novels and was mostly bored. But when any strange men happened to be around, she would become very lively and obliging and do something with her eyes that left me at a complete loss as to what she meant to express by it. It wasn't until I heard from her in conversation that the only coquetry permissible to a young lady is with her eyes that I was able to explain to myself those strange, unnatural ocular gestures, which didn't seem to astonish anyone else in the least. Lyubochka, too, had already started to wear a long dress that almost completely covered her bandy legs, but she was just as much a crybaby as before. Now she dreamed of marrying not a hussar but a singer or a musician, and with that goal was diligently studying music. St-Jérôme, knowing that his time in our home would end with the last of my examinations, had found himself a position with some count, and after that regarded our household with something like disdain. He was rarely at home, had started to smoke cigarettes, which at the time were a great foppery, and constantly whistled cheerful tunes through a visiting card. Mimi grew more and more despondent with each passing day, and from the time that we had started to grow up no longer expected anything good from anyone or anything.

When I came in to dinner, I found only Mimi, Katenka, Lyubochka and St-Jérôme at the table. Papa wasn't home and Volodya was studying for an examination with some classmates in his room and had asked that dinner be brought to him there. The head of the table had lately been occupied for the most part by Mimi, whom none of us respected, and dinner had lost much of its charm. It was no longer, as it had been in *maman*'s or Grandmother's time, a kind of ritual that at a certain hour brought the whole family together and divided the day in two. Now we permitted ourselves to arrive late, to come only for the second course, to drink wine from tumblers (following the example of St-Jérôme himself), to slouch in our chairs, to get up without finishing, and to take various other liberties of the kind. Dinner had ceased to be the joyful family ceremony that it had been before. How much better it was in Petrovskoye when at two o'clock everyone was sitting in the drawing room, washed and dressed for dinner and anticipating the appointed hour in pleasant conversation. The very moment the clock started to whirr in the pantry to strike two, Foka would quietly step into the room with a napkin over his arm and a dignified, even slightly dour expression on his face. 'Dinner is ready!' he would intone in a loud, drawling voice, and then all of us with happy, contented faces – the older ones in front and the younger ones behind – would with a swish of starched skirts and a creak of boots and shoes go to the dining room and take our customary places, quietly chatting among ourselves. Or how much better in Moscow, where everyone would stand quietly talking around the table set in the salon while waiting for Grandmother, whom Gavrilo had just gone to inform that the meal was ready. And then a door would suddenly open and the rustling of a dress and the shuffling of feet would be heard, and Grandmother, in a mobcap with some extravagant lilac bow on the side, would sail out of her room with, depending on the state of her health at the time, a radiant smile or a grim sidelong glance. Gavrilo would rush over to her chair, the other chairs would scrape, and feeling a chill run down your spine (a precursor of appetite), you would pick up your slightly damp starched napkin, nibble on a crust of bread, and then with eager, joyful anticipation, rubbing your palms together under the table, watch the steaming bowls of soup the butler would serve by rank, age and Grandmother's special favour.

But now I experienced neither happiness nor excitement on coming in to dinner.

The chatter of Mimi, St-Jérôme and the girls about what awful boots the Russian teacher had been wearing, or that the young Kornakov princesses now had dresses with flounces, and so on – that chatter, which before had inspired in me a genuine scorn that I made no effort to hide, especially in regard to Lyubochka and Katenka, now failed to upset my virtuous new mood. I was exceptionally mild. Smiling, I listened to them in a particularly amiable way, respectfully asked them to pass the kvass, and agreed with St-Jérôme, who corrected a phrase I had used during the meal, explaining that it's more elegant to say *je puis* than *je peux*.[11] I must admit, however, that it was a little disagreeable that no one paid any attention to my mildness and virtue. After dinner Lyubochka showed me a piece of paper on which she had listed all her sins. I found that to be very good, but said that it would have been even better to list them all in her soul, although 'none of that is really the point'.

'Whyever not?' Lyubochka asked.

'Well, it's all right, too – you wouldn't understand,' I said, and then went up to my room after telling St-Jérôme I was going to study, but actually in the hour and a half left before confession to make a list of my own duties and occupations for the rest of my life, and to commit to paper the purpose of my life and the rules by which I should always act without backsliding.

FIVE
Rules

I got out a sheet of paper, wishing first to make a list of my obligations and activities for the coming year. The paper needed to be lined. Since I couldn't find a ruler, I used a Latin dictionary instead. But besides leaving an oblong puddle of ink on the paper after I drew my pen along its edge and removed it, the dictionary didn't reach the whole length of the sheet, and the line curved around its soft corner. I got out another sheet and, by moving the dictionary along it, made lines of a sort. Dividing my obligations into three kinds – to myself, to my family, and to God – I started to list those to myself, but they proved so numerous and of so many kinds and subdivisions that I saw that I would first have to write *Rules of Life* and only then make the list. I got out six more sheets, bound them together in a booklet, and at the top of the first page wrote *Rules of Life*. But the words were written so crookedly and unevenly that I wondered if I shouldn't write them again, and for a long time I stared at the tattered list and misshapen title in dismay. Why is everything so beautiful and clear in my mind, yet so distorted on paper and in life in general whenever I try to apply to it something I've been thinking about?

'The confessor is here. Please come down for the rules,'[12] Nikolay entered to tell me.

I stuck the booklet in my desk, looked in the mirror, combed my hair forward, which I was convinced gave me a thoughtful look, and went downstairs to the sitting room, where a table was already set with an icon and lighted wax tapers. Papa came in through the other door at the same time. The confessor, a grey-haired monk with a stern, elderly face, blessed him, and Papa kissed his small, wide, lean hand. I did the same.

'Call *Woldemar*,' Papa said. 'Where is he? Oh, never mind. He's taking Communion at the university.'

'He's studying with the prince,' Katenka said, looking at Lyubochka. Lyubochka suddenly blushed for some reason, scowled and, pretending that something was hurting her, left the room. I went out after her. She stopped in the drawing room and wrote something else on her piece of paper with a pencil.

'What, did you commit another sin?' I asked.

'No, it's nothing. I was just writing,' she answered with a blush.

Just then the voice of Dmitry saying goodbye to Volodya was heard in the entry room.

'So, everything's a temptation for you,' Katenka said to Lyubochka as she came into the drawing room.

I couldn't understand what had happened to my sister; she was so mortified that tears welled in her eyes, and her embarrassment reached the point where it turned into vexation with herself and with Katenka, who apparently had been teasing her.

'It's obvious that you're a *foreigner*' – nothing was more offensive to Katenka than being called a foreigner, which is why Lyubochka used the word – 'to upset me on purpose right before such a sacrament,' she said in a pompous voice. 'You must realize that it isn't a joke.'

'You know what she wrote, Nikolenka?' Katenka asked, offended at having been called a foreigner. 'She wrote –'

'I never thought you would be so malicious,' Lyubochka said, starting to whimper and step away from us. 'At such a moment and on purpose. She's forever leading me into sin. I don't tease you about your feelings and heartaches.'

SIX

Confession

With those and other scattered thoughts of the kind, I returned to
the sitting room after all the others had gathered there, and just
as the confessor, now standing, was preparing to recite the prayer
that precedes confession. But as soon as the monk's severe, expressive voice rang out in the general silence as he began the prayer,
and especially when he spoke to us the words, 'Reveal all your
trespasses without shame, concealment or excuse and your soul
will be purified in the sight of God, but if you conceal anything,
you will be committing a grievous sin,' I felt the return of the same
awed trepidation I had felt that morning at the thought of the
impending sacrament. I even took pleasure in being conscious of
that state and tried to hold on to it, stopping all the thoughts that
came into my mind and intensifying my sense of fear.

The first to confess was Papa. He was in Grandmother's room
a very long time, during which all of us in the sitting room either
said nothing or whispered among ourselves about who would
go next. At last the voice of the monk reciting a prayer was heard
by the door, along with Papa's footsteps. The door creaked and
he came out, coughing and shrugging a shoulder, as was his
habit, and not looking at us.

'Well, now you go, Lyuba, and be sure to tell everything.
You're my great sinner, you know,' Papa said merrily, squeezing
her cheek.

Lyubochka turned pale and then blushed, took her list out of
her apron, put it back, and then lowering her head and drawing
in her neck as if expecting a blow from above, she went through
the door. She wasn't gone very long, but her shoulders were
shaking from her sobs as she emerged.

Finally it was my turn after pretty Katenka came out of the door with a smile. With the same dull fear and deliberate wish to stimulate the fear more and more in myself, I entered the half-lit room. Standing in front of a lectern, the confessor slowly turned his face towards me.

I spent no more than five minutes in Grandmother's room, but came back out a happy and, according to my beliefs at the time, a completely pure, morally reborn and new person. Even though I was struck disagreeably by all the old circumstances of life – the same rooms, the same furniture, the same body (I would have liked everything external to change the same way it seemed to me that I had changed within) – even so, I remained in that joyful mood until I went to bed.

As I was starting to fall asleep while going over in my mind all the sins of which I had been cleansed, I suddenly remembered a shameful one that I had kept to myself during confession. The words of the prayer that had preceded confession came back to me and sounded unceasingly in my ears. My serenity was gone in an instant. I heard 'but if you conceal anything, you will be committing a grievous sin' over and over, and saw myself as a sinner so terrible that no punishment could be sufficient. I tossed and turned a long time, thinking about my situation and expecting divine retribution at any moment, or even instant death, an idea that filled me with indescribable terror. But then a happy thought suddenly came to me: when it was light to walk or drive to the confessor at the monastery and confess again. And I grew calm.

SEVEN
My Trip to the Monastery

Afraid I might oversleep, I awoke several times in the night, and then was out of bed before six. There was barely a glimmer in the windows. I put on my clothes and my boots, which lay in a dirty heap by the bed, since Nikolay hadn't had a chance to collect them yet, and then, without saying my prayers or washing, I went out onto the street alone for the first time in my life.

The icy, misty dawn was turning red beyond the green roof of the big house across the street. A quite severe morning frost had frozen the mud and rivulets, and it stung my feet and nipped at my face and hands. I had been counting on a cab for a quick drive to the monastery and back, but there weren't any on our lane yet, and on Arbat Street there were only some carts going by and a couple of bricklayers walking along the footpath in conversation. After a thousand paces or so, I started to come upon servant men and women with baskets on their way to market, a barrel wagon going for water, a pie-seller at a crossing, and an open bakery, and then at last, by the Arbat Gate, a driver, a little old man swaying back and forth asleep on the seat of his rickety, bluish, patchwork, low-sprung droshky. Probably not completely awake, he asked for only twenty kopeks to the monastery and back, but then he came to, and as I was about to get in, he struck his little horse with the ends of his reins and started to drive away without me. 'I can't, sir. I've got to feed the horse!' he mumbled.

I finally convinced him to stop after offering him forty kopeks. He reined in the horse, carefully looked me over, and then said, 'Get in, sir!' I'll admit I was a little afraid he might take me off to some remote lane and rob me. Grabbing hold of the collar of his ragged peasant coat and pitifully exposing as I did so his wrinkled neck above his severely hunched back, I climbed onto the bluish, bobbing, swaying seat and we set off down Vozdvi-zhenka Street. As we were driving I noticed that the rear of the droshky was upholstered with a piece of the same striped green-ish material the driver's peasant coat was made of, and for some reason that circumstance put me at ease, and I stopped being afraid that he would take me away and rob me.

The sun was already quite high when we got to the monastery, and it brightly gilded the cupolas of the churches. There was still frost in the shade, but the road was completely covered with swift, turbid rivulets, and the horse splashed through the thawed mud. Once inside the monastery wall, I asked the first person I saw where I could find the confessor.

'That's his cell over there,' a passing young monk said, stop-ping for a moment and pointing to a little cottage with a porch.

'I thank you kindly,' I said.

But what could the other monks have been thinking as they came out of a church one after another and looked at me? I was neither grown-up nor child. My face wasn't washed, my hair wasn't combed, my clothes were flecked with down, and my boots hadn't been cleaned and were still muddy. To what class of person were the monks mentally assigning me? For they were looking at me with care. I continued, however, in the direction indicated by the young monk.

A little old man in black with thick grey eyebrows met me on the narrow path leading to the cells and asked me what I wanted.

For a moment, I was going to say 'nothing' and run back to the cab and drive home, but despite his prominent eyebrows the old man's face inspired trust. I said that I needed to see my confessor and gave his name.

'Come with me, *young master*, I'll show you the way,' he said, evidently having guessed my standing at once and turning around. 'The father's at matins and will be back shortly.'

He opened the door and led me through a tidy vestibule and entryway across a clean linen floor mat to the cell.

'Wait here,' he said with a warm, reassuring expression and went out.

The room in which I found myself was very small and extra-ordinarily neat. The only items of furniture were an oilcloth-covered table standing between two small double-hinged windows with a pot of geraniums on each sill, a small stand with icons and a little lamp hanging in front, an armchair, and two other chairs. In one corner was a wall clock with little flowers painted on its face and brass weights suspended on chains. Two cassocks hung from nails in a partition (with the bed very likely behind) that was attached to the ceiling with whitewashed wooden posts.

The windows looked onto a white wall five feet away. Between them and the wall was a small lilac bush. No sound reached the room from the outside, and in the silence the pleasant, regular tick-tock of the pendulum seemed loud. No sooner was I by myself in that quiet corner than all my former thoughts and memories abruptly slipped away as if they had never been, and I fell into an inexpressibly pleasurable reverie. The yellowed nankeen cassocks with their worn linings, the scuffed black leather book bindings with their bronze hasps, the dull-green plants with their carefully watered soil and washed leaves, and especially the monotonously intermittent sound of the pendulum all spoke distinctly of a new life, one that until then had been unknown to me, a life of solitude, prayer and quiet, serene happiness.

'The months pass, and then the years,' I thought, 'and he's always alone, always serene, and always feels that his conscience is clear before God, and that his prayers have been heard.' I sat in the chair about half an hour, trying to be still and breathe quietly, so I wouldn't disturb the harmony of sound that was saying so much to me. And the pendulum continued to knock in the same way – harder to the left, softer to the right.

EIGHT

My Second Confession

The confessor's footsteps roused me from my reverie.

'Hello,' he said, arranging his long grey hair with his hand. 'What can I do for you?'

I asked him to bless me, and with special pleasure kissed his small sallow hand.

When I explained my request to him, he said nothing but went over to the icons and began the confession.

After it was over and I had overcome my shame and said everything that was in my heart, he placed his hands on my head and in his soft, resonant voice said, 'May the blessing of our heavenly Father be upon you, my son, and may he preserve in you forever your faith, mildness and humility. Amen.'

I was utterly happy. Tears of happiness welled in my eyes, and I kissed a fold of the monk's thin woollen cassock and lifted my head. His face was utterly serene.

Sensing my pleasure in that feeling of tenderness and afraid of somehow dispelling it, I quickly parted with the confessor and, staring straight ahead to avoid any distraction, came back outside the walls and took my place in the swaying droshky. But the jolting of the carriage and the variety of things flashing before my eyes quickly dispelled the feeling anyway, and I was already imagining that the confessor was most likely thinking that he had never in his life met such a beautiful young soul and never would again, since there were no others like it. I was convinced of that, and the conviction produced in me the sort of gaiety that has to be shared.

I felt a terrific urge to speak to someone, and since there wasn't anyone there but the driver, I spoke to him.

'Was I long, then?' I asked.

'I don't know, fairly long, but the horse should have been fed long ago. I work at *night*, you see,' the little old driver replied, apparently thanks to the sunshine now quite cheerful in comparison with before.

'To me it seemed I was only gone a minute,' I said. 'You know why I went to the monastery?' I added, moving to the hollowed part of the bench that was closer to the old driver.

'What business is that of ours? Whatever the fare says, that's where we go,' he replied.

'No, all the same, why do you think?' I persisted.

'Well, probably to bury someone, and you went to buy a plot,' he said.

'No, brother. You know why I went?'

'I can't know the answer to that, sir,' he answered.

The driver's voice seemed so kind to me that I decided for his edification to tell him the reason for my trip and even the feeling I had experienced.

'You want me to tell you? Well, you see . . .'

And I told him everything and described all my beautiful feelings. Even now the memory of it makes me blush.

'Right, sir,' the driver dubiously replied.

After that he was silent a long time and sat without moving, except to adjust the skirt of his coat, which kept coming out from under his striped leg in its tall boot as the latter bounced along the droshky's footboard. I had already decided that he was thinking the same thoughts about me as the confessor – that a beautiful young person like me was to be found nowhere else in the world – when he suddenly addressed me.

'Well, sir, that's a matter for gentlemen.'

'What?' I asked.

'That matter of yours, it's a matter for gentlemen,' he repeated in a toothless mumble.

'No, he didn't understand me,' I thought, and said nothing more to him all the way home.

Although it wasn't a feeling of tenderness and piety but rather of satisfaction with myself at having experienced them that stayed with me the whole way, despite the variety of people out and about in the brilliant sunshine, that feeling, too, vanished completely the moment I got home. I didn't have the forty kopeks to pay the driver. The butler Gavrilo, to whom I was already in debt, wouldn't lend me any more. Seeing me run across the yard twice as I tried to obtain the money, and probably guessing what I was up to, the driver got down from his droshky and, even though he had seemed kind to me, started to talk loudly about scoundrels who don't pay their fares, obviously intending to sting me.

Everyone else was still asleep, so there was no one besides the servants from whom I could borrow the money. Finally, after the most solemn promise, which I could see in his eyes he didn't believe, but accepted anyway since he liked me and remembered the good deed I had done him, Vasily paid the driver for me. The feeling was thus dispelled like smoke. When I started to get dressed for church in order to take Communion with everyone else, and it turned out that my clothes hadn't been altered and no longer fitted, I committed a host of other sins. Putting on different clothes, I set out for Communion in a peculiar state of hurried thought and a complete lack of faith in my beautiful tendencies.

NINE

How I Prepared for
My Examination

Papa, Lyubochka, Mimi and Katenka left for the country on Thursday of Bright week, with Volodya and me and St-Jérôme remaining behind in Grandmother's big house. The mood I was in on confession day and during the trip to the monastery had completely passed, leaving only a vague, if pleasant, memory, which was gradually replaced by the new impressions of our life of freedom.

The booklet entitled *Rules of Life* was put away with my lesson copybooks. Although the idea of compiling rules for all the circumstances of life and always following them was one that attracted me as both extraordinarily simple and great, and one, moreover, that I intended to put into practice, I once again seemed to forget that it needed to be done at once, and kept postponing it for another time. I did, on the other hand, take comfort in the fact that every thought entering my mind would thenceforth fit under one of the subheadings of my rules and obligations, whether in relation to myself, or to my family, or to God. 'So, I'll assign that there, along with numerous other thoughts that will come to me later on the subject,' I would say to myself. I often ask myself now when was I better and more right: then, when I believed in the omnipotence of the human intellect, or now when, having lost the strength of growth, I doubt the intellect's power and significance. And I'm unable to give myself a definite answer.

The awareness of freedom, and the springtime feeling of anticipation about which I've already spoken, excited me to such an extent that I absolutely could not take myself in hand, and thus prepared for my examinations very poorly. I would be

studying in the classroom in the morning, and know it was
essential to work, since there was an examination the next day
on a subject for which two whole questions remained to be read,
when a spring fragrance would suddenly waft through the
window, and it would seem quite necessary just then to recall
something, and my hands would let go of the book by themselves, and my feet would start to move by themselves and walk
back and forth, and in my mind, as if someone had tripped a
spring and set a machine in motion – in my mind so many cheerful daydreams would begin to rush by so easily and naturally
and with such speed that it was all I could do to note their
splendour. And an hour and then two would pass by unnoticed.
Or I would be sitting over a book again and somehow concentrating all my attention on what I was reading, but then suddenly
hear female steps in the hallway and the rustle of a dress, and
everything would slip from my mind and there would be no
possibility of remaining in my seat, even though I knew very
well that besides Gasha, Grandmother's old chambermaid, there
couldn't be anyone else there. 'But what if *she* has suddenly
come?' I would think. 'What if it's now about to begin and I
miss it?' and I would run out into the hallway and see that it
was indeed Gasha. But for a long time afterwards I wouldn't be
able to concentrate again. The spring had been tripped and a
terrific tumult let loose. Or in the evening I would be sitting
alone in my room with a tallow candle and leave off reading for
a moment to snip the candlewick or to adjust the way I was
sitting in my chair, and I would notice that it was dark in the
doorways and all the corners, and hear that it was silent all over
the house, and again it would be impossible not to stop and
listen to the silence, or gaze into a dark room through an open
door, or remain sitting a long time in that motionless position,
or go downstairs and walk around all the empty rooms. Often
in the evening I would also sit unnoticed for a long time in the
salon, listening to 'The Nightingale'[13] softly picked out with two
fingers by Gasha alone at the piano in the light of a tallow candle.
And if the moon was out, it was absolutely impossible not to get
out of bed and sit on the windowsill facing the front garden and
look out at the gleaming roof of Shaposhnikov's house,[14] and at

the graceful belfry of our parish church, and at the dark shadows cast by the fence and a bush on the path in the garden, and remain there so long that it would be hard to get up even at ten the next morning.

So that if it hadn't been for the teachers who continued to visit me, or St-Jérôme, who would reluctantly prick my pride from time to time, or – the main thing – my wish to seem like a capable fellow in my friend Nekhlyudov's eyes by passing the examinations with distinction, a very important thing according to his notions – if it hadn't been for those things, springtime and freedom would have made me forget even what I knew before, and I wouldn't have been able to pass the examinations for anything.

TEN
The History Examination

I entered the large university hall for the first time on 16 April,[15] escorted by St-Jérôme. We had driven there in our quite elegant phaeton. I was wearing a tailcoat, something I had never done before, and all my clothes, even my linen and stockings, were of the newest and finest. After the doorman had helped me off with my overcoat and I stood before him in the full beauty of my dress, I even started to feel a little ashamed that I was so dazzling. But no sooner did I step onto the bright parquet floor of the crowded hall, and see hundreds of young men in tailcoats and gymnasium[16] uniforms, a few of whom glanced indifferently at me, and at the far end of the hall, important professors casually walking about near the tables or sitting in big armchairs, than I was at once disappointed in my hope of attracting general attention to myself. The expression on my face, which at home and then in the foyer had indicated something like regret that I possessed, in spite of myself, such a noble and imposing appearance, was now replaced by one of the greatest timidity and a kind of dejection. I even fell to the other extreme and was very glad to see an exceptionally badly, even sloppily dressed gentleman, not yet old but almost completely grey, who was sitting at a rear bench apart from the others. I immediately sat down near him and began to inspect those who had come for the examination and to draw my conclusions about them. There were many different faces and figures among them, but according to my ideas at the time, they could all be easily divided into three kinds.

There were those like me who had come to the examinations with their family tutors or parents, including the youngest Ivin with the familiar Herr Frost, and Ilenka Grap with his old father.

They all had downy chins, wore their linen turned out, sat quietly without opening the books and copybooks they had brought with them, and gazed with obvious timidity at the professors and the examination tables. The second kind of examinee was the young men in gymnasium uniforms, of whom many already shaved. They were mostly acquainted with one other, talked loudly, referred to the professors by their first names and patronymics, prepared questions on the spot, passed their copybooks back and forth to each other, walked around among the benches, and brought in pasties and sandwiches from the foyer and ate them at once, lowering their heads to the level of the desktop only slightly to do so. The third and last kind of examinee, although there weren't many of them, was the quite old ones in tailcoats but more often in frock coats without visible linen. They behaved with the utmost seriousness, sat by themselves and looked very sombre. The one who had given me comfort by undoubtedly being dressed worse than I was belonged to the last kind. Leaning on both arms with his tousled, partially grey hair sticking out between his fingers as he read a book, he glanced at me for an instant with his gleaming, not entirely charitable eyes, frowning gloomily and continuing to stick a shiny elbow in my direction, so I wouldn't be able to come any closer. The gymnasium students, on the other hand, were too sociable, and I was a little intimidated by them. One of them thrust a book in my hand and said, 'Pass it to him over there.' Another going by me said, 'Let me through, old chap.' A third, climbing over the desktop, leaned on my shoulder as if it were a bench. All that seemed boorish and unpleasant to me: I regarded myself as far superior to those gymnasium students, and felt that they shouldn't have allowed themselves to be so familiar with me. At last, they started to call out our names. The gymnasium students went up boldly, answered well for the the most part, and returned cheerfully. Our company was much more timid and answered less well, I think. Of the old ones, a few answered superbly, while others did so very poorly. When the name Semyonov was called, my neighbour with the grey hair and gleaming eyes climbed over my legs with a rude push and went up to the table. It was clear from the professors' look that he had answered excellently and confidently. Returning to his place, he calmly picked up his copybooks and left without waiting to see what mark he had been given. There were several times when the sound of a voice calling a name made me tremble, but it wasn't my turn in the alphabet yet, although they had reached the names starting with K.[17] 'Ikonin and Tenyev!' someone suddenly shouted from the professors' corner. A chill ran over my scalp and down my spine.

'Who's that? Which one's Bartenyev?' they started to say around me.

'Ikonin, go ahead, they're calling you. But who this Bartenyev-Mordenyev[18] is, I have no idea. Own up,' said a tall, rosy-cheeked gymnasium student behind me.

'That's you,' St-Jérôme said.

'My name's Irtenyev,' I explained to the rosy-cheeked student. 'Did they really call Irtenyev?'

'Why, yes. What's keeping you? Look at this dandy!' he added just audibly enough for me to hear as I came out from behind the bench. Ahead of me walked Ikonin, a tall young man of about twenty-five who belonged to the third kind, the old ones. He was wearing a tight-fitting olive tailcoat and a dark-blue satin cravat, over which his long blond hair was carefully combed à la moujik.[19] I had noticed his appearance, even on the benches. He was garrulous and not bad-looking, although I was struck by the strange red hair that he had allowed to grow on his throat and by his even stranger habit of constantly unbuttoning his waistcoat and scratching his chest under his shirt.

Ikonin and I went up to a table at which three professors were sitting. Not one of them responded to our bows. A young professor was shuffling the questions like a deck of cards, another with a star on his tailcoat[20] was gazing at a gymnasium student, who was saying something very rapidly about Charlemagne, adding 'finally' after each word, while the third professor, a little old man in spectacles, dipped his head, glanced up at us over his spectacles and pointed to the questions. I sensed that his gaze was directed at both Ikonin and me jointly, and that there was something about us he didn't like (perhaps it was Ikonin's throat hair), since after looking at the two of us again, he made an impatient movement with his head for us to hurry up and take our questions. I was annoyed and offended; first, that none of them had responded to our bows and, second, that they had apparently combined Ikonin and me in a single concept of 'examinees', and were already prejudiced against me on account of his throat hair. I took a question without being shy about it and was preparing to answer, but the professor indicated Ikonin with his eyes. I read over my question. It was one I knew the answer to and, calmly waiting my turn, I observed what was taking place in front of me. Ikonin wasn't abashed in the least and even took his question too boldly, moving the whole side of his body to do so, shook his hair, and briskly read what was written on the card. He was, I think, about to open his mouth to answer, when the professor with the star, after letting the gymnasium student go with praise, suddenly looked at him. Ikonin stopped as if he had just remembered something. The general silence lasted about two minutes.

'Well?' the spectacled professor said.

Ikonin opened his mouth and then fell silent again.

'You're not the only one here. Do you intend to answer or not?' the young professor said, but Ikonin didn't even look at him. He stared at the question and said nothing at all. The spectacled professor looked at him through his spectacles and then over them and then without them, since he had managed during that time to take them off, carefully wipe the lenses, and put them back on. Ikonin said nothing at all. Suddenly a little smile flickered on his face. He shook his hair, moved his whole body towards the table again, put the question back, looked at all the professors one after another and then at me, turned around, and strode jauntily back to the benches. The professors stared at each other.

'Well, there's a good one for you!' the young professor said. 'He's self-paying!'[21]

I moved closer to the table, but the professors continued to talk among themselves almost in a whisper, as if none of them even suspected I was there. I was quite convinced at the time that all three of them were extraordinarily interested in whether I would pass the examination and pass it well, and that it was only from self-importance that they pretended to be completely indifferent and not to notice me.

When the spectacled professor indifferently addressed me, inviting me to answer the question, I looked straight at him, feeling a little ashamed of him for being so hypocritical with me, and faltered slightly at the beginning of my answer. But then it got easier and easier, and since the question was about Russian history, of which I had an excellent knowledge, I ended brilliantly and even got so carried away by my desire to impress on the professors that I was no Ikonin and shouldn't be confused with him, that I offered to take another question. But, nodding his head, the professor said, 'Fine, sir,' and entered something in his register. Returning to the benches, I immediately learned from the gymasium students, who, goodness knows how, were aware of everything, that I had received a five.

ELEVEN

The Mathematics Examination

Besides Grap, whom I considered beneath my friendship, and Ivin, who for some reason kept avoiding me, I made many new acquaintances at the following examinations, and a few of them had started to greet me. Ikonin was even glad to see me, and informed me that he would be re-examined in history, and that the history professor had had it in for him since last year's examination, when he had supposedly also 'flustered' him. Semyonov, who hoped to enter the mathematics department, just as I did, and who remained aloof from everyone to the end of the examinations, sat in silence by himself, leaning on his elbows with his fingers stuck in his grey hair, while passing his sessions with distinction. He was ranked second, while first was a student from Gymnasium No. 1, a tall, skinny, very pale brunet with his cheek wrapped in a black cravat and his forehead covered with pimples. His hands, however, were slender and beautiful, with unusually long fingers and nails so badly bitten that the ends appeared to be bound with threads. All that seemed very fine to me, and, just as it should have been with the 'first gymnasium student'. He talked with everyone the same way all the others did, and made his acquaintance, but even so there was, as it seemed to me, something exceptional and *magnetic*[22] about his walk and the movement of his lips and dark eyes.

I had arrived for the mathematics examination earlier than usual. I had a decent knowledge of the subject, although there were two questions in algebra that I had somehow hidden from my teacher, and that were a complete mystery to me. They were, as I recall now, the theory of combinations and Newton's binomial theorem. I sat down on a rear bench and started to look them over. But the noisy room, which I wasn't used to, and my awareness that there wasn't enough time kept me from reading with any insight.

'There he is. Over here, Nekhlyudov,' I heard Volodya's familiar voice.

I turned around and saw him and Dmitry in unbuttoned frock coats waving their hands as they came towards me between the benches. It was immediately apparent that they were second-year students who were at home at the university. The look of their unbuttoned frock coats alone expressed scorn for our matriculating brother and inspired in him both envy and respect. It was extremely flattering to think that everyone around could see that I was acquainted with two second-year students, and I quickly stood up to greet them.

Volodya couldn't help expressing his sense of superiority.

'Ah, you poor wretch!' he said. 'You still haven't been called up?'

'No.'

'What are you reading? Did you actually not prepare?'

'Not completely on two questions. This is what I don't understand.'

'What? That?' Volodya said and started to explain Newton's binomial to me, but he did it in such a haphazard, unclear way that after seeing the doubt about his knowledge in my eyes, he looked at Dmitry, and obviously seeing the same thing in his eyes, too, he turned red, but continued to say something I was unable to follow.

'No, stop, Volodya. Let me go over it with him, if there's time,' Dmitry said, and after a glance in the professors' direction, he sat down beside me.

I noticed at once that my friend was in the complacently mild mood that always came over him when he was happy with himself, and that I was especially fond of in him. Since he knew mathematics well and expressed himself clearly, he went over the question with me so splendidly that I remember the answer to this day. But hardly had he finished than St-Jérôme said in a loud whisper, '*À vous, Nicolas!*'[23] and, following Ikonin, I stepped out from behind the desk without looking at the second question. I went over to the table where two professors were sitting and next to which a gymnasium student was standing by the blackboard. Noisily breaking the chalk on it, he was briskly deriving some formula, and continued to write even after the professor said 'That's enough' and told us to take our own questions. 'What if it's the theory of combinations?' I thought, picking a question from the soft stack of cards with trembling fingers. Instead of choosing, Ikonin reached in the same way as before with the whole side of his body, took the top card with the same bold gesture, looked at it, and angrily frowned.

'I always get the fiendish ones!' he muttered.

I looked at my own.

A disaster! It was the theory of combinations!

'What did you get?' Ikonin asked.

I showed him.

'That one I know,' he said.

'You want to trade?'

'No, all the same, I'm just not in the mood,' Ikonin barely managed to whisper before the professor asked us to go to the blackboard.

'Well, that's it,' I thought. 'Instead of the brilliant examination I had meant to do, I'll be covered with shame forever, worse than Ikonin.' But suddenly Ikonin turned to me right in front of the professor, grabbed my question out of my hand, and gave me his own. I looked at the card. It was Newton's binomial.

The professor wasn't old and had a pleasant, clever expression that mostly came from his uncommonly prominent brow.

'What's this, gentlemen, are you trading questions?' he said.

'No, he was just showing me his, Mr Professor,' Ikonin deftly replied, and the words 'Mr Professor' were again the last ones that he spoke in that place, for once more he glanced at the professors and at me as he walked by, smiled, and then shrugged with an expression that said, 'It doesn't matter, brother!' I later learned that it was the third year Ikonin had come for the examinations.

My answer to the question I had just gone over with Dmitry was excellent, and the professor even told me that it was better than anyone could have expected and gave me a five.

TWELVE
The Latin Examination

Everything went superbly until the Latin examination. The gymnasium student with the wrapped cheek was first, Semyonov was second and I was third. I had even begun to take pride in it and to seriously think that, despite my youth, I wasn't a joke at all.

There had been nervous talk as early as the first examination about the Latin professor, who was supposed to be a monster who enjoyed seeing young people fail, especially if they were self-paying, and who apparently spoke only Latin or Greek. St-Jérôme, who had been my Latin teacher, was encouraging, and it seemed to me, too, that since I could translate Cicero and several odes of Horace[24] without a dictionary and had an excellent knowledge of Zumpt,[25] I was as well prepared as anyone, but it turned out to be otherwise. The only thing heard all morning was the downfall of those who had gone before: one had received a zero, another a one, a third had been berated and threatened with ejection, and so on and so forth. Only Semyonov and the first gymnasium student calmly went up and, as usual, came back with fives. I could already see disaster looming when Ikonin and I were called to the little table behind which the terrifying professor was seated all by himself. He was a small, thin, sallow man with long greasy hair and an extremely pensive physiognomy.

He gave Ikonin a book of Cicero's speeches and made him translate one.

To my great surprise, Ikonin not only read it but even translated several lines with help from the professor, who gave him hints. Sensing my superiority to such a feeble rival, I couldn't

help smiling, and even did so a bit derisively when it came to
parsing and Ikonin had lapsed as before into obviously hopeless
silence. I had meant to please the professor with that clever,
slightly mocking grin, but it had the opposite effect.

'You probably know better, since you're smiling,' the professor said to me in bad Russian. 'We'll see. You tell me, then.'

I learned afterwards that the Latin professor had taken Ikonin
under his wing, and that Ikonin even lodged with him. I at once
answered the question about syntax that had been posed to
Ikonin, but the professor made a long face and looked away.

'All right, sir, your turn will come and then we'll see what you
know,' he said without looking at me, and then started to explain
to Ikonin what he had been asking about.

'You can go,' he added, and I saw him enter a four for Ikonin
in his register. 'Well,' I thought, 'he's not at all as strict as they've
been saying.' After Ikonin's departure, the professor, for a full
five minutes that seemed like five hours to me, rearranged his
books and questions, blew his nose, adjusted his armchair, sat
back in it, looked along the sides of the hall and then all around
it – just not at me. All that simulation wasn't enough for him,
however, so he opened a book and pretended to read it as if I
weren't there at all. I stepped closer and coughed.

'Ah, yes! You still here? Well, translate something,' he said,
handing me a book.

'No, wait, this one's better.' He leafed through a volume of
Horace and opened it at a passage that I thought no one would
ever be able to translate.

'I haven't prepared that,' I said.

'So you want to answer what you've already memorized?
That's good! No, you translate this.'

Somehow I started to make sense of it, but at every one of
my enquiring glances the professor only shook his head with a
sigh and said, 'No.' Finally, he shut the book with such nervous
haste that he slammed it on his finger. Angrily removing the
latter, he gave me a question about grammar and, leaning back
in his armchair, fell silent in the most ominous way. I was about
to answer, but the expression on his face hobbled my tongue
and whatever I said seemed wrong to me.

'That's wrong, wrong, completely wrong!' he suddenly said in his vile accent, quickly changing his position and resting his elbows on the table, while fiddling with the gold ring that sat loosely on a thin finger of his left hand. 'That's no way to prepare for an institution of higher learning, gentlemen. You just want to wear the student jacket and blue collar. You pick up some superficial knowledge and think that you can be students. No, gentlemen, you have to learn the subject thoroughly,' and so on and so forth.

The whole time he was delivering that speech in broken Russian, I stared dully at his lowered eyes. First I was over-whelmed by disappointment at not being third, then by the fear that I hadn't passed the examination at all, and finally by a sense of injustice, wounded pride and undeserved humiliation, feelings that were further inflamed and made venomous by my contempt for the professor, who, according to my ideas, was not *comme il faut*, as I realized looking at his short, thick, round fingernails. Watching me and seeing my trembling lips and tear-filled eyes, he very likely interpreted my agitation as a plea to raise my mark, and as if taking pity on me (but also in the presence of another professor, who had come over in the meantime) he said, 'All right, sir. Even though you don't deserve it, I'll give you a pass-ing mark (meaning a two) out of consideration for your young age and in the hope that once you're at the university you won't be so flippant.'

That last sentence, delivered in the presence of the other professor, who looked at me as if he, too, were saying, 'Yes, that's right, young man!' completely undid me. There was a moment when my eyes clouded over and the terrifying professor seemed to be sitting at his table somewhere off in the distance, and the wild idea entered my mind with terrible one-sided clarity, 'What if . . . ? What would happen if . . . ?' But for some reason I didn't do anything, but only bowed automatically to both professors with particular courtesy, smiled, I think, the same little smile as Ikonin, and stepped away from the table.

The injustice affected me so powerfully at the time that if I had been free to do as I liked, I would have gone to no more examinations. I lost all ambition (I could no longer think of being third) and let the rest of the examinations slip by without effort or even anxiety. Even so, my average was four plus, although I no longer cared about that. I had decided on my own behalf, and proved very clearly to myself, that it was quite foolish and even *mauvais genre*[26] to try to be first, that what one needed was to be like Volodya, neither too good nor too bad. I intended to hold to that at the university from then on, even if it did mean departing for the first time from the views of my friend.

I was already thinking only about the uniform, the cocked hat, my own droshky, my own room and – the main thing – my freedom.

THIRTEEN
I'm a Grown-up

Actually, those thoughts had their charm, too.

Coming home on 8 May from my last examination, in religion, I found a familiar apprentice from Rozanov's,[27] who had earlier brought a loosely basted uniform frock coat of lustrous black cloth with the lapels marked in chalk, but this time came with a completely finished garment with shiny gold buttons wrapped in tissue.

Putting on the new clothes and finding them excellent, despite St-Jérôme's insistence that the coat puckered at the back, I went downstairs to see Volodya with a delighted smile involuntarily spreading across my face, and feeling (but pretending not to notice) the eager gazes directed at me by the servants from the entry room and hallway. Gavrilo, the butler, caught me in the hallway, congratulated me on entering the university, gave me, on Papa's orders, four white twenty-five-rouble banknotes, and said that the coachman Kuzma, the droshky and the dark-bay Beauty would, again on Papa's orders, thenceforth be entirely at my disposal. I was so delighted by that unexpected good fortune that it was quite impossible to feign indifference to Gavrilo, and a bit beside myself and breathless, I said the first thing that popped into my mind – that 'Beauty's a fine trotter,' I think it was. Noticing the heads peering out of the doors of the entry room and the hallway, and no longer having the strength to resist, I cantered through the salon in my new frock coat with its shiny gold buttons. As I was going into Volodya's room, I heard behind me the voices of Dubkov and Nekhlyudov, who had come to congratulate me and propose going somewhere for dinner and champagne in my honour. Dmitry said that even though he didn't like to drink champagne, he would go with us to drink *Bruderschaft*[28] with me, and Dubkov said that for some reason I looked just like a colonel, while Volodya didn't congratulate me, but merely said very coldly that we would now be able to leave for the country the day after tomorrow. It was as if he was happy about my matriculation, but also a little put out that I was now as grown-up as he was. St-Jérôme, who had also come in to see us, said with a great flourish that his duties were now at an end, that he didn't know if they had been carried out well or ill, but that he had done all that he could, and the next day would be moving to the home of his count. In response to everything said to me, I felt the appearance on my face, in spite of myself, of a sweet, happy, rather fatuously self-satisfied smile, and I noticed that it even imparted itself to everyone who talked to me.

And so my tutor was gone, I had my own droshky, my name had been published in the list of new students, I had a sword on my belt and the policemen in the corner booths might sometimes salute me . . . I was a grown-up and, I think, happy.

We decided to dine at Yar's[29] between four and five, but since Volodya had gone with Dubkov to his place, and Dmitry had, in keeping with his own custom, gone somewhere else after saying that he had business to take care of before dinner, I could spend the remaining two hours as I liked. I walked around the rooms quite a long time, gazing at myself in all the mirrors, first with the frock coat buttoned, then with it completely unbuttoned, then with it buttoned only at the top, and each way seemed excellent to me. And then, ashamed though I was about being too pleased, I still couldn't resist, and went out to the stable and carriage barn to look at Beauty, Kuzma and the droshky. After that I walked around the rooms again, gazing in the mirrors, counting the money in my pocket and continuing to smile just as happily. But less than an hour passed before I began to feel a certain tedium or regret that no one else was seeing me in that brilliant state, and I wanted movement and activity. I therefore ordered the droshky harnessed, having concluded that the best thing would be a drive to Kuznetsky Most for some shopping.

I remembered that when Volodya entered the university he bought himself some Victor Adam[30] lithographs of horses and tobacco and pipes, and it seemed essential to me that I do the same.

Accompanied by glances on every side and by bright sunlight on my buttons, the cockade of my hat and my sword, I arrived at Kuznetsky Most and stopped at Daziaro's[31] picture shop. I went inside and looked around. I didn't want to buy Adam horses, lest I be twitted for aping Volodya, but, embarrassed about disturbing the obliging shopkeepers, I quickly chose a woman's head in gouache that had been in the window, and paid twenty roubles for it. But after I had paid, it still seemed a shame to me that I had bothered the two handsomely dressed shop-keepers with such a trifle, and it also seemed that they were regarding me a little too casually. Wishing to give them a sense of who I was, I turned my attention to a little silver article lying in the vitrine, and on being told that it was a *porte-crayon*[32] and cost eighteen roubles, I asked them to wrap it in tissue. After I had paid for it and learned that good tobacco and chibouks could be found at the tobacco shop next door, I bowed graciously to both shopkeepers and went outside with the picture under my arm. In the neighbouring shop, whose street sign depicted a Negro smoking a cigar, I bought, also from a desire not to copy anyone else, not Zhukov's but some sultan's tobacco, a Stam-bouline pipe, and two chibouks[33] of linden and rosewood. As I was crossing from the shop to the droshky, I saw Semyonov dressed in an ordinary frock coat pass by at a rapid pace with his head down. It annoyed me that he hadn't recognized me. I called out 'Drive up!' rather loudly, got in the droshky and over-took him.

'Good day, sir,' I said.

'My respects to you,' he replied, continuing to walk.

'Why aren't you wearing your uniform?' I asked.

Semyonov stopped, squinted at me in silence, while baring his white teeth as if the sun were hurting his eyes, but really to show his indifference to my droshky and uniform, and then continued on his way.

Coming back from Kuznetsky Most I stopped at a pastry

shop on Tverskaya Street and, although I meant to give the impression that I was primarily interested in the shop's newspapers, I couldn't help myself and started to eat one sweet pastry after another. Despite my embarrassment about the gentleman staring at me in curiosity from behind his paper, I consumed some eight pastries with extraordinary speed, sampling everything in the shop.

I felt a little heartburn after I got home, but I didn't pay any attention to it and set about examining my purchases. I disliked the picture so much that I not only didn't frame it and hang it in my room as Volodya had done, but even carefully hid it behind my chest of drawers where no one else could see it. I didn't like the *porte-crayon* either. I put it in my desk, consoling myself with the thought that it was a substantial thing made of silver and very useful for a student to have. The smoking supplies, however, I decided to put to use at once.

Unsealing the four-ounce pouch and carefully filling the Stambouline bowl with the reddish-yellow fine-cut sultan's tobacco, I touched it with burning tinder, took the chibouk between my middle and ring finger (a position that I especially liked) and began to draw in the smoke.

The tobacco had a very pleasant aroma, but it tasted bitter and made me gasp. Bracing myself, however, I drew in the smoke quite a long time, trying to blow rings and inhale. The room was soon completely filled with blue clouds of smoke, the pipe had started to make a wheezing sound and the hot tobacco to bounce up and down, and I felt slightly dizzy with an acrid taste in my mouth. I was about to stop and see how I looked in the mirror with the pipe, when to my astonishment I began to stagger and the room started to spin, and in the mirror, over to which I had got with difficulty, I saw that my face had turned as white as a sheet. I had barely managed to fall back onto the sofa when I was overcome by such nausea and weakness that I started to imagine that the pipe was a deadly thing for me and that I was dying. I was seriously frightened and about to call the servants for help and send for a doctor.

The terror was short-lived, however. I quickly realized what was wrong and with a terrible headache lay weakly on the sofa a long time, gazing dully at the 'Bostanjoglo'[34] crest on the tobacco pouch and at the pipe lying on the floor among the ashes and what remained of the pastries, and in disappointment sadly thought, 'I'm probably not completely grown up if I can't smoke like the others, and, as they do, hold a chibouk between my middle and ring fingers, inhale and blow smoke through my light-brown moustache.'

Dmitry, coming by for me sometime after four, found me in that unpleasant state. After a glass of water, however, I had almost completely recovered and was ready to go with him.

'Why do you want to smoke?' he said, looking at the traces of the episode. 'It's just silly and a waste of money. I promised myself never to do it . . . But let's hurry, since we still have to stop by Dubkov's.'

FOURTEEN

What Volodya and Dubkov
Were Doing

As soon as Dmitry had entered my room I could tell from his face, walk and the characteristic way he had in a bad mood of blinking and jerking his head to the side with a grimace, as if adjusting his cravat, that he was in the coldly obstinate mood that came over him whenever he was upset with himself, and that always had a chilling effect on my feeling for him. I had recently begun to observe and reflect on my friend's character, but our friendship wasn't changed in the least by that: it was still so young and strong that however I might regard Dmitry, I still couldn't help but see him as perfect. There were two different people in him and both were excellent to me. One, of whom I was passionately fond, was kind, affectionate, mild, cheerful and aware of those likeable qualities. When he was in that mood, his whole appearance, the sound of his voice and all of his movements said, 'I'm mild and virtuous and take pleasure in being mild and virtuous, and you can all see that.' The other, whom I was only now starting to recognize and whose nobility I admired, was cold, severe with himself and others, proud, fanatically religious and pedantically moral. At the moment he was the second person.

With the candour that was an essential condition of our relationship, I told him after we got into his phaeton that it was sad and painful to see him in such a difficult, unpleasant mood on a day of such happiness for me.

'You're probably upset about something. Why don't you tell me what it is?' I asked him.

'Nikolenka!' he answered without hurrying, while nervously turning his head to the side and blinking. 'If I gave my word to hide nothing from you, then there's no reason for you to suspect me of doing so. One can't always be in the same mood, and if something's upset me, then I myself am unable to say what it is.'

'What a remarkably frank and honest character,' I thought, and said no more.

We arrived at Dubkov's in silence. His apartment was exceptionally fine, or so it seemed to me. Everywhere were rugs, pictures, curtains, multicoloured wallpapers, portraits, and bentwood and Voltaire armchairs, and on the walls, guns, pistols, tobacco pouches and cardboard wild-animal heads of some kind. Seeing Dubkov's study, I realized whom Volodya had been imitating in the decoration of his own room. Dubkov and Volodya were playing cards when we came in. Some gentleman unfamiliar to me (and probably unimportant, judging by his self-effacing posture) sat by the table and kept a very close watch on their play. Dubkov was wearing a silk dressing gown and soft shoes. Volodya had removed his frock coat and was sitting across from him on the couch, and was very involved in the game, judging by his flushed face and the discontented glance he shot at us while interrupting his play for a second. Seeing me, he flushed even more.

'Well, it's your deal,' he said to Dubkov. I realized that my learning that he played cards was disagreeable to him. But there was no embarrassment in his expression; rather, it seemed to be saying, 'Yes, I play, and it only astonishes you because you're still young. It not only isn't bad, it's what we should be doing at our age.'

I sensed that at once and understood.

Dubkov, however, didn't deal the cards but stood up, shook our hands, sat us down and offered us pipes, which we declined.

'So, then, he, our Diplomat, is the hero of the festivities,' he said. 'My goodness, but he really does look just like a colonel!'

'Hmm!' I mooed, feeling the fatuously self-satisfied smile spread across my face again.

I respected Dubkov as only a sixteen-year-old boy could respect a twenty-seven-year-old adjutant who was described by all the grown-ups as an exceptionally decent young man with excellent French and fine dancing abilities, and who, while despising my youth in his heart, was clearly making an effort to hide that.

Despite my respect for him, it was – goodness knows why – difficult and awkward for me to look him in the eye the whole time we were acquainted. I noticed afterwards that it's hard for me to look three kinds of people in the eye: those who are much worse than I am, those who are much better, and those with whom I've been unable to speak about something of which we're both aware. Dubkov may have been both better and worse than I was, but there was definitely the fact that he often lied without acknowledging it, and that I had noticed that weakness in him and obviously couldn't bring myself to talk to him about it.

'How about another hand?' Volodya said, shrugging his shoulder like Papa and shuffling the cards.

'He just won't give up!' Dubkov said. 'Let's finish later. Well, all right, just one more, then.'

I watched their hands as they played. Volodya's were large and beautiful. The bend of his thumb and the curve of his other fingers as he held the cards were so like Papa's that it even seemed to me for a while that Volodya was holding his hands that way on purpose in order to look like a grown-up. But it was immediately clear to me from a glance at his face that he wasn't thinking about anything but the game. Dubkov, by contrast, had small, plump hands whose soft, extraordinarily nimble fingers curled inward – just the sort of hands on which you find rings and that belong to people who like handmade articles and owning beautiful things. Volodya had evidently lost, because, after looking at his cards, the third gentleman observed that 'Vladimir Petrovich' was terribly unlucky, and Dubkov got out a portfolio, wrote something in a little notebook and, after showing Volodya what he had written, asked, 'Correct?'

'Correct!' Volodya said, glancing at the notebook with feigned indifference. 'Now let's get going.'

Volodya took Dubkov in his droshky, and Dmitry took me in his phaeton.

'What game were they playing?' I asked Dmitry.

'Piquet.[35] It's a stupid game. In fact, all games are stupid.'

'Do they play for large amounts?'

'Not really, but it's still bad.'

'You don't play?'

'No. I promised myself I wouldn't, whereas Dubkov can't help trying to win off people.'

'Then that's bad of him. Volodya probably doesn't play as well as he does?'

'Clearly not. It isn't good, but there wasn't anything really wrong going on there. Dubkov loves to play and knows how to, but he's still a fine person.'

'Oh, I certainly didn't mean that . . . ,' I said.

'Right, and you shouldn't think that there's anything bad about him, for he is, in fact, an outstanding person. And I'm very fond of him and always will be, despite his weaknesses.'

For some reason it seemed to me that precisely because Dmitry had stood up for Dubkov so emphatically, he no longer liked or respected him, but that he wouldn't admit it from stubbornness and a fear of being accused of fickleness. He was one of those people who love their friends their whole lives, not so much because the friends remain forever dear to them, but because once they have, even by mistake, grown fond of someone, they consider it dishonourable to stop caring about him.

FIFTEEN

I Am Feted

Dubkov and Volodya knew everyone at Yar's by name, and everyone from the doorman to the manager treated them with great respect. We were at once given a special room and served a wonderful dinner selected by Dubkov from the French menu. A bottle of chilled champagne, about which I tried to be as nonchalant as possible, was already waiting. The dinner passed very pleasantly and merrily, even though Dubkov, as was his habit, told the strangest stories, allegedly true, such as the time his grandmother used a blunderbuss to kill three robbers who had attacked her (making me blush and look down and turn away); and even though Volodya noticeably cringed every time I tried to say something (which was unfair, since I don't recall saying anything particularly embarrassing). After the champagne was poured everyone congratulated me, and I linked arms with Dubkov and Dmitry and drank *Bruderschaft* with them and kissed them. Since I didn't know to whom the bottle of champagne belonged (it belonged to everyone, as was later explained) and I wanted to treat my friends with my own money, which I kept fingering in my pocket, I quietly got out a ten-rouble note and, after calling the waiter over, gave it to him and, in a whisper but loud enough for everyone to hear, since they were all looking at me in silence, I told him to bring 'another half-bottle of champagne, please'. Volodya blushed and writhed so much and looked at me and the others with such dismay that I realized my blunder, but the half-bottle was brought anyway, and we consumed it with great pleasure and continued to enjoy ourselves. Dubkov spun yarns without stopping, and Volodya, too, told such funny stories and told them well, which I had never expected it of him, and we laughed a lot. What made them – that is, Volodya and Dubkov – so amusing was the way they copied and embellished well-known jokes. 'Were you abroad, then?' one of them would ask. 'No, I wasn't,' the other would reply, 'but my brother plays the violin.' They attained such perfection in that kind of nonsense humour that they would tell the joke itself as 'My brother never played the violin, either.' They answered each other's questions the same way, and sometimes even without the question tried to combine the most disparate things and speak the nonsense with a straight face, which was very funny. I was starting to grasp how it worked and wanted to say something funny, too, but they all winced or looked away when I spoke, and the joke would fall flat. Dubkov said, 'You aren't making any sense, brother Diplomat,' but I was feeling so good from the champagne and the grown-up company that the comment hardly stung me. Although he had drunk as much as the rest of us, Dmitry alone remained in a dour, serious mood, which dampened the general merriment a bit.

'Listen, gentlemen, after dinner we'll have to take Diplomat in hand,' Dubkov said. 'Why don't we go to *Auntie*'s and deal with him there?'

'You know Nekhlyudov won't go,' Volodya said.

'What a milksop you are, what an intolerable milksop!' Dubkov said to Dmitry. 'Come along with us and you'll see what a fine lady Auntie is.'

'Not only won't I go, but I won't let him go, either,' Dmitry replied, turning red.

'Who? Diplomat? But you want to go, don't you, Diplomat? Why, he was radiant at the mere mention of Auntie.'

'It's not that I won't let him,' Dmitry went on, getting up from his place and starting to walk around the room without looking at me, 'but that I don't advise him to go and wish that he wouldn't. He's no longer a child, and if he wants to, then he can go by himself without the two of you. And you really ought to be ashamed of yourself, Dubkov. Whenever you're up to no good, you want others to do the same.'

'But what's so terrible about my inviting all of you to Auntie's for a cup of tea?' Dubkov asked, winking at Volodya. 'Well, if going with us is so unpleasant, then let Volodya and me go by ourselves. You'll go, won't you, Volodya?'

'Uh-huh!' Volodya confirmed. 'We'll stop by there, and then go back to my place for more piquet.'

'So, do you want to go with them or not?' Dmitry asked, coming over to me.

'No,' I answered, sliding over on the sofa so he could sit down beside me, which he did. 'I just don't want to, and if you don't advise it, then I certainly won't.' 'No,' I added after a pause, 'it wasn't true when I said that I didn't want to go with them, but I'm happy not to.'

'Which is excellent,' Dmitry said. 'Live your own way, and don't dance to anyone else's tune – that's the best way.'

Not only did that little spat not spoil our fun, it even increased it. Dmitry suddenly recovered the mild mood I liked so much. The feeling that he had done something good had that effect on him, as I later noticed more than once. He was pleased with himself for defending me. He became exceptionally merry, ordered another bottle of champagne (which was against his rule), invited a strange gentleman into our room for a drink, sang *Gaudeamus igitur*,[36] asking everyone to join in, and suggested driving out to Sokolniki,[37] at which point Dubkov objected that that would be just too sentimental.

'Let's have a good time today,' Dmitry said with a smile. 'In honour of his matriculation, I'll get drunk for the first time, and so be it.' That merriment sat rather strangely on Dmitry. He was like a family tutor or kind father who's pleased with his children and has relaxed and wants to entertain them, yet at the same time show that it's possible to have fun honourably and decently. Even so, that unexpected merriment infected me and apparently the others, too, and all the more since each of us had by then drunk close to half a bottle of champagne.

In that pleasant mood I went out to the main room to light a cigarette Dubkov had given me.

When I got up from my seat, I noticed that I was a little dizzy and that my arms and legs moved naturally only when I concentrated on them. Otherwise, my legs would wander sideways and my arms would produce gesticulations of some kind. I focused all my attention on those appendages, ordering my arms to lift themselves up and button my frock coat and smooth my hair (during which they tossed my elbows terrifically high) and my legs to walk through the door, which they did, although they put my feet down either too hard or not hard enough, especially the left one, which kept getting up on tiptoe. A voice called out, 'Where are you going? They'll bring a candle.' I surmised that it belonged to Volodya and took pleasure in having done so, but only gave him a little smile in reply and continued on my way.

SIXTEEN
A Quarrel

Sitting and eating something at a small table in the main room was a short, stocky civilian gentleman with a red moustache. Sitting next to him was a tall brunet without a moustache. They were speaking French. Their glances gave me pause, but I decided, even so, to light my cigarette off the candle standing in front of them. With my face to the side to avoid their gaze, I went over to the table and started to light the cigarette. After it was lit, I couldn't help myself and looked at the gentleman who was dining. His grey eyes were staring at me with a hostile expression. I was about to turn away when his red moustache moved and he said in French, 'I don't care for smoking, sir, while I'm dining.'

I mumbled something unintelligible.

'That's right, sir, I don't care for it,' the gentleman with the moustache continued in a severe tone, after a quick glance at the gentleman without a moustache, as if inviting him to admire the working over he was about to give me. 'And I also don't care, sir, for people who are so impolite as to come over and smoke under your nose – I don't care for them, either.' I realized at once that the gentleman was giving me a good scold, even though it had seemed to me from the start that I was very much in the wrong in regard to him.

'I didn't think that it would bother you,' I said.

'And you didn't think that you were a boor, either, but I did!' the gentleman yelled.

'What right have you to yell?' I said, sensing that I was being insulted and getting angry myself.

'This right: that I'll never allow anyone to be disrespectful to me and will always teach brave fellows like you a lesson. What's your name, sir, and where do you live?'

I was so enraged that my lips trembled and my breath came in starts. But I still felt myself in the wrong, probably for having drunk so much champagne, and said nothing rude to the gentleman at all, but on the contrary told him my last name and our address in the most submissive way.

'My name is Kolpikov, sir, and be more courteous in the future. You'll hear from me – *vous aurez de mes nouvelles*,' he concluded, since the whole conversation had been in French.

Trying to make my voice as firm as possible, I merely said, 'I'm very glad,' and then turned around and went back to our room with the cigarette, which had managed to go out.

I said nothing about what had happened to me either to my brother or to our friends, all the more since they were engaged in some heated dispute of their own, but instead sat down in a corner by myself and reflected on the strange episode. The words 'you, sir, are a boor' (*un mal élevé, monsieur*) rang in my ears and made me more and more indignant. My intoxication had completely passed. As I meditated on how I had acted in the affair, the terrible thought suddenly came to me that I had acted like a coward. 'What right did he have to attack me? Why didn't he just say that I was disturbing him? Doesn't that mean he was in the wrong? When he called me a boor, why didn't I just say to him, "A boor, sir, is someone who permits himself such rudeness"? Or why didn't I just shout at him, "Silence!" That would have been excellent! Why didn't I challenge him to a duel? No, I didn't do any of that, but swallowed the insult like a miserable little coward.' 'You, sir, are a boor' rang unceasingly and gallingly in my ears. 'No, I can't leave it there,' I thought and got up with the firm intention of going back to the gentleman and saying some terrible thing to him, and perhaps even bashing him in the head with the candlestick, if it came to that. I imagined the last idea with the greatest of pleasure, but it wasn't without a strong sense of fear that I entered the main room again. Fortunately, Mr Kolpikov had already left and the only person there was a serving boy clearing the table. I was about to tell him what had happened and explain that I hadn't been in the wrong in any way, but for some reason I changed my mind and went back to our room in the gloomiest of moods.

'What's happened to our Diplomat?' Dubkov said. 'He's probably deciding the fate of Europe.'

'Oh, leave me alone,' I said in a sulky voice, turning away. Immediately after that, as I was walking about the room, I for some reason started to reflect that Dubkov wasn't a good person at all. 'What about the endless joking and the name "Diplomat"? There's nothing kind about that. All he wants is to win money off Volodya and visit some "Auntie" or other . . . There's nothing pleasant about him. Everything he says is either a lie or some vulgarity, and he's always making fun of people. I think he's just stupid, and a bad person, too.' I spent five minutes or so brooding like that, and for some reason feeling more and more hostile towards Dubkov. He paid no attention to me, however, which made me even more furious. I was even angry with Volodya and Dmitry for talking to him.

'You know what, gentlemen? The Diplomat needs a good dousing,' Dubkov said with a smile that struck me as mocking and even treacherous. 'He's in a bad way. He truly is.'

'And you, sir, could use a good dousing, too, since you're in a bad way yourself,' I retorted with a spiteful grin, forgetting that he and I were now on familiar terms.

The retort probably surprised Dubkov, but he indifferently turned away and continued his conversation with Volodya and Dmitry.

I was going to try to join in, but I sensed that I absolutely would not be able to pretend and went off to my corner again, remaining there until it was time to leave.

After we had settled up and were putting on our overcoats, Dubkov said to Dmitry, 'Well, then, where are Orestes and Pylades[38] off to? Probably home to talk about "love". How much better than your sour friendship for us to call on a nice auntie.'

'How dare you talk like that and laugh at us?' I immediately replied, going up very close to him and waving my arms. 'How dare you laugh at feelings you don't understand! I won't allow it! Silence!' I shouted, and then fell silent, breathing hard from agitation and not knowing what else to say. Dubkov was at first astonished, and then tried to smile and treat it as a joke, but in the end it frightened him and he looked away, to my great surprise.

'I'm not laughing at you and your feelings at all. It's just the way I talk,' he meekly replied.

'That's just it!' I yelled, but at the same time I felt ashamed of myself and sorry for Dubkov, whose flushed, embarrassed face expressed genuine distress.

'What's the matter with you?' Volodya and Dmitry started asking together. 'No one meant to offend you.'

'No, he was trying to insult me.'

'What a desperate gentleman your brother is,' Dubkov said as he was already on his way out of the door and wouldn't be able to hear my reply.

I might perhaps have run after him to abuse him with more rude remarks, but at that moment the serving boy who had been present during the affair with Kolpikov offered me my overcoat and I immediately calmed down, although I simulated enough residual anger to Dmitry for the instant calming not to seem odd. Dubkov and I ran into each other the next day in Volodya's room and didn't mention the episode, although we remained on formal terms and found it even harder to look each other in the eye than before.

The memory of the quarrel with Kolpikov, who failed to give me *de ses nouvelles* either the next day or any day after that, was for many years a terribly vivid and painful one. For five years or so I would writhe and audibly moan every time I recalled the unavenged offence, comforting myself, however, with satisfaction at what a brave fellow I had shown myself to be in the business with Dubkov. It was only much later that I began to regard that business altogether differently and to remember the quarrel with Kolpikov for the pleasure of its comedy, and to regret the undeserved insult I had inflicted on the 'decent fellow' Dubkov.

When I told Dmitry the same evening about the adventure with Kolpikov, whose appearance I described in detail, he was quite amazed.

'Why it's the same fellow!' he said. 'Can you imagine? This

Kolpikov is a famous rascal and cheat, but mainly a coward who was forced out of his regiment by his comrades for refusing to fight after being slapped. Where did he find the pluck?' he added, looking at me with a kindly smile. 'Did he really only call you a "boor"?'

'Yes.'

'It's bad, but still no disaster!' Dmitry consoled me.

It was only later when I was able to reflect calmly about the situation that I reached the fairly plausible conclusion that Kolpikov, sensing that he could attack me with impunity, had in the presence of the brunet without a moustache avenged the slap he had received years before, just as I had in my turn immediately avenged his 'boor' on the innocent Dubkov.

SEVENTEEN

I Get Ready to Make
Some Calls

My first thought on waking the next morning was the adventure
with Kolpikov, and I moaned again and ran around the room,
but there was nothing to be done about it, and anyway it was
my last day in Moscow and on Papa's orders I had to make the
calls he had written down on a piece of paper for me. His worry
for us was not so much our morality and education as our social
connections. In his rapid scrawl he had written: '1) Prince Ivan
Ivanovich *without fail*, 2) the Ivins *without fail*, 3) Prince
Mikhailo, 4) and Princess Nekhlyudova and Mme Valakhina, if
you have time. And, obviously, the university warden, rector and
professors.'

Dmitry talked me out of the university calls, saying that they
were not only unnecessary but even inappropriate; the rest,
however, all had to be made that day. Of those, I was especially
daunted by the first two with the words 'without fail' written
next to them. Prince Ivan Ivanovich was a general-in-chief, an
old man and a rich one, and lived by himself. That meant that
I, a sixteen-year-old student, would inevitably have direct dealings with him that could not – I had a premonition – be flattering to me. The Ivins were rich people, too, and their father was
an important civilian general[39] who had come to see us only
once in Grandmother's time. After she died, however, I noticed
that the youngest Ivin was avoiding us and apparently giving
himself airs. The oldest, I knew from hearsay, had already
finished the law course and was working in Petersburg; the
middle one, Sergey, whom I had idolized, was also in Petersburg,
where he was a big, fat cadet in the Corps of Pages.[40]

Not only didn't I care in my youth for relations with people who considered themselves above me, but those relations were even an unbearable agony for me, thanks to my constant fear of being insulted, and the exertion of all my mental powers to show my independence. I did, however, have to make up for ignoring Papa's last order by obeying his first ones. I was walking around my room looking over my clothes, sword and hat laid out on the chairs and getting ready to go, when old man Grap came in to congratulate me, bringing Ilenka with him. Grap the father was a Russianized German, an intolerable hypocrite and flatterer, and often intoxicated. Most of the time he came only to ask for something, and Papa would sometimes sit him down in the study but never invite him to dine with us. His abasement and begging were so blended with a certain external good will and ease in our home that everyone attached great merit to his apparent devotion to us, but I just didn't like him and always felt ashamed for him whenever he spoke.

I was quite unhappy about the arrival of those guests and made no attempt to hide it. I had got so used to looking down on Ilenka, and he had got so used to giving us the right to do so, that it was a little unpleasant for me that he was as much a student as I was. It seemed to me that he was slightly embarrassed about that equality, too. I greeted them coldly, without asking them to sit down, since I felt awkward about it, thinking that they could certainly sit without an invitation from me, and ordered the droshky harnessed. Ilenka was a kind, very honest and by no means stupid young man, but he was also what is known as a bit touched. He was constantly subject without any apparent reason to one extreme mood or another, whether tearfulness, hilarity or sensitivity about every little thing, and he now seemed to be in the last mood. He said nothing, looked venomously at me and his father, and when addressed merely smiled the stiff little smile behind which he was used to hiding all his feelings, but especially the feeling of shame for his father that he couldn't help experiencing around us.

'So, then, Nikolay Petrovich, sir,' the old man said, while following me around the room as I got dressed, and twirling in his stubby fingers with deferential slowness a silver snuffbox given to him by my grandmother. 'As soon as I heard from my

son that you, sir, had passed your examinations so brilliantly
– your intellect is known to everyone – I at once ran over to
congratulate you, dear fellow. After all, I once carried you on
my shoulder, and, as God is my witness, I love you all as if you
were my own, and my Ilenka kept asking to come and see you.
He's got quite used to you, too.'

Ilenka was at that moment sitting silently by the window and
supposedly examining my cocked hat, while angrily, if barely
noticeably, muttering something to himself under his breath.

'Well, and I wanted to ask you, Nikolay Petrovich,' the old
man continued, 'about my own Ilyusha; that is, did he do well,
too? He said that you and he will be together, so don't abandon
him, look after him, advise him.'

'What do you mean? He got excellent marks!' I replied, glancing at Ilenka, who blushed and stopped moving his lips when
he felt my gaze on him.

'Couldn't he spend the day with you?' the old man said with
such a simpering smile it was as if he were quite afraid of me,
although he kept so close to me wherever I happened to move
that there wasn't a moment when I wasn't aware of the wine
and tobacco reek he emitted. I was vexed that he had put me in
such a false position with his son, and that he was keeping me
from attending to what at the moment was a very important
activity for me: getting dressed. The main thing, however, was
the maddening reek of alcohol, which so upset me that I said
very coldly that I couldn't be with Ilenka, since I would be out
all day.

'But didn't you want to go to Sister's, Papa?' Ilenka said with
a smile, but without looking at me. 'And I've got things to do,
as well.' I felt even more vexed and embarrassed, and to compen-
sate in some way for my refusal, I quickly added that I wouldn't
be at home, since I had to be at *Prince* Ivan Ivanovich's, at *Princess* Kornakova's and at Mr Ivin's, the one who occupied such
an important post, and that I would probably be dining at *Princess* Nekhlyudova's. I thought that if they knew how important
the people I was going to see were, they couldn't make any more
claim on me. As they were getting ready to go, I invited Ilenka
to come by another time, but he just mumbled something and

smiled stiffly. It was clear that he would never set foot in my
door again.

I left immediately after them to make my calls. Volodya,
whom I had asked that morning to join me so I wouldn't feel so
awkward on my own, declined on the grounds that it would be
just too sentimental for two 'little brothers' to drive around
together in the same 'little droshky'.

EIGHTEEN
The Valakhins

And so I set out by myself. The first call, by proximity, was at the Valakhins on Sivtsev Vrazhek Lane. I hadn't seen Sonyechka for three years and my infatuation had obviously long since passed, although a vivid and touching memory of that childhood love remained in my heart. There had been times in those three years when I recalled her with such force and clarity that tears came to my eyes and I felt myself in love again, but they only lasted a few moments and were slow to return.

I knew that Sonyechka and her mother had spent some two years abroad, where, it was said, their stagecoach had overturned and Sonyechka had cut her face on one of its windows and apparently been quite disfigured. On my way to their house I vividly recalled the former Sonyechka and wondered about the one I was about to see. Because of her two years abroad, I for some reason imagined her as exceptionally tall with a beautiful waist, and as serious and proud yet exceptionally attractive. My imagination refused to picture her with a face disfigured by scars; on the contrary, having heard somewhere of an ardent lover who remained true to the object of his desire despite her disfigurement by smallpox,[41] I tried to think that I was in love with Sonyechka in order to have the merit of remaining true to her in spite of her scars. I wasn't actually in love as I drove up to the Valakhins', but having stirred those old memories in myself, I was quite ready to fall in love again and very much wanted to, all the more since after seeing all my friends in love, I had long been ashamed of lagging so far behind.

The Valakhins lived in a trim little wooden house entered through a yard. I rang the bell – at the time a great rarity in

Moscow – and a tiny, neatly dressed little boy opened the door. Either he didn't know how or didn't want to tell me if the masters were at home, and leaving me alone in the dark entry room, he ran off down an even darker hallway.

I remained alone quite a long time in that dark room, where, besides the front door and the door to the hallway, there was another closed door, and I was partly surprised by the gloomy character of the house and partly inclined to believe that it had to be that way with people who had just returned from abroad. About five minutes later the door to the salon was opened from inside by the same little boy, who led me through it to a tidy but modest drawing room where Sonyechka immediately joined me.

She was seventeen. She was very short and very thin, and her face had a sallow, unhealthy colour. There weren't any scars to be seen on it, but her charming, prominent eyes and bright, cheerfully good-natured smile were the same ones I had known and loved as a child. I hadn't expected her to be that way at all, and therefore couldn't immediately lavish on her the feeling that I had prepared on the way there. She shook my hand in the English manner, which was then just as great a rarity as the doorbell, frankly shook it, and sat me down next to herself on the sofa.

'Oh, how happy I am to see you, dear *Nicolas*,' she said, gazing into my face with such a sincere expression of pleasure that I heard in the words 'dear *Nicolas*' a friendly rather than patronizing tone. To my surprise she was, after her trip abroad, even simpler, sweeter and more kindred in address than before. I detected two small scars by her nose and one eyebrow, but her marvellous eyes and smile were completely in accord with my memory and sparkled in the same old way.

'Oh, how you've changed!' she said. 'You're all grown up! Well, and me? How do you find me?'

'Oh, I wouldn't have recognized you,' I replied, even though I was thinking at that moment that I would always have recognized her. I felt myself once again in the merrily carefree mood that I had been in five years before when she and I had danced the *Grossvater* at Grandmother's ball.

'What, have I become so unattractive?' she asked with a shake of her little head.

'Oh no, not at all. You've grown a bit and are older,' I hastened to answer, 'but on the contrary . . . and even . . .'

'Oh well, it's no matter. You remember our dances and games and St-Jérôme and Mme Dorat?' (I didn't remember any Mme Dorat; carried away in enjoyment of her childhood memories, Sonyechka had apparently mixed them up.) 'Oh, it was a wonderful time,' she continued, and the same smile – or an even better one than I had carried in my memory – and the same eyes sparkled before me. As she spoke I managed a thought about the position I was in at that moment, and concluded to myself that I was at that moment in love. No sooner did I reach that conclusion than my happy, carefree mood instantly vanished, and a kind of fog covered everything before me, even her eyes and smile, and I felt embarrassed about something and blushed and lost the ability to speak.

'The times are different now,' she went on, sighing and raising her eyebrows a little. 'Everything's got much worse, and we have too, isn't that right, *Nicolas*?'

Unable to reply, I looked at her in silence.

'Where are all the Ivins and Kornakovs now? You remember?' she continued, gazing with a certain curiosity at my frightened, blushing face. 'It was a wonderful time!'

I was still unable to reply.

I was temporarily delivered from that difficult position by the entry into the room of the elder Valakhina. I stood, bowed and again acquired the ability to speak, although, on the other hand, an odd change took place in Sonyechka with her mother's arrival. All her cheerfulness and warmth disappeared and even her smile was different, and except for her height, she abruptly turned into the young lady returned from abroad I had imagined I would find in her. There didn't seem to be any reason at all for the change, since her mother smiled just as pleasantly, and all her movements expressed the same gentleness as before. Mme Valakhina sat down on a small couch and indicated a place next to her. She said something to her daughter in English, and Sonyechka immediately left, which made it even easier for me.

She then asked about my relatives, about my brother and about
my father, and told me about her own misfortune – the loss of
her husband, and then, sensing at the end that she had nothing
more to tell me, she gazed at me in silence, as if to say, 'If you
get up now, bow and leave, you'll be doing very well, my dear,'
but a strange thing happened to me. Sonyechka had returned
with some work and taken a seat in a different corner of the
drawing room where I could sense her looking at me. During
Mme Valakhina's story about the loss of her husband, I remembered once again that I was in love and thought, too, that the
mother had very likely already guessed it, and another attack of
shyness beset me, one so strong that I no longer felt capable of
moving any of my limbs naturally. I knew that in order to stand
up and leave I would have to think about where to put my feet
and what to do with my head and hands; in a word, I felt much
the same thing I had felt the previous evening after the half-bottle
of champagne. I had a foreboding that I wouldn't be able to
manage any of it and thus *could not* stand up, and, in fact, *could
not*. Mme Valakhina was probably surprised by my bright-red
face and complete immobility, but I decided it would be better
to sit in that inane position than risk standing up and making
some sort of ludicrous exit. So I sat there quite a long time,
hoping that some unanticipated event would extricate me from
that position. The event presented itself in the person of an unattractive young man who came into the room with the air of a
member of the household and politely bowed to me. Mme Valakhina got up and said with an apology that she had to speak to
her *homme d'affaires*,[42] the whole time gazing at me with a
puzzled look that said, 'If you want to sit there forever, I won't
chase you out.' Making a terrific effort, I somehow got to my
feet, although bowing was beyond my ability, and on my way
out to the accompanying sympathetic gazes of mother and
daughter, I tripped over a chair that wasn't even in my way, and
tripped over it because all my attention had been focused on not
tripping over the rug that lay under my feet. Once I was outside
in the fresh air, however, and after I had writhed and moaned so
loudly that even Kuzma had asked me several times 'How
can I help?' the feeling evaporated, and I began to reflect quite

calmly on my love for Sonyechka and her relationship with her mother, which had seemed so strange. When I mentioned to my father afterwards about noticing that Mme Valakhina and her daughter weren't on good terms, he said, 'Yes, she torments her with her awful stinginess, the poor thing, and it's strange, since she used to be such a charming, sweet, wonderful woman!' he added with stronger feeling than he could have had for a mere relation. 'I can't understand why she's changed so much. You didn't see her private secretary or whatever he is there, did you? And what's a Russian gentlewoman doing with a private secretary, anyway?' he said, as he angrily stepped away from me.

'I did see him,' I answered.

'Well, was he good-looking, at least?'

'No, he wasn't good-looking at all.'

'It makes no sense,' Papa said, angrily shrugging his shoulder and coughing . . .

'So I'm in love,' I thought as I continued on my way in my droshky.

NINETEEN
The Kornakovs

The second call on my way was at the Kornakovs. They occupied the *bel étage*[43] of a large building on Arbat Street. The stairway was exceptionally smart and neat, but not luxurious. There were striped hemp mats secured with gleaming brass rods lying everywhere, but no flowers or mirrors. The salon, over whose brightly polished floor I crossed to get to the drawing room, was just as austerely, coldly and neatly furnished. Everything shone and had a sturdy if not particularly new look, but there weren't any pictures or curtains or other ornaments visible anywhere. I found several young princesses in the drawing room. They were all sitting so primly and idly that you could tell at once that they sat that way only when they had company.

'*Maman* will be out in a moment,' the oldest one said after coming over to sit down beside me. For a quarter of an hour she engaged me in conversation so adroitly and fluently that it never flagged for a moment. But it was too obvious that she was trying to divert me, so I didn't like her. She told me in passing that their brother Stepan – the one they called 'Étienne' and who two years before had been enrolled in the Cadet School[44] – had already received his commission. When she spoke of her brother, and especially of the fact that he had joined the hussars against his mother's wishes, she made a frightened face and all the younger princesses, who were sitting quietly, made frightened faces too; when she spoke of Grandmother's passing, she made a sad face and all the younger princesses made sad faces too; and when she recalled my striking St-Jérôme and being led away, she laughed and showed her bad teeth, and all the other princesses laughed and showed their bad teeth too.

Then their mother came in – the same small, spare woman with restless eyes and the habit of looking at others whenever she was talking to you. She took my hand and raised her own to my lips to kiss, which, not considering it necessary, I certainly wouldn't have done otherwise.

'How glad I am to see you,' she began with her usual volubility, while turning around to look at her daughters. 'He really does look like his *maman*. Isn't that true, *Lise*?'

Lise said that it was true, although I knew for certain that there wasn't the least resemblance between Mama and me.

'Well, you certainly have become very grown-up! And my Étienne, you remember him, since he's your second cousin . . . No, not your second, but what, *Lise*? My mother was Varvara Dmitriyevna, daughter of Dmitry Nikolayevich, and your grandmother was Natalya Nikolayevna.'

'Then they're third cousins, *maman*,' the oldest princess said.

'Oh, you're always getting everything mixed up!' her mother yelled angrily. 'No, definitely not third cousins but *issus de germains*,[45] that's what you and my little Étienne are. Did you know that he's already an officer? Only it's bad that he has so much freedom now. You young people need to be kept firmly in hand and that's all! Now don't be cross with your old aunt for speaking the truth to you. I was strict with Étienne, and found it necessary to be.

'So, here's how we're related,' she continued. 'Prince Ivan Ivanych is my uncle and your mother's uncle. So it follows that she and I were first, or no, second cousins – yes, that's right. Well, tell me then, my friend, have you been to see *Prinz* Ivan?'

I said that I hadn't, but would be going later in the day.

'Oh, how can that be!' she exclaimed. 'That should have been the first call you made! Why, *Prinz* Ivan is the same thing as a father to you, you know. He hasn't any children of his own, which means that you and my children are his only heirs. You should respect him for his years and his position in society and everything else. I know that kinship no longer counts with you young people today and that you don't care for old people, but you listen to me, your old auntie, because I love you and I loved your *maman* and I loved your grandmother, too, very, very much and respected her. No, you go and see him and you do so without fail, without fail.'

I said that I certainly would, and since the present call had, in my opinion, already lasted long enough, I stood up and was about to leave when she stopped me.

'No, wait a moment. Where's your father, *Lise*? Call him in here. He'll be so glad to see you,' she continued to me.

About two minutes later Prince Mikhailo really did come into the room. He was a short, stocky gentleman, very sloppily dressed, unshaven and with such an indifferent expression on his face that it even looked like a stupid one. He wasn't in the least glad to see me, or if he was he didn't show it. But the princess, of whom he was obviously very afraid, said to him, 'Isn't it true how much *Woldemar* (she had apparently forgotten my name) looks like his *maman*?' and made such a gesture with her eyes that the prince, obviously guessing what she wanted, came over to me with the same impassive, even disgruntled expression on his face and offered me his unshaven cheek, which I was obliged to kiss.

'You still aren't dressed and have to go out!' the princess started to say to him immediately afterwards in the wrathful tone that seemed customary to her with her household. 'You want to make people angry with you again, you want to antagonize them again?'

'Right away, right away, Mama,' Prince Mikhailo said and left the room. I bowed and left, too.

It was the first time I heard that we were Prince Ivan Ivanych's heirs, and the news struck me unpleasantly.

TWENTY
The Ivins

It made thinking about the looming, essential call even more oppressive. But before going to the Prince's I had to stop at the Ivins along the way. They lived on Tverskaya Street in a beautiful house of enormous size. It wasn't without fear that I went up the front steps, at the top of which stood a doorman with a mace.

'Are they at home?' I asked.

'Whom do you want? The general's son is in,' the doorman replied.

'And the general himself?' I pluckily asked.

'You'll have to be announced. What is your command?' the doorman said and rang. A footman's feet in gaiters appeared on the stairway. I was so intimidated, although I have no idea why, that I told the footman not to announce me to the general, since I would see his son first. As I climbed the grand staircase, it seemed to me that I had been made terribly small, and not in the figurative but the actual meaning of the word. It was the same way I had felt driving up to the large front steps in my droshky: it seemed to me that the droshky and the horse and the driver had all been reduced in size. The general's son was asleep on a sofa with an open book in front of him when I entered his room. His tutor, Herr Frost, who was still in their home, came into the room after me with his gallant stride and woke his charge. Ivin expressed no particular joy on seeing me, and I noticed that while conversing with me he directed his gaze at my eyebrows. Although he was very polite, it seemed to me that he was just trying to divert me the same way the young princess had and felt no particular interest in me, having no need of my acquaintance, since he very likely had his own, different circle of friends. I divined all that mainly from the fact that he looked at my eyebrows. In short, his attitude towards me, however unpleasant it is for me to admit, was virtually the same as my own towards Ilenka. I was starting to get irritated and intercept every glance of Ivin's, and whenever his and Frost's eyes met, I took it to mean, 'Why did he come to see us?'

After we had talked a while, Ivin said that his mother and father were at home and asked if I wouldn't like to go downstairs with him and see them.

'Just a moment and I'll get dressed,' he added, going into another room, even though he was well dressed in his own room in a new frock coat and white waistcoat. He returned a few minutes later in a uniform coat buttoned all the way up, and we went downstairs. The front rooms we passed through were extraordinarily large with high ceilings and, it seemed to me, luxuriously decorated, all in mirrors and marble and gold and muslin dust covers. Mme Ivina entered a small room behind the drawing room at the same time that we did. She greeted me in a warmly kindred way, sat me down next to herself and asked with sympathetic concern about everyone in our family.

I had only seen Mme Ivina briefly a few times before, but now I looked at her carefully and liked her very much. She was short and slender with a very pale complexion and seemed to be permanently sad and weary. Her smile was wistful but extraordinarily kind. Her eyes were large, tired and slightly slanted, which gave her an even more wistful and appealing expression. She sat with her back straight but somehow let her whole body sag, and all her gestures drooped. Her speech was languid, but the timbre of her voice with its blurred pronunciation of *r* and *l* was very pleasant. She wasn't just trying to divert me. My answers about my relatives evidently had a melancholy interest for her, as if while listening to me she were sadly recalling better times. Her son went off somewhere, and she silently gazed at me for a minute or two, and then suddenly started to cry. I sat there beside her and had no idea at all what to say or do. She continued to cry without looking at me. First I was sorry for her, and then I thought, 'Perhaps I should console her, but how?' and finally I became vexed with her for putting me in such an awkward position. 'Do I really look so pitiful,' I thought, 'or is she doing it on purpose just to see how I'll act in such a situation?

'To leave now would be awkward, as if I were running from her tears,' I continued to think. I shifted in my chair, if only to remind her of my presence.

'Oh, how silly of me!' she said, glancing at me and starting to smile. 'There are days when you just cry for no reason at all.'

She started to look for her handkerchief next to her on the sofa, and then suddenly started to cry even harder.

'Oh, my goodness! How ridiculous of me to keep crying. I loved your mother so much, and she and I . . . were such friends . . . and . . .'

She found her handkerchief, covered her face with it and continued to cry. The awkwardness of my position returned and lasted a long time. I felt both annoyed and even more sorry for her. Her tears seemed genuine, and I kept thinking that she wasn't so much crying about my mother as about the fact that things weren't good for her now, but that once, in those days, they had been much better. I don't know how it would have ended, had not the young Ivin come back in and said that the old Ivin was asking for her. She got up and was about to go when Ivin himself came into the room. He was a short, sturdy gentleman with thick black eyebrows, completely grey close-cropped hair and an extraordinarily hard, severe set to his mouth.

I stood and bowed to him, but Ivin, who had three stars on his green coat, not only didn't respond to my bow but barely glanced at me, so that I suddenly felt I wasn't a human being but some object undeserving of attention – a chair or a window, or if a human being, then one who was no different at all from a chair or a window.

'But you still haven't written to the countess, my dear,' he said to his wife in French with an impassive but hard expression on his face.

'Goodbye, *Monsieur Irteneff*,' Mme Ivina said with a proud nod, while looking, just like her son, at my eyebrows. I bowed again to her and to her husband, and once again my bow had the same effect on the old Ivin as if a window had just been opened or shut. The student Ivin saw me out, however, and on the way told me that he might transfer to Petersburg University, since his father had received an appointment in the capital (he named a very important position).

'Well, it may be what Papa wished,' I grumbled to myself as I got into the droshky, 'but I'll never set foot in that house again. That ninny looks at me and starts to cry as if I were some sort of wretch, while Ivin, the swine, won't acknowledge my bow. I'll give him . . .' Just what I intended to give him I've absolutely no idea, but those were the words that came out.

Afterwards I frequently had to endure the admonitions of my father, who said it was essential to *cultivate* that acquaintance, and that I couldn't expect someone in Ivin's position to concern himself with a boy like me, but I held firmly to my own view of it a long time, just the same.

TWENTY-ONE
Prince Ivan Ivanych

'Well, now to Nikitinskaya Street for our last call,' I said to Kuzma, and we set off for the home of Prince Ivan Ivanych.

Having at that point passed through the ordeal of several calls, I was becoming more self-confident, and as I drove up to the prince's was even in a fairly calm mood – until I suddenly remembered Princess Kornakova's words about my being an heir, and saw two carriages by the front steps and felt my earlier timidity return.

It seemed to me that the old doorman who opened the door for me, and the footman who took my overcoat, and the three ladies and two gentlemen whom I found in the drawing room, and especially Prince Ivan Ivanych himself, who was sitting on the sofa in a civilian frock coat – it seemed to me that they all regarded me as an heir and therefore with hostility. The prince was very affectionate with me, kissed me – that is, put his soft, dry, cold lips against my cheek for a second – enquired about my studies and plans, joked with me, asked me if I had written any more verses like the ones I wrote for Grandmother's name-day, and said that I should stay for dinner. But the more affectionate he was, the more it seemed to me that he was doing it only to keep from showing how disagreeable it was for him to think of me as his heir. Because of the false teeth that filled his mouth, he had the habit of raising his upper lip towards his nose after he said something and producing a slight snuffling sound, as if he were drawing his lip up to his nostrils, and whenever he did that now it seemed to me that he was saying to himself, 'You, you boy, as if I needed you to tell me that you're my heir, my heir,' and so on.

When we were children, we called Prince Ivan Ivanych 'Grandfather', but now that I was an heir I couldn't bring myself to say 'Grandfather' to him, whereas to address him as 'your highness', as one of the gentlemen there was doing, seemed demeaning to me, so I tried the whole time of our conversation to call him nothing at all. But I was made most uncomfortable by the old princess, his sister, who was his heir, too, and who lived in his house. I sat next to her at dinner and the whole time assumed that she wasn't talking to me because she resented me for being as much an heir of the prince as she was, and that the prince wasn't paying any attention to our side of the table because we – the princess and I – were heirs and equally repellent to him.

'Yes, you won't believe how unpleasant it was for me,' I said to Dmitry later that day, wishing to brag to him about my distaste at being an heir (a very laudable feeling, I thought) – 'you won't believe how unpleasant it was to spend those two whole hours at the prince's today. He's a splendid man and was very affectionate with me,' I said, wanting to impress on my friend in passing that I wasn't saying any of it because I had felt humiliated by the prince, 'but the idea that people could regard me the same way they do the princess who lives in his house and grovels at his feet is a dreadful one. He's a wonderful old man and is extraordinarily kind and considerate with everyone, so it was painful to see how badly he *maltreats* the princess. Money's a vile thing and the bane of all relationships! You know, I think it would be far better to have a frank talk with the prince,' I said, 'and tell him that I respect him as a man, but that I'm not thinking about the inheritance, and ask him not to leave me anything, for that would be the only way I could visit him.'

Dmitry didn't burst out laughing when I told him that, but instead lapsed into thought, and then, after remaining silent a few minutes, he said to me, 'You know what? You're wrong. Or rather, you shouldn't assume at all that everyone regards you the same way they do that princess of yours, or if you do assume that, then assume further that you do know what they might think about you, and that those thoughts of theirs are so remote from you that you hold them in contempt and won't do anything on their basis. You assume that they assume that you assume this . . . In short,' he concluded, sensing that he was getting muddled, 'it would be far better to assume nothing at all.'

My friend was absolutely right. It was only much, much later that experience taught me how harmful it is to think – and even more harmful to say – a great deal that seems very noble but should remain forever hidden from everyone in the heart of each, and how rarely noble words correspond to noble actions. I'm convinced that once a good intention has been uttered, it is for that very reason difficult, if not in most cases even impossible, to carry it out. But how to resist giving voice to the smugly noble impulses of youth? It's only long afterwards that you remember and regret them, much as you might regret a flower you picked – you couldn't resist – before it had bloomed, and then afterwards saw faded and trampled on the ground.

When it turned out the next morning before we left for the country that I had squandered all my money on various pictures and Stambouline pipes, I, who had just been telling Dmitry, my friend, that money is the bane of all relationships, took the twenty-five paper roubles he offered me for the journey and then for a very long time failed to pay him back.

TWENTY-TWO

A Heart-to-Heart Talk
with My Friend

Our conversation took place in Dmitry's phaeton on our way to Kuntsevo.[46] After advising me not to call on his mother that morning, he had come by after dinner to take me to spend the whole evening and even all night at the dacha[47] where his family lived. It was only after we had driven out of the city, and the dirty, motley streets and deafening clatter of the cobblestone pavement had been replaced by a broad vista of open fields and the soft crunch of the phaeton's wheels on the dusty road, and I was surrounded on every side by fragrant spring air and space – it was only then that I started to recover from the various new impressions and awareness of freedom that had so completely confused me the last two days. Dmitry was mild and amiable and didn't keep adjusting his cravat with his neck, or nervously blink or squint. I was pleased with the noble sentiments I had shared with him, supposing that on their account he had completely forgiven me for the shameful episode with Kolpikov and didn't scorn me for it, and we chatted amiably about many other heartfelt things that are usually left unsaid, whatever the circumstances. Dmitry talked about his family, with whom I was still unacquainted – about his mother, aunt and sister, and about the one whom Volodya and Dubkov considered my friend's passion and referred to as the 'redhead'. Of his mother he spoke with rather cold and solemn praise, as if to forestall any objection on the subject; of his aunt, he spoke with delight but also a certain condescension; of his sister he said very little, as if he were embarrassed to talk about her with me; but of the 'redhead', whose name was Lyubov Sergeyevna, and who was a no longer young woman living in the Nekhlyudov household thanks to some sort of family connection, he spoke with animation.

'Yes, she's a remarkable young woman,' he said, blushing in embarrassment, but at the same time looking me in the eye with greater boldness, 'or no longer young, but quite old and not good-looking at all, but it's so foolish, such nonsense to care about beauty! I can't understand it, it's so silly,' he said, as if he had just discovered the most extraordinary new truth. 'But what a soul, heart and principles . . . I'm sure you won't find another young woman like her in the world today.' I don't know from whom Dmitry acquired the habit of saying that everything good is rare in the world today, but he liked to repeat that expression and somehow it suited him. 'Only I'm afraid,' he calmly resumed, having utterly demolished with his reason any who might be so foolish as to love beauty, 'I'm afraid that you won't understand or appreciate her right away: she's modest and even reticent, and doesn't like to show off her wonderful, excellent qualities. Take Mama, who, as you'll see, is an excellent and clever woman – she has known Lyubov Sergeyevna for several years and can't understand her and doesn't want to. Even yesterday I . . . I'll tell you why I was out of sorts when you asked. The day before yesterday Lyubov Sergeyevna wanted me to go with her to see Ivan Yakovlevich[48] – you've probably heard about Ivan Yakovlevich, who's supposed to be insane, but who's actually a remarkable man. Lyubov Sergeyevna is extremely religious, I should tell you, and understands Ivan Yakovlevich perfectly. She goes to see him often and talks to him and gives him money for the poor that she herself has earned. She's an amazing woman, as you'll see. Well, I went with her to see Ivan Yakovlevich, and am very grateful to her that I met that remarkable man. But Mama just doesn't want to understand that and regards it as superstition. And yesterday she and I had an argument for the first time in our lives, and quite a heated one,' he concluded with a shuddering movement of his head, as if recalling how he felt during the argument.

'Well, what's your view of it, then? That is, what do you think will come of it? Or don't you talk to Lyubov Sergeyevna about the future and where your love or friendship will lead?' I asked, wishing to distract him from his unpleasant memory.

'Are you asking if I'm thinking of marrying her?' he said, blushing again but turning to look me boldly in the face.

'Well, really,' I thought, reassuring myself, 'it's just fine. We're *grown-ups*, two friends riding in a phaeton and discussing our future lives. Anyone would enjoy looking at and listening to us.'

'Well, why not?' he went on after I had replied in the affirmative. 'After all, my goal, like that of any reasonable person, is to be as happy and good as possible, and with her – but only if it's what she wants after I'm completely independent – I'll be both happier and better than with the greatest beauty in the world.'

Absorbed in conversation, we didn't notice that we were approaching Kuntsevo, nor see that the sky was starting to cloud over, and that it was about to rain. The sun was already low on our right above the old trees of the Kuntsevo orchard, and half its brilliant red disc was covered by a grey, weakly translucent storm cloud, while from the other half fragmented rays burst forth in fiery sprays to illuminate with startling brightness the orchard's old trees, their dense green crowns motionless against the clear, luminous azure of the sky. The brilliance of the light in that part of the sky was in stark contrast to the dark purple cloud spread before us over a young birch grove on the horizon.

Already visible a little to the right behind the trees and shrubs were the varicoloured roofs of the dachas, some reflecting brilliant sunlight, others taking on the sombre aspect of the sky's other half. Below us on the left lay a still, blue pond surrounded by pale-green crack willows darkly reflected in its dull, seemingly convex surface. Spread out on a low hill behind the pond was a blackening fallow field transected by the straight line of an untilled, bright-green boundary strip reaching all the way to the horizon, now leaden with the gathering storm. On either side of the soft road along which the phaeton rhythmically swayed, juicy tufts of rye shone a crisp green, and here and there were already beginning to push up spikes. The air was completely still with a fresh fragrance, and the motionless green of the trees, leaves and rye was unusually bright and clean. It seemed that every leaf and blade of grass was living its own separate, full and happy life. Near the road I noticed a blackish path winding through the dark-green rye now almost knee-high, and for some reason the path reminded me with extraordinary vividness of our village, and then, by an odd linkage of thought, the memory of the village reminded me extraordinarily vividly of Sonyechka and that I was in love with her.

Despite my friendship with Dmitry and the pleasure his candour had given me, I didn't want to know any more about his feelings and intentions in regard to Lyubov Sergeyevna, but urgently wanted to tell him about my own love for Sonyechka, which seemed to me to be of a much loftier kind. But for some reason I decided not to tell him just then how fine I thought it would be when, after marrying Sonyechka, I would live in the country and have little children who would crawl around the floor and call me Papa, and how glad I would be when he and his wife, Lyubov Sergeyevna, came to visit me in their travelling clothes – instead of all that I said, while pointing to the setting sun, 'Look, Dmitry, how beautiful it is!'

Dmitry said nothing, evidently displeased that in response to his admission, which very likely had cost him an effort, I had directed his attention to nature, to which he was mostly cold. Nature had a completely different effect on him than on me: he was impressed not so much by its beauty as by its fascination; he loved it more with his mind than his heart.

'I'm very happy,' I immediately added, paying no attention to the fact that he was clearly preoccupied with his own thoughts and completely indifferent to whatever I might say. 'I told you once, you remember, about a young lady I was in love with as a child – well, I saw her again today,' I continued with animation, 'and now I'm definitely in love with her . . .'

And despite the expression of indifference on his face, I did tell him about my love and all my plans for future married happiness. And it's strange that the instant I told him in detail about the strength of my feeling, I sensed it start to wane.

The shower caught us just as we had turned onto an avenue of birches leading up to the house. But it didn't soak us. I only knew that it was raining because several drops had fallen on my nose and hand, and because something had begun to smack the sticky young leaves of the birches, which, letting their luxuriant branches hang still, seemed to draw in those pure, clear drops with a pleasure that expressed itself in the strong fragrance with which they filled the avenue. We got out of the phaeton and ran through the garden to the house. But right by the entrance we met four ladies coming with rapid steps in the opposite direction, two of them with handiwork, one with a book and another with a Bolognese.[49] Dmitry at once introduced me to his mother, sister, aunt and Lyubov Sergeyevna. They stopped for a moment, and then the rain began to fall harder and harder.

'Let's go up on the veranda and you can introduce him again,' said the one I took to be Dmitry's mother, and together with the ladies we mounted the stairs.

TWENTY-THREE
The Nekhlyudovs

Of that whole company I was most struck in the first moments by Lyubov Sergeyevna, who, holding the Bolognese in her arms and wearing heavy knitted slippers, went up the stairs after the others, pausing a few times to look back at me intently and then immediately kiss her little dog. She was quite unattractive: red-haired, short, thin, with slightly lopsided hips. Her homely face was made even homelier by her strange coiffure parted on the side (it was the sort of coiffure that women with thinning hair devise for themselves). As hard as I tried out of loyalty to my friend, I still couldn't find a single attractive feature in her. Even her hazel eyes, although good-natured, were tiny and dull and definitely homely, and her hands, that distinguishing feature, although small and not badly formed, were red and rough.

After I had joined them on the veranda, each lady said a few words to me before taking up her work again – all except Dmitry's sister Varenka, who merely gave me a searching look with her large, dark-grey eyes and then started to read out loud from the book she was holding in her lap, having kept her place with her finger.

Princess Marya Ivanovna was a tall, graceful woman of about forty. One might have said more, given the locks of greying hair frankly showing from under her mobcap, but her fresh, remarkably soft face with almost no lines, and especially the lively, merry brilliance of her large eyes, made her seem much younger. Her eyes were hazel and very round, her lips were too thin and somewhat severe, while her nose was quite straight but turned a little to the left. Her hands were ringless and large, almost masculine, with long beautiful fingers. She was wearing a dark-blue high-necked dress that tightly fitted her slender, still young waist, which she clearly meant to show off. She sat remarkably straight, sewing some garment. After I came up onto the veranda she took me by the hand, drew me to herself, as if wishing to get a better look at me, and then, while gazing at me with the same slightly cold, frank gaze that she shared with her son, said that she had long known about me from Dmitry's stories, and that in order for me to get to know them properly, she was inviting me to spend the night.

'Do whatever you're of a mind to do without being the least shy with us, just as we won't be shy with you either. Go for a walk, read, listen or nap, if that's more fun for you,' she added.

Sofya Ivanovna was an old maid and the princess's younger sister, although she seemed older. She had that distinctive, over-stuffed figure met with in short, very stout old maids who wear corsets. It was as if all her vitality had been thrust up with such force that it threatened at any moment to strangle her. She couldn't bring her short, plump little arms together under the arched promontory of her bodice, nor could she see the ever so tightly laced bodice itself.

Although Princess Marya Ivanovna had dark hair and eyes and Sofya Ivanovna was blonde with large, vivacious and at the same time (which is very rare) calm blue eyes, there was a strong family resemblance between the two sisters: the same expression, the same nose and the same lips, although Sofya Ivanovna's were a little broader and fuller and moved to the right when she smiled, while the princess's moved to the left. Judging by her clothes and coiffure, Sofya Ivanovna was apparently still trying to look young and wouldn't have revealed her grey locks, if she had any. Her gaze and the way she addressed me seemed very proud at first and disconcerted me, whereas I was completely at ease with the princess. Perhaps Sofya Ivanovna's stoutness and a certain striking resemblance to a portrait of Catherine the Great gave her a proud look in my eyes, but I was completely disconcerted when she looked at me and said, 'The friends of our friends are our friends.' I calmed down and abruptly changed my view of her, however, when, after saying those words, she fell silent and then opened her mouth and sighed heavily. Probably because of her stoutness, it was her habit after saying a few words to sigh deeply while opening her mouth a little and slightly rolling her large blue eyes. Such sweet good nature was somehow expressed in the habit that after that sigh I lost all my fear of her and even liked her very much. Her eyes were charming, her voice was resonant and pleasing, and even the very round lines of her figure seemed, at that time of my youth, to be not without beauty.

As a friend of my friend, Lyubov Sergeyevna should, I supposed, at that point have immediately said something very amiable and heartfelt, and she even gazed at me quite a long time in silence, as if unsure whether it might not be too amiable to say whatever she had in mind, but then she ended her silence only to ask me what university department I was in. Then she stared at me quite intently again for a long time, evidently wondering whether or not to say that amiable, heartfelt thing, while I, upon noticing her uncertainty, entreated her with a facial expression to say it all, but she only remarked, 'They say that there aren't very many studying the sciences at the university now,' and beckoned to her little dog, Suzette.

The remarks made by Lyubov Sergeyevna the entire evening were for the most part neither to the point nor even related to each other, but I so believed in Dmitry, and he looked so anxiously first at me and then at her with an expression that asked, 'Well, then?' that even though I was convinced in my heart that there was nothing special about her, I was, as often happens, still very far from voicing that thought to myself.

The last member of the family, Varenka, was a very plump young woman of about sixteen. Her only attractive features were her large, dark-grey eyes, extraordinarily like her aunt's in their blend of vivacity and calm attention, her very long chestnut braid, and her extraordinarily soft, beautiful hands.

'I suspect it must be tedious for you, *Monsieur Nicolas*, to hear the story from the middle,' Sofya Ivanovna said to me with her good-natured sigh, while turning over the pieces of the garment she was sewing.

The reading had stopped for a moment while Dmitry went off somewhere.

'Or perhaps you've already read *Rob Roy*?'[50]

If only because of my student's uniform, I felt obliged at the time with people I didn't know well to answer every question, even the simplest one, very 'cleverly' and 'originally', and considered brief, clear answers like 'yes', 'no', 'it's boring', 'it's fun' and so on to be highly disgraceful. After a glance at my fashionable new trousers and the shiny buttons of my frock coat, I replied that I hadn't read *Rob Roy*, but that it was still very interesting for me to listen, since I actually preferred to read books from the middle rather than the beginning.

'It's twice as interesting: you have to guess both what went before and what comes after,' I added with a satisfied grin.

The princess laughed a seemingly unnatural laugh (I soon realized that she had no other).

'Well, I suppose that's true,' she said. 'So, *Nicolas*, will you be in Moscow long? You don't mind if I drop the *monsieur*, do you? When are you leaving?'

'I don't know, perhaps tomorrow, or perhaps we'll stay on a good deal longer,' I said for some reason, even though we would most certainly be leaving the next day.

'I had hoped that you could stay on, both for you and for my Dmitry,' the princess observed, while gazing at something off in the distance. 'Friendship's a fine thing at your age.'

I sensed that everyone was looking at me to see how I would answer, although Varenka pretended to examine her aunt's work. I sensed that I was being given a sort of examination, and that I needed to show myself as advantageously as possible.

'Yes,' I said, 'Dmitry's friendship is helpful to me, even if I'm unable to be of any use to him, since he's a thousand times better than I am.' (Dmitry couldn't hear what I was saying, or else I would have been afraid he would detect the insincerity of my words.)

The princess again laughed the unnatural laugh that was natural to her.

'Well, to hear him tell it,' she said, *c'est vous qui êtes un petit monstre de perfection!*[51]

'*Un monstre de perfection* – that's excellent. I'll have to remember it,' I thought.

'Actually, leaving you out of it, he's a master at that,' she continued after lowering her voice (which especially pleased me) and indicating Lyubov Sergeyevna with her eyes. 'In *poor Auntie*,' as they called Lyubov Sergeyevna among themselves, 'whom with her Suzette I've known for twenty years, he's found perfections that I never suspected . . . Varya, tell them to bring me a glass of water,' she added, once again looking off into the distance, very likely having found it too early or not even necessary to let me in on the family relationships, 'or no, let *him* go. *He* isn't doing anything and you can continue to read. Go right through the door, my friend, and then after fifteen paces stop and say in a loud voice, "Pyotr, bring Marya Ivanovna a glass of water with ice,"' she said to me, softly laughing her unnatural laugh again.

'She probably wants to talk about me,' I thought as I went out. 'She probably wants to say that she's observed that I'm a very, very clever young man.' I hadn't yet gone the fifteen paces when the stout, panting Sofya Ivanovna overtook me with quick, light steps.

'*Merci, mon cher*,'[52] she said. 'I'm going that way and will tell them myself.'

TWENTY-FOUR
Love

Sofya Ivanovna, as I later came to know her, was one of those rare, no longer young women who are born for family life, but whom fate has denied that happiness, and who, as a result of that denial, decide to lavish on a chosen few all the love for children and a husband that has been stored, grown and nurtured in their hearts for so long. And the supply of love in no longer young women of that kind is so inexhaustible that even when the chosen are many, a great deal of love still remains, which they lavish on everyone around them, on all the good and bad people they come across in their lives.

There are three kinds of love:

1) Beautiful love
2) Self-immolating love
3) Practical love

I'm speaking not of the love of a young man for a young woman, or the reverse. I fear such tenderness, and have been so unlucky in life that I never saw in love of that kind a single spark of truth, but only mendacity in which sensuality, conjugal relations, money and a desire to bind or unbind one's hands so muddled the feeling that it was impossible to make any sense of it at all. I'm speaking of a love for others that – depending on the greater or lesser power of the soul – is focused on a single person or on several people or is lavished on many – of love for a mother, a father, a brother, or children, or for a comrade, a woman friend, or a compatriot, of a love for others.

'Beautiful love' is love for the beauty of the feeling itself and

its expression. For people who love this way, the object of love
is lovable only to the extent that he arouses the pleasurable feeling in the awareness and expression of which they find enjoyment.
Those who love with a beautiful love care little about mutuality
or circumstances that have no bearing on the beauty or pleasure
of their feeling. They frequently exchange the objects of their
love, since their main goal is the constant arousal of the pleasurable feeling of love. To sustain that feeling in themselves, they
constantly speak in the most elegant terms of their love not only
to its object but also to everyone else, including those who care
nothing about it. In our country, people of a certain class who
love 'beautifully' not only tell everyone about their love but
invariably do so in French. It's a strange and ridiculous thing to
say, but I'm sure that there have been and still are many people
of a certain milieu, especially women, whose love for their
friends, husbands and children would be destroyed at once, were
they simply forbidden to talk about it in French.

The second kind, 'self-immolating love', is love of the act of
sacrificing oneself for the object of love without considering
whether the object is better or worse off for those sacrifices.
'There's no distress to which I wouldn't subject myself to prove
to the world and to *him* or to *her* the extent of my devotion.'
Such is the formula for this kind of love. People who love this
way never believe in mutuality (since it's worthier to sacrifice
myself for someone who doesn't appreciate me) and are always
sickly, which increases the merit of the sacrifice; they are for the
most part steadfast, since it would be hard for them to forfeit
the value of the sacrifices they've made for the object of their
love; and they're always ready to die to prove to *him* or *her* their
complete devotion, even though they neglect the minor, everyday
demonstrations of love that require no particular eruptions of
self-immolation. They don't care if you ate or slept well or are
enjoying yourself or are healthy, and they'll do nothing to obtain
those comforts for you, even if it's within their power to do so;
but face a bullet, jump into water or fire, or pine away from love
– they're always ready for those, if only given the opportunity.
Moreover, people who are prone to self-immolating love are
always proud of their love, as well as demanding, jealous and

suspicious and, strange to say, ready to wish dangers on their
objects from which to rescue them, calamities about which to
console them, and even vices in which to correct them.

You live alone in the country with your wife, who loves you
with a self-immolating love. You're healthy and secure. You have
things to do that you enjoy, but your loving wife is so weak that
she can manage neither the household, which has been turned
over to the servants, nor the children, who have been given up
to nurses, nor even any occupation that she might like, and all
because she loves nothing but you. She *seems* to be ill, but not
wanting to distress you, she's reluctant to tell you; she *seems* to
be bored, but for your sake she's prepared to be bored her whole
life; it *seems* to oppress her that you're intently absorbed in your
activities (whatever they may be: hunting, books, managing
the estate, service) for she sees that those activities will be your
undoing, but says nothing and endures them. But then you fall
ill, and your loving wife forgets her own illness and, despite your
entreaties not to torment herself needlessly, is continually at your
bedside, and every second you feel on you her compassionate
gaze that says, 'Well, I said as much, but I don't care, and even
so I won't leave you.' In the morning you're a little better and
you go into the next room. It's unheated and a mess. The soup
that's the only thing you can eat hasn't been ordered from the
cook, nor has your medicine been sent for, but although
exhausted by her nocturnal vigil, your loving wife still looks at
you with the same compassionate gaze, walks on tiptoe, and in
a whisper gives the servants vague, unfamiliar instructions. You
want to read, but your loving wife says to you with a sigh that
she knows you won't listen to her and will be angry with her,
although she's quite used to it, but it would be better if you didn't
read. You want to take a walk around the room, but it would
be better if you didn't do that either. You want to talk to a friend
who has come, but it would be better for you not to talk. At
night you have a fever again, and you want to doze off, but your
loving wife, thin, pale and sighing from time to time, sits across
from you in an armchair in the half-light of the night lamp, and
with every little movement, every little sound, provokes feelings
of irritation and impatience in you. You have a servant with

whom you have lived nearly twenty years and are used to, and who takes excellent care of you, and does so with pleasure, since he's well rested during the day and gets paid for his services, but she won't permit him to look after you. She does everything herself with her feeble, inept fingers, which you can't help following with suppressed hostility as they vainly try to open a vial or put out a candle or pour medicine or squeamishly reach towards you. If you're an impatient, irritable sort and ask her to leave, you will, in your illness and exasperation, hear her submissively sighing and weeping on the other side of the door and whispering some sort of nonsense to your man. If in the end you're still alive, your loving wife, who hasn't slept the twenty nights you were ill (as she constantly reminds you), herself falls ill, wastes away, suffers, and is even less capable of any activity, and then, when you're well again, conveys her self-immolating love merely by the meek tedium that she involuntarily imparts to you and everyone around her.

The third kind, 'practical love', strives to satisfy all the needs, desires, whims and even vices of the beloved being. People who love this way always love their whole lives, since the more they love, the more they come to know the object of their love and the easier it is for them to love, that is, to satisfy his desires. Rarely is their love expressed in words, but if it is, then not in a self-satisfied, beautiful way but in an embarrassed, awkward one, since such people are always afraid that they don't love enough. They love even the vices of the beloved being, because those vices give them an opportunity to satisfy ever newer desires. They seek mutuality and even gladly deceive themselves about it and believe in it and are happy if they have it. But they love no less without it, and not only want happiness for the object of their love, but continually try to obtain it for him with all the mental and material means, both great and small, that lie within their power.

It was that kind of practical love for her nephew and niece and for her sister and Lyubov Sergeyevna, and even for me, because Dmitry was fond of me, that shone in Sofya Ivanovna's eyes and in her every word and gesture.

I would come to appreciate Sofya Ivanovna fully only much

later, but even then the question occurred to me why Dmitry, who was trying to understand love in a way quite different from the way young people usually do, and who, moreover, had always had the sweet, loving Sofya Ivanovna before him, had nevertheless suddenly fallen passionately in love with the incomprehensible Lyubov Sergeyevna, while merely supposing that his aunt possessed good qualities, too. The saying would seem to be true: 'A prophet is not without honour, save in his own country.'[53] It's one of two things: either there really is more bad than good in every person, or else people are more receptive to the bad than to the good. Dmitry hadn't known Lyubov Sergeyevna very long, but he had experienced his aunt's love from the day he was born.

TWENTY-FIVE
I Get Acquainted

When I returned to the veranda, they were not, as I had supposed, talking about me at all, although Varenka wasn't reading but had put her book down to argue heatedly with Dmitry, who was pacing back and forth, adjusting his cravat with his neck and scowling. The matter at issue appeared to be Ivan Yakovlevich and superstition, but the argument was too vehement for there not to have been some tacit meaning closer to the whole family. The princess and Lyubov Sergeyevna sat in silence, listening closely to every word, clearly wanting at times to join the argument but restraining themselves, the one allowing Varenka to speak for her and the other, Dmitry. When I came in Varenka glanced at me with an expression of such indifference that it was clear that she was too fiercely involved in the argument to care whether or not I heard what she was saying. The princess, who was obviously on her side, looked at me the same way. But Dmitry started to argue even more heatedly in my presence, while Lyubov Sergeyevna seemed to be quite startled by my entrance and said, without addressing anyone in particular, 'Old people speak the truth: *si jeunesse savait, si vieillesse pouvait.*'[54]

While that maxim didn't stop the argument, it did make me think that Lyubov Sergeyevna and my friend's side was the wrong one. Although I was slightly embarrassed to witness that family discord, I was still happy to see the family's true relations reveal themselves as a result of it, and to feel that my presence hadn't kept them from doing so.

How often it happens that for years you see a family concealed by the same unchanging false curtain of decorum, which hides the members' true relations from you (I've even noticed that the more impenetrable and therefore beautiful the curtain, the coarser the true relations it conceals). But then, quite unexpectedly some question will come up within the circle of that family, sometimes a seemingly insignificant question, about silk lace or a call made with the husband's carriage, and for no apparent reason the argument will grow more and more rancorous until it becomes too confining behind the curtain to examine the matter, and suddenly, to the horror of the arguers themselves and the astonishment of those present, all the true relations burst out, and the curtain, no longer hiding anything, flaps pointlessly between the contending parties, serving only to remind you how long you had been deceived by it. It's often less painful to bang your head with full force against a lintel than to touch, however gingerly, a raw wound. And there is such a raw wound in almost every family. For the Nekhlyudovs, it was Dmitry's strange love for Lyubov Sergeyevna, which aroused in his sister and mother if not envy, then offended family feeling. And that's why the argument about Ivan Yakovlevich and superstition was so important to them all.

'You always try to find in whatever other people laugh at and everyone scorns,' Varenka said in her resonant voice, enunciating every syllable, ' – you always try to find in all that something exceptionally fine.'

'In the first place, only the *silliest person* could speak of scorn for someone as remarkable as Ivan Yakovlevich,' Dmitry replied, convulsively jerking his head away from his sister. 'And in the second, it is on the contrary *you* who make a point of not seeing the good that's standing right in front of you.'

On rejoining us, Sofya Ivanovna looked several times in alarm first at her nephew, then at her niece, then at me, and then, as if she had just said something mentally to herself, heavily sighed a couple of times with her mouth open.

'Varya, please hurry up and get on with the reading,' she said, holding out the book to her and affectionately patting her hand. 'I can't wait to see if he found her again.' (I don't think there was anything in the novel about anyone being found.) 'And you, Mitya, it would be better to wrap up your cheek, my friend, or else your teeth will start aching again,' she said to her nephew, despite the resentful look he gave her, presumably because she had broken the logical thread of his argument. The reading continued.

That little quarrel didn't upset the family's tranquillity at all, nor the rational accord with which that feminine circle was imbued.

The circle, which clearly took its outlook and character from Princess Marya Ivanovna, had an attractive and for me completely new quality of a certain logicality, combined with simplicity and elegance. That quality was expressed for me in the beauty, purity and solidity of their things (the hand bell, the bookbinding, the chairs, the table), in the princess's erect, corseted posture, in her frankly displayed locks of grey hair, in her way of referring to me as 'Nicolas' and 'he' at our first meeting, in their pastimes of reading and sewing, and in the exceptional whiteness of their ladies' hands. (Their hands all had the family feature of a straight line delineating the bright pink flesh on the outside of the palm from the exceptional whiteness of the top of the hand.) But above all, that quality was expressed in the excellent Russian and French of all three, and in their way of clearly articulating every syllable and completing every word and sentence with pedantic exactitude. All that, but especially the fact that in their company I was addressed simply and seriously as a grown-up, and told their opinions while they listened to mine, was so new to me that despite my shiny buttons and blue cuffs, I was constantly afraid someone might suddenly say to me, 'Do you really think it's possible to have a serious conversation with you? Get back to your studies!' It all meant, in any case, that I didn't feel the least shy in their presence. I got up and moved around as I liked and boldly talked to everyone, except Varenka, with whom, for some reason, it still seemed improper or forbidden to be the first to speak.

As she read and I listened to her pleasant, resonant voice and looked first at her and then at the sandy path of the flower garden on which round, darkening spots of rain were forming, and then at the lindens on whose leaves occasional drops were continuing to fall with a smack from the pale, blue-edged cloud above us, and then again at her, and then at the last crimson beams of the setting sun shining on a dense stand of old birches wet from the rain, and then again at her, I thought that she was by no means as bad-looking as I had first thought.

'Too bad I'm already in love,' I thought, 'and that Varenka isn't Sonyechka, for what a good thing it would be to become a member of this family: I would suddenly have a mother, an aunt and a wife.' As I thought that, I stared at Varenka while she read and imagined that I was *magnetizing* her and that she would have to look back at me. She raised her head from the book, looked at me, and on meeting my gaze looked away.

'It's still raining, apparently,' she said.

And I suddenly had a strange feeling: it seemed to me that everything that was happening then was a repetition of something that had happened before; that then, too, there had been a shower and the sun had been setting behind the birches and I had been looking at *her*, and she had been reading, and I had *magnetized* her, and she had glanced back, and it even seemed that I remembered yet another time before that.

'Can she really be *she*?' I thought. 'Is it really *beginning*?' But I quickly decided that she wasn't *she*, and that it wasn't beginning. 'First of all, she isn't good-looking,' I thought, 'but just a young lady, and I've made her acquaintance in the most ordinary way, while that one will be extraordinary, and I'll meet her in some extraordinary place, and then, too, I only like this family so much because I still haven't seen anything yet,' I reasoned, 'whereas there will probably always be such families and I'll meet a great many more of them in my life.'

TWENTY-SIX
I Show Off My Best Side

The reading ended for tea, and the ladies began a conversation between themselves about people and circumstances unfamiliar to me, merely to give me a sense, I thought, of the difference between themselves and me in age and position in society, their affectionate reception notwithstanding. But in the general conversation that I was able to join, I tried to make up for my earlier reticence by putting my uncommon intelligence and originality on display, something I felt my uniform especially obliged me to do. When the conversation turned to dachas, I suddenly declared that Prince Ivan Ivanych owned such an extraordinary one near Moscow that people came all the way from London and Paris to see it, that it had wrought-iron fencing that cost 380,000 roubles, and that Prince Ivan Ivanych was a very close relation of mine and that I had dined with him that afternoon and that he had asked me to be sure to come for the whole summer, but I had refused, since I knew the house very well, having been there several times, and that all those fences and bridges were of no interest to me, since I couldn't stand luxury, especially in the country: I liked the country to be completely like the country . . . After delivering myself of that terribly complicated lie, I grew embarrassed and blushed, so that they certainly all realized that I had been lying. Varenka, who was passing me a cup of tea at the time, and Sofya Ivanovna, who was looking at me as I spoke, both turned away and started to talk about something else with an expression on their faces that I've often noticed in kind people when a very young person has obviously started to tell barefaced lies, and that means, 'Of course, we know he's lying, poor fellow, but whatever for?'

The reason I said that Prince Ivan Ivanych had a dacha was because I couldn't find a better pretext for telling them about being related to him and dining that afternoon at his home, but why I added that the fencing cost 380,000, or that I had often visited him, when I hadn't done so even once, nor could have, since he lived only in Moscow and Naples, as the Nekhlyudovs well knew – why I said all that I have absolutely no idea. Neither in childhood nor in boyhood nor later at a more mature age have I observed the vice of lying in myself – on the contrary, I've been rather too truthful and frank – but in that early period of youth I was often visited, for no apparent reason, by a strange desire to lie in the most desperate way. I say 'desperate' because I lied about things in which it was very easy to catch me out. I think the main reason for that strange proclivity was a boastful desire to show myself to be quite different than I was, combined with a hope, unrealizable in life, that the lies wouldn't be discovered.

Since the shower was over and the early evening weather was calm and clear, the princess suggested going for a walk after tea to the lower orchard to admire her favourite place. Following my rule of always being original, and believing that very clever people like the princess and myself should rise above banal courtesy, I replied that I couldn't stand walks without any purpose, and that if I did like to walk, then it was completely alone. It didn't occur to me at all that that was merely rude. At the time I thought that just as nothing is more deplorable than hackneyed compliments, so nothing is nicer and more original than a certain impolite candour. But, pleased as I was with my reply, I went for a walk with the whole company anyway.

The princess's favourite place was on a small bridge over a narrow little swamp at the very bottom of the orchard in its densest part. The view was very limited but appealing and graceful. We're so used to mixing up art and nature that natural phenomena that we've never encountered in a painting will very often seem unnatural to us, as if nature were unnatural, and, conversely, phenomena that have been depicted too frequently in painting will seem trite to us, while views met with in reality that are too imbued with a single idea or feeling will seem precious. The view from the princess's favourite place was the last kind. It consisted of a small pond with weeds around its edge, a steep slope directly behind it overgrown with immense old trees and shrubs and their varied and often mingled foliage, and, jutting out over the pond at the bottom of the slope, an old birch that held on to the pond's moist bank with part of its thick roots, while resting its crown against a tall, slender aspen and dangling its leafy branches out over the pond's smooth surface, which reflected them and the rest of the surrounding foliage.

'How lovely!' the princess said with a nod, speaking to no one in particular.

'Yes, it's marvellous, only I think it looks terribly like a stage set,' I said, wishing to show that I had my own opinion about everything.

The princess continued to admire the view as if she hadn't heard my remark, and then, addressing her sister and Lyubov Sergeyevna, she pointed out a detail that she was especially fond of: a crooked hanging bough and its reflection. Sofya Ivanovna said that it was all beautiful, and that her sister spent hours there at a time, but it was clear she was only saying that to make the princess happy. I've noticed that people endowed with a capacity for practical love are rarely receptive to the beauties of nature. Lyubov Sergeyevna was delighted, too, and asked in passing, 'What's holding that birch up? Will it remain that way long?' and kept looking at her Suzette, who wagged her fluffy tail and ran on her crooked little legs back and forth across the bridge with such a busy expression that it was as if it were the first time in her life she had been let out of her room. Dmitry began a very logical discussion with his mother about how no view can be beautiful in which the horizon is limited. Varenka said nothing. When I glanced over at her, she was leaning against the bridge's railing and looking straight ahead with her profile towards me. Something had evidently impressed and even moved her, for she seemed to have fallen into a reverie with no awareness either of herself or that she was being observed. There was such rapt attention and calm, clear thought in her large eyes, and such naturalness and, despite her shortness, such majesty in her bearing that I was again struck as if by a memory of her, and once again I asked myself, 'Is it beginning?' And once again I replied to myself that I was already in love with Sonyechka, and that Varenka was only a young lady and my friend's sister. But I liked her at that moment and, as a result, felt a vague wish to do or say some mean little thing to her.

'You know what, Dmitry?' I said to my friend, after moving closer to Varenka so she could hear. 'I find that even if there weren't any mosquitoes, there would still be nothing good about this place, but right now,' I added, while slapping myself on the forehead and actually crushing a mosquito, 'it's really pretty awful.'

'Apparently, you don't care for nature?' Varenka said, without turning her head.

'I find it to be an idle, pointless activity,' I replied, quite pleased that I had indeed managed to say some unpleasant little thing and moreover an original one. Slightly raising her eyebrows for an instant in regret, Varenka continued to look straight ahead just as calmly as before.

I was starting to feel vexed with her, but all the same the faded grey paint of the railing against which she was leaning, the reflection in the dark pond of the jutting birch's overhanging bough and the way the reflection seemed to want to merge with the branches suspended above it, the swampy smell, the sensation on my forehead of the crushed mosquito, and her rapt gaze and majestic pose – all that would afterwards turn up quite often and unexpectedly in my imagination.

TWENTY-SEVEN
Dmitry

When we came back from our walk, Varenka didn't want to sing as she usually did in the evening, and I was so arrogant as to consider myself the reason, imagining that it was because of what I had said to her on the bridge. The Nekhlyudovs usually went off to their rooms early without having supper, but since Dmitry's teeth had started to ache, just as Sofya Ivanovna had predicted, that evening we went up to his room even earlier than usual. Supposing I had done everything that my buttons and blue collar required of me, and that everyone liked me very much, I was in a very pleasant, contented mood. Dmitry, however, was taciturn and morose because of the argument and his toothache. He sat down at his desk, got out his copybooks – his diary and the journal in which it was his habit every evening to record his past and future activities – and wrote in them quite a long time, while continually wincing and touching his cheek.

'Oh, leave me alone!' he shouted at the chambermaid whom Sofya Ivanovna had sent to ask how his teeth were and if he needed to have a poultice made. After saying that a bed would be made up for me directly and that he would be right back, he went to see Lyubov Sergeyevna.

'What a pity Varenka isn't pretty and isn't, in fact, Sonyechka,' I mused after I was left alone in the room. 'How fine it would be after graduating from the university to come to them and offer her my hand. I would say to her, "Princess, I'm no longer young, I cannot love passionately, but I'll always love you like a dear sister." "I already respect you," I would say to her mother, "and you, Sofya Ivanovna, believe that I hold you in very, very high esteem. So tell me simply and directly, Varenka, will you be my wife?" "Yes." And she'll give me her hand, and I'll squeeze it and say, "My love is not in words but in deeds." But what if Dmitry,' it occurred to me, 'should suddenly fall in love with Lyubochka, since she's already in love with him, and he should want to marry her? Then one or the other of us would be unable to do so.[55] And that would be excellent. Here's what I would do then. I would notice it at once, say nothing, and then go to Dmitry and tell him, "It's in vain, my friend, that we've hidden it from each other: you know that my love for your sister will end only with my life, but I am aware of everything. You've taken my finest hope from me and made me unhappy, but do you know how Nikolay Irtenyev repays a lifetime of unhappiness? Take my sister," and I would give him Lyubochka's hand. He would say, "No, that cannot be!" and I would reply, "Prince Nekhlyudov! It is in vain that you wish to be more magnanimous than Nikolay Irtenyev. No one in the world is more magnanimous than he!" And I would bow and withdraw. Dmitry and Lyubochka would run after me in tears and beg me to accept their sacrifice. And I could consent to it and be very, very happy, if only I were in love with Varenka . . .' Those daydreams were so pleasant that I very much wanted to share them with my friend, but despite our vow of mutual candour, I for some reason sensed there was no physical possibility of my doing so.

Dmitry came back from Lyubov Sergeyevna with some tooth drops she had given him, but suffering even more and, as a consequence, even more morose. The bed still hadn't been made up for me, and a boy, Dmitry's servant, came to ask where I would be sleeping.

'Get out of here!' Dmitry shouted, stamping his foot. As soon as the boy left, he started shouting, 'Vaska! Vaska! Vaska!' each time louder than before. 'Vaska! Make up my bed on the floor.'

'Oh no, better for me to sleep on the floor,' I said.

'Well, what does it matter? Make the bed anywhere,' Dmitry continued in the same angry tone. 'Vaska! Why aren't you doing it?'

But Vaska apparently didn't understand what was required of him and stood there without moving.

'Well, what's the matter with you? Make up the bed, make

up the bed! Vaska! Vaska!' Dmitry started shouting, suddenly
flying into something like a rage.

But Vaska, still not understanding and now frightened,
remained where he was.

'So, you have sworn to des . . . to infuriate me?'

And jumping up from his chair and running over to the boy,
Dmitry struck him several times on the head with all his might,
and Vaska ran out of the room. Stopping at the door, Dmitry
glanced back at me, and the expression of rage and cruelty that
had been on his face a second before was replaced by such a
childishly meek, remorseful and loving one that I felt sorry for
him, and as much as I wanted to look away, I couldn't bring
myself to. He said nothing, but silently walked around the room
a long time, occasionally glancing at me with the same expression imploring forgiveness, and then got a copybook out of his
desk, wrote something in it, took off his coat, folded it carefully,
went over to the corner where the icon hung, crossed his large
white hands over his chest and began to pray. He prayed so long
that Vaska managed in the meantime to bring a mattress and
spread it out on the floor, according to my whispered instructions. I undressed and lay down on the bed on the floor and
Dmitry continued to pray as before. Looking at his slightly
round-shouldered back and the soles of his shoes, which were
humbly stuck out in front of me as he prostrated himself, I
loved him even more and kept thinking, 'Shall I tell him my
daydream about our sisters or not?' Ending his prayer, Dmitry
lay down on his bed with his head towards me and, resting on
his elbows, silently gazed at me for a long time with an affectionate, remorseful expression. It was clearly hard for him, but
he seemed to be punishing himself. I looked at him and smiled.
He smiled back.

'Well, why don't you say it, that my behaviour was despic-
able?' he asked. 'Isn't that what you were thinking?'

'Yes,' I answered, for even though I had been thinking about
something else, it really did seem to me that it had in fact been
about that. 'Yes, it was very bad and I never expected it of you,'
I said, taking particular pleasure in the fact that I was using the
familiar form of address. 'Well, how are your teeth?' I added.

'Better. Ah, Nikolenka, my friend!' Dmitry said so affectionately that I think there were tears in his gleaming eyes, 'I
know and feel how bad I am, and God sees how much I want
to be a better person, and I ask Him to make me one, but what
am I to do if I have such an unfortunate, loathsome character?
What am I to do? I try to restrain myself and improve, but it's
impossible to do it suddenly, and impossible alone. I need
someone to support me, to help me. And that's Lyubov
Sergeyevna. She understands me and has helped me a lot with
this. I know from my own journal entries that I've improved
a lot in the last year. Oh, Nikolenka, dear friend!' he continued
with unaccustomed affection and a calmer tone after that
admission, 'how much the influence of a woman like her
means! My goodness, how fine it could be with a friend like
her after I'm on my own! I'm a completely different person
with her.'

And Dmitry immediately began to elaborate on his plans for
marriage, a life in the country and constant work on himself.

'I'll live in the country and you'll come to visit me, it may be,
and you'll be married to Sonyechka,' he said. 'Our children will
play. It may all sound ridiculous and silly, but it really could
happen.'

'Certainly it could and very likely it will!' I said, smiling and
thinking that it would be even better if I married his sister.

'You know what I'll say to you?' he said, after falling silent
for a while. 'You only imagine that you're in love with Sonyechka,
whereas I see that it's nothing and that you still don't know what
real feeling is.'

I didn't object, since I almost agreed with him. We fell silent
again for a while.

'You've probably noticed that I was in a foul mood today and
had a bad argument with Varya. It was terribly unpleasant for
me later, especially because it happened in front of you. Although
her thinking about a lot of things isn't what it should be, she's
a splendid girl, a very fine one, as you'll see when you get to
know her better.'

His shift in the conversation from my not being in love to
praise for his sister delighted me and made me blush, but I still

didn't say anything to him about her, and we continued to talk about other things.

We chattered like that until the second cockcrow, and the pale light of dawn was already visible in the window when Dmitry turned around in his bed to put out the candle.

'Well, let's go to sleep now,' he said.

'Yes,' I replied, 'but there's one other thing.'

'What?'

'Isn't life wonderful?'

'Yes, it is wonderful,' he answered in such a voice that in the darkness I seemed to see his childlike smile and and the expression in his merry, affectionate eyes.

TWENTY-EIGHT

In the Country

Volodya and I left for the country the next day by mail coach. Sorting through various Moscow memories along the way, I recalled Sonyechka Valakhina, but only in the evening after we had gone five stages. 'How strange,' I thought, 'that I'm in love but have completely forgotten about it! I must think about her.' And I started to do so the way it happens on the road, disconnectedly but vividly, reaching the point in my reflections that after I got to the country, I for some reason found it necessary to seem sad and abstracted with the entire household, but especially with Katenka, whom I considered a great expert in such matters, and to whom I gave a hint of the state of my heart. But despite my efforts to pretend to others and myself, and my deliberate adoption of all the signs that I had noticed in other people in love, I only remembered that I was in love two days, and even then not continuously but mainly in the evening; and in the end, as I entered the new round of country life and activities, I completely forgot about my love for Sonyechka.

We arrived in Petrovskoye late at night, and I was in such a deep slumber that I saw neither the house, nor the birch avenue, nor any of the household, all of whom had gone to bed long before and were sound asleep anyway. Stooped old Foka, barefoot with a candle in his hand and wearing some quilted jacket of his wife's, threw back the bolt. Seeing who it was, he trembled with joy, kissed us both on the shoulder, quickly put away his felt sleeping mat and got dressed. I had passed through the outer entrance and up the steps not yet fully awake, but the front-door bolt, the warped floorboards, the bin, the old candlestick streaked with tallow as of old, the shadows from the candle's cold, just

lit wick, the perpetually dusty, never removed double window,
beyond which, as I remembered, a rowan grew – all of it was so
familiar, so full of memories so completely in accord with each
other as to seem united in a single thought, that I suddenly felt
the caress of that dear old house. The question spontaneously
presented itself: how could we, the house and I, have been without each other so long? and I hurried off to see if the other rooms
were still the same. Everything was the same, only it had been
made smaller, lower, while I seemed to have become taller, heav-
ier and coarser. But the house joyfully took me in its embrace
even as I was, and with every floorboard, every window, every
step of the stairway, every creak, it awakened in me a host of
images, feelings and events from the happy, irrecoverable past.
We came to our old bedroom – all the terrors of childhood were
still hidden in its dark corners and doorways; we passed through
it to the drawing room – the same quiet, tender mother's love
suffused everything in it; we crossed the salon – the carefree
clamour of childhood gaiety had, it seemed, merely been
suspended and was waiting to be brought back to life. In the
bedroom behind the sitting room, where Foka led us and made
up our beds, it seemed that everything – the mirror, the screen,
the old wooden icon, every irregularity in the white paper-
covered wall – it seemed that everything there spoke of suffering
and death and of what would never, ever be again.

We lay down, and Foka said good night to us and left.

'Isn't this the room where *maman* died?' Volodya said.

I pretended to be asleep and didn't answer. If I had said
anything, I would have started to cry. When I awoke the next
morning, Papa, in a dressing gown and low, imported boots and
a cigar between his teeth, was sitting on Volodya's bed and
laughing and talking. He jumped up with a merry shrug, came
over to me, slapped me on the back with his large hand and
presented his cheek, pressing it against my lips.

'Well, excellent, thank you, Diplomat!' he said with characteristic jesting affection, while gazing at me with his small,
gleaming eyes. 'Volodya says that you did well in your examinations, like a brave fellow – well, splendid! When you want to
use your head, you're my splendid chap, too. Thank you, my

friend. We'll have a splendid time here now, and then maybe in the winter we'll move to Petersburg. Too bad the coursing season's over, or else I would have shown the two of you a good time. Well, can you still shoot, *Woldemar*? There's plenty of game left and I might even go out with you myself sometime. Well, God willing, we'll move to Petersburg in the winter, and the two of you will see people and make connections. You're my grown-up fellows now. I was just saying to *Woldemar* that the two of you are on your own feet now and my part is done, since you can get along by yourselves, but if you want to consult with me, then do. I'm not your guardian any more but your friend, or at least I'll try to be a friend and comrade and adviser in whatever way I can, and nothing else. How does that suit your philosophy, Koko? Eh? All right or not? Eh?'

Obviously, I said it was excellent and I really thought it was. Papa had that day a kind of especially attractive, gay, happy expression, and the new relationship with me as with an equal, a comrade, made me love him even more.

'Well, tell me then, did you see all the relatives? The Ivins? The old man? What did he say to you?' he proceeded to question me. 'You did see Prince Ivan Ivanych, didn't you?'

And we talked so long without getting dressed that the sun was already starting to move from the sitting-room windows, and Yakov (who was just as old and who still wriggled his fingers behind his back and said 'once again') came in to tell Papa that the buggy was ready.

'Where are you going?' I asked him.

'Oh, I almost forgot,' Papa said with a 'vexed' look and a cough, 'I promised to stop by the Yepifanovs today. You remember Yepifanova, *La belle Flamande*, who used to visit your *maman*? They're splendid people.' And with a diffident shrug, as it seemed to me, he left the room.

Lyubochka had during our chattering already come to the door several times and kept asking, 'May I join us?'[56] but each time Papa had yelled through the door, 'No, you certainly may not, since we aren't dressed.'

'Well, what's so awful about that? I've seen you in your dressing gown before.'

'You can't see your brothers in their "unmentionables",' Papa had yelled to her, 'but if each knocks on the door to you, will that be enough? Go ahead and knock. It would be indecent for them even to talk to you in such dishabille.'

'Oh, how unbearable you all are! At least come down to the drawing room as quickly as you can. Mimi so wants to see you,' Lyubochka had yelled back.

As soon as Papa left, I quickly put on my student frock coat and went down to the drawing room, while Volodya, on the contrary, didn't hurry at all, but sat for a long time upstairs talking to Yakov about where to find snipe and woodcock. As I've said, there was nothing in the world he was more afraid of than tender moments with his little brother or sister or his 'pappie', as he put it, and, in avoiding any expression of feeling, he went to the other extreme of coldness, which often painfully offended those who didn't understand the reason for it. In the entryway I ran into Papa as he was going out to the carriage with short, rapid steps. He was wearing his fashionable new Moscow frock coat and smelled of scent. Catching sight of me, he gaily tipped his head, as if to say, 'Splendid, no?' and I was struck again by the happy expression in his eyes that I had noticed earlier in the morning.

The drawing room was still the same bright, lofty room with its yellowish English piano and large open windows looking out onto merry green trees and reddish-yellow garden paths. After I had kissed Mimi and Lyubochka and was going over to Katenka, it suddenly occurred to me that it wouldn't be proper to kiss her any more, and I came to a halt, blushing in silence. Katenka, however, wasn't embarrassed, and holding out her little white hand, she congratulated me on entering the university. The same thing happened when Volodya came into the room and saw Katenka. It really was hard to decide how, after growing up together and seeing each other every day all that time, we should now greet each other after our first separation. Katenka blushed much more than the rest of us, but Volodya wasn't flustered in the least, and after a slight bow to Katenka, he went to Lyubochka, with whom he also chatted briefly but not seriously, before going out for a walk somewhere by himself.

TWENTY-NINE

Our Relationship with the Girls

Volodya had such a peculiar view of the girls that, although he might take an interest in whether they had enough to eat or slept well or were properly dressed or made mistakes in French that might embarrass him in front of strangers, he wouldn't allow the idea that they could think or feel anything human, and even less the possibility of discussing anything with them. Whenever they happened to address some serious question to him (something they naturally tried to avoid), or asked his opinion of some novel or about his work at the university, he would make a face at them and walk away without speaking, or answer with some fractured French phrase – *com si tri joli*[57] or the like, or make a solemn, deliberately stupid face and utter some word having no meaning or relation to the question at all, or with a blank stare say 'rolls' or 'let's go' or 'cabbage' or something of the kind. Whenever I happened to repeat things to him that Lyubochka or Katenka had told me, he would say, 'Hm! So you're still discussing things with them? No, I can see that you're still in a bad way.'

But it was necessary to see and hear him at that moment to appreciate the deep, unwavering contempt in the sentence. Volodya had been a grown-up for two years and constantly in love with all the pretty women he met, but although he and Katenka saw each other every day, and she had been wearing long dresses for two years and getting prettier with each passing day, the idea that he might fall in love with her never occurred to him. Whether it was because the prosaic memories of childhood – the wagonette, the splash apron, the naughtiness – were still too fresh in his mind, or because of the aversion that very young people have for everything home-bred, or because of the general human tendency to pass by anything good and excellent met with for the first time, so that one says, 'Oh, I'll see a good deal of that in my life' – whatever the reason, at the time he still didn't regard Katenka as a woman.

Volodya was clearly very bored that whole summer, his boredom coming from his scorn for us, which, as I've mentioned, he made no effort to hide. The permanent expression on his face said, 'Ugh! How boring, and no one to talk to!' In the morning he would either go shooting by himself or, without getting dressed until dinner, read a book in his room. If Papa was out, he would even bring the book to dinner, continuing to read without talking to any of us, which made us all feel as if we were somehow at fault. In the evening he would lie with his feet up on the sofa in the drawing room and doze while propped on his arm, or else talk dreadful nonsense with a straight face, and sometimes not altogether decent nonsense either, which made Mimi furious and her face turn red in blotches, while we died of laughter; yet never with anyone in our family, except for Papa and sometimes me, did ever he deign to speak seriously. I involuntarily adopted my brother's view of the girls, although I wasn't as afraid of tenderness as he was, and my scorn for them was still far from being as hard or as deep. I even tried several times from boredom that summer to be friendlier with Lyubochka and Katenka and to talk to them, but each time I found so little capacity in them for logical thought, and such ignorance of the simplest, most ordinary things – such as, for example, what money is, or what's studied at a university, or what war is – and such indifference to the explanation of those things, that those efforts of mine only confirmed my unfavourable opinion even more.

I remember one evening when Lyubochka was practising on the piano for the hundredth time some passage of which we were all sick and tired, and Volodya was dozing on the sofa in the drawing room and from time to time muttering with a sort of malicious sarcasm addressed to no one in particular, 'Ah, there she goes . . . A music lady . . . *Beetkhoven!*' (He pronounced the name with particular sarcasm.) 'Smartly, now . . . And once again . . . That's right . . . ,' and so on. Katenka and I were still sitting at the tea table, and I don't remember quite how, but she started to talk about her favourite subject: love. I was in a philosophical mood and condescendingly started to define it as a desire to acquire in another what you lack in yourself, and so on. But Katenka replied that, on the contrary, it wasn't love any more if the young woman was thinking about marrying a rich man, that in her opinion wealth was the most superficial thing, and that the only true love was the one that could survive separation (which I understood to be an allusion to her love for Dubkov). Volodya, who had apparently been listening to our conversation, suddenly propped himself up on his elbow and yelled questioningly, '*Katenka! Russians?*'

'Perpetual nonsense!' Katenka said.

'*Into a pepperbox?*' Volodya continued, stressing each syllable. And I couldn't help thinking that he was absolutely right.

Besides the general abilities of intellect, sensibility and artistic feeling that are more or less highly developed in individuals, there's a particular ability that's more or less highly developed in various social circles, but especially in families, that I'll call 'understanding'. Its essence is a shared sense of proportion and a common view of things. Two members of the same circle or family who share that ability will always allow the expression of feeling up to a certain point, beyond which both will see empty phrases, and both will see at the same time where praise ends and irony begins, or where enthusiasm ends and affectation begins – all of which may have a quite different appearance to people with another understanding. For two people of the same understanding, every object will in the same way for both present mainly its ridiculous, beautiful or sordid aspect. To facilitate that identical understanding, members of the same circle or family will establish their own language, their own turns of phrase, even their own words to define nuances of concepts that don't exist for other people. In our family, that understanding was developed to the utmost degree between Papa and us brothers. Dubkov, too, somehow fitted into our circle and 'understood', but Dmitry, even though he was much cleverer than Dubkov, was deaf to it. But with no one else did Volodya and I, who had grown up in identical conditions, refine that ability to the extent we did with each other. Even Papa had long since lagged behind, and a great deal was beyond his comprehension that was as clear to us as two times two. For example, the following words and corresponding ideas had, goodness knows how, established themselves for Volodya and me: 'raisins' meant a boastful desire to show that you had money; 'shipshape' (here you had to hold the tips of your fingers together and give particular stress to the 'sh' sounds) meant anything fresh, wholesome, elegant, yet not extravagant; a noun used in the plural meant an unjustified partiality for that thing, and so on and so forth. The meaning, however, really depended more on facial expressions and the general sense of the conversation, so that whatever expression for a new nuance one of us might come up with, the other with just a hint would already understand it in exactly the same way. The girls didn't have our understanding, and that was the main reason for our mental estrangement and the scorn we felt for them.

It may be they had their own 'understanding', but it had so diverged from ours that where we saw empty words they saw feeling, while our irony was for them truth, and so on. At the time, however, I didn't realize that it wasn't their fault, and that the lack of understanding didn't keep them from being fine, clever girls, and so I regarded them with scorn. Moreover, once I had hit upon the idea of candour and carried its application to an extreme in myself, I ascribed secretiveness and dissimulation to the tranquil, trusting nature of Lyubochka, who saw no need at all to dig out and examine all her thoughts and inclinations. For example, that Lyubochka made the sign of the cross over Papa every night before going to bed, that she and Katenka wept in the chapel when they went to celebrate Mama's memorial service, and that Katenka sighed and rolled her eyes while playing the piano all seemed extraordinarily affected to me, and I wondered where they had learned how to dissemble like grown-ups and why they weren't ashamed to do so.

THIRTY
My Occupations

All the same, I was closer to our young ladies that summer than in other years, thanks to the emergence in me of a passion for music. A neighbour had come by that spring to introduce himself, a young man who, as soon as he entered the drawing room, kept looking at the piano and imperceptibly moving his chair towards it as he conversed with Mimi and Katenka. After talking for a while about the weather and the pleasures of country life, he deftly turned the conversation to piano tuners, music and pianos, in the end announcing that he played and quickly demonstrating it with three waltzes, while Lyubochka, Mimi and Katenka stood beside the piano and watched. The young man never returned, but I was much taken by his playing – the way he sat at the piano, the way he shook his hair, and especially the way he had of playing octaves with his left hand, quickly extending his little finger and thumb the width of the octave, slowly drawing them together, and then rapidly extending them again. That graceful gesture, his casual posture, the shaking of his hair, and the attention his talent received from our ladies gave me the idea of playing the piano too. Convincing myself, as a result of that idea, that I had a talent and passion for music, I began to study. In that respect, I acted the same way that millions of the male and especially female sex do who study without a good teacher, a genuine vocation or the least idea of what art may provide and how it should be undertaken so that it will provide something. For me, music, or rather playing the piano, was a way of captivating young ladies with my feeling. After learning with Katenka's help to read music and limbering my thick fingers – a task, by the way, to which I devoted two months of such diligent effort that I even exercised my unruly ring finger at dinner on my knee and in bed on a pillow – I immediately started to play 'pieces' and to do so, obviously, with feeling, *avec âme*, as even Katenka admitted, although with a complete lack of measure.

The choice of pieces was the familiar one – waltzes, galops, romances (*arrangés*) and the like – everything by those nice composers of whom anyone with a little sound taste will make a small pile from the stack of excellent things in a sheet-music shop and say, 'Here's what *not* to play, for nothing worse, more tasteless and inane has ever been put down on paper,' and whom, probably for that reason, you'll find on the piano of every Russian young lady. True, we also had the unfortunate Beethoven sonatas, forever mangled by young ladies, the *Path-étique* and the *Moonlight*,[58] which Lyubochka played in memory of *maman*, and some other good things that Lyubochka's Moscow teacher had given her, but there were also others that he himself had composed, the most absurd marches and galops, which she also played. Katenka and I, however, didn't care for serious things, but preferred '*Le fou*'[59] and 'The Nightingale', which she played so rapidly you couldn't see her fingers, and which I had already begun to play fairly loudly and fluently. I adopted the young man's gestures and often regretted that there wasn't anyone around to see me play. But Liszt and Kalkbrenner[60] quickly proved beyond my strength, and I saw the impossibility of ever catching Katenka. As a result, imagining that classical music would be easier, and also partly for the sake of originality, I suddenly decided that I liked the learned German variety, and even though the *Pathétique* had, to tell the truth, long been loathsome to me in the extreme, I began to express my delight whenever Lyubochka played it, and started to play Beethoven myself and to pronounce it 'Beeetkhoven'. For all that confusion and affectation, however, I did, as I remember now, have something like talent, since music often made a strong impression on me to the point of tears, and I was somehow able to pick out the things I liked on the piano by ear, so that if someone at the time had taught me to regard music as an end and a pleasure in itself rather than a way of captivating young ladies with the speed and sensitivity of my playing, I might, perhaps, really have made a decent musician of myself.

Reading French novels, a large number of which Volodya had brought with him, was my other activity that summer. The *Monte-Cristos* and various *Mystères* had just begun to come out, and I read my fill of Sue, Dumas and Paul de Kock.[61] The most artificial characters and events were as vivid as reality to me, and not only did I not suspect the author of making it up, but he didn't even exist for me, while real, living people and events appeared before me from the printed page. If I hadn't met people anywhere like the characters I was reading about, I never for a moment doubted that I *would*.

Just as a hypochondriac reading a medical book finds the symptoms of every disease in himself, so I found in myself all the passions described in each novel and a resemblance to all the characters – heroes and villains alike. I liked the cunning ideas in those novels and the ardent feelings and magical events and uncomplicated characters – if good, then completely good, or if bad, then completely bad, just as I myself imagined people to be in the early years of my youth. I also liked it very, very much that it was all in French, and that I could memorize the noble words the noble heroes spoke for my own later use in a noble cause. How many different French phrases did I invent with the help of those novels for Kolpikov, should I ever meet him again, or for *her*, when at last I should meet her and declare my love for her? I was prepared to say *such* things to them that they would simply perish on hearing me. I even derived from the novels new ideals of moral virtue I might strive for. Above all, I wanted in all my pursuits and actions to be *noble* (I use the French word, since it has a distinct meaning, as the Germans understood in adopting the word *nobel* without confusing it with the idea of *ehrlich*),[62] and then to be *passionate*, and finally something to which I was already inclined – to be as *comme il faut* as possible. I even tried in my appearance and habits to imitate the heroes possessing those virtues. I remember in one of the many novels I read that summer an extraordinarily passionate hero with thick eyebrows, and I so much wanted to look like him (mentally, I felt myself to be exactly the same) that as I was examining my own eyebrows in the mirror, I got the idea of trimming them a little so they would grow back thicker. But once I started, I realized that I was trimming them more in one place than in the other and kept having to even them out, with the result that I very soon had no eyebrows at all and looked quite ugly. I took comfort, however, in the hope that thick eyebrows like those of the passionate man would quickly grow back, so that my only concern was what to tell everyone when they saw me without any eyebrows. I got some gunpowder from Volodya's room, rubbed eyebrows on with it, and lit it. Although the gunpowder fortunately didn't explode, I did look sufficiently like a singed person that no one detected my ruse, and after I had forgotton all about the passionate man, my eyebrows really did grow back in much thicker.

THIRTY-ONE

Comme il faut

I've alluded several times in the course of this story to the idea behind this French phrase, and I now feel the need to devote an entire chapter to it, for it was one of the most pernicious and false ideas instilled in me by my upbringing and milieu.

The human race may be divided up in many ways – rich and poor, good and evil, military and civilian, clever and stupid, and so on and so forth – but everyone is sure to have his own favourite main subdivision to which he unconsciously refers every new person. Mine at the time I'm writing about was between those who were *comme il faut* and those who were not. The second kind were further subdivided into the not *comme il faut* proper and simple folk. I respected people who were *comme il faut* and regarded them as worthy of equal relations; the second kind I pretended to scorn but in essence loathed, taking something like a personal affront at them; while the third didn't exist for me at all, and were held in complete contempt. My own *comme il faut* consisted, first and foremost, of excellent French, especially in pronunciation. Anyone who pronounced French badly at once aroused a feeling of antipathy in me. 'Why do you want to talk as we do when you don't know how?' I would ask mentally with a venomous sneer. The second condition of *comme il faut* was fingernails – long, pared and clean; the third was knowing how to bow, dance and converse; and the fourth, and very important, was indifference to everything and a constant expression of elegant, supercilious boredom. Besides that, I had certain general signs by which I could, without talking to him, decide to which category a person belonged. Besides his room furnishings, signet, handwriting and carriage, a main one was his feet. The relation of his boots and trousers immediately determined a person's position in my eyes. Someone in boots without heels but with a square toe, and in trousers that were tapered at the bottom without straps, was 'simple', while someone in boots with heels and a narrow round toe, and trousers that had straps and were tapered at the bottom and covered the feet, or that had straps and hung like a valance over the toe, was *mauvais genre*, and so on.

It's strange that the idea of *comme il faut* was instilled to such a degree in me, someone with absolutely no capacity for it. Perhaps it became so firmly rooted because of the great effort I had put into acquiring it. It's terrible to remember how much precious sixteen-year-old time, the best in life, was wasted in doing so. Everyone I imitated – Volodya, Dubkov and most of my acquaintances – seemed to have come by it easily. I regarded them with envy and quietly worked on my French, on the technique of bowing without looking at the person you're bowing to, on conversing and dancing, on the cultivation in myself of indifference to and boredom with everything, and on my fingernails, which I cut back to the quick with scissors – all the while feeling that a great deal of effort still remained to reach my goal. And my room and my desk and my carriage – I didn't know how to arrange any of them so they would be *comme il faut*, although I tried hard, despite my aversion for practical matters. With other people it all seemed to go superbly without any effort, as if it couldn't have been otherwise. Once after intensive but useless work on my nails, I remember asking Dubkov, whose own nails were remarkably fine, if he had had them for a long time, and how he had got them that way. He replied, 'For as long as I can remember I've never done anything to make them that way, and I don't see how a decent person could have nails of any other kind.' That answer greatly distressed me. I didn't know at the time that one of the main conditions of *comme il faut* is hiding the effort by which it is achieved. *Comme il faut* was for me not merely an important virtue, a fine quality, a perfection that I wished to attain, but also an essential condition of life, without which there could be neither happiness nor reputation, nor anything good in the world. I couldn't respect a famous actor or a learned man or a benefactor of the human race if he wasn't *comme il faut*. The *comme il faut* person stood higher and was beyond comparison with the rest; he left it to them to paint their pictures, write their music and books, and do good – he even praised them for it, for why not praise whatever is fine in whomever it is found? – but they weren't on the same level as he was; he was *comme il faut* and they weren't, and that was sufficient. It even seems to me that if we had had a brother, a mother or a father who wasn't *comme il faut*, I would have said it was unfortunate, but that between that person and myself there could be no common ground. But neither the loss of precious time employed in constant worry about observing the – for me – difficult conditions of *comme il faut* at the cost of every other serious activity, nor the antipathy to and contempt for nine tenths of the human race, nor the indifference to anything excellent achieved outside the circle of *comme il faut* – none of that was the principal harm inflicted on me by that idea. The principal harm was the belief that *comme il faut* was an independent position in society, that one didn't have to make the effort to be an official or a carriage maker or a soldier or a learned man, if one was *comme il faut*; that in attaining that quality, one had already fulfilled one's purpose and even stood higher than most.

After many missteps and enthusiasms, most people come at a certain point in youth to the necessity of active involvement in social life, and choose some area of endeavour and devote themselves to it. With the *comme il faut* person, however, that rarely happens. I've known a great many people who are old, proud, self-assured and strict in their judgements, and who, if they should be asked in the next world, 'Who are you and what did you do there?' would be unable to answer in any other way than to say, '*Je fus un homme très comme il faut.*'[63]

That fate awaited me, too.

THIRTY-TWO

Youth

Despite the tangle of ideas in my mind that summer, I was young, innocent, free, and therefore almost happy.

Sometimes, or even quite often, I would get up early. (I slept on the terrace in the open air and the oblique rays of the bright morning sun would wake me.) I would quickly dress, put a towel and a French novel under my arm, and go for a swim in the river in the shade of a birch grove less than half a mile from the house. I would lie down on the grass in the shade and read, from time to time looking up from my book to gaze at the surface of the river, violet in the shade and riffled by a morning breeze, or at the field of yellowing rye on the opposite bank, or at the pale-red rays of morning light tinting, lower and lower, the white trunks of the birches as one after another they moved away from me into the depths of the virgin wood, and enjoy the awareness in myself of exactly same fresh, young power of life that nature was emanating everywhere around me. When grey wisps of morning cloud appeared in the sky and I got chilly from my swim, I would often set out directly through the fields and woods, taking pleasure in soaking my boots in the fresh dew. I would vividly daydream about the heroes of the last novel I had read, and imagine myself a commander or a government minister or a man of great strength or a passionate man, and continually look around in a kind of eager hope of suddenly finding *her* in a little clearing or behind a tree. Whenever on those walks I came upon peasant men or women at their work, I always felt a strong instinctive embarrassment and would try not to be seen, even though 'simple folk' didn't exist for me. When it was already getting hot, but our ladies still hadn't come out for tea, I would often go to the garden or the orchard to eat the ripe vegetables and fruit. That activity gave me one of my chief pleasures. You make your way to the apple orchard and the centre of a tall, dense raspberry bush. Above you is the bright, hot sky and all around, the prickly pale-green of raspberry canes entangled with an undergrowth of weeds. A dark-green nettle with a delicate flowering crown reaches gracefully upwards, while a leggy burdock with unnaturally bristly purple flowers rudely pushes through the canes and higher than your head, here and there touching with the nettle the spreading pale-green boughs of an old apple tree, on top of which round, lustrous, still-green apples ripen in the hot sun. From below, a young cane, lacking leaves and nearly dry, twists upwards towards the sun, and needle-like blades of grass and a thistle break through last year's leaves and, moist with the dew, gleam a lush green in the permanent shade, as if unaware of the bright sun playing in the leaves of the apple tree.

It's always musty in the thicket, and smells of heavy, continuous shade, cobwebs, fallen apples turning black on the mouldy ground, raspberries and sometimes even a forest bug, which you accidentally swallow with a berry, making you quickly pick another. As you move forward, you scare the sparrows that always live in the thicket and hear their hasty chirking and the beating of their rapid little wings against the canes, and you hear, too, the stationary buzzing of a plump bee and, somewhere along the path, the footsteps of the orchard boy, the half-wit Akim, and his endless humming to himself. You think to yourself, 'No, not he nor anyone else in the world will find me here,' and right and left with both hands you pull the juicy berries from their conical white plugs, and consume them one after another with gusto. Your legs are drenched even above your knees, in your mind is the most awful drivel (you silently repeat a thousand times in a row, 'a-and t-imes twen-ty, a-and t-imes sev-en'), your arms are stung with nettles and so are your legs through your soaked trousers, your head is baking in the sunshine that has started to penetrate the thicket, you've long ceased wanting to eat, yet you remain in the thicket and look and listen and think and mechanically pull off the best berries and gulp them down.

I would usually enter the drawing room before eleven, and more often than not after tea when the ladies were already busy at their work. Standing beside the first window with its unbleached canvas shade drawn against the sun, but letting in through the gaps bright sunshine that covers everything it touches with such brilliant, fiery rings that it hurts to look at them, is an embroidery frame with flies quietly crawling across its white linen. Mimi is sitting at the frame and constantly shakes her head in exasperation as she moves from one place to another out of the sunshine, which suddenly breaks through somewhere else and covers first her face and then her hands with a fiery band. Bright rectangles of light limned by the frames of the other three windows fall on the bare drawing-room floor, and lying by old habit in one of the rectangles is Milka, who stares with erect ears at the flies crawling within it. Katenka sits on the sofa knitting or reading out loud, and impatiently waves her little white hands, seemingly translucent in the bright sunshine, or shakes her head with a frown to shoo away a fly that has got in her thick, golden hair and is beating against it. Lyubochka is either walking back and forth in the room with her hands clasped behind her, waiting until they'll all go out to the garden, or else is playing on the piano some piece of which I've long known every note. I sit down somewhere to listen to the music or the reading, and wait for the chance to take my own turn at the piano. After dinner I sometimes favour the girls with a horseback ride (going for walks with them I consider beneath my years and position in society), and those rides, in which I escort them to out-of-the-way places and ravines, are very pleasant. Sometimes adventures happen to us in which I show myself to be a brave fellow, and the ladies admire my riding skill and daring, and regard me as their protector. If we have no company, in the evening after tea on the shaded terrace, or a walk with Papa around the estate, I take my old place in the Voltaire armchair and, listening to Katenka or Lyubochka play, I read and daydream, just as I used to. Sometimes, when I'm alone in the drawing room and Lyubochka is playing some old melody, I involuntarily put down my book and gaze out through the open door of the balcony at the leafy branches hanging from the tall birches on which evening shadows have begun to fall, and at the clear sky in which, if you stare hard, what looks like a dusty yellow spot will suddenly appear and disappear, and then as I listen to the music from the salon, and the squeaking of the gate, and the voices of the peasant women, and the sound of the herd as it comes back to the village, I suddenly vividly recall Natalya Savishna and *maman* and Karl Ivanych and feel sad for a moment. But my heart is at the same time so full of life and hope that the memory merely brushes me with its wing and flies on.

After supper and sometimes an evening stroll in the garden with someone else (I was afraid to walk down the dark avenues alone), I would go off by myself to sleep on the floor of the terrace, which was a great pleasure, despite the millions of mosquitoes that would try to devour me. If the moon was full, I would often spend the whole night sitting on my mattress, gazing at the light and the shadows, listening intently to the silence and the sounds, dreaming of various things, but primarily of a poetical, voluptuous happiness, which at the time seemed the greatest in life, and regretting that, so far, it was only something I could imagine. As soon as everyone had gone off to bed, and the lights had moved from the drawing room to the rooms upstairs, where female voices could be heard along with windows opening and closing, I would go out to the terrace and pace back and forth, eagerly listening to the sounds of the house as it fell asleep. As long as there was a hope, however small and baseless, for even partial happiness of the kind I dreamed, I couldn't calmly construct an imaginary one for myself.

At every sound of barefoot steps, every cough, sigh, movement of a window or rustle of a dress, I would jump up from my bed, look and listen like a thief, and for no apparent reason become agitated. But then the lights would go out in the upstairs windows, the sounds of footsteps and voices would be replaced by snoring, the night watchman would bang his cast-iron bar, the garden would become both gloomier and brighter as the bands of red light falling on it from the upstairs windows disappeared, the last light from the pantry would move towards the entryway, casting its band on the dewy garden, and through the window I would see the stooped figure of Foka in his quilted

jacket, carrying a candle as he went to his own sleeping place. I
often got a great pleasure and thrill from creeping across the
wet grass in the dark shadow of the house to the entryway
window to listen with bated breath to the snoring of the boy
and the wheezing of Foka and his aged voice as he said his
prayers a long, long time, supposing that no one else could hear
him. Finally, he would put out the last candle, shut the window
with a bang and leave me entirely alone, and I would timidly
look around to see if somewhere by the flowers or my bed a
fair-skinned woman wasn't waiting, and then scamper back to
the terrace. And then I would lie down on my bed facing the
garden and, covering up as best I could against the mosquitoes
and bats, I would gaze out into the garden and listen to the
sounds of the night and dream of love and happiness.

Everything would take on a different meaning for me then:
the look of the old birches, on one side their leafy branches
gleaming against the moonlit sky, and on the other glumly hiding
the bushes and the road in their dark shadows; the pond's placid,
glittering brilliance gradually increasing like a sound; the moonlight glistening in the dewdrops on the flowers, which also cast
their graceful shadows on the grey flower bed in front of the
terrace; the chirp of a quail from beyond the pond; the voice of
someone on the main road; the barely audible creak of two old
birches rubbing against each other; the whine of a mosquito
above my ear under the blanket; the fall onto dry leaves of an
apple that had been caught on a branch; and the hopping of
frogs that sometimes came up to the terrace steps, their greenish
backs glimmering somehow mysteriously in the moonlight – all
that would take on a strange new meaning for me, the meaning
of overwhelming beauty and a kind of incomplete happiness.
And then *she* would appear, always sad and beautiful, with a
long dark plait and firm bosom, and with bare arms and voluptuous embraces. She would love me, and I would sacrifice my
whole life for one minute of her love. But the moon would rise
higher and higher in the sky and shine brighter and brighter, the
pond's glittering brilliance would continue to increase like a
sound, growing ever more distinct, the shadows would become
darker and darker, and the light more and more transparent,

and as I looked at and listened to it all, something would tell me that even she with her bare arms and ardent embraces was still far, far from being all there was of happiness, that even love for her was still far, far from being all there was of goodness; and the longer I gazed at the high, full moon, the more exalted true beauty and goodness seemed to be, and the purer they became, and the closer they were to Him, the source of all that is beautiful and good, and tears of a kind of yearning joy would fill my eyes.

And although I was alone, it would still seem to me that the mystery and majesty of nature, and the bright, alluring circle of the moon, stopped for some reason at a single high, indefinite point in the pale-blue sky, yet shining everywhere as if filling the immensity of space with itself, and I an insignificant worm soiled by every petty, wretched human passion, yet with all the immense, mighty power of imagination and love – it would still seem to me in those moments that nature and the moon and I were one and the same.

THIRTY-THREE

Our Neighbours

I was quite surprised the day after our arrival to hear Papa call our neighbours the Yepifanovs splendid people, and even more surprised that he was going to see them. We had been involved in a protracted lawsuit with them about some land. As a child I had heard Papa lose his temper more than once over the suit, curse the Yepifanovs and summon various people in order, as I understood it, to enlist them in his defence; I had heard Yakov refer to them as our enemies and as 'evil people'; and I remember *maman* asking that in her home and in her presence those people never even be mentioned.

I had in keeping with those facts formed in childhood such a firm, clear idea of the Yepifanovs as 'foes' ready to stab or strangle not only Papa but any son of his, should they come across him, and as 'evil people' in the absolute sense, that on seeing Avdotya Vasilyevna Yepifanova, *La belle Flamande*, taking care of Mama before she died, it was hard for me to believe she was from the same evil family, and I continued to hold the lowest opinion of them. Although we saw them frequently that summer, I remained strangely prejudiced against them all. But here, in essence, is who the Yepifanovs were. The family consisted of the mother, a fifty-year-old widow still fresh and gay; her beautiful daughter, Avdotya Vasilyevna; and her son, the stutterer Pyotr Vasilyevich, a retired lieutenant and bachelor of quite serious character.

Before her husband died, Anna Dmitriyevna Yepifanova had for some twenty years lived apart from him, sometimes in Petersburg, where she had relatives, but mostly in her own village of Mytishchi,[64] which was no more than two miles from us. Such horrors were told in the district about her way of life that Messalina[65] seemed like an innocent babe in comparison, which is why Mama had asked that not even Yepifanova's name be mentioned in her home. But speaking without the least irony, it was impossible to believe a tenth of that most malicious of all forms of gossip, the gossip of country neighbours. Although the serf clerk Mityusha was living in her home when I came to know Anna Dmitriyevna, and although he stood behind her chair at dinner in a Circassian-style frock coat and was always pomaded and curled and had a handsome mouth and eyes that Anna Dmitriyevna would, in his presence but in French, often invite her guests to admire, there was nothing remotely like what rumour continued to hold. Anna Dmitriyevna had, I think, really changed her way of life completely some ten years before, when she had called her dutiful son Petrushka back home from the service. Her estate was small, just over a hundred serfs, and her expenditures during her life of merriment had been great, so that ten years earlier, obviously after being mortgaged and re-mortgaged, the estate was in arrears and would unavoidably have to be put up for auction. Assuming in those extreme circumstances that the trusteeship, property inventory, arrival of the court officer and other unpleasant events were happening not so much from her non-payment of the interest as from the fact that she was a woman, Anna Dmitriyevna wrote to her son at his regiment, asking him to come to her rescue. Even though Pyotr Vasilyevich's career in the service was going so well that he soon hoped to have his own living, he gave it all up, retired and, as a dutiful son who regarded his first obligation to be the comfort of his mother in her old age (as he wrote to her in complete sincerity), he returned to the country.

Despite his ugly face, awkwardness and stutter, Pyotr Vasilyevich was a man of exceptionally firm principles and uncommonly practical mind. One way or another, by means of small loans, deals, petitions and promises, he held on to the estate. Having turned himself into a landowner, Pyotr Vasilyevich put on his father's fur-lined coat, which had been kept in the storeroom, sold his carriages and horses, discouraged company at Mytishchi, dug ponds, increased the cultivated share, reduced the peasant allotment, cut down his grove with his own people and sold it for a profit – and put his affairs in order. Pyotr Vasilyevich gave himself his word and kept it that until all his debts had been paid he would not wear anything but his father's coat and another canvas affair he had sewn for himself, nor drive in anything but a cart behind peasant horses. He tried to extend that stoical way of life to the whole family, at least to the extent allowed by his deferential regard for his mother, which he took as his duty. In the drawing room he stutteringly fawned on Anna Dmitriyevna, carrying out her every wish and rebuking those who failed to follow her orders, but alone in his study and office he would strictly call to account anyone who brought a duck to the table without his approval, or sent a peasant at Anna Dmitri-yevna's order to ask about a neighbour's health, or dispatched peasant girls to the woods to pick raspberries instead of weeding the garden.

In four years or so all the debts were paid off and Pyotr Vasil-yevich took a trip to Moscow, returning with new clothes and a tarantass.[66] Yet despite the flourishing state of his affairs, he retained the same stoical inclinations, taking, it appeared, a grim pride in them both with his family and with outsiders, and frequently stuttering that 'anyone who really wants to see me will be glad to see me in a sheepskin coat and eat cabbage soup and porridge. It's what I eat, too,' he would add. Every word and gesture expressed his proud awareness of his sacrifice for his mother's sake and his redemption of the estate, along with his contempt for others who had done nothing of the sort.

The mother and daughter had completely different characters from Pyotr Vasilyevich's and were in many respects unlike each other, too. The mother was a woman of the most pleasant sort, always merry with company in the same good-natured way. Everything merry and nice made her truly happy. She even had to the highest degree the ability to enjoy the sight of young people having fun – a quality met with in only the most good-natured older people. Her daughter, Avdotya Vasilyevna, was, on the contrary, a person of serious character, or rather of that special indifferently vague and, without any basis for it, haughty disposition often found in unmarried beauties. But when she wanted to be merry, then her merriment was rather strange – she would laugh at herself, or at the person she was talking to, or at all of society, none of which she probably meant to do. I was frequently surprised and wondered what she meant when she used phrases like 'Yes, I'm terribly good-looking,' 'Well, of course, everyone's in love with me,' and so on. Anna Dmitriyevna was always active, with a passion for decorating her little house and garden, and for flowers, canaries and pretty knick-knacks. Her rooms and garden were small and modest, but everything was arranged so neatly and tidily, and it all had so much of that easy gaiety that a good waltz or polka conveys, that the expression 'little toy', often used in praise by her guests, in fact suited Anna Dmitriyevna's garden and rooms exceptionally well. And she herself was a little toy – short, slim, with a fresh colour to her face and pretty little hands, and always merry and always becomingly dressed. Only the slightly too prominent purple veins of her hands diminished the general effect. Avdotya Vasilyevna, on the contrary, almost never did anything, and not only didn't care for knick-knacks or flowers, but even spent too little time on herself, and was always running off to get dressed whenever company came. On returning to the room, however, she was extraordinarily attractive, except for the cold, unchanging expression of her eyes and smile that all very beautiful faces share. Her graceful figure and the strict regularity of her lovely face always seemed to be saying, 'You may look at me, if you like.'

Yet in spite of the mother's vivacious character and the daughter's indifferently vague demeanour, something told you that the first had never – not before and not now – ever loved anything that wasn't pretty and gay, while Avdotya Vasilyevna was one of those natures that, once they fall in love, will sacrifice their whole lives for the ones they fall in love with.

THIRTY-FOUR
Father's Marriage

My father was forty-eight when he took Avdotya Vasilyevna Yepifanova to be his second wife.

When he arrived in the country by himself with the girls that spring, Papa was, I imagine, in the special restlessly happy and sociable mood that usually visits gamblers who have sworn off after large winnings. He sensed that he still had a lot of unspent good luck, which, if he wasn't going use it on cards, he could use for success in life. Then, too, it was spring and he had an unexpectedly large amount of money and was completely alone and bored. While discussing business with Yakov, and recalling the endless litigation with the Yepifanovs, as well as the beauty Avdotya Vasilyevna, whom he hadn't seen in a long time, he probably said, 'You know, Yakov Kharlampych, rather than trouble ourselves over the lawsuit, I think I'll just let them have the damned land. Eh? What do you think?'

I imagine Yakov's fingers wriggling behind his back in dismay at such an idea and his proving that 'once again, Pyotr Aleksandrovich, our cause is just'.

But Papa ordered the buggy to be harnessed, put on his fashionable olive fur-trimmed overcoat, combed what was left of his hair, sprinkled his handkerchief with scent and, in a mood made merry by the belief that he was acting nobly, but mainly by the hope of seeing a pretty woman, he set off for the neighbours' estate.

I know only that Papa failed on that first visit to find Pyotr Vasilyevich at home, since he was out in the fields, and so spent two hours alone with the ladies. I imagine him showering them with compliments and charming them as he tapped his foot in its soft boot, lisped slightly and gazed at them with sweet little eyes. And I imagine the merry old woman suddenly taking a tender liking to him, and her cold, beautiful daughter cheering up as well.

When a housemaid ran up out of breath to tell Pyotr Vasilyevich that old Irtenyev himself had come, I imagine him angrily replying, 'Well, so what if he has?' and then returning to the house as quietly as possible, and perhaps after entering his study even putting on his filthiest coat and sending word to the cook that by no means should he dare, even if his mistress ordered it, to add anything for dinner.

I often saw Papa and Yepifanov together afterwards and therefore can vividly picture their first meeting. I imagine that despite Papa's offer of an amicable end to the lawsuit, Pyotr Vasilyevich, who was surprised by nothing, was sullen and angry about having sacrificed his career for his mother, whereas Papa had done nothing of the sort, and that Papa, as if not noticing the sullenness, was playful and gay and treated him as if he were an astonishing wag, which sometimes offended Pyotr Vasilyevich, although he couldn't help submitting to it. Papa, with his penchant for turning everything into a joke, for some reason called Pyotr Vasilyevich a colonel and, despite the latter's pointing out once in my presence, while stuttering worse than usual and turning red in vexation, that he wasn't a c-c-colonel but a l-l-lieutenant, Papa had within five minutes called him a colonel again.

Lyubochka told me that before our arrival in the country, they saw the Yepifanovs every day, and that it had been enormous fun. Papa, with his ability to arrange everything originally, humorously and yet simply and elegantly, had organized first coursing, then fishing, then fireworks of some kind, for all of which the Yepifanovs had been present. And it would, according to Lyubochka, have been even more fun, had it not been for the unbearable Pyotr Vasilyevich, who sulked and stuttered and tried to spoil everything.

After Volodya and I arrived, however, the Yepifanovs came to see us only twice, and we all went to see them only once. But after St Peter's day, Papa's name-day, for which they had come to celebrate along with a great many other guests, our relations with the Yepifanovs for some reason broke off completely, and only Papa continued to visit them.

In the short time that I saw Papa together with Dunyechka, as her mother called her, this is what I managed to observe. He was constantly in the same happy mood that had impressed me the day after our arrival. He was so merry, young, full of life and happy that beams of that happiness fell on everyone around him and infected others with the same mood, in spite of themselves. He was never more than a step away from Avdotya Vasilyevna when she was in the room, and would compliment her in such a saccharine way that I was embarrassed for him, or would gaze at her in silence, sometimes shrugging his shoulder and coughing in a sort of complacently ardent way, or would whisper to her with a smile, but all of it with the 'just joking' expression that was characteristic of him in the most serious matters.

Avdotya Vasilyevna seemed to have adopted from Papa the expression of happiness that at the time shone in her large blue eyes almost continuously, except in the moments when she would suddenly become so shy that for me, who knew the feeling, it was pitiful and painful to look at her. It was apparent then that she was intimidated by every glance and gesture, and felt that everyone was staring at her, thinking only about her, and finding everything about her indecent. She would glance around at everyone in dismay, the colour would come and go in her face, she would start to talk loudly and boldly, inanities for the most part, and then, sensing that they were inanities and that Papa and all the others had heard her, she would blush even harder. When that happened, however, Papa wouldn't even notice the inanities but, with a cough, would continue to gaze at her with merry delight and no less ardently. I noticed that those attacks of shyness, although they could come upon her for no reason, often occurred immediately after some young and beautiful woman had been mentioned in Papa's presence. The frequent shifts from pensiveness to the sort of strange, awkward gaiety that I've already mentioned, her repeating of Papa's favourite words and expressions, the continuation with others of conversations started with Papa – all that would, if one of the *dramatis personae* hadn't been my father and I had been a little older, have made his and Avdotya Vasilyevna's relationship clear to me, but at the time I suspected nothing, not even when in my presence Papa received a letter from Pyotr Vasilyevich that upset him very much, and he stopped going to see the Yepifanovs for the rest of the summer.

But then at the end of August he started to see them again, and the day before Volodya and I were to leave for Moscow, Papa announced that he and Avdotya Vasilyevna Yepifanova were going to be married.

THIRTY-FIVE

How We Took the News

Everyone in the house knew about the situation the day before the official announcement and had made their various judgements. Mimi stayed in her room all day and wept, Katenka remained with her and came out only for dinner with a sort of offended expression that she had clearly adopted from her mother, while Lyubochka was very gay, and at dinner said that she knew a wonderful secret but couldn't tell anyone.

'There's nothing wonderful about your secret,' Volodya said, not sharing her pleasure. 'If you were capable of thinking seriously about anything, you would realize that on the contrary it's very bad.'

Lyubochka stared at him in amazement and said nothing.

Volodya wanted to take me by the arm after dinner, but very likely afraid that it would look like tender feeling, he merely touched my elbow and indicated the salon with his head.

'You know the secret Lyubochka was talking about?' he asked after making sure that we were alone.

Volodya and I rarely talked face to face or about anything serious, so when it did happen we felt a kind of mutual awkwardness and, as Volodya said, our pupils would begin to dance. But this time in response to the embarrassment apparent in my eyes, he continued to gaze at me with a sober expression that said, 'There's nothing to be embarrassed about; we're brothers, after all, and have an important family matter to discuss.' I understood, and he continued.

'You know that Papa's marrying Yepifanova?'

I nodded, since I had heard about it.

'Well, it's very bad,' Volodya went on.

'How so?'

'How so?' he asked in vexation. 'What a very pleasant thing to have a stuttering uncle of that ilk, the colonel, and all the rest of that family. She may seem kind enough now, but who knows what's to come? It may not make any difference to us, perhaps, but Lyubochka will have to enter society soon. It won't be so pleasant with that sort of *belle-mère*;[67] why, even her French is bad, and what sort of manners could she teach Lyubochka? She's a *poissarde*[68] and nothing more, a decent one, I suppose, but a *poissarde*, nevertheless,' Volodya concluded, evidently quite taken with the epithet *poissarde*.

Strange as it was to hear Volodya passing judgement on Papa's choice so coolly, it seemed to me that he was right.

'But why does Papa want to get married at all?' I asked.

'It isn't really clear, so goodness only knows. All I can say is that Pyotr Vasilyevich had been trying to get him to and demanded it, and that Papa didn't want to, but then got some maggot about chivalry – it isn't really clear. I'm only beginning to understand our father now,' Volodya continued (that he referred to him as 'our' father and not as 'Papa' stung me painfully) ' – that he's a fine man, kind and clever, but so thoughtless and fickle . . . It's amazing! He can't look at a woman calmly. You know, don't you, that he's never met a woman he hasn't fallen in love with? Including Mimi.'

'What?'

'That's right. I recently found out that he was in love with her when she was young, and wrote poems to her, and that there was something between them. Mimi suffers to this day,' Volodya said, starting to laugh.

'That's impossible!' I said in astonishment.

'But the main thing', Volodya went on, serious again and abruptly switching to French, 'is how pleased such a marriage is going to make all our relatives! There will probably be children, too, you know.'

I was so struck by Volodya's common sense and foresight that I didn't know how to reply.

At that moment Lyubochka came over to us.

'So you do know?' she asked us with a joyful face.

'Yes,' Volodya said, 'only I'm surprised, Lyubochka. After all, you're no longer a little child, so how can you be glad that Papa's marrying some trash?'

Lyubochka suddenly made a serious face and grew thoughtful.

'Volodya! What do you mean "marrying trash"? How dare you talk that way about Avdotya Vasilyevna? If Papa's marrying her, that means she isn't trash.'

'No, not trash, I didn't mean that, but all the same –'

'There isn't any "all the same",' Lyubochka interrupted him, starting to get angry. 'I didn't call the young lady you're in love with trash; how can you talk that way about Papa and a fine woman? Even if you are my older brother, don't talk to me like that, you mustn't talk like that.'

'But why can't I discuss – '

'Because you may not,' Lyubochka interrupted him again. 'You may not discuss a father like ours that way. Mimi might do it, but not you, an older brother.'

'No, you still don't understand anything,' Volodya said contemptuously. 'But understand this. Is it a good thing that some "Dunyechka" Yepifanova is taking the place of your deceased *maman*?'

Lyubochka was silent for a moment and then her eyes suddenly filled with tears.

'I knew you were proud, but I never thought you could be so mean,' she said and walked away.

'Cabbage,' Volodya said with a comically solemn face and vacant look. 'See what happens when you try to discuss something with them?' he added, as if reproaching himself for having forgotten himself so badly as to condescend to a conversation with Lyubochka.

The weather the next day was poor, and neither Papa nor the ladies had yet come out for tea when I entered the drawing room. There had been a cold autumn rain the night before, and across the sky hurtled remnants of the cloud that had emptied itself, and through which the sun, already fairly high, shone as a faintly luminous disc. It was windy, damp and chilly. The door to the garden was open, and the puddles left by the rain on the moisture-darkened terrace floor were beginning to dry. The open door shook on its iron hook in the wind, the paths were wet and muddy, and the old birches with their bare white branches, the bushes, the grass, the nettles, the blackcurrant, and the elder with the pale side of its leaves turned up all shook in place, as if trying to break free of their roots, while round yellow leaves, swirling and overtaking each other, blew in from the linden avenue and fell on the wet road and the wet, dark-green rowen[69] of the meadow. My thoughts were on my father's impending marriage, regarded from Volodya's point of view. The future of our sister, ourselves and Father himself didn't seem to promise anything good. I was indignant at the thought that a woman who was an outsider and a stranger and above all *young* – a mere *young lady* – would in many ways, and without any right at all, suddenly assume the place of whom? Of my deceased mama! It saddened me, and Papa seemed more and more in the wrong to me. And then I heard his and Volodya's voices in the waiters' room. I didn't want to see my father just then, and stepped away from the door, but Lyubochka came out to get me, saying that he was asking for me.

He was standing in the drawing room, leaning with his hand on the piano and looking impatiently and at the same time sombrely in my direction. His face no longer had the expression of youth and happiness that I had seen on it that whole time; rather, it was sad. Volodya was walking about the room with a pipe in his hand. I went over to Papa and greeted him.

'Well, my friends,' Father said resolutely, lifting his head and using that special abrupt tone in which things are said that are obviously unpleasant but already beyond judgement, 'I think you know that I'm marrying Avdotya Vasilyevna.' He was silent for a moment. 'I never meant to marry again after your *maman*, but . . . ,' he paused for a moment again, 'but . . . but it seems to be my fate. Dunyechka is a kind, sweet young woman who really isn't so young; I hope, children, that you'll come to love her, for she already loves you from her heart and is a good person. Now as for the two of you,' he said, addressing Volodya and me, as if hurrying to speak before we could interrupt, 'it's time for you to be on your way, while I'll stay here until the new year, and then come back to Moscow,' again he paused, 'with a new wife and Lyubochka.' It hurt me to see Father as if losing heart and standing guilty before us, and I moved closer to him, but Volodya continued to smoke and walk around the room with his head bowed.

'So then, my friends, that's what your old fellow has come up with,' Papa concluded, turning red, coughing and offering Volodya and me his hand. There were tears in his eyes when he said that, and I noticed that the hand he held out to Volodya, who at the moment was on the other side of the room, trembled a little. The sight of that trembling hand struck me painfully, and the strange thought came to me and struck me even harder that Papa had served in 1812[70] and was known to have been a courageous officer. I took his large, veiny hand and kissed it. He squeezed my own hard and, starting to sob, suddenly took Lyubochka's dark head in his two hands and began kissing her eyes. Volodya pretended to drop his pipe and, as he bent over to pick it up, furtively rubbed his eyes with his fist before slipping out of the room.

THIRTY-SIX

The University

The wedding was to be in two weeks, but our lectures were about to start and Volodya and I returned to Moscow at the beginning of September. The Nekhlyudovs had also come back from the country. Dmitry immediately dropped by to see me (on parting we had promised to write to each other, but obviously hadn't done so even once), and we decided that the next day he would take me to the university for my first lectures.

The day was sunny and bright.

No sooner had I entered the lecture hall than I felt my identity disappear in the throng of merry young people surging through all the doors and hallways in the bright sunshine that came through the large windows. The feeling of membership of that immense society was very pleasant. But of all those people only a few were known to me, and even with them the acquaintance was limited to a nod and the words, 'Hello, Irtenyev!' Yet everywhere around me they were shaking hands and jostling each other, and friendly words, smiles, goodwill and jokes rained down on every side. I felt all around me the bond linking that youthful society, although with sadness I sensed that it had somehow passed me by. But that was only a momentary impression. As a result of it and the vexation it produced, I quickly found it to be even a very good thing that I didn't belong to that whole society, that I should instead have my own circle of respectable people, and I took a seat on the third bench, where Count B., Baron Z, Prince R., Ivin and some other gentlemen of that kind were sitting, and of whom I knew Ivin and Count B. But those gentlemen also looked at me in a way that made me feel that I didn't entirely belong to their society, either. I started to observe everything taking place around me. Semyonov, with his tousled grey hair and white teeth and unbuttoned frock coat, was sitting not far from me, leaning on his elbows and chewing on his pen. His cheek still wrapped in a black cravat, the gymnasium student who had the highest score in the entrance examinations was sitting on the first bench and playing with a little silver watch key attached to his satin waistcoat. Ikonin, who had matriculated after all, was sitting on a balcony bench dressed in piped light-blue trousers that covered his entire boot, and laughing and shouting that he was on Parnassus.[71] Ilenka, who to my amazement had bowed not only coolly but even with disdain, as if wishing to remind me that we were all equal there, was sitting in front of me with his skinny legs up on the bench in a particularly careless way (for my benefit, as it seemed to me) and talking to another student, while occasionally glancing back at me. Ivin's party next to me was speaking French. Those gentlemen seemed terribly stupid to me. Every word of their conversation seemed not only pointless but wrong – simply not French ('*Ce n'est pas français*,'[72] I said to myself), and the postures, speech and actions of Semyonov, Ilenka and the others seemed ignoble to me, not respectable, not *comme il faut*.

I didn't belong to any party, and feeling isolated and incapable of overcoming it, I started to get angry. A student on the bench in front of me was chewing on his fingers, all red hangnails, and I was so disgusted by it that I even moved to another seat, farther away. But in my heart, as I remember, I was very sad that first day.

After the professor entered and everyone stopped fidgeting and was silent, I remember extending my satirical gaze to him, too, and it struck me that he had begun his lecture with an introductory sentence that in my opinion made no sense at all. I wanted the lecture to be so clever from beginning to end that it would be impossible to add or subtract a single word. Disappointed in that, under the heading 'First Lecture' in the handsomely bound copybook I had brought with me, I immediately drew eighteen profiles joined in a petal-shaped circle, only occasionally moving my hand across the paper, so the professor (who, I was confident, was very aware of me) would think I was taking notes. Having decided at that first lecture that writing down everything every professor said was not only unnecessary but would even be silly, I kept to that rule for the rest of the year.

I didn't feel quite so isolated at the following lectures, and made many new acquaintances, shook hands and engaged in conversation, but even so a genuine intimacy for some reason never developed between me and my classmates, and it still often happened to me to feel sad in my heart and dissemble. With the party of Ivin and the aristocrats, as everyone called them, I couldn't get any closer, because, as I recall now, I was unfriendly and rude to them and bowed only when they bowed to me, and they clearly had very little need of my friendship anyway. But with the majority it happened for a completely different reason. As soon as I sensed that a classmate had begun to favour me, I immediately let him know that I dined at Prince Ivan Ivanych's and had my own droshky. I only said it to show myself to the greatest advantage, so the classmate would like me even more, but to my surprise the news about the droshky and my connection to Prince Ivan Ivanych resulted almost every time in the classmate suddenly becoming aloof and cold.

Among us was a state-supported student named Operov, a modest, very capable and diligent young man who always offered his hand like a board, without bending his fingers or making any movement at all, so that our wittier classmates sometimes gave him their own hands in the same way and called it shaking hands 'little-board' style. I almost always sat beside him and we often talked. I especially liked Operov's unintimidated views of the professors. He defined very clearly and precisely the merits and defects of the teaching of each, and sometimes even made fun of them, which had an especially strange, startling effect on me coming from his tiny little mouth, and said in his quiet little voice. Despite that, however, he carefully copied down all the lectures without exception in his minuscule handwriting. He and I were becoming friends and had decided to study together, and his tiny grey, near-sighted eyes had begun to turn to me with pleasure whenever I came to sit down beside him. But I found it necessary once in conversation to explain to him that my mama, as she was dying, had asked my father never to put us in a state school, and that I was becoming convinced that all the state students might well know at lot, but that for me 'they ... they weren't at all the thing, *ce ne sont pas des gens comme il faut,*' I said, faltering and sensing that for some reason I was blushing. Operov said nothing, but at the following lectures he didn't greet me first, didn't offer me his little board, didn't converse, and when I sat down he lowered his head a finger's length from his copybooks, as if poring over them. I was surprised by his sudden coldness. But *pour un jeune homme de bonne maison* I considered it unbecoming to ingratiate myself with the 'state student Operov' and left him alone, although, I'll admit, his coldness did sadden me. Once, I arrived before he did, and since the lecture was by a popular professor and attended by students who didn't make coming to lectures a regular practice, so that almost all the seats were taken, I sat down in Operov's place, put my copybooks on the writing stand and went back out. When I returned to the lecture hall I saw that my copybooks had been removed to the back bench, and that Operov was sitting in his usual place. I pointed out to him that I had already put my copybooks there.

'I have no idea,' he answered, suddenly turning red and not looking at me.

'I'm telling you I put my copybooks there,' I said, feigning anger in order to intimidate him with my pluck. 'Everyone saw,' I added, glancing around at the other students, but although many of them were looking at me with curiosity, none of them said anything.

'Places aren't hired out here, so whoever comes first can sit in them,' Operov said, angrily rearranging himself in his seat and glancing indignantly at me for an instant.

'That means you're a boor,' I said.

Operov appeared to mutter something. I think it may even have been, 'And you're a stupid boy,' but I didn't hear it clearly. And what would have been the good if I had? To quarrel like *manants*[74] of some sort and no more? (I was quite pleased with the word *manant*, and it was my response and solution to a good many confused situations.) I might perhaps have said something else, but just then the door slammed and the professor, dressed

in a blue frock coat, quickly mounted the dais after a bow and
a scrape.

However, before the examinations when I needed his copybooks, Operov, remembering his promise, offered them to me
and invited me to study with him.

THIRTY-SEVEN
Matters of the Heart

I was quite occupied with matters of the heart that winter. I fell in love three times. Once was a passion for a very buxom lady I had seen at Freitag's riding hall and, as a result, I would go to watch her every Tuesday and Friday, the days she rode. But since I was always afraid that she might see me, I would stand so far away from her, and run so soon from the place where she was supposed to pass, and turn away so casually whenever she happened to gaze in my direction, that I never got a good look at her face, and to this day cannot say if she really was attractive or not.

Dubkov was acquainted with the lady, and after hearing about my passion from Dmitry, and catching me lurking in the hall behind the servants and the fur coats they were holding, he offered to introduce me to her, which so terrified me that I dashed headlong out of the place, and from the mere idea that he had told her about me, didn't dare return, not even as far as the servants, lest I ran into her.

When I was infatuated with women I didn't know, especially married ones, I was overcome with a shyness that was a thousand times greater than any I had felt with Sonyechka. More than anything in the world, I was afraid that the object might find out about my love and even my existence. I thought that if she did find out about my feelings for her, she would be so offended that she would never forgive me. And really if that rider had known in detail how, as I watched from behind the servants, I imagined carrying her off to live in the country, and what I imagined I would do with her there, she might justifiably have been very offended. I couldn't grasp that without knowing me, she wouldn't suddenly be able to divine all my thoughts about her, and that there was therefore nothing shameful about simply making her acquaintance.

The second time I fell in love was with Sonyechka again after seeing her when she visited my sister. My earlier infatuation with her had long since passed, but I fell in love once more as a result of Lyubochka's giving me a copybook with some verses that Sonyechka had copied out, and in which a number of gloomily amorous passages from Lermontov's 'Demon'[75] had been under-lined in red ink and marked with pressed flowers. Recalling that Volodya had the year before kissed the coin purse of his young lady, I thought I would try the same, and after I was alone in my room and daydreaming while gazing at one of the flowers and touching it to my lips, I really did experience a sort of pleasantly tearful mood, and was in love again for several days, or so I supposed.

The third time I fell in love that winter was with a young lady with whom Volodya was also in love and who came to visit us. In the young lady, as I remember her now, there was nothing fine at all, certainly nothing of the sort that usually appealed to me. She was the daughter of a famously clever and learned Moscow lady, small, slender, with long chestnut English curls and a limpid profile. Everyone said that the young lady was even cleverer and more learned than her mother, but I couldn't judge that at all, since feeling something like abject terror at the thought of her cleverness and learning, I had only talked to her once, and then with indescribable awe. But the delight expressed by Volodya, who was never shy about expressing it in the pres-ence of others, communicated itself with such force that I, too, fell passionately in love. Sensing that Volodya wouldn't be pleased by the news that 'two little brothers were in love with the same young lady', I didn't tell him. For me, however, the greatest pleasure in the feeling came from the thought that our love was so pure that even if its object was the same charming creature, we were still friends and ready, if necessary, to sacrifice ourselves for each other. Actually, in regard to a readiness for sacrifice, Volodya did not, I think, entirely share my view, since he was so passionately in love with the young lady that he wanted to slap and call out to a duel a certain real diplomat, who, it was said, was planning to marry her. But it would have been a very pleasurable thing for me to sacrifice my own feeling, perhaps because it wouldn't have taken much effort: I had only had one affected conversation with the young lady about the merits of classical music, and my love, however hard I tried to sustain it, was gone by the following week.

THIRTY-EIGHT

Society

The society amusements to which I had dreamed of devoting myself in imitation of my older brother after entering the university were a complete disappointment to me that winter. Volodya danced a great deal, and Papa also went to balls with his young wife, but I was evidently regarded as still too young or as ill-suited for such diversions, and so no one introduced me to the houses where the balls were given. Despite my vow of candour with Dmitry, I didn't tell him or anyone else how much I wanted to go to balls, and how hurt and distressed I was to have been left out and, apparently, regarded as a sort of philosopher, which as a result is what I pretended to be.

There was, however, a soirée at Princess Kornakova's that winter. She herself invited us all, including me, and I was to attend my first ball. Before we were to go, Volodya came to my room to see what I was wearing. That action greatly astonished and puzzled me. It seemed to me at that time that the desire to be well dressed was quite shameful and should be concealed; he, however, regarded it as so natural and necessary that he quite frankly told me that he was afraid I might embarrass myself. He directed me to put on patent-leather boots without fail, was horrified that I wanted to wear suede gloves, re-attached my watch in a certain distinctive way, and took me to a barber on Kuznetsky Most. They curled my hair. Volodya stepped back to look at me from a distance.

'It's all right now, but can the cowlicks really not be smoothed down?' he asked the barber.

But however much *Monsieur Charles* lubricated my cowlicks with some sticky substance, they still stood up when I put on my hat, and in general my coiffed figure looked even worse to me than before. My one saving grace was an affectation of nonchalance. Only in that form did my appearance resemble anything.

Volodya was apparently of the same view, since he asked me to comb out the curls, and after I had done so and it still wasn't any good, he didn't look at me any more and was silent and dejected the whole way to the Kornakovs'.

Volodya and I entered their home boldly enough, but when Princess Kornakova invited me to join the dancing and I for some reason said that I didn't dance, even though I had gone there with the express purpose of dancing a great deal, I lost heart and, keeping to myself among unfamiliar people, I fell into my usual unrelenting, insurmountable shyness. I stood in silence in the same spot all evening.

During a waltz one of the young princesses came over to me and, with the formal courtesy that she shared with the rest of her family, asked me why I wasn't dancing. I remember being disconcerted by her question, but at the same time and completely involuntarily, a complacent smile spread across my face, and in the most florid French, replete with parentheses, I started to talk such rubbish that even now, many years later, I'm embarrassed to recall it. Very likely, it was the effect of the music, which stimulated my nerves and drowned out, as I supposed, the not wholly intelligible part of my speech. I said something about high society, about the shallowness of men and women, and in the end got so muddled that I stopped in the middle of a word of some sentence that there wasn't any possibility of finishing.

Even the young princess with her well-bred poise was dismayed and gave me a reproachful glance. I smiled in reply. At that critical moment, Volodya, noticing that I was speaking with some vehemence, and very likely wanting to know just how I was making up in conversation for my failure to dance, came over with Dubkov. Seeing my grinning face and the princess's startled expression, and hearing the terrible rubbish with which I ended, he blushed and turned away. The young princess left me standing where I was. Even though I continued to smile, I was at that moment so painfully aware of my stupidity I was ready to sink into the floor, and I realized that whatever it took, I needed to move from my spot and say something and somehow rescue my situation. I went over to Dubkov and asked him if he had managed to dance many waltzes with 'her'. It was seemingly playful and merry, but essentially I was pleading for help from the same person at whom I had shouted 'Silence!' during our dinner at Yar's. Dubkov pretended he hadn't heard me and looked away. I then went over to Volodya and said with an effort, trying at the same time to give my voice a jocular tone, 'Well, then, Volodya, have you quite worn yourself out?' But he only looked at me as if to say, 'You don't talk to me that way when we're alone,' and walked off without a word, evidently afraid that I might somehow attach myself to him.

'My goodness, even my brother is abandoning me!' I thought.

For some reason, however, I didn't have the strength to go. I stood morosely in the same spot until the end of the evening, and it was only when everyone was getting ready to leave and had crowded into the entry room, and a servant, while helping me with my overcoat, had caught the brim of my hat so that it tipped up, that I managed a rueful laugh through my tears and said to no one in particular, 'Comme c'est gracieux.'[76]

THIRTY-NINE

A Carousal

Although, thanks to Dmitry, I still hadn't abandoned myself to the traditional student amusements known as 'carousals', I did happen to take part in one such entertainment that winter, and the feeling I got from it wasn't entirely pleasant. Here's how it was. Once at a lecture at the beginning of the year, Baron Z., a tall blond young man with a regular face of utterly serious mien, invited us all to his home for a comradely evening. 'Us all' meant those of his classmates who were more or less *comme il faut*, which obviously didn't include Grap, Semyonov, Operov or any other gentlemen of that sort. Volodya smiled with disdain when he heard that I was going to a carousal with the first-year students, but I anticipated great and exceptional pleasure from that, to me, still completely unknown pastime, and I arrived at Baron Z.'s punctually at eight, the appointed time.

Baron Z., in an unbuttoned frock coat and white waistcoat, received his guests in the brightly lit salon and drawing room of the small house in which he lived with his parents, who had turned the front rooms over to him for the evening's festivities. Visible in the hallway were the dresses and heads of curious chambermaids, and glimpsed once in the pantry was the gown of a lady whom I took to be the baroness herself. There were around twenty guests, all of them students, except for Herr Frost, who had come with Ivin, and a certain tall, ruddy civilian gentleman, who was in charge of the revels and had been introduced to everyone as a relative of the baron's and a former student of Dorpat University.[77] The excessively bright lighting and dully formal arrangement of the front rooms at first had such a chilling effect on the young company that everyone involuntarily stood back against the walls, except for a few bold spirits and the Dorpat student, who, with his waistcoat already unbuttoned, seemed to be in both rooms at once and in every corner of each room, and to fill them with his pleasant, resonant, unceasing tenor. But the rest of the company remained silent for the most part, or else talked modestly about professors, studies, examinations and other serious but uninteresting topics. Although they tried not to show it, all without exception were watching the door of the pantry with expressions that said, 'Isn't it time we began?' I, too, felt it was time and awaited the *beginning* with happy impatience.

After the servants had served everyone tea, the Dorpat student asked Frost in Russian, 'Do you know how to make a rum punch with burnt sugar and spices, Frost?'

'O, ja,'[78] Frost replied, flexing his calves, and the Dorpat student then said to him, in Russian again, 'Then you take care of that business' (they were both graduates of Dorpat University and on familiar terms), and Frost, with great strides of his muscular bowed legs, started to go back and forth between the drawing room and the pantry, and the pantry and the drawing room, and soon a big soup tureen appeared on the table with a nine-pound loaf of sugar resting on top on three crossed student swords. Baron Z. had meanwhile been going around to all the guests, who had gathered in the drawing room to look at the tureen, saying the same thing to everyone with an invariably serious face: 'Let's all pass the cup around student-style, gentlemen, and drink *Bruderschaft*, or else there won't be any comradeship at all in our year. And unbutton or completely take off your coats, just as he's done.' The Dorpat student had indeed taken off his coat and, after rolling up his white shirtsleeves above his white elbows and planting his feet in a resolute stance, was already lighting the rum in the tureen.

'Gentlemen, put out the candles!' the Dorpat student suddenly shouted so masterfully and loudly as would only have been necessary, had we all been shouting, too. But we were gazing in silence at the tureen and at the Dorpat student's white shirt, all of us feeling that the solemn moment had arrived.

'*Löschen Sie die Lichter aus, Frost!*'[79] the Dorpat student shouted again in German, his excitement evidently getting the better of him. Frost and the rest of us proceeded to put out the candles. The room turned dark, with only the white sleeves and the hands supporting the loaf of sugar on the swords illuminated by the bluish flame. The Dorpat student's loud tenor was no longer alone, since talk and laughter had started up in every corner of the room. Many had taken off their coats (especially those who were wearing fresh shirts of fine quality), and I did the same, realizing that it had *begun*. Although it still wasn't any fun, I was sure everything would be fine, once we had each drunk a glass of the beverage they were preparing.

At last it was ready. Spilling it all over the table, the Dorpat student ladled the punch into glasses and shouted, 'All right, gentlemen, let's begin!' After each of us had taken a sticky glassful, the Dorpat student and Frost began to sing a German song with the exclamation *juchhe!*[80] frequently repeated. We awkwardly joined in, started to clink our glasses, shouted something, praised the punch and drank the strong, sweet fluid, both with our arms linked in *Bruderschaft* and without. There was nothing left to anticipate, for the carousal was already in full swing. I had finished one glass of the punch, another had been poured for me, my temples were throbbing, the flame seemed to have turned crimson and there was shouting and laughter all around, yet not only did it not seem like much fun, but I was even sure that we were all bored, and that for some reason we all considered it necessary to pretend to be having fun. The only one who wasn't pretending, perhaps, was the Dorpat student, who became more and more flushed and ubiquitous, filling the empty glasses of everyone and spilling more and more punch on the table, which had turned sweet and sticky. I don't remember how or what came after what, but I do remember being terribly fond of the Dorpat student and Frost that evening, learning a German song by heart and kissing them both on their sugary lips. I also remember hating the Dorpat student that evening and wanting to throw a chair at him, but resisting the urge. I remember that besides the same feeling of disobedience in all my appendages that I had experienced during the dinner at Yar's, my head ached and spun so much that I was in great fear of dying that very moment. I remember, too, that for some reason we all got down on the floor, moved our arms in imitation of rowing and sang 'Down Mother Volga', and that I was thinking the whole time that there was no reason for any of it. I also remember lying on the floor with interlocked legs and wrestling, Gypsy-style, and spraining someone's neck and thinking that it wouldn't have happened if he hadn't been drunk. I remember, too, that we had supper and drank something else, that I went outside for some fresh air and that my head felt cold, and that I noticed, as we were leaving, that it was terribly dark, that the footboard of the droshky was tilted and slippery, and that it was impossible to hold on to Kuzma, since he had become weaker and was swaying like a rag doll. But the main thing I remember is the constant feeling I had the whole evening that I was doing a foolish thing in pretending to have such fun, and to like drinking so much and not even think about being drunk, and that the others were all doing an equally foolish thing in pretending the same. It seemed to me that it was just as individually unpleasant for them as it was for me, but because each of us supposed himself to be the only one who was experiencing that unpleasant feeling, we found it necessary to pretend to be having fun so as not to upset the general merriment. Furthermore, strange although it is to say, I considered it necessary to pretend simply because three bottles of champagne at ten roubles a piece had been poured into the tureen along with ten bottles of rum at four roubles a piece, for a total of seventy roubles, in addition to the supper. So convinced was I of it all that I was quite amazed at the lecture the next day when those who had been at Baron Z.'s carousal were not only not ashamed to remember what they had done there, but even talked about it so the other students could hear. They said that it had been a most excellent carousal, that the Dorpat students were splendid fellows for such affairs, and that forty bottles of rum had been drunk by twenty people, many of whom had passed out under the tables. I couldn't see why they not only talked about it, but even made up lies against themselves.

FORTY

My Friendship with the Nekhlyudovs

That winter I not only saw a lot of Dmitry, who came by often, but also of his whole family, with whom I was becoming friends.

The Nekhlyudovs – mother, aunt and daughter – spent their evenings at home, and the princess liked to have young visitors – the sort of men who were, she said, able to pass an entire evening without cards or dancing. Evidently, however, there weren't many such men, since I rarely met any other guests there, although I visited the Nekhlyudovs nearly every evening. I got used to the people in the family, to their various moods, and formed a clear idea for myself of their mutual relations, grew accustomed to their rooms and furnishings and, when there weren't any other guests, felt completely at ease, except during the times I was alone with Varenka. It always seemed to me that as a not very beautiful young woman she should very much want me to fall in love with her. But that awkwardness with her soon began to pass, too. She showed so naturally that it made no difference to her whether she was talking to me or to her brother or to Lyubov Sergeyevna that I got into the habit of regarding her simply as someone with whom it was in no way shameful or dangerous to express the pleasure taken in her company. The whole time of my acquaintance with her she would, from one day to the next, seem to me to be either very ugly or not bad-looking at all, but never did I ask myself if I was in love with her. Although I did converse with her directly, I more often addressed my words to Lyubov Sergeyevna or to Dmitry in her presence, and I especially liked the second way. I took great pleasure in speaking in her presence, in listening to her sing and, indeed, in just knowing she was in the same room, but thoughts about what kind of relationship she and I might have later on, or daydreams about sacrificing myself for my friend, should he fall in love with my sister, now rarely occurred to me. And if they did, then being content with the present I would unconsciously avoid any thought of the future.

Yet for all that intimacy I continued to regard it my certain duty to conceal from all the Nekhlyudovs, but especially from Varenka, my real feelings and inclinations, and thus to present myself as a completely different young man than I actually was, or than I actually could have been. I tried to seem passionate and enthusiastic, to gasp in amazement and make impassioned gestures whenever I had supposedly taken a liking to something, but at the same time to appear indifferent to any unusual occurrence I witnessed or was told about. I also tried to be a fierce mocker for whom nothing was sacred, but at the same time a subtle observer, logical in all my actions, precise and painstaking, yet disdainful of everything material. I can safely say I was much better in reality than the strange creature I tried to make of myself, but all the same the Nekhlyudovs grew to like me, even as the person I pretended to be, although fortunately without, I think, believing any of the pretence. Only Lyubov Sergeyevna, who considered me a great egoist, atheist and mocker, didn't seem to like me, and often argued with me, got angry and baffled me with her incoherent, disjointed phrases. But Dmitry continued to have the same strange, more than friendly relations with her, and said that no one understood her, and that she had done an extraordinary amount of good for him. Their friendship continued to distress the rest of the family in exactly the same way as before.

Talking to me once about that relationship, so incomprehensible to everyone, Varenka explained it this way.

'Dmitry's vain. He's inordinately proud, and for all his cleverness very fond of praise and astonishment, and always likes to be first, and in the innocence of her heart *Auntie* is lost in admiration of him, and lacks the tact to hide it, and it comes out as flattery, only not feigned but sincere.'

Varenka's reasoning stayed with me and, considering it afterwards, I couldn't help thinking that she was very clever, and I gladly raised my opinion of her. But although that elevation, a result of the intellect and other qualities I had found in her, was carried out gladly, it was done with something like a strict sense of moderation, and never reached delight, the highest point of elevation. Thus, when Sofya Ivanovna, who never tired of talking about her niece, told me how four years before in the country when she was a child, Varenka had without permission given away all her dresses and shoes to peasant children, so that they had to be got back, I didn't at once see that fact as deserving a further elevation of my view of her, but instead silently scoffed at her for having such an impractical view of things.

When the Nekhlyudovs had other guests, with Volodya and Dubkov sometimes among them, I would withdraw into the background with a sort of calm, contented awareness of my place as a household member, and not take part in the conversations but merely listen to what the others were saying. And everything they said seemed so unbelievably inane that I was privately amazed at how people as clever and logical as the princess and her whole family could listen to those inanities and respond to them. If it had occurred to me then to compare what the others were saying with what I myself had said when I was alone with the Nekhlyudovs, I probably wouldn't have been amazed at all. And I would have been even less amazed, had I thought that our own Avdotya Vasilyevna, Lyubochka and Katenka were no different from other women and in no way inferior to them, or remembered the things that Dubkov, Katenka and Avdotya Vasilyevna spent whole evenings talking about with merry smiles, or how Dubkov, on taking exception to something, would almost every time recite with feeling the lines '*Au banquet de la vie, infortuné convive . . .*'[81] or passages from the 'Demon', and in general what rubbish all of them talked, and what pleasure it gave them for hours on end.

Varenka would obviously pay less attention to me when they had company than when we were alone, and then there would be neither the reading nor the music that I was so fond of listening to. When talking to guests, she lost for me her principal charm – her calm rationality and simplicity. I remember how oddly struck I was by the conversations she had with Volodya about the theatre and the weather. I knew that Volodya avoided and despised banalities more than anything in the world, and that Varenka, too, had always laughed at conversations feigning an interest in the weather, and so on – then why when they were together did they both constantly utter the most intolerable platitudes, and do so, moreover, as if they were ashamed of one another? Each time after those conversations I would be secretly furious with Varenka and the next day make fun of the previous evening's guests, but then find even greater pleasure in being alone again in the Nekhlyudov family circle.

Be that as it may, I was starting to find it more enjoyable to be with Dmitry in his mother's drawing room than alone by ourselves.

FORTY-ONE

My Friendship with Nekhlyudov

At the time, my friendship with Dmitry was in fact hanging by a thread. I had been thinking about him too long not to find flaws. In first youth we love passionately only those who are perfect, but as soon as the fog of passion little by little starts to lift, or the clear light of reason begins, in spite of us, to shine through the fog, so that we see the object of our passion as he is with his virtues and flaws, then those flaws, as something unexpected, stand out vividly, exaggeratedly, and our appetite for novelty and our hope that perfection may not be impossible in someone else spur not only a cooling but even a hostility towards our previous object of passion, and without regret we cast him aside and hurry on in search of new perfection. If that didn't happen to me in regard to Dmitry, then I owe it only to his stubborn, pedantic and more rational than heartfelt attachment, which I would have been ashamed to betray. We were, moreover, bound to each other by our strange rule of candour. Having grown apart, we were too afraid of leaving in each other's power all the shameful personal secrets we had confided, even though our rule of candour had obviously not been observed for a long time, and had often inhibited us and produced strange relations between us.

Almost every time I visited Dmitry that winter I would find there his university classmate Bezobedov, with whom he studied. Bezobedov was a skinny, pockmarked little person with tiny freckled hands and a mass of uncombed red hair, who was always dishevelled, dirty and ill-bred, and even a poor student. Dmitry's relationship with him, like the one with Lyubov Sergeyevna, made no sense to me. There was no one in the university who looked worse than Bezobedov, but that fact was probably the very reason why Dmitry had chosen him from among all his classmates, and took pleasure in offering him his friendship in defiance of everyone else. Expressed in all his relations with Bezobedov was the proud feeling, 'Well, it makes no difference to me who you are; everyone's the same to me, and if I like him, then that means he's all right.'

I was amazed at the ease with which Dmitry kept forcing himself, and the way the miserable Bezobedov put up with the awkwardnes of his position. I disliked that friendship very much.

Once I arrived at Dmitry's in order to spend the evening with him talking in his mother's drawing room and listening to Varenka sing or read, and found Bezobedov already upstairs. Dmitry curtly told me that he couldn't come down, since, as I could see, he had company.

'What fun is it down there, anyway?' he added. 'Much better to sit here and chat.' Even though the thought of spending two hours with Bezobedov didn't entice me at all, I couldn't bring myself to go down to the drawing room alone, and quietly irritated by my friend's quirks, I sat in a rocking chair and silently began to rock. I was annoyed with Dmitry and Bezobedov for depriving me of the pleasure of going downstairs, and I waited for Bezobedov's quick departure, and silently fumed at him and Dmitry as I listened to their conversation. 'Such a pleasant guest! Go ahead and sit with him!' I thought, after a servant brought tea and Dmitry had to ask Bezobedov five times to take a glass, since the timid fellow felt obliged to refuse the first and second and say, 'No, you go ahead.' Clearly forcing himself, Dmitry occupied his guest with conversation into which he tried in vain to draw me several times. I remained grimly silent.

'There's no point in that "Let no one suspect that I'm bored" face,' I mentally said to Dmitry, as I silently, steadily rocked. Taking a certain pleasure in it, I more and more fanned in myself a feeling of quiet loathing for my friend. 'What a fool,' I thought. 'He could spend an enjoyable evening with his nice relatives, but no, he's up here with this lout, and it's getting late and soon it will be too late to go down to the drawing room,' and I shot a glance at him from around the back of my chair. His arm and the way he was sitting and his neck and especially the back of his head and his knees seemed so repellent and offensive to me that I might that minute have enjoyed doing something mean to him, even something genuinely mean.

At last Bezobedov got up, but Dmitry couldn't just let such a pleasant guest go; he invited him to spend the night, which Bezobedov fortunately declined to do and left.

After seeing him out, Dmitry came back, rubbing his palms together with a smug little smile – very likely because he had stood firm yet had at last been delivered from boredom – and started to walk about the room, glancing at me from time to time. That was even more repellent. 'How dare he walk about and smile?' I thought.

'Why are you so angry?' he suddenly asked, stopping in front of me.

'I'm not angry at all,' I replied, as people invariably do in such situations, 'only it vexes me to see you pretending to me and to Bezobedov and to yourself.'

'What rubbish! I never pretend to anyone.'

'I haven't forgotten our rule of candour,' I said, 'and I'm telling you frankly how certain I am that you can't stand this Bezobedov any more than I can, because he's a dullard and goodness knows what else, but you enjoy showing off to him.'

'No! And in the first place, Bezobedov is an excellent person –'

'And I'm saying, you do! And I'll even say that your friendship with Lyubov Sergeyevna is also based on the fact that she considers you a god.'

'And I'm telling you it isn't.'

'And I'm telling you it is, because I recognize it in myself,' I answered with the heat of pent-up vexation, but still hoping to disarm him with that frank admission. 'I've told you before, and I'll repeat that it always seems to me that I'm fond of people who say pleasant things to me, but then when I take a good look at it, I see that there's no real affection, after all.'

'No,' Dmitry continued, adjusting his cravat with an angry movement of his chin, 'when I like someone, neither praise nor abuse can change the way I feel.'

'That's not true! When I admitted to you that after Papa called me trash, I hated him for it for a time and wished he were dead, in exactly the same way that you –'

'Speak for yourself. It's a pity if you're such a –'

'On the contrary!' I cried, jumping up from the chair and looking him in the eye with desperate pluck. 'What you're saying isn't good; did you really not say about my brother – I won't remind you what it was, because that would be unfair – but did you really not say to me . . . ? I'll tell you exactly how I understand you now.'

And trying to hurt him more painfully than he had hurt me, I started to prove to him that he didn't care about anyone, and said all the things with which I felt I had the right to reproach him. I was quite satisfied that I had said it all to him, completely forgetting that the only possible purpose for doing so – his admitting the flaws I had exposed – couldn't be achieved when he was angry. But when he was calm and might have acknowledged them, I never would have said anything.

The argument was already turning into a quarrel, when Dmitry suddenly fell silent and walked away from me into the other room. Continuing to speak, I started after him, but he ignored me. I knew that a quick temper was in his column of vices, and that he was now trying to get a hold of himself. I cursed all his lists.

So that's what our rule about 'telling each other everything we felt, and never telling anyone else about each other' had led to. In our enthusiasm for candour we had sometimes made the most disgraceful admissions, shamefully passing off an assumption or daydream as a desire or feeling – for example, what I had just said to him then. And those admissions not only failed to strengthen the bond between us, but dried up our feeling for each other and pushed us apart, and now pride had suddenly kept him from making the most trivial admission, and in the heat of our argument we had made use of weapons that we ourselves had given each other, and that inflicted terrific pain.

FORTY-TWO

Our Stepmother

Although Papa hadn't meant to bring his wife to Moscow until the new year, he came in October, in the autumn, when there was still excellent riding to be had with the dogs. He had changed his mind, he said, because a case of his was supposed to be heard in the Senate,[82] but Mimi's version was that Avdotya Vasilyevna had been so bored in the country, had talked so much about Moscow and had pretended to be so unwell that Papa had decided to carry out her wish.

'Because she never loved him, but only buzzed about her love in everyone's ears, so she could marry a rich man,' Mimi added with a wistful sigh, as if to say, 'Not what *some people* would have done for him, had he been able to appreciate them.'

Some people were unfair to Avdotya Vasilyevna. Her love for Papa, a passionate, devoted, self-immolating love, was apparent in her every word, gesture and glance. But that love didn't at all keep her, along with her desire not to be separated from her beloved husband, from wanting an extraordinary bonnet from Madame Annette's, or a hat with an extraordinary light-blue ostrich feather, or a dark-blue dress of Venetian velvet that would artfully display her graceful white bosom and arms, till then revealed to no one but her husband and the chambermaids. Katenka took her mother's side, obviously, whereas strange, facetious relations were immediately established between us and our stepmother from the day of her arrival. No sooner had she stepped from the coach than Volodya shambled over to her with a solemn face and vacant look and said with a bow and a scrape, as if he were introducing someone, 'I have the honour to welcome our sweet mama and kiss her hand.'

'Ah, dear little son!' Avdotya Vasilyevna said, smiling her beautiful, unchanging smile.

'Don't forget your second little son,' I said, going over to her, too, and trying, in spite of myself, to imitate Volodya's voice and demeanour.

If we and our stepmother had been confident of our mutual attachment, that demeanour might have meant casualness about showing signs of affection; if we had been ill-disposed towards each other, it might have meant irony, a contempt for dissembling or a desire to hide our real attitude from Papa, who was standing nearby; or it might have meant any number of other thoughts and feelings. But in the present instance that expression, which was very much in keeping with Avdotya Vasilyevna's own spirit, meant exactly nothing and served only to conceal the absence of any relations at all. Afterwards, I often noticed falsely jovial relations of the kind in other families, where the members had a premonition that the true relations might not be very good, but between us and Avdotya Vasilyevna those relations were established involuntarily. We almost never departed from them, and were invariably affectedly courteous with her, spoke French, bowed and scraped and called her *chère maman*, to which she always replied with jokes of the same kind and her beautiful, unchanging smile. The tearful Lyubochka, with her bandy legs and guileless conversation, was the only one who came to love our stepmother, and she tried quite naïvely and sometimes awkwardly to bring her into closer relations with the rest of us; in return, the only one in the whole world for whom, besides her passionate love for Papa, Avdotya Vasilyevna had even a drop of affection was Lyubochka. Avdotya Vasilyevna even treated her with a kind of delighted wonder and deferential respect that quite astonished me.

In the beginning, Avdotya Vasilyevna often liked to refer, while identifying herself as a stepmother, to how children and other household members always regard such a person badly and unjustly, and how difficult her own position was as a result. Yet even though she foresaw all the unpleasantness of that position, she did nothing to avoid it: to be affectionate with one, to give gifts to another, not to be peevish, all of which would have been quite easy for her, since she was by nature undemanding and very kind. Not only did she not do any of that, however, but on the contrary, in anticipation of the unpleasantness of her position, although without any provocation, she mounted her defence and, in assuming that the whole household wanted to do nasty things to her and insult her in every way, she saw design in everything and concluded that the most dignified thing would be for her to endure it all in silence, by her inaction obviously not gaining any love, but not provoking any hostility either. There was, moreover, so little capacity in her for that 'understanding' of which I've already spoken, and which was developed to the highest degree in our family, and her habits were so at odds with those that had taken root among us, that she was for those reasons alone already at a disadvantage. In our orderly home with its regular routine she continued to live as if she had just moved in: she got up and went to bed sometimes early and sometimes late, she came out for dinner or she didn't, she had supper or she didn't. When there wasn't any company, she almost always went around half-dressed and wasn't embarrassed to be seen by us and even the servants in a white underskirt with a shawl thrown over her bare arms. At first I liked that simplicity, but then, because of it, I quickly lost the remaining respect I had for her. Even stranger to us was that she was two completely different women with company and without: the first, in its presence, was a youthful, healthy, cold beauty, superbly dressed, neither clever nor stupid, but gay; the second, in its absence, was a worn-out, melancholy, no longer young woman, sloppy and bored, although loving. Seeing her flushed from the cold, smiling and happy in the awareness of her beauty as she came back from calls and, after removing her hat, went to look at herself in the mirror; or embarrassed yet proud before the servants as she went out to the coach with a rustle of her magnificent low-cut ball gown; or at the little soirées at home in a high-necked silk dress with exquisite lace next to her tender skin as she beamed her beautiful, unchanging smile in every direction – seeing her like that, I would often wonder what those who were delighted with her would have said, had they seen her as I did when, spending the evening at home waiting for her husband to come back from

the club after midnight, she would walk around the dimly lit
rooms like a wraith in some house wrap with her hair uncombed.
She would go over to the piano and, frowning with effort, play
on it the only waltz she knew, or pick up a novel and, after reading a few lines from the middle, throw it down, or, not wanting
to disturb the servants, go into the pantry by herself to get a
pickle or some cold veal and eat it while standing next to the
little pantry window, or, tired and depressed again, aimlessly
wander from room to room. But what estranged her and us most
was the lack of 'understanding', which was mainly expressed in
her characteristic manner of gracious attention, whenever others
spoke to her of things beyond her grasp. It wasn't her fault that
it had become an unconscious habit to smile slightly with just
her lips and to tip her head to the side whenever she was told
things that were of little interest to her (and besides herself and
her husband, nothing interested her), but that smile and tipping
of her head, constantly repeated, became unbearable. Her merriment, as if laughing at itself, at you and at all of society, was
awkward, too, and failed to communicate itself to anyone, and
her sensitivity was much too affected. But the chief thing was
that she wasn't ashamed to talk constantly to any and all about
her love for Papa. Although she was certainly telling the truth
when she said that her love for her husband was her whole life,
and although she proved it with her whole life, the incessant,
unselfconscious repetition of it was, to our way of thinking,
offensive, and we were embarrassed for her whenever she spoke
of it in front of strangers – even more embarrassed than we were
about her mistakes in French.

She loved her husband more than anything in the world, and
her husband loved her, especially in the beginning when he saw
that he wasn't the only one who was pleased with her. Her one
purpose in life had been to obtain her husband's love, yet she
seemed to do on purpose what could only be unpleasant for
him, and all of it with the goal of proving to him the whole
power of her love and her readiness for self-sacrifice.

She loved finery, and my father enjoyed seeing her in society
as a beauty who elicited astonishment and praise, yet she sacrificed her passion for finery for his sake, and got more and more

used to staying home in a grey smock. Papa, who had always considered freedom and equality essential conditions of family relations, hoped that his favourite Lyubochka and his good young wife would become sincere friends, but Avdotya Vasilyevna sacrificed herself, and felt it necessary to treat the 'real mistress of the house', as she called Lyubochka, with unseemly deference, which painfully offended Papa. He gambled a lot that winter, towards the end losing a great deal, and not wishing, as ever, to mix his gambling and his family life, he kept his gambling affairs to himself. Avdotya Vasilyevna sacrificed herself, and although sometimes unwell and towards the end of the winter even pregnant, she considered it her duty to totter out to meet Papa in her grey smock with her hair uncombed, even at four or five in the morning, when he, sometimes worn out and ashamed of his losses, came back from the club after the eighth fine.[83] She would absently ask him if his luck had been good, and then listen with gracious attention and a smile and a nod to what he told her about his activities at the club, and to his asking her for the hundredth time never to wait up for him. Yet although the losses and gains, on which, according to his play, Papa's whole fortune depended, didn't interest her in the least, she would once again be the first every night to meet him when he came back from the club. Besides her passion for self-sacrifice, she was impelled to those meetings by the still hidden jealousy from which she suffered to an intense degree. No one in the world could have convinced her that Papa was coming back from the club and not from a lover. She tried to detect in his face his amorous secrets and, finding nothing there, would sigh with a certain pleasure in her sorrow, and indulge in the contemplation of her unhappiness.

As a result of those and many other unceasing sacrifices, there was in Papa's treatment of his wife in the last months of that winter, during which he lost a great deal and was out of sorts most of the time, an intermittent feeling of 'quiet loathing' – a sort of stifled aversion to the object of his affection that was manifest in an unconscious urge to inflict on it every kind of petty mental distress.

FORTY-THREE
New Comrades

The winter had passed imperceptibly, the thaw had come and the examination schedule had already been posted, when I suddenly remembered that I would have to answer about the eighteen subjects for which I had gone to lectures without listening, taking notes or preparing a single one. It's strange that a question as obvious as how I would pass my examinations never occurred to me. But I was in such a fog that whole winter from my delight at being grown-up and *comme il faut* that when the question of how I would pass finally did occur to me, I compared myself to my classmates and thought, 'Well, they'll have to take examinations, too, and most of them aren't *comme il faut*, which means that I'll have another advantage over them and will certainly pass.' The only reason I even attended the lectures was because I had got used to it, and because Papa ordered me out of the house. I also had many acquaintances at the university and often enjoyed myself there. I liked the noise and talk and laughter in the lecture halls, and sitting on the rear bench during lectures and daydreaming and observing my classmates with the drone of the professor's voice in the background, or running off from time to time to Materne's[84] for vodka and a snack with someone, and then, aware that I could be rebuked for it, entering the lecture room after the professor with a cautious squeak of the door. I also liked taking part in pranks as one boisterous class after another filled the hallways. It was all great fun.

When everyone started coming to lectures more regularly, and the physics professor had concluded his course and taken leave of us until the examination, and the students had collected their copybooks and begun to study in small groups, I sensed that I, too, should be studying. Operov, with whom I remained on bowing terms, even though our relations had been very cool, not only offered to share his copybooks but also invited me to study with him and some other students, as I've mentioned. I expressed my thanks and agreed to do so, hoping by that honour to smooth over our earlier rift completely, and asking only that they be sure to come each time to my house, since I had good rooms.

Their answer was that we would take turns, studying first at one person's place and then at another's, and wherever was closer. The first time was at Zukhin's, a little room behind a partition in a large building on Trubnoy Boulevard.[85] I arrived late that first day after they had already begun to read. The little room was filled with smoke, and not even from decent tobacco, but from the cheap shag Zukhin was using. On the table were a decanter of vodka, a wineglass, bread, salt and a mutton bone.

Without getting up, Zukhin invited me to help myself to some vodka and take off my frock coat.

'You aren't used to such fare, I think,' he added.

They were all wearing dirty calico shirts and dickies. Trying not to show my disdain, I removed my coat and lay down on the sofa in a 'comradely' way. Only occasionally consulting the copybooks, Zukhin recited, while the others broke in with questions, which he answered concisely, cleverly and exactly. I started to listen and, not understanding much, since I didn't know what had preceded it, I asked a question.

'You shouldn't even listen, old man, if you don't know that,' Zukhin said. 'I'll give you the copybooks and you can go over it for tomorrow; otherwise, there's no use explaining.'

I started to feel ashamed of my ignorance, but feeling, too, that Zukhin's comment was fair, I stopped listening and occupied myself with observing those new comrades. In the subdivision of people into *comme il faut* and not *comme il faut* they belonged, obviously, to the second category, and as a result provoked not only disdain in me but also a certain resentment, since even though they weren't *comme il faut*, they still seemed to regard me as an equal and even to patronize me in a good-natured way. The disdain was in reaction to their feet and dirty hands and chewed fingernails, the long nail Operov had let grow on his little finger, their pink shirts and dickies, the abuse which they affectionately directed at each other, the filthy room, Zukhin's habit of constantly blowing his nose while pressing one nostril with his finger, but especially their speech, their way of using and stressing certain words. For instance, they would say 'cretin' instead of 'fool', 'as though' instead of 'as if', 'magnificent' instead of 'excellent', 'propulsive' instead of 'driving', and the like, which seemed uncouth and bookish to me. But that *comme if faut* resentment was provoked even more by the stress they gave to certain Russian and especially foreign words: they said 'máchine' and not 'machíne', 'enterprísing' and not 'énterprising', 'íntentionally' and not 'inténtionally', 'firepláce' and not 'fíreplace', 'Shakespéare' and not 'Shákespeare', and so on and so forth.

However, despite their insurmountably repellent appearance for me then, I did have a sense of something good in those people and, envying the merry camaraderie that united them, I was drawn to them and wanted to be closer to them, as hard as it was for me. The meek, honest Operov I already knew, but I now took an extraordinary liking to the lively, exceptionally clever Zukhin, who was evidently the leader of the circle. He was a short, stocky brunet with a slightly plump and always shiny but extraordinarily clever, animated and independent face, whose expression came mainly from the not high but prominent brow that extended over his deep-set dark eyes, his short bristly hair and his heavy dark beard, which always looked unshaven. He appeared not to think about himself (which I've always especially liked in people), but it was clear that his mind was always engaged. He had one of those expressive faces that a few hours after you've first seen them will all of a sudden take on a completely different cast. That happened to me with Zukhin towards the end of the evening. New lines appeared in his face, his eyes sank deeper, his smile changed and his whole aspect was so altered that it was hard for me to recognize him as the same person.

After we had finished reading, Zukhin, the other students and I each drank a glass of vodka in proof of our wish to become comrades, and almost completely emptied the decanter. Zukhin asked if anyone had a twenty-five kopek piece, so the old woman who looked after him could go out for more. I offered my own money, but Zukhin, as if not hearing me, turned to Operov, who got out a beaded coin purse and gave him the required sum.

'Watch out you don't start drinking,' said Operov, who hadn't drunk anything himself.

'Have no fear,' Zukhin answered, sucking the marrow from the mutton bone. I remember thinking then, 'The reason he's so clever is that he eats a lot of marrow.'[86] 'Have no fear,' Zukhin said again with a little smile, and his smile was the kind that you involuntarily notice and are grateful for, 'although if I should, it won't be a disaster. But now we'll see, brother, who gets the better of whom, he or I. It's all in here, brother,' he added, boastfully tapping himself on the forehead. 'Semyonov's the one who ought to worry, since he's been drinking pretty hard.'

It was, in fact, the same Semyonov with the grey hair who had cheered me at the first examination by looking worse than I did, and who had been ranked second in the entrance examinations. In the first month of his studenthood he had faithfully come to all the lectures, but then just before the beginning of the review period he had started to drink, and by the end of the term he was no longer to be seen at the university at all.

'Where is he?' someone asked.

'I've lost track,' Zukhin replied. 'The last I saw of him was when he and I tore up the Lisbon[87] together. That was a magnificent thing! And then there was some incident, apparently. What a brain! What fire in the fellow! What an intellect! It will be a pity if he fails. But fail he certainly will, since with his urges he's not the kind to stick around the university.'

After talking a while longer and agreeing to meet the following days at Zukhin's, since his place was the closest for everyone, we went our separate ways. When we were outside, it embarrassed me a little that the rest of them were walking, while I alone had a droshky, so I sheepishly offered Operov a ride. Zukhin had come outside with us and, after borrowing a silver rouble from Operov, went off somewhere by himself to spend the night. As we were driving, Operov told me a lot about

Zukhin's character and way of life, and after I got home I lay
awake a long time thinking about my new acquaintances. Before
falling asleep, I wavered a long time between, on the one hand,
the respect to which their knowledge, simplicity, honesty and
the poetry of their youth and daring inclined me, and on the
other, their uncouth appearance, which repelled me. For all my
desire to do so, it was at the time simply impossible for me to
be close to them. We had a completely different understanding
of things. There were numerous nuances that constituted the
whole charm and meaning of life for me, but that were completely
unintelligible to them, and vice versa. The main reason for the
impossibility of intimacy, however, was the twenty-rouble cloth
of my frock coat, my droshky and my fine linen shirt. That reason
was especially important to me: it seemed to me that I was
involuntarily insulting them with the signs of my wealth. I felt
guilty around them and, first abasing myself and then chafing
at the unfairness of it and shifting to arrogance, I couldn't in
any way enter into equal, sincere relations with them. And the
rough, profligate side of Zukhin's character was at the time so
muffled for me by the strong poetry of daring I sensed in him
that it didn't affect me unpleasantly at all.

For the next two weeks I went almost every evening to
Zukhin's to study with them. I studied very little, because, as
I've already said, I had fallen behind and, not having the strength
to work by myself to catch up with them, I only pretended to
listen to and understand what they were reading. I think they
saw through my dissembling, since I noticed that they often left
out the parts they themselves already knew and never asked me
any questions.

Drawn into their way of life and finding so much in it that
was poetic, I became more tolerant of the uncouthness of that
circle with each passing day. Only my word of honour to Dmitry
not to go drinking with them kept me from taking part in their
pleasures.

Once I wanted to boast to them of my knowledge of literature,
especially French literature, and started a conversation on the
topic. To my surprise, it turned out that although they used the
Russian titles of the foreign works, they had read a great deal

more than I had, and knew and appreciated English and even
Spanish authors and Lesage,[88] whom I hadn't even heard of
before that. Pushkin and Zhukovsky[89] were literature for them
and not, as they were for me, books in yellow bindings read and
learned in childhood. They held Dumas, Sue and Féval[90] in
equally low regard, and judged literature much better and more
clearly than I did, especially Zukhin, as I couldn't help admitting.
I had no advantage over them in my knowledge of music, either.
To my even greater surprise, Operov played the violin, another
student studying with us played the cello and the piano, and
both of them were members of the university orchestra and had
a respectable knowledge and appreciation of good music. In a
word, except for my pronunciation of French and German,
everything that I had intended to boast to them about they knew
better than I, and weren't conceited about at all. I might have
boasted of my position in society, but unlike Volodya I had none.
So what was the pinnacle from which I regarded them? My
acquaintance with Prince Ivan Ivanych? My pronunciation of
French? My droshky? My fine linen shirt? My fingernails? Wasn't
it all just rubbish? Or so it would sometimes dimly begin to seem
to me under the influence of my envy of the camaraderie and
good-natured youthful merriment I saw before me. They were
all on familiar terms. The simplicity of their treatment of each
other verged on rudeness, yet always apparent beneath that
rough exterior was a fear of offending each other even a little.
'Scoundrel' or 'swine', although used by them in an affectionate
way, only grated on me and gave me a pretext for inward scoff-
ing, but the words didn't offend them or keep them from being
on the friendliest and most sincere footing. They were very tact-
ful and circumspect in their treatment of each other, as only
happens with the very poor and the very young. But the main
thing was the sense I had of something generous and wild in
Zukhin's character, and in his adventures at the Lisbon. I had
an intimation that those bouts had been quite different from the
humbug with the flaming rum and champagne that I had
witnessed at Baron Z.'s.

FORTY-FOUR

Zukhin and Semyonov

I don't know which caste Zukhin belonged to, but I do know that he was from the S. gymnasium, had no means at all, and seemed not to be a nobleman. He was at the time around eighteen, although he looked much older. He was exceptionally clever and quick: it was easier for him to take in an entire complex subject at once, anticipating all its components and corollaries, than arrive by conscious deliberation at the laws from which those corollaries had been deduced. He knew he was clever and was proud of it, and as a result of that pride he treated everyone in the same straightforward, good-natured way. He had very likely experienced a great deal in his life. Love, friendship, business and money were already reflected in his passionate, receptive nature. Whether in small measure or in the lowest strata of society, there was nothing, once he had experienced it, that he wouldn't have regarded either with contempt or with a kind of indifference and lack of concern produced by the too great ease with which everything came to him. It seemed that he undertook everything new with such ardour merely to be able, after he had achieved his goal, to scorn whatever it was he had achieved, and his capable nature always achieved the goal and thus obtained the right to scorn it. It was the same with his studies: working little, taking no notes, he knew mathematics superbly, and wasn't boasting when he said he would get the better of the professor. It seemed to him there was a lot of nonsense in what he was taught, but with the unconscious practical cunning characteristic of his nature, he immediately went along with whatever the professors required, and they all liked him. He was direct in his relations with the authorities, and the authorities respected him.

He not only didn't like and respect his own field, but even regarded with contempt anyone who seriously studied what had come so easily to him. The sciences, as he understood them, didn't engage a tenth part of his ability; life in his student's position offered him nothing to which he might have completely devoted himself, but his ardent, 'enterprising' (as he would have said) nature demanded life, and he gave himself up to whatever drinking his means permitted, surrendering to it with passionate fervour and a desire to use himself up to 'the limit of my strength'. And then, just before the examinations, Operov's prediction came true. Zukhin disappeared for a couple of weeks, so that towards the end we studied at another student's. But then pale, dissipated, with trembling hands, he arrived in the auditorium for his first examination and passed on to the second year in brilliant form.

At the beginning of the year there had been eight or so in Zukhin's band of revellers. Among them were Ikonin and Semyonov, but the first withdrew because he couldn't tolerate the frantic revelry to which they devoted themselves, while the second left because it seemed insufficient to him. Everyone regarded them with something like awe and told each other stories about their escapades.

The escapades' main heroes were Zukhin and, towards the end of the year, Semyonov. Everyone eventually came to look on the latter even with a kind of horror, and when he turned up at the lectures, which happened infrequently enough, there was excitement in the room.

Semyonov ended his drinking career just before the examinations in a most energetic and original way, as I myself witnessed, thanks to my acquaintance with Zukhin. Here's what happened. One evening just after we had all gathered at Zukhin's, and Operov had placed a tallow candle in a bottle next to himself to go with the one already there in a candlestick, and then lowered his head over the minuscule handwriting in his physics copybook and begun to read in his thin little voice, the landlady came in to tell Zukhin that someone was there with a message for him.

Zukhin went out and quickly returned with a thoughtful

expression on his face and two ten-rouble notes in his hand, along with the opened message written on grey wrapping paper.

'Gentlemen! An extraordinary event!' he said, raising his head and looking at us with something like a triumphantly serious gaze.

'Did you get some tutoring money?' Operov asked as he leafed through his copybook.

'Let's get on with the reading,' someone else said.

'No, gentlemen! No more reading for me,' Zukhin continued in the same tone. 'I tell you, it's an inconceivable event! Semyonov has sent a soldier with twenty roubles he borrowed from me once, and written that if I want to see him, I had better come to the barracks. Do you realize what this means?' he added, looking at each of us in turn. We were all silent. 'I'm going over to see him right now,' Zukhin continued. 'Anyone who wants to can come along.'

We immediately put our frock coats back on and got ready to visit Semyonov.

'Won't it be awkward,' Operov asked in his thin little voice, 'if we all barge in and stare at him like some curiosity?'

I completely agreed with Operov's observation, especially as it concerned me, since I was barely acquainted with Semyonov, but it was such a pleasure to know that I was taking part in a shared comradely activity, and I so wanted to see Semyonov himself, that I didn't say anything.

'Rubbish!' Zukhin said. 'What's so awkward about going to say goodbye to a comrade, wherever he might be? It's nothing. Anyone who wants to can come.'

We hired cabs, put the soldier in with us, and set off. The duty non-commissioned officer didn't want to let us in, but Zukhin somehow persuaded him, and the soldier who had brought the message led us to a large room, dark except for the faint illumination of a few night lamps, with bunks along either side on which new recruits with shaven foreheads were sitting or lying in grey overcoats. I had been struck on entering the barracks by a particularly oppressive smell and by the sound of several hundred people snoring, and, as we crossed the room between the bunks

behind our guide and Zukhin, who with a firm stride went on
ahead, I peered anxiously at each recruit, applying what remained
in my memory of the hardy, solidly built figure of Semyonov
with his long, tousled, almost grey hair, white teeth and sombre,
gleaming eyes. In the farthest corner of the barracks near the
last little clay pot filled with dark oil in which a charred and
twisted wick dimly smoked, Zukhin quickened his pace and then
suddenly stopped.

'Hello, Semyonov,' he said to a recruit with a shaven forehead
like the others, who was sitting in heavy soldier's long underwear
with a grey overcoat over his shoulders and his feet on the bunk,
while talking to another recruit and eating something. It was
him with his grey hair cropped short and his forehead shaved
blue, yet with the same sombre, energetic expression that his
face always had. Afraid that my staring might offend him, I
looked away. Operov, seeming to share my opinion, stood behind
everyone else, but the sound of Semyonov's voice and of his
customary clipped speech as he greeted Zukhin and the others
put us completely at ease, and we hurried forward to extend – I
my hand, and Operov his 'little board', but as we were doing
that, Semyonov reached out with his own large, dark hand,
thereby sparing us the unpleasant feeling of seeming to do him
an honour. He spoke reluctantly and calmly, as always.

'Hello, Zukhin. Thanks for coming. Sit down, gentlemen! Let
them, Kudryashka,' he said to the recruit with whom he had
been having supper and talking. 'You and I will finish our conversation later. Go ahead and sit down. So, were you surprised,
Zukhin? Eh?'

'Nothing you've ever done has surprised me,' Zukhin
answered, sitting beside him on the bunk with an expression
rather like that of a doctor sitting down on the bed of a patient,
'although I would have been if you had turned up for the examinations – that I can say. Well, tell us where you went off to, and
how this all came about.'

'Where did I go off to?' Semyonov answered in his deep,
strong voice. 'I went off to taverns, pot-houses and inns, for the
most part. Sit down, gentlemen, all of you, there's plenty of room.
Pull your legs up there, you!' he yelled commandingly, revealing

his white teeth for an instant, at a recruit who was lying on the bunk to his left and watching us with idle curiosity, his hands behind his head. 'Well, I was on a spree. A bad one. But good,' he continued, with each clipped sentence changing the expression on his energetic face. 'You know about the incident with the merchant. The rascal died. They wanted to kick me out. What little money I had, I squandered. But all that would have been nothing. A huge pile of debts remained – and nasty ones. I had no way to pay them. Well, that's it.'

'How did you ever come up with such an idea?' Zukhin asked.

'This way: I was on a spree at the Yaroslavl, you know, on Stozhenka,[91] with some merchant gent. He was a recruit supplier.[92] I said, "Give me a thousand roubles and I'll go." And I did.'

'But how could that be? – you're a nobleman,' Zukhin said.

'That was nothing! Kirill Ivanov made all the arrangements.'

'Who's Kirill Ivanov?'

'The one who bought me,' he said with a strange, amused, mocking glint in his eyes, and what looked like a smile. 'They got permission from the Senate.[93] I had another spree, paid off my debts and went. That's all there is to it. After all, they can't flog me[94] . . . I've got five roubles left . . . Perhaps there'll be a war . . .'

And then with a sombre gleam in his eyes and a constantly changing expression on his energetic face, he started to tell Zukhin about his strange, incomprehensible adventures.

When they wouldn't let us stay in the barracks any longer, we began to say our goodbyes. He shook all our hands with a firm grip and without getting up to see us out he said, 'Come again sometime, gentlemen. They say they won't move us out until next month,' he added, once more seeming to smile.

Zukhin moved a few steps away, then turned back. Wanting to see their parting, I stopped, too, and saw Zukhin take some money out of his pocket and offer it, but Semyonov pushed his hand away. Then I saw them embrace and heard Zukhin say quite loudly as he came back towards us, 'Farewell, Wizard! It's certain I won't finish the year, but you'll be an officer.'

Semyonov, who never laughed, responded with loud, ringing laughter that struck me extraordinarily painfully. We left.

The whole way home, which we walked, Zukhin remained silent and kept lightly blowing his nose, putting his finger first to one nostril and then to the other. When we arrived at his place he immediately left us, and drank from that day until the examinations began.

FORTY-FIVE

I Fail

At last it was time for the first examination, on differential and integral calculus, but I was still in a strange fog with no clear account to myself of what awaited me. The idea would occur to me in the evenings after the society of Zukhin and my other classmates that I needed to change something about my convictions, that something about them was wrong and not good, but the next morning in the light of day I would be *comme il faut* again and quite satisfied with that, and not want to make any changes in myself at all.

It was in that mood that I arrived for the first examination. I sat down on a bench on the side where the princes, counts and barons were sitting and started to speak to them in French, and, strange as it is to say, the thought never entered my mind that I would soon have to answer on a subject about which I knew nothing. I casually watched those going up to be examined and even allowed myself to taunt a few of them.

'Well, then Grap,' I said to Ilenka as he came back from the table, 'were you scared to death?'

'Let's see how you do,' he replied. Since entering the university, Ilenka had completely rebelled against my influence, didn't smile when I spoke to him and was ill disposed towards me.

I smiled scornfully at Ilenka's reply, although the doubt he expressed did scare me for a moment. But the fog covered up the feeling again, and I remained disengaged and indifferent, even promising to go for a snack at Materne's with Baron Z. as soon as I had been examined – as if the latter were the most trivial thing. When I was called up with Ikonin, I straightened the skirts of my uniform and coolly went up to the examination table.

A slight shiver of fear ran down my spine only when the young professor, the same one who had given me the entrance examination, looked directly at me as I reached for the postal paper on which the questions had been written. Ikonin, although he took his question with the same swing of his body as at the previous examinations, did answer something, if very poorly, while I did what he had done at the entrance examinations, but did it even worse, since I took another question and had no answer for that one either. The professor looked at me with regret and then said in a quiet but firm voice, 'You won't pass into the second year, Mr Irtenyev. Don't bother to come to the other examinations. The department needs to be weeded out. The same goes for you, Mr Ikonin,' he added.

Ikonin begged as if for alms for permission to be re-examined, but the professor replied that he couldn't do in two days what he had failed to do in the course of a year, and there was no way he would pass on. Ikonin implored him again, mournfully, abjectly, but the professor again refused.

'You may go, gentlemen,' he said in the same quiet but firm voice.

It was only then that I decided to step away from the table, ashamed that by my presence I had seemed to be a party to Ikonin's demeaning pleas. I don't remember crossing the hall past the other students, or what I replied to their questions, or going out to the foyer, or how I got home. I was insulted, humiliated and truly unhappy.

I didn't come out of my room for three days, saw no one, found pleasure in tears, just as I had in childhood, and cried a great deal. I looked for pistols with which to shoot myself, should I really want to. I thought that Ilenka Grap would spit in my face if he ran into me, and would be right to do so, that Operov would be glad of my disaster and tell everyone about it, that Kolpikov had been absolutely right to disgrace me at Yar's, that my inane chatter with the young Princess Kornakova couldn't have ended any differently, and so on and so forth. All the painful, humiliating moments in my life came back to me one after another, and I tried to find someone else to blame for my unhappiness: I decided it had all been done on purpose, and invented a whole intrigue to thwart me, and muttered against my professors, my classmates, Volodya, Dmitry and Papa, too, for having sent me to the university, and against Providence for having let me live to see such a disgrace. Finally, sensing my utter downfall in the eyes of everyone who knew me, I asked Papa to let me join the hussars or go to the Caucasus. He was displeased with me, but seeing my anguish, he consoled me by saying that however bad it might be, it could all still be made right if I transferred to another department. Volodya, who didn't see anything so awful in my misfortune either, said that at least in another department I wouldn't be ashamed in front of my new classmates.

Our ladies didn't understand at all, and either didn't want to or were unable to grasp what an examination was, and what to pass one meant, and were only sorry for me because they could see my grief.

Dmitry came by every day and was extraordinarily affectionate and mild the whole time, although it did for that very reason seem to me that his feelings for me had cooled. It was painful and insulting that on coming up to my room, he would sit down beside me without a word but with a little of the demeanour of a doctor at the bedside of a gravely ill patient. Sofya Ivanovna and Varenka sent books with him that I had wanted, and asked me to come and see them, although in their solicitude I saw proud – and for me insulting – condescension to someone who had already slipped too far. After three days I grew somewhat calmer, although I still didn't go out anywhere until we left for the country, but instead wandered aimlessly from room to room brooding about my calamity and trying to avoid the rest of the household.

I brooded and brooded, and finally late one night as I was sitting downstairs by myself listening to Avdotya Vasilyevna play her waltz, I suddenly jumped to my feet, ran upstairs, got out the booklet in which I had written my *Rules of Life*, opened it and was overcome with remorse and a sense of moral urgency. I began to weep, but no longer tears of despair. Recovering, I resolved to rewrite my rules of life, quite certain that I would never do anything bad, nor spend a single moment in idleness, nor ever betray my rules again.

Whether that urgency would last, what it consisted of and what new foundations it laid for my spiritual development, I'll tell in the next, happier part of youth.[95]

24 September 1856
Yasnaya Polyana[96]

Notes

CHILDHOOD

1. *Auf, Kinder, auf*: 'Up, children, up.' *'S ist Zeit*: 'It's time.' *Die Mutter ist schon im Saal*: 'Mother's already in the salon.'
2. *Nu, nun, Faulenzer*: 'Well, then, lazybones.'
3. *Ach, lassen Sie*: 'Oh, leave me alone.'
4. *Sind Sie bald fertig?*: 'Will you be ready soon?'
5. *Histoire des voyages* (*History of Travels*, Paris, 1746–52): The two volumes are from the fifteen-volume *Histoire générale des voyages, ou nouvelle collection de toutes les relations des voyages par mer et par terre* (*General History of Travels, or New Collection of All Accounts of Travel by Land and Sea*) by the Abbé Prévost (1697–1763). The presence on the shelf of even a remnant of that monumental series may be taken as a sign of the broad European culture of the Irtenyev family and milieu, and perhaps of their Enlightenment sympathies.
6. *Seven Years War* (1756–63): Fought in Europe, India and North America between France, Austria, Russia, Saxony and Sweden on the one side, and Prussia, England and Hanover on the other.
7. *Northern Bee* (*Severnaya pchela*): An influential newspaper of patriotic stamp published in St Petersburg from 1825 to 1864 by the journalist and novelist Faddey Bulgarin (1789–1859). The country's first privately owned periodical, it was addressed to the emergent middle class and offered political news and literary reviews, as well as works by the leading writers of the day, beginning with the poet Alexander Pushkin (1799–1837).
8. *Lieber Karl Ivanych*: 'Dear Karl Ivanych.'
9. *dinner* (*obed*): The principal meal of the day, served early to mid-afternoon and consisting of at least three courses, starting with soup. As Tolstoy makes clear here and elsewhere, the meal had

an important social as well as nutritional function, being the only time during the day when the entire family came together.

10. *études by Clementi*: The études or exercises of the distinguished Italian composer, piano virtuoso, conductor, music publisher, piano manufacturer, piano teacher and long-time London resident Muzio Clementi (1752–1832) remain standard works of musical pedagogy.

11. *Ich danke*: 'I thank you.'

12. *trustee bank (sokhrannaya kazna)*: The large-scale financial arm of the Trustee *Council (Sovet opekunsky)*, which offered the nobility and other landowners long-term, low-interest mortgages secured by 'stone' buildings, factories and estates, including the serfs residing thereon. It is implied that Papa is expecting the disbursement of new loans to help pay off an older one, and that the family's properties are of substantial size, given the sums in question.

13. *Wo kommen sie her?*: 'Where are you coming from?' *Ich komme vom Kaffeehaus*: 'I'm coming from the coffee house.' *Haben Sie die Zeitung nicht gelesen?*: 'Haven't you read the paper?'

14. *Nikolay nodded affirmatively*: The energy of his descriptive impulse bursting a structural seam, Tolstoy shifts here and in the rest of the account of the conversation in Nikolay's room from the limited, first-person mode generally employed in the trilogy (whereby the narrator recounts only what he himself has witnessed or been told) to an omniscient mode, since with the door closed (and moreover closed twice) the eavesdropping Nikolenka could not have seen Karl Ivanych and Nikolay's gestures and postures, or what Nikolay was doing with his hands. The logical lapse is brief and of little importance, but it reminds us that for all the young author's extraordinary insight and skill, his narrative technique, at least in this early episode, was not yet under perfect control.

15. *Von al-len Lei-den-schaf-ten die grau-samste ist . . . Haben sie geschrieben?*: 'Of all pas-sions the cru-el-lest . . . Have you written that?' *Die grausamste ist die Un-dank-bar-keit . . . Ein grosses U*: 'The cruellist is In-grat-i-tude . . . A capital I.'

16. *Punctum*: 'Period' or 'full stop'.

17. *holy fool (yurodivy)*: A phenomenon of Russian Orthodox Christian culture from as early as the fourteenth century, holy fools were adherents of a radical asceticism (imitation of the sufferings of Christ), who engaged in self-mortification and were believed by many to have prophetic powers. Feigning mental debility, perhaps

to combat the sin of pride in themselves, holy fools commonly
lived as wandering mendicants relying on the generosity of any
who would give them shelter. Although discouraged by the church
after the sixteenth century due to concerns about imposture,
deception and even genuine insanity, the practice survived into
the nineteenth. The image of Grisha involves many of these issues
– issues of light and dark, of authenticity and the nature and power
of faith.

18. *Parlez donc français*: 'Speak French.'

19. *Mangez donc avec du pain*: 'Eat that with some bread.' *Comment
est-ce que vous tenez votre fourchette?*: 'Is that the way to hold
your fork?'

20. *boss* (*bolshak*, literally, 'big one') is what he called all males without distinction. (Tolstoy's note.)

21. *je suis payée pour y croire*: 'I have reason to believe it.'

22. *Klepper*: A small, pony-like breed of Finnish or Baltic origin.

23. *treat*: It was (and is) a common practice to reward Borzois (Russian
wolfhounds) for proper hunting discipline with an occasional
treat. Milka's behaviour is thus a mark of her experience, alert
intelligence and confidence in her master.

24. *The wood had acquired a voice and the hounds were in full
pursuit*: The sentence set apart here by Tolstoy has, like the
chapter itself, strong affinities with the poem 'Hunting with
Hounds' (*Psovaya okhota*, 1846) by Nikolay Nekrasov (1821–
77), the influential editor who accepted *Childhood* for
publication in his magazine, *The Contemporary*, and who did
much to foster the young Tolstoy's career (see the Introduction).
Be that as it may, the hunting terms used by Tolstoy in this
chapter were well established. As elsewhere in the narrative, his
language is scrupulously exact in its representation of the partic-
ulars of social and material life, even as he responds to a variety
of literary antecedents and influences, while developing his own
distinctive forms and themes.

25. *Robinson Suisse*: Isabelle de Montolieu's widely read French adaptation (Paris, 1814) of *Der Schweizerische Robinson* (Zurich,
1812–13) by Johann David Wyss (1743–1818). The book is, of
course, also well known in English as *The Swiss Family Robinson*
(London, 1814). The children's game is thus pan-European in the
broadest sense.

26. *C'est un geste de femme de chambre*: 'That is the gesture of a
chambermaid.'

27. *caste* (*soslovie*): Although there may be some conceptual overlap,

the term used here and elsewhere in the text refers not to class in the modern, post-Marxian sense, but to the largely hereditary social categories or 'estates' established with various privileges and obligations as a matter of Russian law: nobles, clergy, honoured citizens, merchants, miscellaneous ranks (*raznochintsy*), town residents, Cossacks and peasants. The Irtenyevs and their circle belong, like Tolstoy himself, to the highest caste or estate, that of the nobility.

28. *à bonnes fortunes*: 'successful'.

29. '*Do Not Wake Me, a Bride*' and '*Not Alone*': Russian folk songs. N. S. Semyonova (1787–1876) was a well-known Russian opera singer who performed from 1809 into the 1830s.

30. *John Field* (1782–1837): A celebrated Irish composer and piano virtuoso, who invented the nocturne form and who, after an apprenticeship with Muzio Clementi and a series of successful European tours, lived in Russia from 1804 to 1837, first in St Petersburg and then in Moscow, performing in the country's finest halls and giving private lessons in the homes of the wealthy. His Concerto No. 2 in A-flat Major dates from 1816.

31. *britzka*: A long, open Russian carriage similar to a phaeton, with a folding top over the rear seat and a front seat facing the rear.

32. *et puis au fond c'est un très bon diable*: 'and besides, at bottom he's a very decent devil.'

33. *Church Slavonic*: The Russian variant of the liturgical language used by Orthodox Slavs, much as Latin was once used instead of the vernacular in the Roman Catholic church.

34. *take out a pastille . . . Ochakov incense . . . marched against the Turks*: The Russo-Turkish Wars were waged intermittently from the late seventeenth to the second half of the nineteenth century. The episode meant here is the war of 1787–91, successfully fought by Marshal Alexander Suvorov for Tsarina Catherine II, the Great (1729–96). *Ochakov*: a city in the Ukraine occupied by the Ottoman Turks and captured in 1788 by Russian forces under the command of Catherine's favourite, Grigory Potemkin (or Potyomkin). *pastille*: Natalya Savishna seems to have lit the incense for the humblest of reasons: to perfume the air in a house without indoor plumbing after Nikolenka's use of a commode or 'necessary'.

35. *everyone had gathered . . . a last few minutes together*: It is a Russian custom to sit briefly in silence before starting a journey.

36. *kisses on the shoulder*: It was the custom of serfs to kiss their masters on the shoulder as a mark of affection and respect, but also in acknowledgement of their dependent status.

37. *coupon*: At the end of each lesson private teachers were given coupons or tickets, which they would then present to their employers at the end of the month for the total due for their services.

38. *Dmitriev nor Derzhavin*: Ivan Dmitriev (1760–1837) was a minor poet of the Sentimentalist school. Gavrila Derzhavin (1743–1816) was perhaps the most important Russian poet of the late eighteenth century. Both figures were out of fashion by the time of the narrative (the late 1830s to mid-1840s), which is perhaps why Tolstoy has included them here: to further locate the late eighteenth-century culture of the Irtenyevs and their milieu.

39. *office* (*moleben* in Russian or Paraklesis in Greek Orthodox terminology): A brief service of supplication or thanksgiving to the Theotokos (Mother of God) or for the intercession of a saint, offered on special occasions in church or wherever such occasions may warrant.

40. *ma bonne tante*: 'my good aunt.'

41. *un garçon qui promet*: 'a promising boy.'

42. *je vous demande un peu*: 'I simply ask you.'

43. *Racine, Corneille, Boileau, Molière and Fénelon*: Jean Racine (1639–99), Pierre Corneille (1606–84) and Molière (1622–73) were leading dramatists, the first two known for their tragedies and the last, for his comedies; Nicolas Boileau (1636–1711) was a poet and influential neoclassical critic; François Fénelon (1651–1715) was a poet and Quietist theologian of somewhat liberal tendency.

44. *Ségur*: Louis Philippe, comte de Ségur (1753–1830), was a French diplomat, historian and memoirist of revolutionary and later Bonapartist sympathies, who from 1785 to 1789 served in St Petersburg, where he was a member of Catherine the Great's inner circle.

45. *Goethe, Schiller and Byron*: Johann Wolfgang von Goethe (1749–1832) a German poet, novelist, dramatist and polymath, is regarded as the supreme master of German literature. Johann Christoph Friedrich von Schiller (1759–1805) a German poet, dramatist, historian and philosopher, who is generally considered to be one of the most important representatives of German classicism. George Gordon, sixth Baron Byron, or more simply, Lord Byron (1788–1824), was an English poet and perhaps the most influential member of the Romantic movement.

46. *ma bonne amie*: 'my good friend.'

47. *un parfait honnête homme*: 'a perfectly decent man.'

48. *lexicons*: These may, as some suppose, be the partial 1786 translation of the so-called *Lexicon of the French Academy* by the

diplomat Ivan Tatishchev (1743–1802), or, in a more probable and interesting link, they may be the three large volumes of the unfinished *Russian Historical, Geographic, Political and Civil Lexicon* of the historian, geographer and ethnologist Vasily Tatishchev (1686–1750), published in 1793 by the great bibliophile Alexey Musin-Pushkin (1744–1817), whose grandson Alexander Musin-Pushkin (1827–1903) was a childhood friend of Tolstoy's and the likely model for Seryozha. Tolstoy would, in that case, be turning Seryozha upside down on a pedestal of words in more ways than one.

49. *Quelle charmante enfant!*: 'What a delightful child!'

50. *Voyez, ma chère … Voyez comme ce jeune homme s'est fait élégant pour danser avec votre fille*: 'Look, my dear … Look how elegant this young man has made himself to dance with your daughter.'

51. *Danube Maiden*: *Das Donauweibchen* (1798), a Romantic opera by the Viennese composer Ferdinand Kauer (1751–1831), was very popular in Moscow and St Petersburg in the first decades of the nineteenth century.

52. *Vous êtes une habitante de Moscou?*: 'Are you a resident of Moscow?' *Et moi, je n'ai encore jamais fréquenté la capitale*: 'As for me, I have never *frequented* the capital before.'

53. *vis-à-vis*: Literally, 'face to face', but here meaning across from each other.

54. *Rose ou hortie?*: 'Rose or nettle?' *Hortie* is an older spelling of the modern *ortie*.

55. *Il ne fallait pas danser, si vous ne savez pas!*: 'You shouldn't dance if you don't know how!' Papa's use of the formal pronoun may increase the severity of his rebuke.

56. *Grossvater* (grandfather): A traditional theme and dance signalling the evening's end.

57. *La belle Flamande* ('The beautiful Flemish woman'): It has been suggested that the source of this odd phrase is Laurence Sterne's *Sentimental Journey* (1767), which Tolstoy was translating while he worked on 'Childhood', but it may be wiser – and more Tolstoyan – to look for its meaning in the personality of Papa himself and see it as a typically facetious, if not wholly intelligible allusion by him to the 1818 *contredanse* of the same name by the well-known Belgian *maître de danse* (dance master) Charles Sacré (1785–1831), who choreographed it, along with seventeen others, for balls given in Brussels by the Duke of Wellington and the Prince of Orange. With that kind of topical association, appropriate for Papa's generation and caste, the phrase would have been

both flattering and whimsically grandiose, and thus entirely in keeping with his distinctive sense of humour.

58. *Benjamin*: The youngest son of Jacob in the story of Joseph (Genesis 37–50).

59. *band* (*venchik*): It was a Russian Orthodox custom to place across the brow of the deceased a satin or paper ribbon containing images of the Saviour, the Theotokos and St John the Apostle.

60. *Nasha* (or *Nashik*): A shortened form of Natasha, the diminutive of Natalya. Its similarity to the feminine form of the Russian word for 'our' (*nasha*) would naturally reinforce the little girl's usage and its intimate force – not to mention the modern reader's perhaps anachronistic sense of dramatic irony: personal name, family member, chattel.

61. *kutya*: A dish of sweetened rice and raisins traditionally served at Russian Orthodox funerals and wakes, perhaps as a token of the sweetness of eternal life awaiting all true believers.

BOYHOOD

1. *Serpukhov*: A small town on the Oka river about sixty miles south of Moscow.

2. *gouverneur*: 'governor' or 'tutor'. *des enfants de bonne maison*: 'children from a good home'. *menin*: 'inferior' or 'domestic'.

3. *Geselle*: 'journeyman'.

4. *Ulm*: The Battle of Ulm of October 1805 in southern Germany (Bavaria) ended with the rout and capture by Napoleon of the Austrian army sent against him; *Austerlitz*: the Battle of Austerlitz of December 1805 in Moravia saw the decisive defeat by Napoleon of an Austro-Russian army led by Tsar Alexander I (1777–1825); *Wagram*: the Battle of Wagram near Vienna of July 1809 ended with the defeat of a third Austrian army by Napoleon.

5. *aber der Franzose warf sein Gewehr und rief pardon*: 'But the Frenchman threw down his musket and asked for mercy.'

6. *auf und ab*: 'back and forth'.

7. *'Qui vive?' sagte er auf einmal ... 'Qui vive?' sagte er zum zweiten Mal ... 'Qui vive?' sagte er zum dritten Mal*: '"Who's there?" he said all of a sudden ... "Who's there?" he said a second time ... "Who's there?" he said a third time.'

8. *'Amalia!' sagte auf einmal mein Vater*: '"Amalia!" my father said at once.'

9. *Franz*: After the Battle of Austerlitz, the last Holy Roman Emperor Franz II (1768–1835) dissolved that nominal empire, restyling himself, meanwhile, as Franz I, Emperor of the Austrian Empire, which he ruled from 1804 until his death.

10. *Überrock*: 'overcoat'.

11. *Nachtwächter*: 'night watchman'.

12. *Macht auf!*: 'Open up!'

13. *Macht auf im Namen des Gesetzes!*: 'Open up in the name of the law!'

14. *Ich gab ein Hieb*: 'I gave him a blow.'

15. *Ems* (or *Bad Ems*): A Rhineland resort town on the Lahn river. It was in the nineteenth century a fashionable destination for the Russian nobility and other foreigners, thanks to its charm, reputedly healthful waters and social prestige. For Karl Ivanych it was thus a very good place to look for a position.

16. *Lundi, de 2 à 3, Maître d'Histoire et de Géographie*: 'Monday, from 2 to 3, Teacher of History and Geography.'

17. *Smaragdov*: Sergey N. Smaragdov (1805–71) taught at the elite Alexander Lyceum in Tsarskoye Selo and was the author of a number of popular history texts for secondary school students, including a *Guide to Understanding the Middle Ages* (St Petersburg, 1841).

18. *Kaydanov's history*: Ivan K. Kaydanov (1782–1843) was a distinguished Russian pedagogue who also taught at the Alexander Lyceum, where his students included Pushkin, among other later renowned literary and political figures. He, too, published several standard history textbooks for secondary school students, including a *History of the Middle Ages* (St Petersburg, 1831).

19. *given me a two*: Five was the highest mark in the Russian grading system, just as it is today. One is the lowest.

20. *St Louis*: Louis IX (1214–70) was crowned king of France in 1226 at the age of twelve, with his mother, Blanche of Castile, ruling as regent until his majority. He took part in two disastrous crusades: in 1248, when he was captured and ransomed, and in 1270, when he died on his way to the Holy Land.

21. *Voyons, messieurs! Faites votre toilette et descendons*: 'Let's see, gentlemen! Get straightened up and we'll go downstairs.'

22. *petits jeux*: 'drawing-room games'.

23. *Lange Nase*: 'long nose'.

24. *C'est bien*: 'Very well.'

25. *Avgust Antonych*: St-Jérôme's Russified first name and patronymic; that is, 'Auguste, son of Antoine'.

26. *Oh mon père, oh mon bienfaiteur, donne-moi pour la dernière fois ta bénédiction et que la volonté de dieu soit faite*: 'Oh, my father, oh, my benefactor, give me your blessing for the last time and let God's will be done!'

27. *À genoux!*: 'On your knees!'

28. *C'est ainsi que vous obéissez à votre seconde mère, c'est ainsi que vous reconnaissez ses bontés?*: 'This is how you obey your second mother, this is how you acknowledge her benevolence?'

29. *Tranquillisez-vous au nom du ciel, madame la comtesse*: 'Calm yourself, in heaven's name, Madame Countess.'

30. *fouetter*: 'to flog' or 'to whip'.

31. *with an accent circonflexe*: Lengthening the final vowel.

32. *Spaniard flea*: The phrase should be taken as an example of Karl Ivanych's characteristic malapropisms. In the Russian, Tolstoy has him say 'Champagne fly', with a confusion of *shampanskaya* ('champagne') and *shpanskaya* ('Spaniard') in a phrase thus intended to mean 'Spanish fly', possibly in the sense of an irritant, since the well-known preparation was used as a blister-inducing agent in nineteenth-century medicine.

33. *mauvais sujet, vilain garnement*: 'worthless boy', 'nasty imp'.

34. *Krohn*: The brewing establishment of Abram Krohn, founded in St Petersburg in 1795 with support from Catherine the Great, produced both beer and *mead*, a usually mild alcoholic beverage made from honey mixed with water, hops and spices.

35. *Schelling*: If the German Idealist philosopher Friedrich Wilhelm Joseph von Schelling (1775–1854) never subscribed to the radical solipsism attributed to him here, he was certainly interested in the problem of the relation of subjectivity and the world, and in the nature and grounding of subjective images or representations, especially as they are embodied in art.

36. *religion (zakon bozhy)*: Part of the basic curriculum of Russian elementary and secondary schools of the day and thus a fit subject for a university entrance examination. It included the history of the Christian church in general and the Russian Orthodox church in particular, Orthodox dogma (catechism), the forms and significance of the Orthodox liturgy and prayers, and the truths of religion and the personal ethical responsibilities that followed from them.

37. *le fond de la bouteille*: 'the last drops' or 'dregs'.

38. *jeu perlé*: 'exquisite playing'.

39. *Votre grande-mère est morte*: 'Your grandmother is dead.'

40. *comme il faut*: There are several ways to render this key expression. Literally, it means 'as is necessary' or 'as it should be', but

the broader, idiomatic sense is 'proper', 'decent' or 'respectable' and, in Tolstoy's subsequent analysis, an aesthetic rather than ethical category that derives from the received taste, manners and forms of the Irtenyev milieu, and that is a decidedly negative principle in the recurring dialectic of Nikolenka's psychological, social and moral development, as Tolstoy makes clear.

41. *un homme comme il faut*: 'a respectable man'.

42. *á la coq*: 'cock-style', that is, with a pompadour or quiff like a cockerel's crest or comb.

43. *si je suis timide*: 'if I am shy.'

44. *Savez-vous d'où vient votre timidité? D'un excès d'amour propre, mon cher*: 'Do you know what your shyness comes from? From too much pride, my dear.'

45. *the week before Lent* (*maslenitsa* or 'butter week'): The seven days of partial fasting (dairy but no meat) that precede Lent or the Great Fast, as it is called in the Russian Orthodox church. It corresponds to Shrovetide, but lasts twice as long and entails different procedures and restrictions.

46. *Karr*: Jean-Baptiste Alphonse Karr (1808–90) was a French editor, critic, novelist and author of pithy aphorisms, and an enduring favourite of Tolstoy's.

YOUTH

1. *Bright week*: The first week after Easter in the Russian Orthodox calendar. *Thomas week*: the second week after. *Passion week*: the first week before. *fast*: in nineteenth-century Russia, confession was normally made once a year and preceded by a special fast during Passion week in preparation for both confession and Communion.

2. *the son coming for the father*: A fracturing characteristic of Karl Ivanych, who seems to have combined it with a German idiom, of the traditional Russian expression 'the grandson has come for the grandfather', meaning that the fresh wet snow of winter's end has arrived to take away the older, drier accumulation.

3. *Francoeur's*: Louis-Benjamin Francoeur (1773–1849) was a distinguished French mathematician, whose *Algèbre supérieure* (*Advanced Algebra*, 1838) was widely used in Russia.

4. *bricks and salt pyramids . . . goose wing*: It was common to place salt between double window frames to absorb moisture and prevent fogging. The dusting tool is a dried *goose wing*.

5. *droshky*: A low, open carriage with a bench on which the passen-

gers rode sideways, or else facing forward astride the seat, as on a saddle, with their feet resting on iron bars below.

6. *Sparrow Hills*: A Moscow park district on the south side of the Moscow river.

7. *Pedotti's*: A well-known pastry shop established in the 1820s near the Kremlin on the fashionable street known as Kuznetsky Most (Blacksmith Bridge).

8. *Rappo*: Karl Rappo (1800–54) was an Austrian juggler and strong man who performed in Moscow in 1839 to great acclaim.

9. *Mazeppa*: Ivan Mazeppa (1644–1709) was a Cossack hetman who fought for Ukrainian independence and was ultimately defeated by Peter I, the Great (1672–1725), in the Battle of Poltava (1709). Mazeppa was celebrated in eponymous Romantic poems by Byron (1819) and Victor Hugo (1829) and portrayed more darkly in Pushkin's patriotic 'Poltava' (1828–9). In Pushkin, the elderly Mazeppa captivates and elopes with the much younger *Maria*, the beautiful daughter of a wealthy nobleman.

10. *Synod*: Established in 1721 by Peter the Great as an instrument of control over the Russian Orthodox church and surviving until the 1917 revolution, the Holy Synod was a council of high-ranking clergy and laymen appointed by the tsar, and the ultimate authority in all religious and in many social matters, including divorce. *Georgia*: The Caucasian principality was at the time part of the Russian empire.

11. *je puis . . . je peux*: Alternative present indicative forms of the verb *pouvoir* ('to be able'). The first variant is a less common but more formal literary usage.

12. *rules (pravila)*: The admonitions, instructions and prayers preceding confession. Tolstoy's use of the same term to denote two orders of moral practice – both a modern, rationalist technique of ethical self-improvement (making lists and keeping diaries, with Benjamin Franklin's *Autobiography* as the model) and an ancient tradition of spiritual principles, obligations and procedures – would seem to be deliberate.

13. *'The Nightingale'* (1826): A still popular romance composed by Aleksandr Alyabev (1787–1851) with words by the poet Anton Delvig (1798–1831), a classmate of Pushkin's at the Alexander Lyceum.

14. *Shaposhnikov's house*: Tolstoy very likely had in mind the home of Kondraty Shaposhnikov (1778–1855), a prominent merchant who served as head of the Moscow city administration from 1841 to 1843 and lived in the central Moscow district of the narrative.

15. *16 April*: Tolstoy seems to have forgotten that 'Bright week came quite late in April' the year Nikolenka took his university entrance examinations, since the date given here for their start suggests that, in fact, it came quite early.

16. *gymnasium* (*gimnaziya*): A type of German-inspired and classically oriented secondary school with a rigorous eight-year curriculum, first established in Russia at the beginning of the nineteenth century.

17. *names starting with K*: The names are evidently being called in reverse order.

18. *Bartenyev-Mordenyev*: The second part of the imagined name is mildly insulting, since it derives from *morda*, the Russian for 'snout', 'muzzle' or 'ugly mug'.

19. *à la moujik*: 'peasant-style' or long and straight with a fringe.

20. *star on his tailcoat*: A single star on a university uniform lapel indicated the rank of state councillor, the fifth class or grade in the fourteen-grade Table of symmetrical court, civil and military ranks established by Peter the Great in 1722. In the early 1840s a state councillor was the equivalent of a major in the army.

21. *self-paying*: University students were of two kinds in the 1840s: 'self-paying' (*svoyekoshtny*) were those who, like the narrator, were responsible for their own tuition and expenses, while 'state-supported' (*kazennokoshtny*) were those whose educational and other expenses were paid from a variety of public funds. Since university admission was in principle merit-based (it depended on entrance-examination performance) and secured, moreover, by assistance for students who were not from propertied or wealthy families (the children of clergy or of low-ranking civil servants, for example, or those from the impoverished nobility), the university student population was – as Tolstoy makes clear in a number of ways – more diverse than in any institution or circle outside it, and thus permitted a degree of caste interaction on equal terms unusual elsewhere in mid-nineteenth-century Russian society.

22. *magnetic* (the archaic *magnetichesky*): Tolstoy has set off the adjective here and elsewhere because it is being used not in the ordinary sense of 'highly attractive' (as it might be in English), but rather in reference to the theory of 'animal magnetism' advocated by the physician and early investigator of hypnotism Franz Anton Mesmer (1734–1815) – in reference, that is, to the already long-discredited but still popular notion of mental and spiritual forces known as Mesmerism.

23. *À vous, Nicolas*: 'Your turn, Nikolay.'

24. *Cicero . . . Horace*: Marcus Tullius Cicero (106–43 BC) was a Roman philosopher and statesman and one of Rome's greatest orators and prose stylists. Horace (Quintus Horatius Flaccus, 65–8 BC) was one of Rome's greatest poets.

25. *Zumpt*: Karl Gottlob Zumpt (1792–1849) was a German philologist and professor of Latin at the University of Berlin. His *Lateinische Grammatik* (1818) was widely used outside Germany, including in Russia, where it appeared in translation in 1835.

26. *mauvais genre*: 'bad form' or 'boorish'.

27. *Rozanov's*: A well-known Moscow tailor.

28. *Bruderschaft*: 'brotherhood', but here meaning the celebration with a drink of the decision to switch to the familiar or *thou* or *tu* form with the greater intimacy it signifies.

29. *Yar's*: A celebrated French restaurant, opened on Kuznetsky Most in 1826. It was a favourite of many writers, including Alexander Herzen, Ivan Turgenev and Pushkin, who, for example, recalled its excellent cold veal and truffles in his wistful lyric 'Highway Complaints' (1829).

30. *Victor Adam* (1801–70): A popular neoclassical French painter and lithographer known for prints of historical and mythological scenes, equestrian portraits (of Russian tsars, for example) and renderings of horses and dogs.

31. *Daziaro's*: The Italian Giuseppe Daziaro (1806–65) opened his first picture shop in Moscow on Kuznetsky Most in 1829, following soon afterwards with branches in St Petersburg and Paris. The shops sold, along with prints, paintings, daguerreotypes and other 'artistic works', art and stationery supplies, paints of the firm's own manufacture, and drawing and writing implements and paper.

32. *porte-crayon*: 'pencil-holder', that is, a device into which leads could be inserted from either end to make the immediate ancestor of the modern mechanical pencil.

33. *Zhukov's . . . chibouks*: Zhukov's was a cheap tobacco packaged in the first half of the nineteenth century in the Moscow and St Petersburg factories of Vasily Zhukov (1796–1881). *sultan's*: a variety of better-quality Russian-grown tobacco. *Stambouline pipe*: a short Turkish pipe. *chibouk*: a Turkish pipe with a very long wooden stem and a clay or meerschaum bowl.

34. *Bostanjoglo*: The oldest and largest manufacturer of tobacco products in Moscow, founded in 1820 by the Ukrainian Greek Mikhail Bostanjoglo.

35. *Piquet*: 'Picket', a French game for two players dating at least to

the seventeenth century and very popular in France and Russia in the nineteenth. The purpose is to take tricks, which are given a point value, with the first player to reach 100 in a hand declared the winner, and the loser obliged, in the gambling version, to pay the difference between his own score and that of his opponent if both reach 100, or the total of both scores plus 100, if he does not. Volodya's debt to Dubkov may thus have been quite large.

36. *Gaudeamus igitur*: A Latin song in ten exhausting stanzas dating from the late Middle Ages that celebrates youth but acknowledges its brevity, and is traditionally sung by university students, usually at graduation: *Gaudeamus igitur / Juvenes dum sumus. / Post jucundam juventutem / Post molestam senectutem / Nos habebit humus* . . . 'Let us rejoice then / While we are young. / After a merry youth, / After a troubled old age, / The earth will have us . . .'

37. *Sokolniki*: A large park in central Moscow first laid out in the time of Peter the Great with lawns, flowerbeds, ponds and tree-lined avenues.

38. *Orestes and Pylades*: An allusion to the proverbial friendship in Greek mythology between Orestes – son of Agamemnon and Clytemnestra and the title character of Aeschylus's *Oresteia* trilogy – and Pylades, the younger cousin with whom Orestes was raised and who became his adviser and eventual brother-in-law after marrying Orestes' sister Elektra.

39. *civilian general*: A civil servant of the fourth grade or higher in the Petrine Table of Ranks.

40. *Corps of Pages* (*Corps des Pages*): An elite military school for the nobility established (or reorganized) in St Petersburg in 1802 by Alexander I. Admission, usually at the age of fifteen, required not only high noble status but also the passing of difficult examinations with an emphasis on mathematics and foreign languages. Graduates had the right to join the regiment of their choice and often went on to distinguished military and sometimes civil careers.

41. *smallpox*: Perhaps an allusion to *Julie, ou la nouvelle Héloïse* (*Julie, or the New Eloise*, 1761) by Tolstoy's favourite Jean-Jacques Rousseau (1712–78).

42. *homme d'affaires*: 'personal secretary'.

43. *bel étage*: In a large home or building, the first floor (or *piano nobile*) above the ground floor containing the salon, drawing room and other reception rooms, as well as the bedrooms.

44. *Cadet School (Yunkerskaya shkola)*: Founded in 1823 in St Petersburg on the initiative of the future Tsar Nicholas I (1796–1855) to train children of the nobility for military service, it was reorganized in 1838 as a 'self-paying' secondary institution to supply officers for the cuirassiers (heavy cavalry), uhlans (lancers) and hussars (light cavalry).

45. *issus de germains*: 'second cousins' or relatives who share a great-grandparent or a pair of them.

46. *Kuntsevo*: A suburb south-east of Moscow, but today a district within the city limits.

47. *dacha*: 'suburban' or 'country home'.

48. *Ivan Yakovlevich*: Ivan Yakovlevich Koreysha (1783–1861) was a holy fool revered even today by some Russian Orthodox Christians and described by Tolstoy in a note to the second edition of *Youth* as 'a famous madman who lived in Moscow a long time and enjoyed among the Moscow ladies the reputation of a seer'. The argument between Dmitry and his mother, resumed in the next chapter between Dmitry and his sister, may thus be seen to echo, in its ostensible meaning, the argument in *Childhood* between Papa and *maman* in regard to Grisha.

49. *Bolognese* (or Bichon Bolonais): A fluffy white lapdog not much larger than a cat. The breed dates from thirteenth-century Italy, if not from Roman times, and would in Tolstoy's Russia very likely have evoked much the same associations of cuteness and privilege as it does today.

50. *Rob Roy*: An enormously popular novel by Sir Walter Scott (1771–1832), first published in 1817, whose subject is the early eighteenth-century Scottish rebellion by Robert Roy McGregor (1671–1734). It was translated into French in 1822 and into Russian in 1829. Varenka could thus have been reading from either translation.

51. *c'est vous qui êtes un petit monstre de perfection*: 'it's you who are a little monster of perfection.'

52. *Merci, mon cher*: 'Thank you, my dear.'

53. *A prophet is not without honour, save in his own country*: The common saying comes from Matthew 13:57.

54. *si jeunesse savait, si vieillesse pouvait*: 'if youth only knew, if age only could.' Lyubov Sergeyevna's characteristic *non sequitur* is a French bromide dating from at least the sixteenth century, if not from Horace.

55. *Then one or the other of us would be unable to do so*: A double marriage between two sets of siblings of the kind Nikolenka is

imagining was forbidden as a matter of law on the pedantic ground that either couple would be marrying 'blood relatives', even if there had been no prior consanguinity.

56. *May I join us?*: 'Us' is not a typographical error or a solecism, but an expression of Lyubochka's social tact and nice sense of language (and of Tolstoy's ear for dialogue and its undercurrents and nuances): she badly wants to take part in the activities of 'our' family (a 'we'), since she's a member of it, too.

57. *com si tri joli*: That is, *comme c'est très joli* or 'how very pretty it is'.

58. *Beethoven sonatas . . . the Pathétique and the Moonlight*: The sonatas by Ludwig van Beethoven (1770–1827) are the No. 8 in C minor, opus 13 (1798), named *Pathétique* in 1799, and the No. 14 in C-sharp minor, opus 27, No. 2 (1801), named *Moonlight* in 1832.

59. *'Le fou'*: 'The Madman', opus 136 (1837), a 'dramatic scene' for piano by the German Romantic pianist and composer Friedrich Wilhelm Kalkbrenner (1785–1849).

60. *Liszt*: Franz Liszt (1811–86) was a prolific and influential Hungarian composer and wildly popular piano virtuoso. *Kalkbrenner*: See note 59 above.

61. *Sue, Dumas and Paul de Kock*: Eugène Sue (1804–57) was a French writer of socialist sympathies who published his popular ten-volume *roman-feuilleton* or serialized novel *Les Mystères de Paris* (*The Mysteries of Paris*, 1842–3) in the weekly *Journal des débats* (*Journal of Debates*). The story's hero is a nobleman of admirable moral, intellectual and physical qualities, who with his almost equally admirable companions helps a variety of people while disguised as a French worker. Alexandre Dumas (1802–70) was a widely read author of historical novels of high adventure, including *Les Trois mousquetaires* (*The Three Musketeers*, 1844) and the rest of the now classic D'Artagnan series, and *Le Comte de Monte-Cristo* (*The Count of Monte-Cristo*, 1845–6), still beloved today. Paul de Kock (1793–1871) was the prolific author of novels depicting scenes of bourgeois Parisian life that were extremely popular in the first half of the nineteenth century, especially outside France.

62. *nobel . . . ehrlich*: The French adjective *noble*, like the German *nobel*, differed at the time from the German *ehrlich* and the Russian *blagorodny* in its connotation of generosity of spirit and nobility of character, as opposed to honesty or honourability or nobility of birth alone.

63. *Je fus un homme très comme il faut*: 'I was a very well-bred (or respectable) man.'

64. *Mytishchi*: The name means 'customs duties' or 'tolls'.

65. *Messalina*: Valeria Messalina (*c.* AD 17–48) was the third wife of the Roman emperor Claudius and an epitome of dissoluteness, immorality and extreme ruthlessness.

66. *tarantass*: A light, closed carriage mounted on two parallel poles extending from front to rear, which allowed the replacement of its wheels with runners in the winter – just the sort of vehicle that would appeal to a man of Pyotr Vasilyevich's smug practicality.

67. *belle-mère*: 'stepmother'.

68. *poissarde*: 'fishwife'.

69. *rowen (otava)*: The early autumn regrowth after the last mowing. The Russian word is, like the English, an unusual one, but as such a reflection of Tolstoy's wide knowledge and terminological precision.

70. *1812*: The year of Napoleon's disastrous invasion of Russia.

71. *Parnassus*: Mount Parnassus in central Greece was, in Greek mythology, sacred to Apollo and the abode of the three muses of poetry, music and learning.

72. *Ce n'est pas français*: 'That isn't French.'

73. *ce ne sont pas des gens comme il faut*: 'they aren't respectable [or well-bred] people.'

74. *manants*: 'churls' or 'yokels'.

75. '*Demon*' (1839): A narrative poem by the Romantic poet Mikhail Lermontov (1815–41), begun while he was at the Cadet School and not published in complete form until 1860, although it did appear in a censored version in 1842 and was circulated in hand copies before that. It is the story of the tragic love of a fallen angel, an 'exile from heaven', for a mortal woman, and is told in sensuous verse with voluptuous images of seduction and of the lush alpine Caucasus landscape where the story takes place.

76. *Comme c'est gracieux*: 'How graceful.'

77. *Dorpat University*: The university of the Estonian city of Dorpat, or Tartu as it is called today, was founded in 1632 and is one of the oldest and finest in Eastern Europe.

78. *O, ja*: 'Oh, yes.'

79. *Löschen Sie die Lichter aus, Frost!*: 'Put out the lights, Frost!'

80. *juchhe!*: 'Hurrah!'

81. *Au banquet de la vie, infortuné convive . . .* : The French poet Nicolas Joseph Laurent Gilbert (1751–80) wrote his widely popular '*Adieux à la vie*' ('Farewell to Life') on his deathbed. The

seventh stanza reads, '*Au banquet de la vie, infortuné convive, / J'apparus un jour, et je meurs; / Je meurs, et sur ma tombe, où lentement j'arrive, / Nul ne viendra verser des pleurs*': 'At life's gay banquet placed, a poor unhappy guest, / One day I pass, then disappear; / I die, and on the tomb where I at length shall rest / No friend will come to shed a tear' (trans. Oliver Wendell Holmes, Sr, 1858).

82. *Senate*: The principal legislative, judicial and administrative arm of the Russian monarchy, and as such the country's court of last resort.

83. *eighth fine*: It was the practice at the venerable Moscow English Club – of which Tolstoy would become a member in the 1860s, and to which Papa presumably belongs – to impose incremental fines on any who remained after the club's official closing time of 1 a.m.

84. *Materne's*: Philippe Materne's delicatessen and café, located in the 1830s and 1840s near the university building on Mokhovaya Street, was one of the best in the city.

85. *Trubnoy Boulevard*: Sretensky Boulevard in central Moscow today.

86. *marrow*: A pun in Russian, where the word for 'marrow' also means 'brain'.

87. *Lisbon*: A well-known Moscow tavern.

88. *Lesage*: Alain-René Lesage (1668–1747) was a French novelist and playwright, and the author of the classic picaresque tale *L'Histoire de Gil Blas de Santillane* (1715–35).

89. *Zhukovsky*: Vasily Zhukovsky (1783–1852) was a leading Russian poet and influential translator of English and German Sentimental and Romantic verse.

90. *Féval*: Paul Féval (1816–87) was a French novelist and dramatist known for swashbuckling fiction and, under the pseudonym Sir Francis Trolopp, for his immensely popular, Sue-like *Les Mystères de Londres* (*The Mysteries of London*, 1844).

91. *Stozhenka* (or Ostozhenka): A street in central Moscow.

92. *recruit supplier*: A speculator who, after paying Semyonov to enlist in the army (Semyonov may exaggerate the sum), will receive a voucher or receipt from the state, which he will then sell to someone else, who will use it to avoid the catastrophe of conscription, which at the time entailed twenty years of service in the ranks for those castes subject to it by law.

93. *permission from the Senate*: Nobles as a caste not only had no military obligation but were prohibited from volunteering for

service in the ranks, except with permission of the Senate, which through its Department of Heraldry was responsible for all matters pertaining to changes in estate affiliation and function.

94. *flog me*: Nobles were exempt from corporal punishment as a matter of law.

95. *I'll tell in the next, happier part of youth*: Tolstoy never wrote the last part – to be called *Young Manhood* (*Molodost*) – of his projected *Four Periods of Growth* (*Chetyre epokhi razvitiya*).

96. *Yasnaya Polyana* (Clear Glade): Tolstoy's ancestral estate, about 125 miles south of Moscow, near the city of Tula.

THE STORY OF PENGUIN CLASSICS

Before 1946 ... 'Classics' are mainly the domain of academics and students; readable editions for everyone else are almost unheard of. This all changes when a little-known classicist, E. V. Rieu, presents Penguin founder Allen Lane with the translation of Homer's *Odyssey* that he has been working on in his spare time.

1946 Penguin Classics debuts with *The Odyssey*, which promptly sells three million copies. Suddenly, classics are no longer for the privileged few.

1950s Rieu, now series editor, turns to professional writers for the best modern, readable translations, including Dorothy L. Sayers's *Inferno* and Robert Graves's unexpurgated *Twelve Caesars*.

1960s The Classics are given the distinctive black covers that have remained a constant throughout the life of the series. Rieu retires in 1964, hailing the Penguin Classics list as 'the greatest educative force of the twentieth century.'

1970s A new generation of translators swells the Penguin Classics ranks, introducing readers of English to classics of world literature from more than twenty languages. The list grows to encompass more history, philosophy, science, religion and politics.

1980s The Penguin American Library launches with titles such as *Uncle Tom's Cabin*, and joins forces with Penguin Classics to provide the most comprehensive library of world literature available from any paperback publisher.

1990s The launch of Penguin Audiobooks brings the classics to a listening audience for the first time, and in 1999 the worldwide launch of the Penguin Classics website extends their reach to the global online community.

The 21st Century Penguin Classics are completely redesigned for the first time in nearly twenty years. This world-famous series now consists of more than 1300 titles, making the widest range of the best books ever written available to millions – and constantly redefining what makes a 'classic'.

The Odyssey continues ...

The best books ever written

PENGUIN CLASSICS

SINCE 1946

Find out more at www.penguinclassics.com